Dead Man's Rules

by

Rebecca Grace

Dead Man's Rules

Cover Art by *Kim Mendoza*

The Wild Rose Press, Inc.
PO Box 708
Adams Basin, NY 14410-0708
Visit us at www.thewildrosepress.com

Publishing History
First Crimson Rose Edition, 2014
Print ISBN 978-1-61217-268-4
Digital ISBN 978-1-61217-269-1

Published in the United States of America

"I didn't come for vacation." Her eyes flashed with irritation but she waved a hand as though realizing how curt she sounded. "I mean, I came to see Mom, but I want to do a story on the handprint. I need to."

His insides knotted, as his breakfast churned in his stomach. Poor Lottie. She would be hurt if she realized her daughter's real reason for coming. He didn't ask why she needed to do the story. He knew. Ego.

Reaching down, she pulled a reporter's notebook from her bag. "Riggins' story didn't quote anyone who knew Marco. If you won't do an interview, do you know anyone who might talk to me?"

Why had he wondered what she might think about him? She was only after her damn story. Acid boiled in his stomach. This woman was no Gary Riggins, content to do a half-assed job. She would dig, pry, and eventually she might uncover some ugly truths. And she would spill it all out on national television. She could hurt a good many people, just as she destroyed the homecoming for that little actor in her last story. But he hadn't known the kid. He would know anyone she hurt in Rio Rojo. And it was his sworn duty to protect the citizens of his county.

He might as well have struck her. Her chin snapped up and her body grew rigid. He drew back at the determination he saw grow in her bright eyes along with her rising voice.

"Don't try to tell me what I should do. It's time someone found out who murdered Marco Gonzales. Yes, I said, murdered, Sheriff. If you don't want to help me investigate, I'll do it on my own."

Praise for Rebecca Grace

Dedication

To my sister, Lillie, and my brothers, John and Richard, who are always there for me.

Prologue

The shotgun blast reverberated around the shadowy room. Marco Gonzales staggered backward, his hand clutching at the pain that tore at his throat. Warm blood gushed from his wound, bathing his palm and fingers. How strange that he was still alive. He'd expected a gunshot at this close range to kill him instantly.

The stench of gunpowder filled his nostrils as he took a deep, painful, shuddering breath. He opened his lips, but no words came out, not that he could hear anything over the ringing in his ears from the gunfire.

He'd expected to be afraid, but instead all he felt was the weighty, incredible sadness that had settled on him hours ago. Even this pain wasn't as overwhelming.

There were so many things he wanted to say, needed to say, but he'd known he would never speak now, even if he'd gotten the chance. He tried to think of what and who he was leaving behind, and the thoughts only increased the load of melancholy.

If only...

But it was too late for that thought.

How fitting to die here where he'd first learned to live. Where he'd first dared to dream. Where he'd first discovered the joys of love.

As he tried to step forward, he stumbled over something on the floor and flung out his bloody hand to steady himself. For an instant he braced himself against the wall and then his knees buckled. He crumpled to the floor, sinking into a pool of sticky blood.

A face appeared in the doorway, grim features outlined by the lantern on the floor. Marco made no sound. He knew rescue was not at hand.

Not now.

Not ever.

He'd always considered himself a man of many words, and so many had poured out of him over the years, but now only three words came to him...

Chapter One

"Help me."

A ghostly figure illuminated by candlelight gasped the words in a rasping voice. His eyes glowed in a shadowy face as he opened his mouth again.

"Please."

A large hand lifted toward her, coated in something dark and sinister.

Blood!

Cere Medina jerked up in bed, heart pounding.

Not again.

She blinked the spooky image from her head. This was the second straight night of that horrific dream. Shadows danced on the walls of a dimly lit room. *Lit by what? A candle? A flashlight?* At the center of the light stood the ghostly apparition with burning eyes and a dripping hand.

What could it mean? Stress at work? She blew out a sigh of disgust. No, she'd been in broadcasting for eight years. Tension was a normal part of being a reporter. Reacting to the quick pace and steady pressure was a challenge she relished.

Her breathing slowed and Cere glanced toward the nightstand. The red digital numbers showed 4:10. If she fell back asleep, she'd get two more hours before the alarm rang. If not, she'd be groggy for what promised to be a hell of a busy day.

After punching her pillows, she sank back. Familiar noises emerged—background sounds that were part of living in Santa Monica. From a distance came the hum of the constant flow of traffic on the San Diego Freeway. If she concentrated, she could hear the low rumbling of waves crashing on the beach three blocks away. An ambulance siren sang a mournful wail in the distance. Normal sounds. Why did she feel so jittery and agitated?

Damn dream.

She inhaled slowly and steadily, hoping that deep breathing might relax her. She waited for the scent of ocean air to fill her nostrils.

Wait.

She smelled… not ocean air. *Smoke.*

Cere shot up again. Where was that smoke coming from? A fire nearby? Maybe the reason for the siren she'd heard? She leaned toward the open window. The ocean breeze floated in, filling her nose with cool salty air. The smoke was…

Behind her. She twisted around and spotted a shaft of light coming from the end of the hall just as the smoke detector blared and sent her bolting from the bed.

Oh, hell.

The kitchen light cast shadows along the hall as she scampered toward it. One foot came down on something unexpected and she jerked forward, twisting her ankle. Looking down, she kicked away a stiletto sandal from the middle of the hall.

"Freeda!" She stomped into the kitchen where darkening eggs sizzled in a skillet. Plumes of smoke billowed up from the pan. After flipping off the burner she tapped on the stove fan. The eggs couldn't be salvaged so she grabbed the pan and dumped its singed contents into the sink, turning on the faucet. Overhead the alarm still blared.

"Wasss goin' on?" Freeda's hoarse voice came from the hallway. Her cousin staggered out of the bathroom, rubbing her ear. Her glazed eyes tried to focus on the ceiling. "Wasss makin' that noise?"

"Surely you recognize the smoke alarm by now." Cere grabbed a towel and waved it at the alarm to blow away the smoke and stop the noise. It was at times like this she wished she was taller than five-foot-four.

"I was cookin' breakfast." Freeda wobbled into the kitchen and frowned at the sodden eggs in the sink.

"Sweetie, how many times do I have to tell you not to put something on to cook and leave?" A final swat with the towel silenced the alarm, but the scent of burned eggs still permeated the room. Cere flicked the towel a few more times.

"I'm hungry. All I've eaten since yesterday is peanuts and olives and I have a big day coming."

"We both do."

They were assigned to cover one of the biggest Hollywood stories of the year—a custody hearing involving multi-millionaire child actor, Randy Waverly. Cere went to bed early so she'd be fresh, but here she was at four AM dealing with her drunken cousin.

Freeda opened the pantry and yanked out a bag of corn chips and a can of bean dip. "Gotta get somethin' in my stomach." She tugged open the bag and chips cascaded around the counter while the can tumbled out of her hand and rolled across the floor.

Cere caught the can and pulled the aluminum ring

to open it. With a sigh, she set it on the counter and helped Freeda onto a stool.

Swaying like a flag pole on a windy day, Freeda scooped dip with several chips and stuffed the fistful into her mouth. "Big day coming."

Freeda probably hadn't thought of the big day until now. She wore a skin-tight black dress and dangly silver earrings. Party clothes. While her olive face was scrubbed to shiny smoothness, remnants of smudged lipstick and black rings around her eyes illustrated the dramatic make up she'd tried to remove. Her hair drooped around her face in black ringlets.

"Let me fix something warm for you." Cere hit the button on the automatic coffee maker, already loaded for the morning. She rinsed the skillet and removed a carton of eggs from the refrigerator.

For an instant as a red spot glowed below the burner on the range she again saw the pleading eyes of the man in her dream. She blinked them away and cracked eggs into a bowl. That stupid dream wasn't going to bother her.

Slowly the scent of fresh coffee and warm toast replaced the stench of burning eggs. She placed a plate of scrambled eggs and toast on the counter and removed the chips and dip from a slumping Freeda whose ringlets now dangled close to the can.

Freeda leaned her face on one hand and attacked the eggs with the other. "Thanks for fixing breakfast. You take such good care of me. Sorry I woke you."

"I was awake. I had another bad dream."

"Hey, wow!" Freeda jerked up. "Same guy, needing help? Tell me everything you remember."

Cere poured them both cups of coffee and took the

other stool at the counter. She regretted revealing her earlier dreams. Her cousin had been raised by their grandmother who loved the supernatural.

"No big deal. I'm just stressed out. The network bigwigs are supposed to be in town today from New York. Hopefully they'll watch our Waverly coverage and realize I'm better than Gail Martin." Just saying the name of the network correspondent made her throat tighten.

"Ten times better! I swear she got that network gig 'cause she's sleeping with someone. Hell, I'd sleep with someone for a network job. Wouldn't you?"

Cere started to shake her head, then laughed. "Well, someone cute, maybe, but he has to get me a job somewhere besides *Scope*." The gossipy news program was at the bottom of the network totem pole, even if it had a huge following. Being a tabloid reporter wasn't why she became a journalist.

"Hey, babe, maybe if you get promoted we could move to New York." Freeda's dark eyes grew big and almost focused. "I can freelance there as easily as here."

"You could look for a full time job."

"Maybe." Since losing her last job, Freeda lived in Cere's guest room. She worked from time to time as a freelance television news producer, but claimed her real job was writing a screen play. So far she hadn't finished much beyond a loose synopsis that kept changing. She spent most of her time partying.

"Perhaps your job with Channel 10 will work into something full time."

Freeda glanced up from a forkful of eggs, a sly smile turning up her full lips at the corners. "You hopin' I'll get somethin' full time so you can get rid of me?"

"Nena would never hear of it." Cere reached over to catch a ringlet that dangled close to the plate and tucked it behind Freeda's ear. Ever since her ten-year-old cousin arrived in California to live with their grandmother, carrying nothing but a battered Barbie suitcase and a dirty pink, stuffed poodle, the two had been inseparable. Nena made them pledge to look out for each other, but Cere did most of the "looking out." Not that she minded. She couldn't imagine life without Freeda.

"Let's go back to your dream." Freeda waved her fork, flicking pieces of egg around them.

Patiently, Cere wiped up clumps that fell on the counter. "It's the same guy and we're in a dark room and he wants help."

"Nena says it means something if you keep having the same dream. We should go see her, let her analyze it. What are you doing tomorrow? Let's drive to Santa Barbara."

"Hello?" Cere rapped a knuckle on Freeda's bent head. "Remember Randy Waverly? We'll *both* be at the Santa Monica courthouse. Did you forget he's supposed to testify today? I don't understand how you could go drinking…" She stopped as Freeda flashed an impish grin.

"You shoulda reminded Audrey. It was her idea."

Wonderful! Probably the biggest story of the year and her photographer would be hung over. With a sigh she slid off her stool. "I better head to the office. Maybe I can do an early blog on what to expect."

"You're so dedicated." Freeda let her fork clatter to

the plate and shoved herself to her feet. "I better get some sleep."

"Good idea. He's due to arrive first thing. I'll save you a spot in case you're late."

"Thanks for saving my butt. Again." She turned and thumped down the hall, leaving a lump of eggs to harden on her plate and toast crumbs scattered around the counter.

Cere cleared the counter, rinsed the dishes and put them in the dishwasher. At least Freeda's drama had eliminated some of the anxiety caused by her dream. For an instant, as she walked down the hall to shower, Cere could see those eyes.

"Help me. You're the only one who can."

****

The rapping at the door jerked Sheriff Rafe Tafoya away from his first cup of coffee. Ginny! Fear that his daughter might be ill propelled him to his feet and to the front door. Relief and surprise surged through him when he recognized the outline of his neighbor, Lottie Medina, through the sheer drapes of his front door.

"Lottie, you okay?" he asked as he pulled the door open.

She was a retired school teacher who lived around the corner and kept fit with her morning jogs. Today, her normally smiling countenance was pale and a frown slashed across her brow. Her concerned look jerked his protective instincts to life.

"I'm fine," she said, though she sounded breathless and she cast a quick look back over her shoulder. "I'm sorry to bother you, but I saw your light on so I jogged over. I'm probably just spooked."

"Spooked?" He looked beyond her. The streets of

Rio Rojo were quiet, not unusual for six in the morning in the small New Mexico town.

She choked out a laugh. "I am being silly. That's what thirty years of living in the city will do to you."

"Come on in."

Lottie stepped inside and took a deep breath as though catching the rich aroma of his strong coffee. "I hope I didn't wake Ginny," she said, looking toward the narrow hallway that led to the bedrooms.

"She spent the night at Mom's since I had to do early morning rounds. Come on in. I just made a fresh pot of coffee. Tell me, what has you spooked?"

She glanced out the wide front window one last time before following him through the living and dining rooms. "Have you seen that big black van that's been around town lately?"

Rafe had spent a dozen years as a police officer in Los Angeles and he prided himself on his powers of observation. "Big black van? No, I can't say that I have."

"I've seen it a few times. It has out of state license plates. Now I'm probably being silly, like I said." She drew a quick, sharp breath as she sank onto a chair at the kitchen table. "When I came out to run this morning, I saw it parked down my street and as I ran past, I realized there was someone sitting in it. Watching me. Well, maybe not watching. I am the only fool out this early so he might have simply been sitting there. But why on a residential street three blocks from downtown? Anyway, I did my run, but as I was coming back, there it was again, parked a few blocks over and the guy was still in it. He had moved. So I thought, did he know where I was running? That's probably me being paranoid. I lived too many years in Los Angeles where you pay attention to strange details. But you police officers were always the ones telling us to watch out for things like that."

Rafe poured her a steaming cup of coffee and placed the cup on the table before retrieving milk from the refrigerator. He pushed a small tray of sugar and sweetener across the table toward her. "No cream, sorry. I don't blame you for being paranoid, and there is a good reason we tell people that. And Rio Rojo may not be a big city, but that's what makes unknown people more noticeable." Their shared past in California was part of why they had become friends since her arrival. Like him she had grown up here before leaving for the city. Maybe it was telling they had both come back.

"It could be an innocent reason," she said, making a face as she stirred sweetener into her coffee. "It just seemed out of place. Why would a stranger be parked on two different streets, when I was running by? Then I saw your lights so I came over."

He started toward the door, but she shook her head. "He's gone. I looked back when I started knocking and he left before you opened the door."

"I'll keep a watch out," he said with a nod as he slid back onto the chair where he'd been earlier.

"I'm really sorry I had to bother you. I mean, what if you had a lady guest?"

Rafe almost choked as he took a sip of coffee. "Lady guest?"

She gave him a coy smile. "You never know."

He grunted and shook his head. "In this town, I know. I think I dated every girl within five years of my age before I left. And don't you start trying to set me up with people. I get enough of it from Mom."

"You're lucky your Aunt Rosalie is not still around. When we were in high school, she was the queen of matchmaking. I never had to look for a date because she would always find someone for both of us. If she was still with us, she'd be searching from Taos to Albuquerque to find the right woman for you."

He didn't want to encourage her, but he was pleased to see her earlier tension had eased. At least she was now smiling. This was the Lottie he knew and enjoyed. "Are you saying she'd set *us* up?"

She laughed. "Goodness no. She'd find a way to get my Cere out here and introduce the two of you."

Cere Medina. TV star. He knew how proud Lottie was of her journalist daughter, but he'd watched her reports and all he could think was *no thanks.* "Well, I hear you've got the hottest romance in town, dating the mayor?"

She made a face. "Don't tell me you listen to that crazy gossip. And we're just friends." But her giggle was more like a teenager than a retired fifty-something. Then she sobered. "You know what? I think I saw that car last night too, when Bradley and I were coming out of Gennaro's Restaurant. Oh, my gosh. You don't think I have someone following me, do you?"

Chapter Two

"Here they come!"

The shout was a war cry—a call to arms. A long black limousine provided the objective, with cameras and microphones the weapons of choice. Cere eyed the gathering swarm of warriors preparing to storm the castle—except these warriors wore expensive suits and designer ensembles instead of armor.

Another day of battle on the news front.

She drew a deep breath and hurtled into the thick of the crowd, hoping for a glimpse of little Randy. The custody battle had waged for three days, but this was the first time he was expected to appear and tell the judge his side.

Switching on her microphone she searched the frantic throng until she located Audrey Jones. Her photographer's statuesque height was invaluable in tight situations. Cere didn't see Freeda, but this was every woman for herself. Ducking around thrusting microphones and waving cell phones, Cere maneuvered her way to the front. She swung out her elbow to clear a spot for Audrey to join her and photograph Randy as he emerged from the limo.

The boy was shorter than she expected, a skinny kid with flaxen hair in a blue suit that appeared to be too big, even though it was probably custom-made. The public adored Randy for his rubbery face and wide blue eyes, which exuded glee on the screen. He'd made millions in a string of comedies, but today his thin lips pinched together, his cherubic face as pale as his hair. His willowy, platinum-haired mother kept her arm around his small shoulders as though issuing her visible claim to the boy.

The media army surrounded the pair as they fought their way up the steps and into the sanctuary offered by the courthouse. Around Cere, still photographers frantically focused and snapped pictures. Television cameramen shouldering compact equipment jostled for the best position. Microphones with colorful logos thrust forward like swords. Boom mikes dangled overhead like vultures about to pounce. Cere shoved her hand microphone at the pair, battling to be heard over the others.

"Randy, who do you want to live with?" she shouted.

He blinked, blue eyes growing larger, but he didn't answer.

"Where's your dad?" Gail Martin, the frail network correspondent, jostled aside the reporter next to her with the zeal of a linebacker.

"Are you going to testify?"

"What are you going to say?"

"Hey, Randy, look over here."

The boy's eyes flashed with fear as he contemplated the stampede of reporters and cameras. His mother shielded him, ignoring the questions. A cadre of attorneys and police officers fought to shove the crowd aside and keep the pair shuffling toward the doors of the courthouse. As quickly as they arrived, the two were swept inside, and the media army retreated.

"Damn!" Cere grimaced in pain as her gaze lowered to her black Italian pumps. During the fray, someone had stepped on her foot. The scuffed blemish on the expensive leather hurt worse than her mashed toe. She leaned down to rub it.

Audrey appeared beside her. "You should have worn Reeboks."

"Probably. Did you get anything good?"

"Great shots of the kid. Wanna see it, or do you want it downloaded to your laptop?" She hefted the video camera from her shoulder with one hand, tanned arms displaying fine muscular tone.

Turning to the courthouse, Cere waved her hand in frustration. "I want to be in there. I want to hear what they tell the judge."

"Now what? Another day of waiting? Writing a running blog and keeping up with Twitter fans?" Audrey scanned the activity outside the courthouse as she shoved her blue baseball cap higher on her forehead. Her blonde ponytail poked through the back.

Around them reporters and photographers were setting out lawn chairs under a green awning as though preparing for a giant picnic. Most were already tapping on laptop keyboards or texting into cell phones.

Cere pulled out her phone. "Go ahead and transfer the video to my laptop and send in video of the kid." She hated waiting, but she could send a preliminary report for the web to use with Audrey's pictures.

"You want tonight's lead," Audrey teased as she unlocked the van to retrieve Cere's laptop. "You're wearing your new Prada jacket."

Cere didn't react to Audrey's baiting, though she had paid special attention to her wardrobe and hair,

15

which was why she'd chosen the Italian pumps over running shoes. She'd carefully selected the navy blazer, beige linen slacks and a sleeveless pink shell. She'd also taken care with her make-up, using a light shade of green to enhance her brown eyes and blush to make her face look less round. She was pleased she'd had the foresight to have her customary auburn streaks put into her shoulder-length brown tresses a couple of weeks early.

"It *is* the lead." She waved at the throng of reporters. "Look at this circus."

Their van was one of several dozen emblazoned with bright logos that lined a side street near the courthouse. Rows of microwave trucks sent up towering masts, while across the street, several bulky satellite trucks pointed their dishes into space. Lines of cable snaked across the street which was closed at both ends by barricades. She held up her phone, snapped a picture of the media crowd and emailed it to the web producer.

Reporters stood in front of the courthouse to deliver reports for local and cable stations but Cere didn't have to worry about going "live." *Scope* was a syndicated news program broadcast every weekday. Their ongoing work would be uploaded on the *Scope* website and their full edited report would appear on the evening program.

Cere watched with disguised envy as Gail barked orders at her photographer in front of the courthouse. Why was Gail the network star while she couldn't get noticed? Could it be the woman's wild mane of honey-colored hair and willowy figure? People called Cere cute and curvy, but men didn't stare at her when she walked into a room—not like Gail.

Freeda, wrapped in a black leather coat, popped her head around the corner of the van. Her dark eyes were rimmed with black eyeliner that only emphasized their bloodshot nature. "Hey, guys, where is the network star today?"

Cere put her finger to her lips and gestured at Gail's producer who was setting up a chair nearby. Because they worked for the same network, Cere and Gail sat near each other, though Cere knew the reason was Audrey's video. Gail's camera person always seemed to be out of position, while Cere made certain her photographer got a good spot.

Audrey appeared from the back of the van and shook a finger at Freeda. "You look as bad as I feel. Nice outfit. Cere, didn't you buy that last week?"

She drew a quick breath and jerked around as Freeda removed her coat, displaying a beige Kate Spade sweater and black knit St. John skirt. Damn! Her cousin was always dipping into her closet, but she'd hoped to save the ensemble for an important occasion.

"I had to rush," Freeda replied without apology. "So the kid's already inside, huh? Damn, I missed it."

As though noticing Cere's clenched hands, Audrey thrust the laptop at her. "Video's all here, babe. Great stuff."

With a sigh, she took the computer and set up a folding chair at the edge of the awning. She placed the laptop on her knees and called up the video file. Freeda leaned over her shoulder.

"Good, I wanna see how it went down."

"Do you mind if I watch too?" Gail walked over to join them.

Cere bit her tongue and tapped the "play" icon. The pictures showed Randy emerge from the car with wide, startled eyes. The crowd moved in, and Audrey's lens caught the mess for a moment before zeroing in on the boy's tense face. Cere's voice sounded shrill as she shouted her question and she grimaced. Better remember to bring her voice down a notch next time.

Freeda giggled at the chaotic scene. "Damned media parasites."

"As if you wouldn't have been right in the thick of it," Cere said.

"Nice video," Gail cooed. "Mind if I get a copy?"

"Sure, when I'm finished with my report." In a proprietary gesture, she pulled the computer closer to her and began tapping the keyboard.

Freeda turned her attention to her phone and began texting. "*Muchos gracias.* Just like I was there. Shall I ask my EP if he wants to buy that video?"

"You work for a competing network," Gail protested, looking from one to the other. "You two are going to get into trouble sharing, and *you* weren't even there!"

They didn't work on the same story often and never shared video without permission, but Gail was getting angry. Cere shook her head at Freeda. "Not this time."

"I'm gonna sack out in the front seat," Audrey said with a yawn. "I'll keep my camera handy. Call me if they come out."

Cere didn't look up from her keyboard. "You set up your tripod outside the courthouse in case there's a news conference and sent in the video, right?"

Audrey barked out her answer with a grin and

salute. "Yes'm, drill sergeant!"

"You think she'd take a chance of slacking when she's working with the scourge of photojournalists everywhere?" Freeda teased.

"What?" Cere looked from Freeda to Audrey but both were smiling.

Freeda winked. "People know better than to argue with you, right, Audrey?"

Audrey tilted her head toward Cere and saluted again. "Yes'm, drill sergeant!"

"Screw you both. The guys can call me stubborn and aggressive all they want. I'm just being meticulous—"

Freeda snorted. "And killing the competition. Climbing fences, getting locked into restricted areas. Normal things."

Cere knew that while some journalists disapproved of her tactics, her bosses trusted her to get a good story. A few feet away, Gail smiled as she focused on her computer, obviously enjoying the exchange.

Cere had heard enough. She waved at Audrey. "Go take your damn nap. I need to send this in." As she sat up after finishing her report, Freeda leaned toward her.

"Mind if I borrow your computer? I left mine somewhere last night."

"The computer I let you borrow? You lost it?"

Freeda flicked her hand like swatting a fly. "Misplaced it. May I borrow yours to check in?"

The computer was an old laptop, but Cere was tempted to say no. Sooner or later her cousin had to stop being so careless.

Gail snapped her fingers to get their attention. "I would like to look at that video again."

Cere forced a smile. "Sure, Gail. I'll give it to you when she's done." She handed the computer to Freeda who plopped on the ground cross-legged. Hopefully grass stains would come out of the new skirt—if she got the item back before Freeda traded it.

For now clothes weren't her main concern. She needed a new story or a different angle. With dozens of hungry reporters around, she didn't intend to get stuck in the crowd. She was going to make that leap to the network—one way or another.

"I need to talk to the parents." She pounded her thigh with her fist in frustration. An exclusive interview would put her on the network news.

"Good luck," Freeda said, without looking up. "I've been trying all week."

"His dad is out of town," Gail added with a smirk. "My producer learned that Richard Waverly was spotted in Italy this morning."

Cere noted the emphasis on "my producer." Why couldn't *Scope* provide her with a producer to make calls?

On the ground, Freeda was oblivious to their conversation. She was engrossed with the computer so Cere used her phone to check whether her report and pictures had been posted online.

After a few minutes, Gail began to pace, and finally stopped above Freeda, her body vibrating with tension. "Are you almost finished?"

"Huh?" Freeda glanced up in confusion.

"I need that laptop to view Audrey's video."

"Oh, sure." Freeda turned to Cere. "Do you have a printer in the van?"

"No, why?"

"I want to print this story so I can finish reading it. Remember the Palladium? That old dance hall in New Mexico near where your mom is living? There's a story about it. Remember how scared we got when we went out there ghost hunting as kids?"

"What?" She leaned over her cousin's shoulder. Instead of a script, Freeda was reading what looked like a webpage.

"What the hell are you doing?" Gail cried.

Freeda ignored her and grinned at Cere. "Your mom emailed you a link to a Santa Fe newspaper."

"You're reading my email?" She had to fight to keep anger out of her tone.

Nonplussed, Freeda gestured at the laptop. "Remember? Some kid told a story about the place being haunted. The ghost was a guy who left a bloody handprint on the wall when he killed himself."

Cere looked beyond her at a picture. She'd been twelve years old, and their evening ghost hunting expedition with several cousins haunted her dreams for weeks. Now the building looked like a long pile of sagging rocks with boarded up windows.

Freeda enlarged the picture and another beside it. "There's the ghost." She pointed at a grainy black and white photo of a young man. "Meet Marco Gonzales."

"I need the damn computer," Gail insisted.

Her demanding voice faded as the day grew still. Cere's stomach clenched and her breath caught as goose bumps rose on her skin. She stumbled backward.

"What?" Freeda asked, noting her alarm.

Despite the faded image, Cere knew Marco. His eyes burned from the screen.

"That… that's the man in my dream."

Chapter Three

Rafe spotted short bursts of dust plumes in the distance and turned his Jeep Grand Cherokee off the highway beside a tilted wooden sign. The letters on the sign were barely readable, and rust had taken a toll on the "no trespassing" sign that hung nearby on the barbed wire fence. Someone had used the metal sign for target practice. Fresh tire tracks in the dirt provided confirmation that someone had ignored the sign and driven to the Palladium.

The owners needed to put a locked gate on the road. That might not keep out determined teenagers who wouldn't hesitate to climb over or through the barbed wire, but it might deter casual interlopers. He chased away kids all the time, but he understood the allure. How many times had he been out there as a kid? Hell, he'd made a business out of leading the curious to the dance hall in search of the elusive ghost of Marco Gonzales. No one ever witnessed anything supernatural, but no one asked for their money back either. The spookiness fulfilled all promises of a frightening adventure.

As he rounded a bend, the long stone two-story structure with its pitched, rusting tin roof came into view. It hadn't been used in at least thirty years and the interior was a major disaster waiting to happen. The floor boards were rotting when he was young. Now they had to be dangerous.

Why the hell didn't the owners tear it down? The interior was a smelly mess of bird and cow droppings and the walls were scarred by graffiti. One day someone was going to get hurt in there. Things hadn't been so bad until recently, when a Santa Fe newspaper reporter dredged up the old story. This was the fourth time in two weeks he'd had to chase someone away.

The sun glinted off a black Cadillac Escalade parked in the gravel parking lot. Texas license plates. This wouldn't be good. Expensive cars often meant jerks. Hopefully it wasn't a bunch of rich kids on a joy ride. Or perhaps…could this be the vehicle that frightened Lottie?

He saw no sign of anyone as he stopped his patrol vehicle beside the big SUV. The afternoon air caught him like a hot blanket as he stepped outside. Its stillness could hypnotize with its silence. Nary a rustle came from the grove of cottonwood trees that bordered a pond beyond the building.

A loud crack broke the stillness. He trotted around the building to the wooden veranda that bordered the back end and stretched along the side overlooking the pond. A tall lanky man hunched over a boarded up window in the back. He pulled at the rotting slats with a crow bar. Fresh scratches in the peeling paint of the back door indicated he might have first tried to pry off a metal latch. The thick door had refused to budge and so had the thick padlock.

"Can I help you there?" Rafe called. He took a long step over a broken stair and climbed onto the rotting wood planks that formed the floor of the veranda.

The man jerked back, whirling toward him. While

he'd been sheriff for little more than a year, Rafe had grown up in Rio Rojo and knew almost everyone in the Verde Valley. This man was a stranger. He was dressed all in black, from his cowboy hat to his narrow western-style shirt, black jeans, and polished cowboy boots. Even his sunglasses were a dark shade of black.

A cowboy? No. Those designer jeans had never seen the back of a horse and his boots were the type purchased in a high end Santa Fe shop.

"This place is closed," Rafe said when he didn't answer. "Didn't you see the 'no trespassing' sign at the turn off?"

The man's placid face didn't move. Rafe put him at around forty, despite a thatch of gray hair protruding from the hat. He was of equal height, right around six feet tall, or perhaps it was the heel on the boots that made him seem taller.

"I suggest you get in your fancy SUV and get the hell out of here before I arrest you on trespassing or vandalism charges."

The man lowered the crowbar, but still didn't speak and despite the shady porch, he didn't remove the glasses.

Tired of waiting for a reply, Rafe stretched out his upturned palm. "Got some ID?"

The crowbar fell to the wood boards with a clatter as the man reached into his back pocket with his left hand. He moved so quickly Rafe found himself placing his hand on the top of his gun.

The stranger produced a black wallet that looked like rich leather, embossed with the initials "DV" and retrieved a license to hand to Rafe. "Name's Diego Diaz." His voice was harsh, raspy, and carried the twang of a Texas accent.

"What does DV stand for?" He gestured at the wallet as he glanced at the Texas license.

The man looked at it as though seeing it for the first time. "Velasquez is my middle name." He cleared his throat though his reply still came out hoarse. "People call me D-V."

"Uh-huh." The picture depicted the man wearing a black eye patch. The green of his other eye was a startling contrast to the deep golden hue of his skin. His hair was on the long side, curling over his ears, streaked with gray and black. Rafe started to return the license, but the age caught his attention.

"How old are you?" He felt as though he was carding a teenager with a fake ID.

"Fifty-seven," the man replied without missing a beat. That agreed with the license, but his smooth face showed no wrinkles.

"What are you doing here?" He waved at the window as he handed back the license.

"You're the police chief in Rio Rojo?" Diaz put away the license and tucked the wallet back into his pocket.

"I'm Sheriff Rafe Tafoya. This is county land. What are you doing here?"

The man hesitated, then nodded. "I saw a story in the paper about this place, and I was curious so I drove over."

"From Texas? That's at least a four-hour drive."

His quick laugh was gruff. "I was at a meeting in Santa Fe. Don't mean any harm, Sheriff. Just passin' through, as they say."

"I suggest you keep passing. This is private

property and the owners pay my salary to keep people out."

"Who are the owners?" Diaz asked.

"You interested in buying it?"

Again, that quick harsh laugh. "Maybe. Wanna give me a tour as a potential buyer?"

"I may run in your ass for trespassing if you don't get back in your fancy vehicle and get the hell out of here."

Diaz held up a hand. "Hey, son, I'm not looking for trouble. I can have my business manager finish the deal."

Sarcasm dripped from his tone, but Rafe let it ride. He wanted the stranger gone. Not being able to see the man's eyes bothered him. Maybe he'd spent too many years in Los Angeles dealing with smart alecks in shades.

"Want me to fix that board?" Diaz asked.

"I'll send someone to do it. Just hit the road."

The man picked up the crowbar and slung it over his shoulder. To Rafe's surprise, Diaz smiled as he walked by. He moved with a slight limp, faltering as he stepped around the broken step.

"One more quick question, though," Rafe said, as the man reached the ground. "Were you parked over on Maple Street this morning?"

The man jerked his head up. "Huh?"

"Someone said they saw a big black vehicle parked on Maple earlier today. Was that you?"

Again the strange grin came. "Like you said, Sheriff, you're not police chief, are you? Shouldn't *he* be asking me questions if there's some sort of problem? Not that it matters. If I was parked on that street, it might have been I was visiting an old friend."

Rafe bristled, but he didn't reply. He had a feeling the man wanted another excuse to verbally spar. Instead he followed as the man ambled toward the Cadillac, whistling. He tossed in the crowbar, hopped into the vehicle and waved back as though knowing he was being watched. Only when the dust plumes dissipated as the man turned onto the highway did Rafe get into his Jeep to continue his rounds.

****

"They're coming out," someone called from across the grass. Reporters and photographers scrambled from their chairs. Grabbing microphones, notepads and cameras, the media throng rushed toward the courthouse.

"Oh, hell," Freeda shouted, jumping to her feet.

Cere still reeled from her discovery about Marco Gonzales and the words took a few seconds to reach her consciousness. She blinked away the spooky image as she closed her computer.

Damn! Audrey was asleep in the van. Cere glanced around in case the shouts had wakened her. Gail and her producer sprinted across the lawn, but Audrey was nowhere to be seen. Cere banged on the side of the van and opened the door to yank at Audrey's foot, making her moan.

"I told you they'd be out early. Hurry! Get up!"

As a groggy Audrey rose, Cere spied movement from the side of the courthouse. A door opened and a familiar cherubic face poked out. She froze as the black limo turned the corner not far from the door.

"What are you doing?" Freeda cried, but didn't wait for a reply. She dashed toward the crowd which was already jockeying for positions at the front of the courthouse.

Audrey grabbed her camera, and Cere jabbed her finger at the side door, which was now fully open. "Let's go that way."

The photographer's eyes widened and she nodded without saying a word. The limo glided to a stop near the side entrance, but no one else seemed to notice. Walking with determined steps but not fast enough to draw attention, Cere and Audrey moved toward the waiting limo. The chauffeur stepped out and waited.

The pair reached the door as Randy and his mother stepped through it. Cere thrust her microphone toward the boy, knowing Audrey would be ready. "Did you testify?"

His mother pulled her son behind her and faced Cere, wide blue eyes startled. "No, he didn't. The case is settled. We didn't want to make him choose."

"We're going home." Little Randy flashed his familiar smile as he peered around his mother's waist.

A rotund man in a blue suit whom Cere recognized as their attorney shot her a furious look. He grabbed the woman's arm and hustled her and Randy toward the car.

Without missing a beat, Cere whirled to the blue-suited man. "What was the settlement?"

"There was no settlement. A statement will be issued from my office later," he snapped.

Audrey's camera followed the group into the limo and then the car as it glided toward the intersection of a main thoroughfare. Shouts erupted around the building and news crews swarmed toward the limo.

"Let's follow it." Cere grabbed Audrey's arm as

heavy traffic immediately stalled the car's progress.

"I'll never get the van out."

Freeda appeared, dangling car keys. "I parked across the street since I arrived late. I'll drive, but we share all video."

"No problem." Cere's expensive heels dug into the wet grass as they jogged, but she didn't hesitate. Catching the limo could get her the lead on the national broadcast and put her in front of the corporate brass. *Take that, Gail!*

They darted across the street, and she flung herself into the back seat of Freeda's Honda so Audrey could take the front. Freeda grabbed a ticket off her windshield and slid in. Audrey began shooting the instant Freeda steered the car onto the street. Skillfully, she maneuvered her way through traffic to a spot behind the limo much to Audrey's shouted delight.

The limo led them east to the 405 Freeway, then north to Sunset Boulevard where they wound through the curves of Beverly Hills. It finally turned onto a side street and stopped in a driveway. Freeda whipped the car around in a U-turn.

As Randy and his mother emerged from the limo, Audrey steadied herself on the door and began shooting. The woman glanced toward the street, face pale, her lips pulled into a thin line. The boy stood frozen for a moment, looking bewildered.

"Zoom in on his face," Cere called to Audrey.

The door to the house opened, and a tall, familiar figure appeared. Richard Waverly had starred in dozens of movies and there was no mistaking his thick blond, wavy hair.

"Daddy," the boy shouted and ran toward him.

The man caught Randy in his arms. "Welcome home, buddy boy."

The woman gestured toward the street as Waverly looked up. He put his arm around her and Randy in a protective motion and they walked toward the house. The portly attorney glared at the three women as he climbed from the limo, but Audrey kept recording.

Cere waved a fist in triumph. "They can issue all the statements they want."

"Yup, we got the real story right here." Audrey tapped her camera off as the door to the house closed.

"I bet everyone complains about us following the limo and interrupting the family reunion," Freeda added with a delighted giggle.

"Only after they ask if they can have the video," Cere said. "I guess Daddy wasn't in Italy after all. Good work, ladies."

The three exchanged high fives and slid back into the car.

Chapter Four

"To the Waverly reunion." Cere lifted her glass of champagne as Freeda and Audrey joined her. They were giddy even though they hadn't drunk a single drop. Audrey's video had won Cere the coveted lead spot on the *Scope* broadcast and had been the headline video for the network. Gail used it in her report, but Cere didn't care. She'd done so many interviews with national TV outlets, her face would be everywhere for the next twenty-four hours.

"Did you call Nena and *Tia* Lottie?" Freeda asked. Cere might be the caretaker, but Freeda made certain they met familial obligations.

"I'll call in the morning. When I sober up." They cheered and drank another gulp of champagne.

"Now that the trial is over, we should go see your mom," Freeda urged. "I've heard New Mexico is beautiful in June."

Cere's champagne glass thumped on the marble table top. "Are you kidding? I can't leave now. Tomorrow I'm calling the Waverlys to see if they'll do an interview."

"The network tried that," Audrey said. "The family left town for Mexico or New Mexico. I overheard a producer telling the bureau chief this afternoon."

"Our network chief?" Cere asked. "What were you doing hanging with the enemies?"

Audrey focused on her champagne glass. "I might as well tell you. The network has asked me to work out of the LA bureau. Alan called when I got back today and I met with the bureau chief. He wants me to start in two weeks."

Cere didn't know if she was pleased or envious. Probably both. If anyone deserved a shot at the network, it was Audrey. Had the brass noticed her efforts too?

"Congratulations!" she said, raising her glass again. "Now we really have something to celebrate."

"I put in a plug for you," Audrey said. "Don't be surprised if they call you next."

"They'll call if I track down the Waverlys and get an interview."

Audrey shook her head. "You never quit, do you?"

Cere drained her glass. "Nope."

Audrey grabbed the bottle and frowned. She lurched to her feet. "We need more champagne and I'm buying the next round." Without waiting for a server, she pushed her way through the crowd toward the bar.

"You okay, babe?" Freeda leaned toward Cere.

She nodded, though her smile dissolved. Audrey deserved a chance, but so did she. "I just need a big story to get noticed."

"We should do that story from the newspaper. Didn't you say Alan loves cold cases and ghosts?"

Scope did a combination of unique stories—from Hollywood gossip to undercover reports, unsolved mysteries and investigations of the occult. Alan Dunn, the executive producer, was always begging for something new.

"Who cares about some old suicide in New

Mexico?"

Freeda tapped her arm. "Hey, according to that article he might not have committed suicide. The story hints at murder. Where do you think the ghost stories originated? He was accused of some crime, sent to jail but swore he was innocent. He said he'd come back and prove it. Maybe that's why he's haunting your dreams."

Cere hadn't thought about Marco Gonzales all day. She waved a hand. "At least my dreams make sense now. I bet I saw his picture when I opened the email and it brought back those scary memories."

"Maybe."

She knew why Freeda was so enthralled. Her cousin's earliest memories were of New Mexico and it still fascinated her. They'd also recently heard rumors that Freeda's father might be living there. Joe Ferguson was constantly on the move, though he turned up every so often to visit Freeda. He'd been doing that ever since leaving her at a New Mexico commune after her mother died. Freeda hadn't remained there long. Nena dispatched Cere's dad to get her granddaughter. During the trip, Cere and Freeda bonded, in part because of their visit to the Palladium.

Freeda reached into her bag and pulled out a sheaf of printed pages. "I don't know... You've been dreaming him for a while."

"Oh, stop it. Show me the damn thing already." She shivered as she viewed the photo of the man in her dream. The caption read, "*Saint or Sinner?*" Had she seen that picture before the dreams started?

The man's face was thin but arresting, with high cheekbones and a determined jaw with the wisp of a goatee. His dark eyes seemed to burn off the page

Rebecca Grace

despite the age of the photo. He stood with his fist in the air, a symbol of protest. His dark beret and Army jacket painted the same picture. Cere could not take her eyes off him. Even now that unreal voice echoed in her ear.

"Help me."

Flipping the page, another blurred picture caught her eye. She studied it—a smudged outline of a palm print, the sort a child might make in finger painting class. Her stomach did a funny jiggle. She didn't need to read the caption to know the hand print was supposedly made with the dying man's blood.

Freeda's voice seemed to come through a fog. "See that? The hand on the wall. It's still there."

The bloody handprint was what she, Freeda and her cousins set out to see at the Palladium. Marco's ghost was only part of the allure.

"What are you guys reading with such interest?" Audrey asked as she swung back into a seat at the table, carrying a fresh bottle of champagne. She refilled glasses as Freeda explained.

"When Cere's folks came to get me, we stayed with her mom's family for a few days. One night a friend of her cousins told us about a ghost that haunted this old building. He offered to drive us out there for five bucks."

Cere touched her wrist to interrupt. "Correction. He invited the boys. They didn't want to take us. Scared little girls, you know."

"Naturally Cere pulled her weight and…"

"Not weight. Money. They didn't have enough, so I volunteered two dollars from my allowance." She didn't add that her hand trembled as she gave them the bills. She'd felt like a scared little girl as they crammed into the boy's Ford.

She gazed at the picture of the Palladium. Was that dilapidated building really the place that haunted her? As a child, she viewed it as a looming skyscraper in the darkness—strange and sinister. Even the misshapen trees around it appeared monstrous. Now they were simply stubby juniper trees.

Freeda tapped the pages. "Kids still go looking for the ghost. We thought we heard him. Remember?"

Cere shivered, and for an instant she was in the claustrophobic room on the second floor of the Palladium. She stood with the small group as they gathered around the handprint. The only light came from a flickering flashlight trained on the spooky, smudged outline.

"When we saw the handprint, those noisy guys shut up," she recalled.

"Total silence," Freeda agreed in a soft tone as though she could feel the quiet too.

Audrey looked from one to the other. "You're freaking me out."

"It was spooky," Cere said. "Then something happened. A creaking? What was it?"

Freeda thrust up her arms in a dramatic gesture. "More of a groan. Maybe a gust of wind made the building creak. Whatever it was, we ran like bats out of hell and all the doors slammed shut."

Cere's throat constricted. She hadn't escaped with the others. The slamming doors closed with her inside that room.

The noise of the bar fell away until she was alone in a space darker than night.

For an instant she feared she was locked inside forever with the ghost. Her shaking fingers felt for the door and found the big round knob. She twisted, but it refused to turn. She shouted, but the footsteps beyond the door faded. In fear she stumbled around the room, feeling the walls for a way out. As she neared the wall where she knew the handprint was, the door behind her swung open with a squeaky sound. A flickering light guided her.

She ran down the stairs well behind the others, hurtling through the open front door. As she dashed toward the car, nearby dark, fat shapes transformed into animated monsters marching toward her. Something grabbed at her legs and she tumbled to the ground. She rolled onto her back, staring up at a star-filled sky. Was that the last sight she would ever see? She looked to the side. The walls of the building towered over her as though reaching out to claim her. To the other side, those dark shapes moved closer.

What was that rustling sound she heard? Chanting?

Fear snatched at her, telling her she was going to be captured. Heart thudding, she waited for the ghost and his unearthly army to claim her...

"I was so damn scared." Cere shivered and shook her head to clear it. She hadn't recalled that awful night in years. She realized her fingers were shaking and put down her tilting glass so the others wouldn't notice.

"Hell, we all were," Freeda agreed. "I still don't know how you got back to the car first."

Cere didn't know either. She'd closed her eyes and kept them shut tight when strong arms lifted her. "Someone carried me. I think it was that stupid kid who took us out there. I was surprised to open my eyes and find myself staring at the car door."

Freeda turned to Audrey and laughed. "Needless to say, we rode back to town in total silence."

"Quite a story."

Freeda pounded on Cere's shoulder. "She's been dreaming of the ghost. He's asking for help."

Ignoring her, Cere pulled the pages closer and began to read the story.

Convicted of burglary as a teenager, Marco Gonzales claimed he was wrongfully accused and promised revenge on the town of Rio Rojo. While in prison he joined an activist group, and when he returned, he preached peace and tolerance as he pushed for civil rights.

However, when a rash of vandalism and burglaries hit the town, Gonzales became a suspect. Businesses were looted and small fires set to cover the thefts. One fire flared out of control and several businesses burned to the ground. Official reports indicate that following the fire, Gonzales was tracked to the Palladium where he killed himself with a shotgun. According to current Sheriff Rafe Tafoya, he was never charged with the final round of crimes, but the burglaries stopped after his death. The money taken in the thefts—said to be thousands of dollars—was never recovered.

Cere lowered the pages and whirled toward Freeda. "Wait a minute! After all these years, no one has ever tried to find the money he stole? What do you suppose happened to it?"

"Exactly! And look at that." Freeda pointed to another picture below the handprint.

"All for love?" Cere read the smudged words

written in Spanish that were described as being below the hand. "Why didn't that kid tell us about that?"

"Too mushy." Freeda giggled and wrinkled her nose. "That story says there may have been a secret woman involved."

"She took the money and split," Audrey offered in a matter-of-fact tone. "Or ran off with some other guy."

Freeda nodded. "Maybe. Why else commit suicide? Unless the lover killed him. Or the woman. See? Romantic mystery, hidden treasure? Just right for *Scope*."

Cere studied the story, but before she could read more, a sudden shout came from the front of the bar where a television set sat high above it.

"Hey, Cere, you got the network lead!"

She looked up, saw the anchorwoman and then her own face. She leaped to her feet and waved her fist in a victory pump.

"Top of the network," Freeda screeched. "What are you going to do to top this?"

Chapter Five

Rafe shoved aside the papers that littered his desk. His stomach churned and he took an antacid from his desk drawer and popped it into his mouth. Damn, he hated paperwork. Countless hours of mindlessly filling out forms. But it was necessary—even more than when he'd been on the police force in Los Angeles. The forms were useful county records that showed what his department did. That could add up to more state or federal funds. Computers were supposed to help. Now he filled out forms and put the information into the computer. Double paperwork.

He pushed his chair back from the desk. Its protesting screech filled the quiet room. He should get that oiled. He rubbed his hand over aching eyes. He was tired, almost too exhausted to get out of the hard, wooden chair and go home. The clock must read midnight, if he could see it. He had been on duty since four that morning.

His office was dark except for the splash of light from his desk lamp. Beyond his office, light spilled into the corridor through the open door to the restroom across the hall. A sudden scraping noise jerked him upright in his chair. Naldo Sanchez, the ancient janitor, shuffled out of the restroom. His thin shoulders drooped as he pushed a galvanized bucket on rollers using a mop handle to maneuver it. Seeing Rafe, he waved.

"I'm done. *Esta limpia.*" He pulled out a red handkerchief and wiped his dark, wrinkled forehead.

If Naldo was finished, the room would be very clean. The old man was undoubtedly the cleanest man in Rio Rojo and took pride in the few janitorial jobs he still did. Despite the late hour and having worked through the evening, Naldo's overalls were neatly pressed even if they were frayed around the cuffs. His gray hair was clipped so short his skull showed in places, an indication he cut his own hair.

Rafe wanted nothing more than to go home and stand under a hot shower but noting the older man's stooped posture, he gestured at the seat across from him. "*Sientese, Viejo.* You shouldn't be here so late. Tell me how you've been."

With a wheeze, Naldo nodded and pushed his bucket aside. He folded the handkerchief into a neat square with bony fingers and put it into his pocket. From another pocket he pulled a plastic water bottle. The liquid in it was the color of watered down tea, but Rafe suspected it was laced with something else. He didn't complain. Naldo did his work better than men half his age.

"Why are you working?" Rafe asked, lifting his feet to his desk and clasping hands across his midsection. "You should be retired. Spending your time fishing."

The grizzled face softened into a toothless grin. "I don't like to fish. This is *mi*..." He waved his hand toward the room. "*Dinero loco.* Spending money."

Rafe grinned. Like so many in Rio Rojo—Anglo and Hispanic—Naldo mixed English with liberal doses of Spanish. *Spanglish.* He couldn't imagine why the old man needed extra money. Naldo's tiny house had been owned by his father and his used pick-up was bought with cash. For years the Sanchez family ran a pawn shop and Naldo had plenty of unclaimed collectibles he could sell any time he needed anything.

"Sure, *Viejo.* You're a rich old man. I still hear rumors you got silver and gold coins buried in your back yard or tucked into a mattress." Rafe worked for Naldo as a boy, helping clean yards and shovel snow from walks. He knew the old man enjoyed the rumors about his supposed wealth.

Naldo cackled and took a long drink from the plastic bottle. "*Me gusto que trabajar.* Keeps me out of trouble." He might be slow in movement, but his brain remained quick, and his brown eyes were sharp. Since becoming sheriff, Rafe had learned that while people seldom paid attention to Naldo, few things happened in town without his knowing.

The phone jangled and Rafe jumped. He jerked his feet from the desk and sat up stiffly, stomach tightening as he reached for the phone. Calls this late usually meant trouble.

"Sheriff's office." Maybe it was Lottie wondering when he'd be by to pick up Ginny. He hadn't intended to make her babysit so long.

"Good, you're still open," said a strange woman's voice. "I'm trying to reach Sheriff Tafoya. Is he in?"

Why would anyone think he might still be in at midnight? "Maybe."

"I need to speak to the sheriff. This is critical."

He sat up straight. She was nearly shouting as noise filtered in from the background. "You have an emergency?"

"My name is Cere Medina and I work for *Scope News Magazine* in Los Angeles."

Tension rippled through his muscles. "Lottie's daughter? Is something wrong with Ginny? Why did Lottie call you?"

"Lottie?" The woman sounded surprised. "You know my mother?"

"Yes. Isn't that why you're calling?"

"No, no...the han..." There was noise behind her and she spoke to someone else. "I got the sheriff, I think."

Her voice sounded slurred and he realized why she was shouting. "Are you in a bar?"

"I work for a television news magazine. I may come out to do a story."

This had to be Lottie's doing. He'd watched her latest report at her mother's house while dropping off Ginny. He'd been drawn by her intense gaze as though she was looking right through the camera lens. Her melodious, fluid voice flowed over him, but her story troubled him. Shots of a frightened boy, a mother in distress. He didn't like her way of telling the story—interfering with what should have been a happy family reunion.

"You're coming here for a story?" He winked at Naldo as he adopted a hint of sarcasm. "A national program is interested in our little town?"

"Well, yes."

Why was she calling at midnight? She sounded half drunk. "What could we have that would be of interest to your audience?"

"The hand on the wall."

His attempt at levity exploded like a bursting

bomb, and Rafe shot to his feet despite his fatigue. "You're joking, right?"

"I saw the hand when I visited my cousins years ago."

Naturally. Maybe she was one of his former customers. This had to be a joke. "I see."

"I read a newspaper story." Eagerness took control of her tone as words spilled out like cards dumped onto a table. "I'd like to follow up and look into whether Marco Gonzales was murdered."

"Marco Gonzales murdered? What the hell are you talking about?" Her words pounded him like punches in the gut. He fished out another antacid tablet from his drawer with his free hand.

"I'd like to investigate. Like solving a cold case?"

"Ah, hell." He paced around his desk, gripping the phone until his hand cramped. Pictures of the frightened boy she'd used in her story popped into his head. If she could tread on a child's privacy, what else might she do? What did Lottie say about how intrepid her daughter was? "Look, it's midnight and I'm on my way home."

"Sure, Sheriff. I'll call you when I get there. We could interview you, you know, like a crime expert. We might even pay…"

"Yeah, right. Good night." He put down the phone and dropped back on his chair, like a deflated balloon. "Damn!"

Naldo emitted a soft belch that echoed like an alarm in the quiet room. Rafe had forgotten he was still there.

"*Que pasa?* They wanna do another story on Marco?" Naldo wiped the back of his hand across his mouth.

"Yeah, but TV this time. She says they'll pay for an interview." Rafe grunted.

"TV, huh? You gonna talk to 'em?"

"Hell, no. Hopefully I can convince her not to do it." Rafe had answered a few questions for the Santa Fe reporter, but mainly tried to dissuade him from writing the story. Television and national exposure would be a nightmare. He'd have to deal with more trespassers—tourists like that Texan, Diaz, whom he'd chased off earlier. He fumbled in his drawer for fresh antacid tablets.

"*Quienese?*" Naldo asked, using his lips to point at the phone. "Who was callin' you?"

Rafe stopped rummaging and glanced across the desk. A hint of a sparkle glistened in the old man's eyes. Damn, another problem. Television was the sort of excitement to stir up a lonely old man's life.

As far as Rafe knew, Naldo had not spoken to Gary Riggins. The reporter relied on old information, rumors, and filled in the blanks with speculation. The townspeople didn't speak to outsiders, but the daughter of a local resident, waving a checkbook and the chance at television fame, might be another story.

"You don't want to get mixed up in this," he warned with a dismissive wave of his hand. "This is going to be big trouble, *Viejo.*"

"*Yo se.* I'm gettin' too damn old *por chisme.*" The old man struggled to his feet and slid the bottle into his pocket. "*Buenos noches.*"

"Good night." Popping the fresh tablets into his mouth, he crunched down hard as he snapped off his light. After a quick pass through the building to make certain all the doors were locked, he stepped outside.

A warm summer breeze brushed his cheeks, holding a promise of warmer days to come. The scent of freshly mowed grass filled his nostrils. The streets were quiet except for the far away barking of a dog. Nearly a block away, Naldo ambled along.

Rafe climbed into his Jeep and drove until he was even with the old man. He stopped and rolled down his window. "Need a ride?"

"Nah. It does me good to walk."

As he drove on, headlights flashed in the rearview mirror. A dark SUV turned onto the street and pulled over beside Naldo, who waved it away. Rafe made a quick U-turn through a parking lot. This might be city jurisdiction, but he wasn't going to take chances. As he came back around, he saw that the vehicle was a black Cadillac Escalade and Naldo was climbing into it. Rafe stopped beside it.

Diaz rolled down the window. Despite the darkness, he still wore sunglasses. In the dark his gravelly voice sounded menacing. "Problem, Sheriff?"

Ignoring the question, Rafe looked beyond him. "You okay, Naldo?"

The weathered face wasn't visible, but the dark outline of his head bobbed. "*Si, si.*"

Diaz grinned. "Just giving the old man a ride home. Not breaking any laws, Sheriff. Not in your county."

"Ees okay," Naldo added. "*Mi amigo.*"

Rafe hesitated before driving on, watching the rearview mirror until the vehicle turned onto Naldo's street, Maple Street, where Lottie had seen the black car. Damn Diaz. He'd been playing games earlier.

He drew a deep breath, listening to the silence of

the town where he'd grown up. He'd come back from Los Angeles for that peace and quiet. Until now the town was just what he wanted. His parents spoiled Ginny and she enjoyed the freedom of small town life along with the attention of numerous relatives. If only he'd been able to convince Carmen sooner... He shook away that train of thought. He'd been as eager to earn big city wages as his wife had been about her opportunity to teach inner city youngsters.

Rio Rojo wasn't perfect. Every town had its legends and the spell of Marco Gonzales had held this town in a vise for years. Rafe never believed in the ghost, never witnessed anything supernatural at the Palladium, though he made it sound that way to make money as a teenager. Now, like a restless ghost stirring, a hot breeze whipped down the street, making the elm trees rustle. A superstitious person might say the spell of Marco was rising, hoping to regain its grip.

As sheriff, he believed in reality. Like Diego Diaz in his black Escalade. He couldn't be detained without a reason but Naldo's acquaintance with the man was surprising. In his years as a police detective, Rafe learned to sense when someone was hiding something. Diaz fit that bill.

Trouble waiting to happen.

So was Cere Medina and her crazy ideas about Marco Gonzales.

Chapter Six

"Exile! I swear we're in exile." Cere guided the rental car northwest along a two-lane highway. "They may call it New Mexico, but the truth is we've been banished from civilization. When was the last time we saw a car?"

Freeda studied the passing countryside. "There weren't that many on the interstate."

More than an hour ago they had turned off northbound Interstate 25 onto the state road that led toward Rio Rojo. They passed through towns nestled in rows of canyons surrounded by parched, rocky hills dotted with scrub brush, ground hugging cacti, juniper and piñon trees. The towns consisted of boarded up buildings, sprawling discount stores and fast food places linked by rows of aging brick houses, newer low profile stucco homes and scattered mobile homes. The hills were populated by cows, scrawny horses, and a few goats. Overhead hovering buzzards circled as they patiently waited for their next meal. Every so often they passed a small cross by the side of the road, surrounded by fading flowers. A ridge of mountains outlined in blue rose along the distant horizon.

Cere pounded a fist on the steering wheel, unable to contain the frustration that had gripped her for two days. "I should go back. File a protest. Alan can't suspend me."

Freeda sighed. "I wondered how long it would take you to start up again. You're not suspended. You're on vacation."

Cere pressed her lips together, her muscles tensing. "I'm in exile. *Scope* gets the glory of a major scoop, Audrey gets a great new gig, you get job offers, and me? I get sent on vacation. Alan as good as told me to leave town or I'd be suspended."

"It's only for two weeks."

"You know why they did it. Richard Waverly is personal friends with the network CEO. They play golf together, I hear."

Freeda's voice grew bored. "And I've heard all this about twenty times. You knew there would be repercussions when we followed the limo. You said so."

"I didn't know Waverly and his lawyer would try to get me fired for interrupting their beautiful family moment. Hah! Any tourist from the street could have gotten that picture of the kid and his dad."

Throwing up her hands, Freeda squirmed in her seat until the car shook. "Enough! How many times are you going to go through it? They sent you on vacation. I say, enjoy it."

"I can't afford to. They could still fire me. Well, I'm not giving up. I'm going to work that Marco story and return with something outstanding. Alan called me the Queen of Chaos. Can you believe it?"

"Everyone calls you that. They just don't do it to your face."

"At least he seemed interested in the Marco story. He might pay my salary if it pans out."

"Old news," Freeda said in a sing song voice.

"Did I tell you he told me to look around for Hollywood connections? Lots of stars are buying up land here. How could anyone *choose* to live here?"

"*Tia* Lottie likes it." Freeda twisted to look out the window and heaved a big sigh. "Dad saw something in it. There's a strange beauty."

Cere's frustration dissipated at the sound of her cousin's voice. How insensitive could she be? Of course Freeda was thinking of her dad.

They entered a narrow canyon lined with craggy sandstone walls. Only the winding two lane road and a rushing creek between thickets of cottonwood and spruce trees fit between the imposing walls.

"Do you remember living here with Uncle Joe?" Cere asked.

"I remember the commune. It has always seemed weird that your mom's family lived so near my dad but they didn't meet until they went to school in Los Angeles."

Cere knew the story from her mother, but she doubted Freeda's dad ever explained it. "I think it's why they became friends at UCLA. Both were from New Mexico. When my dad started dating Mom they set up Uncle Joe with his sister."

"Dad's commune isn't far away. It's near the Colorado border." Freeda tapped a postcard against her knee, probably the card she'd received a month ago from Uncle Joe.

Where was he now? Still in New Mexico? Was that why Freeda insisted on coming? To look for her father?

"Maybe we can go up that way before we go back."

"Maybe." Freeda's normally animated face grew

glum as she glanced at the card. For all her openness, she never wanted to discuss why her father took off and disappeared. Maybe it was time to change the subject.

"I don't remember this place much at all," Cere said. "We only visited one time and my memories are of that dance hall. At least I'm no longer having spooky dreams." Three dream-free nights had convinced her that seeing the picture had triggered the unpleasant memories from her childhood.

"But you're going to do the story."

"Oh, hell, yeah. I called Gary Riggins, who wrote the article, but he's on assignment in Mexico. I left voice mail and talked to his assistant. I brought my video camera so I might have you shoot my interview with him and the sheriff—if he talks to me."

A laugh burbled from Freeda. "You think he'll agree after our drunken phone call?"

Cere wrinkled her nose and stuck out her tongue. "It was your idea. He knows Mom, but I don't think he told her. I kept waiting for a lecture."

"Won't happen. She's just thrilled you're coming."

"I had to get out of town. Take a vacation..." She stopped, as Freeda tilted her head toward her and gave her a warning look. Cere waved her hand. "Okay, I just remember this place scared me last time when we went ghost hunting. Thinking back, it had to be because of that stupid kid who told the ghost story. I think he got a charge out of scaring us."

"I had a crush on him. Ten years old, and I thought he ought to notice me."

Cere rolled her eyes, but she joined in Freeda's quick laughter. "Me too. He was my first crush, except I don't recall his name. All I remember was that he had the longest, curliest eyelashes I'd ever seen."

"His name was Chico."

"So much for first love." She waved at Freeda's purse. "Write down that name. We should look up good old Chico."

"He's probably bald and paunchy with five kids."

Cere reached out and punched her cousin on the arm. "That would be your first thought. If he's still sexy. I don't care how he turned out. Maybe he'll take us to see the hand again."

Freeda punched her back. "Naturally that would be your first thought—the damn story."

Cere guided the car around a rocky outcropping and relief swept through her as the road dipped down a hill to a wide green valley dotted with houses.

"Well, look at that. A rusty welcome sign with what looks like bullet holes. Looks like we made it."

On first glance, Rio Rojo didn't appear any more welcoming than the fading sign. It spread across the valley between sandstone-topped mesas. The town was a conglomeration of paved and gravel streets with small squat buildings that looked like they had been tossed there by some careless giant playing a game of build-a-town.

Freeda put away the postcard and sat up straighter, interest shifting. "Small town, USA. Obligatory junkyard, followed by a cemetery. Wow, look at how tiny it is. And no grass."

"Lots of flowers, though," Cere said. "I wonder if that's where Marco is buried." At Freeda's frown, she turned her attention in another direction. "Look, an old drive-in. It hasn't been used since the 80's. 'Top Gun' was the last movie to show."

The center of town arrived quickly as the highway transformed to Main Street, a wide avenue that hosted a cluster of sandstone and brick buildings—none higher than two stories. Many of the store fronts were empty with wide, dusty windows. Faded facades above the functioning stores bore faint reminders of former owners. An old grocery store building advertised hardware, and what looked like a converted burger stand housed a real estate office. A theater marquee with missing letters offered showings of a movie that was two months old.

"Shades of 1960," Freeda said with a good-natured laugh. "It's like we drove through a time tunnel in that canyon or we're on a tour of the back lot at Universal Studios. If we turn down a street, we'll discover the fronts being held up by two-by-fours. Marco transported us to the *Twilight Zone* while he was haunting your dreams."

"I don't see the shops, bistros, or galleries Alan mentioned." Cere craned her neck as she drove by each side street. "I promised Audrey silver and turquoise earrings. I doubt I'm going to find anything here."

"There's a Walmart." Freeda pointed at a wide lot leading to the big box store. The lot held more cars than they'd seen since leaving the freeway. "They'll have postcards and T-shirts."

Cere grimaced at the scene. "If this story doesn't pan out, maybe we can convince Mom to go to a spa in Santa Fe."

"The ghost won't like that."

"Correct me if I'm wrong, but we're leaving town." Cere pointed at another junk yard followed by open prairie. "You better call Mom and find out where we turn."

"I thought you printed a map." Freeda twisted toward the back seat to find Cere's purse.

"I think I misplaced it when I was printing out the map on how to get to the Palladium."

Freeda sank back onto her seat. "So we have a map on how to get to the story location, but no idea how to get to your mom's house?"

"Something like that," Cere snapped. She knew what Freeda was thinking. She was more interested in the legend of Marco than visiting her mother. "Call her."

Freeda picked up her cell phone, squinted at it and waved it impatiently. "Still no service. It's been that way since Albuquerque."

"Even in town?" Cere pulled over to the side of the road to make a U-turn and stopped. "Hey, I remember that sign. Lockhart Lake. With the cabins and the big trout? We saw that sign when we were headed up toward the Palladium that night."

"You remember that?" Freeda asked, her voice filled with amazement.

Cere's heart began to pound as excitement pulsed through her. "That means it's somewhere on this road. You want to go there before we head to the house?"

"You didn't want to do that story and now you're all over it like gangbusters."

"I need to do something big. I want to be able to call Alan with some ideas and get taken off suspension. Don't you see how important that is?" Cere stiffened and she clenched the wheel as her insides twisted. "My suspension could end up being dismissal."

Freeda blew out a heavy sigh. "Okay, I'm sorry.

Let's do it."

"The directions are in the side pocket of my bag."

Twisting in her seat, Freeda picked up the bag and removed the map along with the folded up copies of the newspaper articles. She studied the printed page.

"Looks like it's five miles out."

She pulled the car back onto the road. "Good. It'll only take a couple of minutes."

"In the meantime, *Tia* is waiting lunch and I gotta pee."

"You can go in the bushes. You've done that plenty of times before."

The far side of Rio Rojo was only slightly different from the canyon entrance. The creek reappeared as a wide flat river on one side. Small houses and mobile homes dotted the other side. Some properties had corrals with horses and cows, old weathered barns or chicken coops. Tiny front lawns were bordered by gravel driveways filled with pick-ups and old cars.

After five miles only a sagging overhead sign and a narrow line of parallel tracks indicated the turn off for the dance hall. The sign carried the faded letters "Pal di m" grooved into gray wooden boards. Amid Freeda's protests, Cere jerked the rental car to the right. It bounced over dirt and gravel bordered by thin wispy grass.

"We're not getting off," Freeda protested. "I really have to pee."

"This whole thing was your idea and you're wimping out? Afraid we'll run into Marco? I just want to look around."

"I'm not scared. Oh, hell, let's go. Maybe there's an outhouse or something."

"It's gonna be a big story." And if it wasn't, she'd find a way to make it important.

They bounced along at least two miles before a large, long building came into view. It sat forlorn and deserted near a huddled group of cottonwood trees. Its sagging rock structure was exactly like the picture in the newspaper. Cere could also see the slanting roof was rusting and the wooden boards of the front entrance were dusty and gray. Boards covered the line of windows. She stared at it, calling up memories from their youthful visit. That night it rose against the dark sky like a hulking monster. Now it hunkered like a wounded animal. She pulled the car to a stop in a gravel parking lot.

"I'm gonna pee behind that bush," Freeda said and launched herself from the car.

Cere moved slower, stepping out and stretching to ease the stiffness caused by the long morning drive. The dry air hit her like a hot, sharp slap across the cheeks, though its warmth felt good on her legs after the car's air-conditioning. "I'm going around back," she called. "I remember that's how we got inside." Cursing at the uneven ground and the rocks that she could feel through the thin sole of her sandals, she rounded the building and drew up short. A man sat on the edge of a slanting stone wall that bordered the stairs up to the building's veranda.

Was that a ghost? Her ghost?

He jerked to his feet at the sound of her footsteps, looking as discomfited as she was.

"What the hell are you doing here?" he asked in a raspy voice.

"I'm sorry… I thought this was public…"

He was tall, lanky, wearing a beaten up black cowboy hat and Oakley sunglasses, even though he stood in the shade. His jeans looked new and the boots resembled the snakeskin designer type Alan wore. His bolo tie had a huge shiny black rock at its center. Onyx?

"This is private property," he grated. "You have no business here."

She stepped forward, wishing she had a business card to offer. "I'm Cere, Lottie Medina's daughter. I'm a reporter with *Scope* TV newsmagazine."

"We're looking for Marco Gonzales," Freeda said behind her. "His ghost wants Cere to help him."

Cere whipped around. "Freeda!" Leave it to her cousin to be so open about their search.

"Hi, I'm Freeda Ferguson."

The dark glasses swiveled from one to the other and his thin lips turned up in a crooked, but sinister smile.

"You girls don't get out of here, you're gonna find more than Marco." His voice lowered to a ghastly whisper. "Don't you know he's dead? He comes back every year on August 17th, the night he died, looking for girls who don't have the sense to realize he was a killer. Lots of bodies buried up there. He killed 'em." He jerked his head toward the hills behind the building.

Cere's heart thumped in a quick rhythm, as though she'd just completed a mile long run. She jumped as Freeda caught her arm.

"Uh... we should get going." For once Freeda's voice sounded unsure.

"Who are you?" The man was spooky, but Cere wasn't going to let him think he frightened her, despite that whiskey rough voice.

He shifted, allowing her to catch sight of a crow bar on the stairs. "I've been called the ghost of Marco Gonzales."

A sudden gust of wind whipped around the side of the building, and a violent shiver surged through her. For a minute she was in her dream with the outstretched hand and the searing eyes pleading for help.

She whirled toward Freeda and as they had when they were children, they turned and ran back to the car. Driving quickly with no regard for bumps or flying rocks, Cere guided the car away from the building, checking the rearview mirror to make certain he wasn't following. Neither said a word until she had turned onto the highway.

"Who the hell was that?" she asked, glancing over at Freeda.

"I don't know, but I'm glad I peed before we saw him. He scared the hell out of me." Freeda shivered and reached over to turn down the air conditioning.

"He wanted to scare us with that talk about the ghost and bodies in the hills." She chewed on a nail, gripping the steering wheel with one hand and then forced herself to place both hands firmly on the wheel. She and her cousin shared that habit of chewing their nails, but she refused to destroy a brand new manicure.

"Maybe this Marco story isn't a good idea."

Cere waved her hand. "I'm not going to let some weirdo scare me. But let's not tell Mom about this Marco thing for now. Let her think I'm here to visit while I nose around."

"I'm not going to argue. I'm sorry I brought the whole thing up."

Cere looked into the rearview mirror one last time.

She could still see the man's sinister smile.

"I'm the ghost of Marco Gonzales."

The heck with that. If Marco was responsible for buried bodies, it would only make the story more interesting.

Chapter Seven

Rafe leaned forward in his normal booth at the *Matador* while his daughter Ginny hopped away to the play area in back. They had breakfast at the restaurant most days, and he had just put in his order. Normally he'd lean back and enjoy that first cup of coffee, but today a restless energy filled him. From the moment Lottie Medina gleefully told him about her daughter's imminent arrival he'd been on edge. He hadn't mentioned the drunken midnight call. Hopefully Cere was coming to see her mother and the Marco reference was a joke.

He looked up as the bell over the door tinkled. Cere would have been recognizable even if her mother wasn't beside her, their arms linked. She had big city woman stamped on her like a mailing label. Sunglasses on her head, a tote bag with a designer logo, and sparkling gems in her ears that were probably diamonds. Her auburn hair was swept back from her face, and the color of her manicured nails was matched on painted toenails. He prided himself on the ability to instantly size up people and he knew her type immediately—spoiled, demanding, used to being the center of attention.

Sleek as a well-groomed cat, Cere glided across the room. Her bright yellow cotton shorts outlined a narrow waistline. Not skin and bones like so many LA women, she exuded health and vitality. The shorts and an avocado-colored, sleeveless shell clung to her curves, which were womanly and nicely rounded in all the right places. She was of medium height and her caramel legs were muscular, not that long, skinny look so many West Coast men favored. The beaded sandals were impractical—strappy models with heels that could probably take out an eye.

What he didn't expect was the burst of energy that emanated from her flashing eyes. They seemed to burst like fireworks as she studied the open room. Her wide engaging smile displayed small white teeth.

A third woman joined them. She was taller than Cere with thick black hair pulled away from her face in a ponytail. She wore a cotton shirt over a tank top, cargo shorts and black hiking boots. All three women giggled like school girls as they settled into a nearby booth. Lottie sat on one side, the younger women across from her. Their voices rang out over the country music that blared from speakers overhead.

Had she noticed him? No, it was foolish to think she'd glance in his direction. He pulled his gaze away as Naldo shuffled by with a broom, sweeping up a child's wayward Cheerios.

"Que tal, Viejo."

Naldo nodded and Rafe gestured him to sit down. He hadn't talked to the old man since their midnight chat.

"Digame about Diaz," he said as Naldo slid into the booth.

Naldo shrugged, his wrinkled face scrunching. "Don't really know him."

"You said you did."

"He used to live here. Long time ago. Before you was born. Left town, maybe forty years ago." His neatly clipped fingernails tapped on the table top and his eyes watched them, avoiding Rafe.

"Is he still around?"

"Nah, gone back to Texas, I think."

"Did he tell you I caught him nosing around the Palladium?"

Naldo's head jerked up, and a sheen of sweat broke out on his dark skin. Fear glistened in the old man's dark eyes for the quick second that they rested on Rafe before he lowered them back to the table. "Don't matter. He's gone."

"Do you know why he was out there?"

"Gonna buy the place, he said." Naldo smiled a broken-toothed grin and pushed himself to his feet. "Here comes Josie with your breakfast."

Rafe watched him shuffle away as a fresh bout of skepticism filled him. Naldo's behavior might set off alarms, except the old man liked sending up false smokescreens. It was why so many rumors abounded about him. Only a visit to his house and a bottle of Jack Daniels might loosen his tongue.

A plate of sausage and biscuits arrived with a very welcome distraction—Ginny. Rafe helped her into the booth as Josie Morales put down her pancakes. When he re-settled, he positioned himself to look away from Lottie and her distracting daughter.

****

Clapping her hands like a little girl, Lottie smiled at Cere and Freeda. "I can't tell you how happy I am you girls came."

"I can't get over how healthy you look, *Tia.* Your

tan is better and I love your hair."

Lottie tugged at whitish blonde curls. "Millie does it. It pays to have a sister-in-law who is a stylist. We're letting it go as close to natural as possible."

Cere smoothed her silk top and stifled a yawn. They had stayed up talking until three in the morning, but her mother expected them to be at this diner by eight. Freeda was right about the surprising changes. Like the short, blunt fingernails. "I can't get over the fact you stopped manicuring your nails."

"It doesn't make sense when I'm working in the garden every day. That's what accounts for the tan too."

"Gardening every day? What would Dad think?"

A faraway look crept into her blue eyes. "He'd be happy. He knew how much I wanted a garden. That damn swimming pool took up our whole backyard."

"Seems to me you loved that damn swimming pool. We couldn't get you out of it in the summer."

"That was my old life. Now I have a garden."

"And rabbits," Freeda chirped. She'd immediately fallen in love with four cages of rabbits in Lottie's backyard. "My dad always wanted to raise bunnies."

Cere turned her attention from their discussion long enough to glance around the café. From the moment they walked in, she knew she wouldn't get her customary breakfast of nonfat yogurt and fresh fruit. The scent of fried onions and bacon hung thick in the air. Velvet paintings, colorful serapes and sombreros hung on the back paneled walls. Carved wooden booths ringed the front half of the restaurant below a line of windows. A counter with round black seats formed a giant U at the center while circular tables filled the rest of the space. A door to one side was marked

"Restrooms." A mix of families in vacation garb and men wearing western shirts or work clothes jammed nearly every booth and filled most of the spots at the counter.

"Coffee?" A chunky young waitress deposited plastic menus on the burgundy Formica table top and gestured with a glass coffee pot at the porcelain cups on the table. She examined Cere with the rapt attention a fan might give a movie star.

All three nodded as Lottie waved across the table. "Josie, this is my niece, Freeda, and my daughter, Cere."

Cere summoned one of her friendliest on-camera smiles. "Josie, it's so nice to meet you." She'd learned that it paid to make friends with waitresses in small town restaurants. They knew all the gossip. Josie might be a good starting point for information.

"I watch you all the time," she gushed as she poured coffee, hazel eyes shining beneath thick coats of black eyeliner and mascara. "I never miss your stories. I'll get water while you study the menu."

Cere frowned at the menu—no fresh fruit, no yogurt. Lots of artery clogging fried or smothered choices. She closed it and glanced across the table, studying the changes in her mother. The lines that once grooved her cheeks and the circles under her eyes were gone. Even her clothes were different. As a high school social studies teacher, she favored skirts and sweaters or pants suits. Casual clothes consisted of pressed capris and crisp cotton shirts. Today she wore jeans and a bright peasant blouse.

Freeda slammed down her menu. "I'm having the breakfast burrito. What do you think, *Tia*?"

"Get it smothered. Frank makes the best green chili in town. That's what I'm getting."

"I may have oatmeal and a banana."

"Cere, we're on vacation. Let's live a little." Freeda jabbed her with an elbow.

"Don't embarrass me by being a city snob, sweetie. This is real food. Homemade."

"Which means fattening. I may be on vacation, but I can't afford to gain weight."

"*Tia* Lottie hasn't gained. This place must agree with you."

"Oh, hell yes!"

Freeda barked out a laugh. "You're cussing? What would *Tio* Del say?"

"He's been gone for three years. I can say whatever I damn well please." As soon as the words came out, she shook her head. "That's wrong. The truth is I miss him horribly. Back home, reminders of him were everywhere. Even going to my favorite restaurant reminded me we'd never go there again. He wanted me to move on with my life so here I am."

Cere reached over and clasped her mother's hand. They had gone through this before the move. She missed having her mother nearby, but her own long hours and irregular work schedule prevented them from getting together much.

"You're happy, Mom? This place can't have much to offer in the way of culture or the arts..."

Her blue eyes sparkled with energy. "I volunteer at the local historical museum and since I went to school with the head librarian, she lets me consult on programs. Many of my old school friends are still here so I have an active social life. Your Aunt Millie wouldn't let me get bored. We've known each other since grammar school so this has been like coming home."

Josie returned with red plastic glasses of iced water. Cere started to ask for bottled water, but one glance at her frowning mother silenced her.

"We're all having the breakfast burritos, smothered," Freeda announced before Cere could speak.

Lottie waggled a finger at Cere as Josie walked away. "Sweetie, a pound or two won't hurt you."

So much for healthy eating. Luckily she'd inherited her mother's slender frame instead of her father's bulk. Still it might be nice to have a few more of the Medina curves, like Freeda.

"So what's on the agenda today, Mom? Are there any galleries? Shopping places?"

Her mother tapped her hair. "Well, it's my day to get my monthly touch up. Do you want to come with me and see Millie? Maybe get your hair done or a manicure?"

Freeda tugged at her unruly curls and burst into laughter. "No one will touch this mess, and I guarantee Cere won't let some small town stylist cut into her two hundred dollar hairdo."

She considered kicking her cousin under the table, but her mother's smile was understanding.

"It looks beautiful on television, sweetie. Maybe you girls can wander around and get acquainted with my world. We'll do something this afternoon and tonight we've been invited to dinner. There are some friends I'd like you to meet. Well, one friend..." She lowered her gaze to the table, her face glowing pink under her tan.

Freeda lurched upright. "A friend? Like a guy? *Tia*, you got a fella?"

Cere's insides did a wild flip flop and she fought to keep her voice from sounding accusatory. "I noticed you're not wearing your wedding ring."

"*Tia*!"

Her mother put her fingers to her lips. "I'm not wearing my rings because I was worried I'd lose them when I do my gardening."

"But you met a guy." Freeda waved her hands up and down.

"Not met." She sat up straight as a board and adopted her teaching demeanor as a sober gaze stopped Freeda's wild gesturing. "I am seeing, well, I've been keeping company with an old friend…someone I've known for years, before I met your father."

Cere fought to keep her composure, but before she could reply, a buzzing sounded and her mother reached for her purse. She extracted her cell phone, gave it a shy smile and held up a finger. "Could you excuse me a minute?" She rose without waiting for an answer and walked toward the back of the restaurant.

Freeda grasped Cere's arm with both hands. "Wow! *Tia* has a guy! She's doing better than we are."

Cere couldn't answer. Was *he* on the phone? Was *he* why her mom insisted they be here so early?

"Something wrong?" Freeda asked.

"No, but why hasn't she told us about him? Who is *he*?" Her attempted smile felt stiff.

"You need to lighten up, babe. Let me out. I'm gonna check the local paper and see if I can find information about the area." Squeezing past Cere, she clomped toward the front of the restaurant where several wooden bins held newspapers and brochures. Typical Freeda. She collected brochures everywhere they went. When they came home, she deposited them in a box and never touched them again.

Cere sensed restlessness in both her mother and Freeda. Maybe this trip had been a mistake. She should have convinced them to go to a spa or take a cruise. Or maybe she was the one on edge. But then she was the one with a job in jeopardy.

Still standing, she glanced around the cafe. She'd come hoping to turn this town into a story and so far it didn't appear promising. But she couldn't afford to return with nothing. Across the room, a barrel-chested man wearing an apron dotted with food stains waddled through a set of swinging doors. He carried a steaming oval plate which he plopped down in front of a paunchy man seated at the counter.

"Jerry, *muchachos,* try these tamales." The man held one out on a spatula and then began putting them on the plates of diners at the counter. "Turned out great today."

A tempting, spicy aroma wafted to the table. Her stomach rumbled. Maybe the burritos were a good idea.

"Oye, amigo. Muy bueno!" The man identified as Jerry smacked his lips together after tasting the offering.

"Yep, great," the skinny man next to him agreed.

A strange sensation ran over Cere as she watched the men, a prickling of the hair along the back of her neck. Swiveling, she discovered a pair of eyes, shiny as polished onyx, focused on her. Her heart thudded and she drew back, startled.

The eyes from her dream?

No. These eyes belonged to a real man and their piercing blackness cut across the short distance between them like sharp edged blades. He sat in a small booth that wrapped around the back wall. Thick black hair curled over his ears. His striking, neatly clipped beard was streaked with thin gray rivers. Deeply tanned, his proud, chiseled face was that of a Native American warrior straight out of central casting for a Hollywood Western. His white cotton shirt outlined large shoulders. A bolo tie held together by a silver and turquoise thunderbird hung loosely at the open neck of his shirt.

He watched her, ignoring the food in front of him. A small plate with half eaten pancakes and a pool of congealing syrup sat across from him, but the other seat at the table was empty.

Cere met his gaze and attempted a smile. During her years at *Scope* she'd grown used to people staring at her or having strangers approach her, but this man's steady gaze was unsettling.

She pointed at the bolo tie. "That's beautiful. Where did you get it?"

A long finger stroked his beard. "Thanks. My cousin makes them."

"Do you have his card?" That would make a perfect gift for Alan.

"She doesn't have cards, but I can put you in touch with her." The man shifted, appearing uncomfortable. "You're Cere Medina."

She nodded. His dark scrutiny made her uneasy.

"You don't remember me?" As he looked down, his long, feathery lashes swept across one tanned cheek, and she flashed back. He was the boy she and Freeda had the crush on.

"You're a friend of my cousins. Chico. I met you years ago." The implication hit her immediately. He led the expedition to the Palladium. Maybe she could get him to take her again so she didn't have to worry about strange, threatening guys. Maybe he'd do an interview.

He tapped his nose as his lips twitched. "Right on the button. Anything else?"

She blinked. *What did that mean?* Suddenly she was aware of her appearance. Her hair was a mess, tied in a ponytail that threatened to fall. In tank top, shorts and sandals, she hardly looked like a national television reporter.

"Think about it," he said, gaze steady.

Oh, damn. That deep voice. She recognized it even as the sun reflected off the badge on his white shirt. She should have guessed it from the moment she found him staring at her. Chico, her old crush, was now Sheriff Rafe Tafoya.

Chapter Eight

Cere stared at the sheriff in disbelief. He was not what she'd expected from their phone conversation. Before she could respond, Lottie returned, her face bright pink. She looked from one to the other and clapped her hands together.

"You've met. I'm so pleased. Rafe is my favorite neighbor. His aunt Rosalie was one of my best friends in high school."

Not anxious to admit their earlier discussion, Cere nodded at him.

Lottie hovered at the edge of the booth. "Hon, I'm sorry, but I need to do something... so I have to run. Josie's wrapping my breakfast to go." She reached over, picked up her purse and pulled out a set of keys. "Here are my car keys and this is the house key. I'll call when I'm done or Millie can bring me home. I hate leaving you girls to eat alone..." She gave the sheriff an expectant look.

He waved at the table and smiled, showing a row of very white, straight teeth. "They're welcome to join me."

Cere eyed the half eaten meal. "Looks like you have company."

"Fickle female. Already deserted me. Please..." His eyes fixed on Cere as he pushed the other dish to the far corner of the table.

"Thanks, Rafe." Lottie scooped up their water glasses and carried them to his table.

Judging by the quick action, Cere sensed that her mother feared resistance. *No way!* Breakfast with him was a perfect opportunity to get started on her story. He'd been hesitant on the phone, but maybe in person she could convince him to talk. She picked up the coffee mugs and set them on his table, aware of his eyes.

"I'll take good care of them," he said with a warm smile.

"Watch out for Freeda. I haven't told you about her. She's from the other side of the family and quite a handful." Lottie glanced around, then back at Cere. "Where is the wild one?"

"Picking up local information." Cere spotted her cousin coming across the restaurant and waved. Freeda's hands were stuffed with brochures and newspapers. She drew up in surprise as she approached and saw the sheriff.

Lottie introduced Freeda, and for once Cere was pleased to have her boisterous cousin around. After all, it had been Freeda's bright idea to call him at midnight. After another apology, Lottie hurried to the counter to get her meal and directed Josie toward their new table. The waitress put down steaming platters as Freeda slid into the booth.

"Yummy." Freeda dug her fork into the mound of green chili before stopping to look up at the sheriff. "Hey, you hung up on us the other night."

He looked from one to the other. "I did?"

She turned to Cere. "That's what you said."

A sudden unease enveloped Cere. His large

presence made her feel small. She offered an apologetic smile. "I'm sorry about the late night call. I'm afraid we had too much to drink."

"No problem." His wide grin crinkled the edges of his eyes.

A quick stirring teased her insides and her breath caught. She hated herself for doing it, but she checked his left hand, resting on the table. No wedding band. She dropped her gaze to the burrito, a huge tortilla drenched in a green chili gravy and sprinkled with grated cheese. It sent up a warm, wonderful, spicy scent.

"So you're friends with my mother?" she asked, picking at the tortilla.

"We have a lot in common. We're both natives who moved to the city and came back. We help each other re-acclimate."

Loathe to admit her mother had not said much about her new life, Cere merely nodded and took a bite. Freeda's assessment was right—yummy.

Her cousin joined the conversation. "What city?"

"I spent seventeen years in Los Angeles. Went away to school and didn't come back until a couple of years ago."

"You can survive in this little burg after LA?" Freeda asked.

"It has its good points." His dark eyes swept around the room. "No rush hour. Easy to get around and everyone knows and looks out for each other."

Freeda followed his gaze. "Are all these little towns like that? Like Rio de los Muertos? Do you know where that is?"

Content to let her get the sheriff into a talkative

mood with rapid fire questions, Cere focused on her food. The burrito was delicious with just the right mixture of eggs, potatoes and spicy pork chili.

Freeda finally smacked her lips and pushed away a clean plate. "That was excellent. I'd heard New Mexico green chili was sublime."

"Frank makes everything himself from old family recipes. He and his relatives have run this place for fifty years."

Cere scanned the café, trying to think of a way to bring up what she really wanted to discuss. Behind the counter a black velvet painting of a matador in full swing rang a bell in her subconscious. "I remember coming here when I was young."

His face lightened, full lips twitching into a smile. "I'd forgotten until a few minutes ago about that visit. Seems I recall a feisty girl who insisted on following the boys around." His deep voice grew teasing.

"Sheriff Tafoya, are you calling our Cere a tomboy? She's the only kid I ever knew who refused to wear blue jeans. Corduroy was as close as she got. She preferred frilly dresses and patent leather Mary Janes."

He laughed, a rumbling sound that caught hold of Cere's senses and held them. "Actually I was thinking she was brave."

His comment provided a perfect opening. "You're talking about the night we visited the Palladium?" She turned to Freeda. "He's the boy who took us out there."

Freeda stared at him for a minute as recognition came into her eyes. "Chico! We both had crushes on you."

He lowered his eyes, lashes flickering across his cheek. "You had to be ten years old."

"I was twelve," Cere corrected, wishing she could kick her cousin. "That night scared the hell out of us."

He laughed, a warm rich sound that shook her insides worse than the thought of ghosts. He sat back on his seat. "Is that why you called me? To see if I remembered that night?"

Cere toyed with her fork, deciding how to proceed. She lifted her eyes to his, offering him the smile she used to win over reluctant interview subjects. "I was serious. I want to do a story on Marco Gonzales."

"She's gotta do it." Freeda began to giggle. "That ghost is after her."

His smile grew stiff and he shook his head. "Sorry, but you won't get any information from me."

"I read a story in the Santa Fe paper that quoted you," Cere said. "You spoke to Gary Riggins. Why not me?"

A sudden shadow crossed his face and his dark eyes glittered. "I realized I made a mistake. I'm sorry the story got written."

Despite the reluctant tone, Cere refused to back down. She met his steely gaze. "Do you ever go out there?"

"To chase kids away. The place is ready to fall."

Perhaps the time had come to try another approach, the understanding reporter. "You're quite the protector," she said with her most brilliant smile, pointing at his badge. "My mother, kids…"

He seemed to relax too as his lashes lowered like a dark feather and he winked. "I suppose you could say that. But what can I say? It's my role in life. The kind of guy I am."

His lopsided grin made her insides perform a wild

flip. Was he flirting? Under the table, Freeda tapped her shin with a quick kick. She obviously thought so, but Cere wanted to warn him off trying to charm her. He'd matured into a fine looking man, but she didn't have time in her busy life for a small town sheriff. Still, she wasn't going to discourage him... not yet.

"You should help her," Freeda said.

The sheriff looked from one to the other with a puzzled smile. "Why?"

"I told you. Marco the ghost is asking her for help. She has to report on it, or he'll keep stalking her."

Rafe jerked upright and put down his coffee cup with a thump. "That's not funny." He could tell from the startled look on Cere's face that she was dismayed by her cousin's comments. She turned and muttered something to Freeda as Josie provided a welcome break, arriving with fresh coffee.

Cere's quick smile of thanks sent an unsettling awareness surging through him. Until the subject of Marco came up, he'd enjoyed the conversation. Freeda was off the wall, but Cere...

He drew a deep breath, shaking off the unwelcome sensations that invaded his body. This wasn't healthy. What the hell was he doing? Flirting with her? No, he was being preachy, as his mother put it. Was that the impression he wanted to give her?

He'd been prepared to dislike her from the moment she marched into the café, giving off that brittle, "look at me, I'm gorgeous and rich" look. Having dealt with pampered and spoiled women for years, he pegged her as the type to expect everything to revolve around her.

When she turned her attention to him with unexpected force, she'd nailed him to the wall. No, it was more like a bug pinned to a scrapbook page.

It wasn't as though Cere would be interested in him. She probably dated lawyers, doctors, or rich business types.

He glanced at Freeda who had grown still. The two women seemed very different. While Cere appeared calm and confident, Freeda's movements were animated and restless. Her voice was loud, as though she didn't care who heard her. Men probably found her interesting with her nicely rounded body, wide, olive shaped eyes, and tousled piles of onyx curls.

Cere, on the other hand, resembled an exotic doll. *Damn, she had beautiful eyes. TV didn't do them justice.* They were brown with gold flecks that grew bold when she was excited. Her gaze fastened on his shirt. *What was she thinking?*

"Have you ever tried to solve the mystery of that hand?" she asked suddenly.

He shifted, and his smile tightened. "Mystery? Is there something you know that I don't?"

"Do you think Marco Gonzales was murdered?"

"Suicide," he corrected, using his official law enforcement tone. "That was the finding by the sheriff and coroner."

"Pffft." Freeda waved her hand and rubbed her thumb and forefinger together. "Back then people could be bought off with a little green."

Cere pointed a red fingernail at her cousin. "Exactly. What about the money? Did he leave buried treasure? That's what you told us when we were kids. Riggins wrote that it has never been found."

Rafe took a sip of coffee and contemplated his answer carefully. "No one knows for certain about lost money. It was another claim exaggerated over the years. I'm sorry I passed it along."

"Why do the stories continue?" A slight furrow appeared on Cere's smooth forehead as she frowned. "Why do people still go out there?"

"Are you thinking of visiting the Palladium? I should warn you. The building is boarded up. It's been condemned and the floorboards are rotting. One of these days someone is going to fall through the upper floor." Enough preaching. He shoved away his coffee cup. "I better get to work. It was nice meeting you both and breakfast is on me."

Freeda rose as he picked up their check and moved out of the booth. He reached for his hat that hung on a curving metal rack at the end of the booth.

"Thanks, Sheriff. I hope we see you again." She gave Cere a wink and waved across the room. "I'm going to the can. Meet you in the parking lot."

As Cere stood, her hand caught his sleeve. "Maybe you should take us out there, Sheriff. We'd like to see the hand in the daylight."

Damn, she was perseverant, but he shook his head, again hoping to discourage her. "I chase people out. I don't give tours. Enjoy your vacation with your mother."

"I didn't come for vacation." Her eyes flashed with irritation but she waved a hand as though realizing how curt she sounded. "I mean, I came to see Mom, but I want to do a story on the handprint. I *need* to."

His insides knotted, as his breakfast churned in his stomach. Poor Lottie. She would be hurt if she realized her daughter's real reason for coming. He didn't ask why she needed to do the story. He knew. Ego.

Reaching down, she pulled a reporter's notebook from her bag. "Riggins story didn't quote anyone who knew Marco. If you won't do an interview, do you know anyone who might talk to me?"

Why had he wondered what she might think about him? She was only after her damn story. Acid boiled in his stomach. This woman was no Gary Riggins, content to do a half-assed job. She would dig, pry, and eventually she might uncover some ugly truths. And she would spill it all out on national television. She could hurt a good many people, just as she destroyed the homecoming for that little actor in her last story. But he hadn't known the kid. He would know anyone she hurt in Rio Rojo. And it was his sworn duty to protect the citizens of his county.

He gritted his teeth as he forced an answer, hoping for one final chance at dissuading her. "No one will talk to you. My advice is to let it go. Relax. Take that vacation with Lottie."

He might as well have struck her. Her chin snapped up and her body grew rigid. He drew back at the determination he saw grow in her bright eyes along with her rising voice.

"Don't try to tell me what I should do. It's time someone found out who murdered Marco Gonzales. Yes, I said, murdered, Sheriff. If you don't want to help me investigate, I'll do it on my own."

Cere's sharp, insistent voice rang out in the silence that came at the end of a song. Rafe sensed heads turning toward them.

"The Palladium is private property." He knew his own voice was being heard too, but hopefully it discouraged any listeners. "The doors are padlocked. If

I catch you out there, I'll arrest you for trespassing."

She didn't flinch. In fact she grew still and stony as a statue. "Where were you yesterday? There was a weird guy out there with a crowbar like he was about to break the damn padlock."

His gut wrenched and he lowered his voice, hoping she took the hint and lowered hers too. "Was he driving a black SUV?"

"We never saw a car. He was an older guy, talked like he was whispering."

He couldn't stifle the curse that burst from his lips before he turned and marched to the counter cash register. He shoved money and the check at Josie. "Can you keep an eye on Ginny until Mom comes to get her?"

"Sure," she said, glancing toward the back where Ginny sat on the floor in the play area, pulling a wooden train.

Starting for the door, he remembered he hadn't said goodbye to Cere. Courtesy made him turn. She sat in the booth again, tapping into her phone. He walked over and put his hand on the table. "Sorry for the outburst, but you better stay away from there. That guy is dangerous."

Wariness entered her eyes as she glanced up. "I figured that." She took out a card from her pocket and handed it to him, giving him a wide smile as though they had not argued. "This is my cell number, Sheriff. Call me. I'll buy coffee and we can talk."

Shocked at the offer, he could only stare, uncertain what he read in her direct gaze. He had no time to think about it. He took the card and stomped out the door, eager to forget her expressive eyes. He had a bigger problem.

Diego Diaz!

If he was inside the Palladium or lurking outside with a crowbar, he was going to jail.

Chapter Nine

With growing interest Cere observed Rafe as he strode across the parking lot. At least six feet tall with long legs and an ass that looked good in tight black jeans, he was a fine physical male specimen. Her adolescent crush had grown into an attractive man.

But she couldn't let his looks distract her. She knew she shocked him. He thought he'd won their argument, but evasive interview subjects were nothing new to her. She honed her skills disarming them. Pulling out all the stops by claiming Marco was murdered surprised him. *Good!* Let him think about it.

So now what? She was tempted to grab Freeda and drive to the dance hall to see if that was where the sheriff headed in such a rush. It would serve that strange man right if she could tell him she'd turned him in. Was he dangerous? She didn't care to find out.

Freeda darted back to the table, nervous energy spilling over. "Hey, guess what? I met a woman in the restroom who used to live in Rio de los Muertos. She has pictures of the old commune, so I'm going over to her house."

"Freeda, we just got here."

"I know. But you want to work on that story…and…hey, what happened to the sexy sheriff? He was really eyeballing you."

"He had business."

"Oh, well, see you at *Tia's* later. Daphne knows her and can give me a lift."

Before Cere could protest, her cousin scooped up the brochures, stuffed them into her bag and hurried to the door. Trust Freeda to make an instant friend and set off in some new direction. What should she do for the rest of the morning? Sitting at her mother's tiny house alone wasn't appealing and she didn't feel like wandering around alone. That left one option—work on her story.

Cere glanced around the café. The breakfast crowd had thinned, but a few men in jeans and work shirts remained at the counter. An old man wielded a mop outside the restroom entrance. Why not conduct research here? What better place to get information than the local diner? She pulled a fistful of cards from her bag along with a pen and small notebook and approached the counter. She took a seat at one end and put down her bag. Turning over a fresh mug on the counter, she gestured for Josie's attention.

With a smile, Cere turned to the men working on half eaten plates of tamales and breakfast burritos. She put down the notebook and rested the pen beside it.

"Hi, I'm Cere Medina from *Scope,* a national TV show. I'm doing a story on Marco Gonzales and the hand on the wall. Did any of you know him?"

"I've seen your reports," the man next to her said with a wide smile. He wore a faded black T-shirt and jeans. Shaggy black hair curled at his neck. She guessed his age at around thirty. "I'm Jerry Orozco. You ever met Angelina Jolie?"

"I've talked to her a number of times," she replied in a light voice that made it sound as though they were best buddies. So what if her interviews consisted of chasing the star through halls with a microphone? She launched into her normal response when asked about her connection to Hollywood celebrities. "It's funny how much those stars are like us. Without fancy clothes and make up, you barely recognize them. I hear Marco was a celebrity around here?"

"Nah," Jerry said, and turned back to his plate.

A round-faced, dark man beyond him shook his head. "Trouble maker. That's what my dad says."

She picked up her pen, heart beginning to thud. Had she hit pay dirt immediately? "What is your name? Did he know Marco?"

"My name's Sam, but my old man never knew him. That was a long time ago."

"You ever talked to Tom Cruise?" The question came from a heavy man seated farther down the counter in a grubby work shirt.

"Whatever happened to Sylvester Stallone?" another man in a green baseball cap asked. His scraggly hair was longer than the others and shot with gray strands. His dark face was leathery beneath gray stubble and he had a long red tattoo down one thin arm. "You never hear about him no more."

Despite the useless questions, Cere retained her bright smile. "Who might be willing to talk to me about Marco? Do you guys know anyone who talked to the reporter who wrote the story in the Santa Fe paper?"

"No one talked to him!" The harsh voice came from the barrel-chested cook who had brought out tamales earlier. He stood at the door to the kitchen and flicked angry eyes along the counter. "No one cares about him no more and no one is gonna say nothin' to you."

Any interest from the men at the counter closed like a door slamming shut. Their smiles disintegrated and they turned away. The man in the green cap rose and nodded, face averted.

"Did you know him?" Cere persisted. He looked older than the others.

"Way before my time. Besides, that newspaper story was crap."

She tried another tack. "What about the Palladium itself? I might do a story on it. They say it's haunted."

All four laughed, and she sensed unease as they looked beyond her. She twisted slightly on her stool and saw that the burly cook had taken up a position at the end of the counter, thick arms folded over his greasy apron.

Cere decided to confront him head on. "What about you? What do you think?"

"Hmph!" The cook cocked his head to the side as pointing out a direction. "You wanna do a story on a haunted house, go on up the canyon to the old Hollister place."

"Frank's right." Jerry jerked a thumb toward the window. "You oughta check that. Like it's not called Hollister Ranch no more. It's Tres Padres." His voice carried a sarcastic note that drew a ripple of laughter.

"Why would I be interested?" Cere asked.

"Could have Hollywood connections," Jerry said. "No one knows who bought the place, but there's lots of heavy equipment going up there. I hear they're rebuilding the old house."

"You can't go camping up at the lake," the cook added. "It's fenced off. Did the same guy buy that land?"

"Someone did," green cap said. "Hell, we used to picnic there when I was a kid."

Cere drained her coffee cup. This was going nowhere. She had no interest in some local land issue. She could sense the conversation shifting.

"You ought to talk to Bradley Foster." The comment came from the old man who had been pushing a mop bucket near the restroom entrance. "Or maybe you did already?"

"Who?" She jerked toward him. The man wore an orange Denver Broncos T-shirt below denim overalls. He was older with gray stubble on his head.

"Knock it off, Naldo," the cook growled, "and get back to work."

The old man turned, shouldered the door and pushed his bucket inside.

"Who is Bradley Foster?" she asked, turning back to the cook.

"Ask your momma." His smug smile made her shiver.

The man in the green cap leaned forward on the counter. "He's the mayor. Knows everyone and everything."

"At least he thinks he does," round-faced Sam added. "For sure he likes the ladies."

They laughed in unison, exchanging glances and the undercurrent that had been running through the room hit her like a slap. Could Bradley Foster be her mother's boyfriend?

She'd had enough. Time to try another course of action—like the local newspaper office. At least it might have old clippings. She slid off the stool and put her notebook into her bag.

"Can anyone tell me where the newspaper office is?"

"Not open yet," the cook said. "Stella's in the back and she don't open until ten. Hey, Stella? Someone's looking for you."

A short, rotund woman emerged from around the corner, holding the hand of a small dark haired girl. The woman had short curly black hair and wore too much eye make-up. Her dark eyes were ringed by very black liner and mascara clumped on impossibly long black lashes.

"Someone asking for me?"

Cere stepped forward, held out her hand and introduced herself. "I'd like to look at your old files. I'm doing a story on the death of Marco Gonzales."

The woman drew straight up and stared hard at Cere. "Marco…" Her voice was breathless.

"I told her it's stupid," the cook said.

Cere ignored the interruption. "I'm certain your files would have stories about his death."

The woman's face grew hard as brown granite. "*Our* files don't go back that far. See, Marco burned down the old newspaper office the night he died."

****

Rafe circled the Palladium in his patrol vehicle, bumping along the rough open country. The old building looked as forlorn and lonely as the first day he'd seen the stranger lurking beside it. Today he saw no sign of Diaz or his black Escalade.

He parked in the back and climbed out. A blast of hot summer air hit his face as he closed the door to the air-conditioned cab. He stood for a moment, listening.

The only sounds were leaves rustling in the distance and turtle doves cooing far overhead. Walking around the building, he stopped to examine the gravel parking lot for tire tracks. A pair of wide marks probably came from the Escalade. As he neared the edge of the old parking lot where the gravel ended and the soft earth of the prairie began, he picked out a line of small footprints. Someone in heels. He shook his head. Crazy Cere Medina. The small bulky footprints that stepped partially over hers were probably made by her cousin.

Reaching the back of the building, he hopped up the steps and cursed. The biscuits and gravy nearly boiled into his throat. Flecks of faded green paint dotted the weathered gray wooden planks by the back door. He yanked open the screen door. The metal latch on the back door had been broken and clumsily repaired. He removed the broken latch and pushed open the door. Sure enough, as he stepped inside he could see where the dust on the floor had been displaced by someone pushing the door wide open. He squinted into the gloomy room after the brightness outside, but he didn't need to see the footprints of cowboy boots in the dust to know Diaz had gotten into the building.

Anger rushed through him. Naldo had lied to him. *Why?* One thing was for certain, Diaz was still around.

Who was that guy?

And what was he really doing in Rio Rojo?

He was going find him and question him if he had to spend all day looking for that arrogant SOB. And one way or another he was going to get some straight answers out of old Naldo.

For the next eight hours he drove from one end of the county to the other, keeping a watch out for the black SUV. He made three trips to the Palladium, only to find it deserted every time. Perhaps Diaz had found what he wanted when he got inside and was really gone. No, he had a feeling the man was still lurking somewhere. When he finally came back to town in the late afternoon, he stopped at the Matador, prepared to grill Naldo.

The dining room was nearly empty and Josie was putting out water glasses and silverware for the dinner crowd. Frank, the owner, was sweeping out the dining room.

"He left early," he replied to Rafe's impatient questioning.

His pulse quickened. "Alone?"

"Yeah, sure. He said he had to meet someone."

Oh, hell, what if he'd spent all day looking for Diaz and the guy had been sitting in town all day?

As Rafe yanked open the door to his Jeep, his police radio crackled to life.

"Sheriff… there's… uh… trouble over at old Naldo's house… someone says he's dead and …there's blood all over."

Chapter Ten

Murder.

It made him sick. Not that Rafe had never smelled the coppery stench of death. Not that he hadn't seen his share of corpses during his years in the LAPD. Four of those years had been in homicide. This was different. Those bodies belonged to strangers. He knew Naldo. And this was Rio Rojo. Things like this didn't happen in his hometown.

"You're thinking he was shot?" he asked Police Chief BJ Foster, trying to ease around the man's bulky frame to get a full look. Rafe could make out well-worn slippers, a length of bloody denim and a dark crimson stain on the floor.

BJ threw up his hands. "Don't really know nothin' yet. Looks like it could be gunshot. Let the doc tell us."

"I know the difference between a gunshot and knife wound."

"Well, you ain't in LA now, so just hold your horses. This is city jurisdiction, so it's not really your concern. It doesn't look like an accident. Could be he shot himself."

Rafe glanced around the tiny, neat kitchen. "I don't see a weapon, so I don't think he did it himself, unless one of your officers picked it up by mistake."

BJ's blue eyes flashed with anger. "My officers didn't touch nothing. We're all wearing gloves and bein' real careful about where we step. Now you're welcome to hang around, if you insist, but this is *my* case."

He stifled a reply, pleased that BJ didn't try to force him out. The two were constantly mixed up in cross-jurisdictional disputes. But he had been to more crime scenes than BJ would ever see in his life. And the man wasn't handling it well. BJ's normally ruddy face carried an unnatural pallor.

The chief hitched up his pants and turned away, blocking Rafe's view. The kitchen was too small to maneuver around and two young officers bent over the corpse. He surveyed the kitchen. Its orderly state stood in stark contrast to the chaos on the floor. Boxes of cereal and rice stood arranged in a line by height on the counter. A frayed dish towel was neatly draped over a towel rack. Everything had been painted white, from the cabinets to the wooden table and chairs. Everything was spotless. Rafe's mother said Naldo kept his house so clean you could eat off the floor. That made the blood on the floor more obscene.

Rafe ran his finger over a jagged scar at the edge of his cheek. A queasiness edged into his stomach. "Want me to take pictures? I have a camera in the pickup."

"My boys can do it."

BJ moved, and Rafe got what he really wanted. He managed to lean over and get a look at the body. Naldo's frail form lay crumpled beside the table, the front of a brown plaid shirt soaked with blood. Rafe couldn't see the wound, but he had seen enough. Even if he had found a gun on the floor, he knew this was no suicide.

Murder.

In Rio Rojo.

Rafe pulled his gaze away and as he did, the flip top of the beige plastic wastebasket caught his eye. With everything else so clean, a reddish brown smudge screamed for attention. Taking a pen from his pocket, he used it to tip the lid. A gun barrel poked through potato peelings.

"BJ, you might want to check this."

BJ whirled toward him. "What the hell you doing?"

"I just noticed this. Looks like the killer tossed the gun in here."

"Killer?" One of the officers jerked up from looking under the table. "No one said anything about a killer. He musta shot himself. Look at all this blood."

Rafe struggled to keep from sounding sarcastic. "Then he threw the gun in the waste basket? Suicide victims don't usually have time to hide their weapons."

The officer shot him a startled look. "Maybe the kid who found him put it there. He said he never came inside, but maybe he lied."

"Why?"

BJ started to reach inside the waste basket, but Rafe caught his hand.

"You ever heard of fingerprints? That gun is evidence. You should call the state crime lab. We're not equipped to handle this sort of thing."

The chief pulled back like he'd had his hand slapped while digging in the cookie jar. "Don't pull crap with me, just 'cause you spent time in the city. We'll deal with this ourselves. You can leave."

Rafe considered arguing, but he looked from BJ to the young officers who appeared ready to vomit on the clean floor. Before long one of them would suggest the same thing and BJ would agree. They were all on edge. Arguing could only make things worse.

Without replying he turned and walked back through the shabby house, saddened by the old man's death. He stopped in the tiny, cramped living room, recalling the past. As a boy, when he'd helped shovel snow, they sat in this room drinking hot chocolate. Naldo would regale him with stories about the pawn shop his father once owned and point out leftover treasures. German cuckoo clocks brought back by returning WWII soldiers, silver bowls and candle sticks, various ceramic artifacts and sculptures had ended up in their possession when borrowers couldn't pay off pawn tickets.

The interior hadn't changed much. Worn, overstuffed furniture was jammed together, giving the room a claustrophobic feel. Even in dim light, the linoleum floor gleamed, and the wooden tables and stained glass lamps looked freshly dusted. Rafe smiled at the one tribute to modern culture. An entertainment center holding a state-of-the-art flat screen television occupied much of one wall.

The glass of an antique curio cabinet shimmered from a narrow hallway, catching Rafe's attention. The door hung open. Like the smudge on the wastebasket, that wasn't like Naldo.

Rafe glanced toward the kitchen. BJ was arguing with his officers as they looked into the trash can. Careful not to disturb anything, Rafe crossed to the cabinet and peered inside. An array of small silver and gold trinkets glittered in the light, but he knew something was missing. The bottom shelf once held a black lacquer box with a white horse painted on the lid.

As a boy he had watched Naldo take out the box and fish an envelope full of dollar bills from it. The old man would hand two crisp dollar bills to Rafe and then carefully replace the envelope in the box and put it back into the cabinet. Nothing else in the neat room appeared to have been touched. Was robbery the motive for Naldo's death? Someone could have known about the money box, or perhaps Naldo had told them, never realizing it was the last thing he would ever say.

Another thought hit him and his stomach turned upside down.

The coins!

Naldo had kept a small brown leather pouch that he swore contained gold coins dating back to the late 1800's. The worn pouch had also been in that box. He'd often told Rafe about them, providing a different story about how he'd acquired them every time. He showed him one once. It had been the color of gold, but whether or not it was real, young Rafe had no idea.

"What the hell are you doing? Get out of there!" BJ had entered from the kitchen. He pointed toward the outer door.

Rafe didn't move. "You might want to check this. His money box is missing."

"Money box?" BJ's brows shot up.

"He used to keep a black wooden box with money and coins in this cabinet. It's gone."

"Don't you start with the crazy rumor about that old man's coins."

Behind him, Officer Joe Hernandez laughed and jerked a thumb at the television set. "He probably sold them for that. Thing must have cost him thousands. Last time I priced sets like that they were running ten times more than his pay as a janitor."

BJ nodded and squared off the entryway to the hall. "Hell, Tafoya, you're getting on my nerves. Maybe I ought to arrest you. You seem to know a hell of a lot. Just happened to find the gun, just happened to notice a box is missing. Just happen to know money might be in it." His face bloomed red.

Rafe drew a deep breath and held back an angry response. He could understand BJ's frustration. He motioned toward the cabinet. "The door was open. When I was a kid and did odd jobs for him, he paid with money from that box. He said it held his valuables."

"How do you know he still kept it there?"

Rafe grimaced and turned away. BJ was right. He hadn't been around lately and maybe he was jumping to faulty conclusions. Perhaps Hernandez was correct about the big TV.

No. Something didn't feel right here. And until they could figure out the truth, better safe than sorry.

"BJ, you know as well as I do that robbery was probably the motive. Everyone claimed he had money hidden in the house or buried in the back yard."

A frightening thought hit him as he considered Naldo's bragging about his money. Had the old man foolishly made those claims to Diaz? *Where the hell was he?* Had he paid a final, deadly visit to Naldo before leaving town?

BJ seemed to weigh Rafe's words before walking over to close the cabinet door. "I know all that."

"Dammit, BJ, don't touch anything!"

The police chief grew so red he appeared ready to explode. "This is my case. Let me do my job. Now get the hell out of here!"

Rafe started to mention Diaz, but given BJ's anger, he turned and stomped out without further protest. He'd talk to him later, once he calmed down.

Stepping outside into a soft evening breeze, Rafe paused, inhaling fresh air like a thirsty man gulping down water after crossing a desert. Small knots of people stood outside the low brick fence that ringed the front of Naldo's house. In nearby yards, neighbors spoke in low voices, anxious eyes on the house. He examined the well-kept front lawn with its ceramic donkey and cart and cement birdbath on one side and a Virgin Mary in a bathtub on the other side of a brick walkway. Plastic sunflowers bordering the bricks seemed comical against the back drop of death. Naldo's Chevy pickup was parked in the gravel drive, and a couple of men lounged against it.

"Did someone kill him?" A voice came out of the darkness as Rafe approached the men near the truck.

Denial was useless. Young Robby Padilla, who found the body and called his office instead of BJ's, had probably already spread the word. The teenager was outside the house talking to anyone who came by when Rafe arrived. His curt order to one of BJ's officers to isolate the boy set the tension level with the police chief before they ever entered the house.

Rafe's queasy stomach still felt like it was inside. "Afraid so. You guys better get out of the yard if you're going to hang around. We don't know who might have touched his truck. They may want to fingerprint it."

The men jerked away as though the vehicle was hot. They retreated to congregate along the edge of the brick wall that separated the yard from a broken city sidewalk.

"Who would kill him?" Jerry Orozco, who lived two houses away, positioned himself on a seat atop the fence.

"You see anything, Jerry?" Rafe had no intention of playing detective, but he could gather information. If Diaz was around with his black SUV, Jerry might have seen him.

"You investigating?" Jerry asked, leaning back, arms folded.

"It's BJ's case. I'm just helping." He studied the watching faces. "Anyone see anything?"

"They were looking for money," one of the other men said, rubbing a dark hand over a stubbly beard. Rafe recognized Bill Langley, who nodded toward the house with his chin. "There was money in that house. Everyone knew he had it from when his dad ran the pawn shop. It wouldn't surprise me if he still had gold or silver too. Remember, he used to have those coins. I saw them once when I was a kid. Don't know if he still had them or if he buried 'em in his yard."

"Hey!" Rafe had known that speculation was coming. "I wouldn't be telling that story if I were you. You want people digging up the place?" He challenged the men and they looked away.

"They killed him for money," Bill repeated.

Rafe walked away, sliding a roll of antacid out of his pocket. He feared they were right about money as the motive. And he feared he knew the culprit.

****

The chirping cell phone was a welcome intrusion. Cere swallowed a yawn as the portly man sitting across from her reached down and pulled up a silver phone. It disappeared in his pudgy hand as he lifted it to his ear. A diamond pinky ring the size of a shelled peanut glittered in the glow of a candle squatting in the center of the table.

Beside Cere, Lottie smiled and smoothed the white linen tablecloth. "That's the problem with dating the mayor," she said in a voice just loud enough for Bradley Foster to hear across the table. "They're always getting called in the middle of dinner."

The gray haired man winked at Lottie, a gesture that drew a smile from Freeda. Cere turned away and stifled a laugh.

Stop that. She should be happy that her mother was going out, but Mayor Foster was not the type of man she'd expect her mother to date. Large, pompous and overbearing, he was nothing like her quiet, scholarly father. The budding romance delighted Freeda, but Cere was having a hard time with it.

"Say that again?" A furrow deepened across the man's forehead. His jowly face grew ruddy. "Dead, yes, but murder?"

"Murder?" Now that got Cere's interest. Suddenly the obligatory dinner with her mother's new beau didn't seem so boring.

Lottie put a finger to her lips, frowning in her most disapproving manner. That look terrified many junior high students over the years, but Cere was seldom cowed.

Bradley put away the phone and pushed back his chair. "This has been pleasant, ladies, but duty calls."

"There's been a murder?" Freeda asked. "I didn't think things like that happened in little places like this."

"We don't know it's murder." He had been trying

97

to charm Cere and Freeda with his blustery talk of the town, but now annoyance flicked in his blue-gray eyes. He picked up the check and took out his wallet. "I better go to the scene."

Tony Gennaro, a lean, silver-haired man her mother had introduced as the restaurant owner, approached as though he had been watching. "Did you find everything satisfactory?" He took the check and credit card being offered by Foster. Alert, sea green eyes rested on Lottie as he asked the question.

"Fine, Tony," she replied with a warm smile. "Wonderful, as usual."

The lanky man flushed with pride and nodded at her. Cere exchanged a knowing smile with Freeda and stifled a giggle.

Bradley hefted himself to his feet. "You ladies stay and have dessert and cappichina on me. I'll send a car to take you home."

Cere bit back laughter at his mispronunciation, but she was already lifting her napkin to her lips. The food had been surprisingly good for a small town restaurant, and she had eaten too much, but she wanted to find out about this murder.

"Who was killed?" Lottie asked, concern visible on her face.

"BJ said it was Naldo Sanchez. You probably don't remember him. Strange old hermit type. Must be in his 70s, so I doubt he was killed. Probably fell down or something." He said a quick goodbye, leaned down and kissed Lottie on the cheek and went to meet Tony at the front of the restaurant.

Freeda leaned over and elbowed her aunt. "Quite a catch, *Tia*. The mayor?"

Her mother emitted a girlish giggle, but it only sparked frustration in Cere. She put down her napkin and pushed back her chair "I don't know about the two of you, but I ate too much to have dessert. I'll walk home. I can use the exercise."

Lottie tilted her head in a disapproving manner. "Cere, you're being a party pooper. You didn't say two words over dinner."

Freeda laughed and leaned forward. "Maybe she's thinking about her own romantic conquest."

"What?" Cere and Lottie cried in unison.

"The sexy sheriff. They really hit it off this morning."

Chapter Eleven

Cere threw her cousin a look that threatened murder, but as usual, Freeda was unfazed.

"He kept flirting with her. I might as well have been a bug on the wall."

Lottie clapped her hands together. "I want to hear all about it."

"Then stay and discuss it." She stood, knowing Freeda was eager to tell the story. The three had spent the afternoon visiting relatives so there was no opportunity for girly gossip.

Tony appeared at the table interrupting their conversation. "Mayor Foster says he's buying dessert. May I suggest our tiramisu? It's my grandmother's recipe."

"Heavenly," Lottie said. "Cere, you should stay and try this."

"I can't eat any more." She patted her stomach that stretched against her knit dress. "We spent all day sitting. I need to walk. But you stay. I know you both love your sweets."

Lottie nodded at Tony. "Two espressos and one dessert. We'll split it." As he left, she looked up at Cere. "Can you find your way home? It's not that far. You go down Main Street two blocks and turn right for three… wait, I'll draw a map."

"I can find it. I did earlier."

"You were in the car. I don't want you wandering around lost." Lottie dug in her purse, brought out paper and pen and began to draw. "Thank you for meeting Bradley, hon. I had such a crush on him when I was a teenager. He was deputy sheriff, and he always looked so handsome in his uniform."

Cere tried to imagine the heavy, jowly man as young and appealing, but the image refused to appear.

"He seems nice," Freeda said. "Kinda like a cuddly teddy bear, but what about Mr. Gennaro?"

Lottie's eyes blinked rapidly, and she looked startled. "Tony? What do you mean?"

"He's giving you the eye, *Tia*."

Lottie flicked her hand in dismissal. "I've known Tony since high school. He's always been a friend, one of the boys. Bradley was special. He would drive me home on snowy days. Sometimes when he saw me at the drug store, we'd have a coke together."

"I guess I should be pleased he never paid attention to you or I wouldn't be here."

Her mother's face grew pink and she looked up. Her voice grew low and conspiratorial, as though sharing a secret. "No. He was married and I was so jealous of his wife." She sighed like a teen with a crush. "I guess he was friendly to everyone, even though I liked to think he took special care of me. In high school, when boys bothered me… he… well… rescued me."

To Cere's surprise, her mother's eyes had a girlish gleam unlike anything she'd ever seen. She'd never considered her mother's life before Del Medina. She had always taken for granted that he was her mother's first and only love.

"Did you date a lot when you were young?" Freeda asked.

"Heavens, no! My parents were strict. I couldn't go out alone so Millie and I double dated. Since she was dating my brother, I was well-chaperoned." She finished her map and handed it to Cere. "Don't get lost. And relax. Sit in the back yard, enjoy the stars. You've been too tense since you arrived."

Cere drew a deep breath. Relaxing at home was the last thing on her mind. When her mother told her about buying a cozy place, Cere had visions of a new townhouse or gingerbread Victorian. Instead, the two bedroom bungalow had the cookie-cutter look of the 1950s and its narrow rooms barely held the family furniture. The only attempt at updating was the addition of a second bathroom. With no air conditioning, the little house would be hot and stuffy.

Cere intended going home, but only to get her car and find out where the Mayor had gone. Maybe this place was the murder capital of New Mexico. This could be a story.

Finding the murder location was easy. She didn't even need her car. The center of town was unnaturally quiet as she hurried along the sidewalk. She didn't see one car before turning toward the residential area. At first she was struck by the silence, then a strange noise seemed to buzz around her. It took her a few seconds to recognize the sound of crickets. But she didn't have time to think about them. As she reached the next intersection, she caught sight of a crowd gathered a few blocks away. Police cars with flashing lights stood like beacons on both sides of the street.

Without hesitation she turned in that direction. As

she approached she could see small knots of people gathered outside a tiny well-kept yard. Bradley Foster stood in front of the house, listening to an overweight man in a police uniform, his jowly face a study in concentration.

Inner excitement stirred as she neared the scene and she felt the thrill of arriving at a breaking news story. She didn't cover murders often, and seldom anyone besides Hollywood stars, but she'd been to crime scenes. She pushed her way to the front of the throng until a short brick fence stopped her. She leaned forward, hoping to hear what the mayor was saying to the uniformed officers.

"Well, well, the media arrives. What brings you out here?"

Cere jumped and turned to find Sheriff Tafoya standing nearby. Much to her dismay, her heart skipped at the sight of him. A cowboy hat cast shadows on his eyes, but his face wore a grim smile.

She feigned disinterest, shrugging her shoulders and gesturing at the people around her. "I'm just an onlooker, like everyone else."

The crowd was a mixture of young and old. Curiosity mingled with anxiety on tense faces. A few children pushed at each other, while others circled the street on bikes.

"Why aren't you inside?" she asked.

"City jurisdiction. I'm an observer too."

"How did he die? Mr. Foster said maybe an accident?"

His full lips drew down, and he shook his head. "He was killed. I saw the gun."

"My mother told me how safe this place is

compared to Los Angeles."

"Safe enough. First murder in years."

"Since Marco Gonzales," said a dark man beside him.

Cere twirled toward the voice. The speaker was the man in the black T-shirt who had been at the restaurant earlier. What was his name?

"Really?" she asked. "You know Marco was murdered, uh, Jerry, right?"

"Hey!" Rafe shot him a hard look. "Don't start that."

Jerry lounged on top of the brick wall at the corner of the yard, and as she studied the men near him, she recognized several others from the café counter. Interesting. Her heart thumped. Maybe they would be more talkative tonight.

"Nobody's goin' to care about Marco no more."

"Why?" she asked, spinning around. The comment came from the man she'd talked to earlier in the green baseball cap. She hadn't learned his name.

"Why go looking for ghosts when you can stay in town and search for treasure?" he said.

Cere's curiosity rose like a building wave.

"Do you think there's treasure buried here? Want to tell me about it?" She didn't have a notebook with her, but she pulled out her mother's map and a pen from her purse.

"Stop it, Bill." Rafe moved to stand between her and the group. "I told you before I don't want to hear that nonsense. Those ridiculous rumors about Naldo burying stuff in his backyard was nothing but talk, and you damn well know it."

"Maybe," another man said, jerking his unshaved

chin at the house. "But I bet there's gold in that house and he was killed for his money."

"The coins probably," Jerry added.

Rafe drew a deep breath. "Will you guys stop? Jerry, Monte, you know better."

"Just saying. She's a curious reporter." Jerry nodded at her as though he was suddenly her friend.

"Hollywood stories," Rafe replied, disgust rippling through his voice.

"I'm a reporter tonight and I'm always looking for interesting stories." She stepped around him to stand beside Jerry and his group.

She directed her gaze at the man Rafe had called Monte. He was tall and wiry with long gray hair that hung to his Led Zepplin T-shirt. He had not been at the restaurant.

"What coins?" she asked.

"Naldo's people used to own a pawn shop," Rafe interrupted. "Years ago. He still had things that people couldn't redeem."

"Gold coins," Jerry repeated. "Had them appraised once and ended up in a fight with the Santa Fe appraiser who said they was worthless."

"Yeah, worthless," Monte added with a grunt, "but the guy was willing to give him a thousand for them. I saw them once and they looked real to me."

Jerry nodded in agreement. "Naldo threw him out. I saw the fight right here." He pointed at the edge of the sidewalk. "Kicked the guy in the ass and chased him to his car with a shovel. Told him he'd rather bury them in his backyard than let that crook have a single one."

Monte leaned toward Cere, eyes wide, eyebrows raising and lowering. "And the next spring, whaddya know? The old man digs up his front and back lawns and puts in fresh sod."

The men laughed, but it carried an uneasy, uncertain ring.

"Ever since, these guys have been convinced he did bury them," Rafe finished in a sarcastic tone.

"You don't think it's true?" Jerry asked. "I'll tell ya, he never showed 'em to no one again. Used to be, if you ran into him in the street, and he needed money, he'd have a silver or gold coin he'd show you and say if he didn't pay you back, he'd give it to you. They looked real, but he hasn't shown them in years."

"Since he dug up the yard," Monte finished, nodding in agreement, gray hair dancing on his thin shoulders.

"Don't believe them," Rafe cautioned in a low voice.

Cere looked from one man to the next. Jerry stared at the yard, dark eyes glittering in the klieg lights that had been put up along the fence. Monte leaned against the pillar where Jerry sat, unlit cigarette in one hand, while Bill, the man in the green baseball cap, stood beside him, hands thrust into the back pockets of jeans that clung to narrow hips.

She couldn't tell if they were teasing. They had joked about Bradley Foster at the café and he *was* dating her mother. A quick glance toward Rafe offered no answers. He shifted and for an instant she caught sight of his eyes under the brim of his hat. His dark eyes glowed and something strange sparked inside her. She grew suddenly aware of his large body next to her and the difference in their heights. Her eyes were level with the badge on his chest.

As if he noticed their close proximity and her eyes on him, he turned away, shaking his head. He ambled around the yard, scanning the yard and house. Was he looking for clues or checking for where the old guy might have hidden the coins? She was tempted to follow him, but given her strange reactions to him, she stayed put.

****

Rafe watched the scene unfold with a sense of unease. He had heard enough from the men and he wasn't certain he wanted to remain near Cere much longer. She smelled too good and he was too aware of her presence as she stood beside him. In a slim black dress with short sleeves and a dipping neckline that gave him a tantalizing view of her cleavage, she raised the temperature in his blood despite cool night air. His uncle Willie waved from across the lawn and he walked over to him.

"The old man? They're certain it's murder?" Willie asked.

His uncle ran the town newspaper and much as Rafe wanted to provide an answer, he knew anything official had to come from the chief or there would be hell to pay. He'd already screwed up with comments to Cere.

"You better get the details from BJ."

"They're ignoring me."

As though on cue, BJ and his dad, Mayor Foster, seemed to notice them and marched forward.

"Old Naldo Sanchez has been shot," the mayor announced. "We've called the state crime boys, and they'll be here in the morning. That's the only statement we can give tonight." His hard gaze pointed at Rafe.

"Did you tell them he'd been murdered?" Rafe asked, wondering what BJ had told the crime lab. He couldn't believe the technicians would wait so long.

Like his son, Bradley's face reddened visibly. "We don't know what happened. We're putting up tape around the scene once the coroner takes out the body. Nothing more to do tonight."

Rafe glanced at the lingering crowd as the Fosters walked away. He doubted a string of yellow tape would hold them back long. "I hope you're keeping someone here all night."

BJ drew up abruptly and whipped around toward him, visibly angry. "We'll lock up."

"The guys out there are talking about that crazy treasure story," Rafe said, stepping forward and lowering his voice. "If you don't keep someone posted, you may come back in the morning and find the damn yard dug up. Someone might even break into the house."

BJ shook his head, but his father grunted. "Damn, he's right. Better keep someone here tonight. Can you lend us a deputy, Rafe?"

He didn't have to think about that request for more than a second. "I'll stay."

BJ kicked at the ground, refusing to look Rafe in the eye, but he nodded. The mayor muttered a quick thanks.

He had several reasons for volunteering. He was curious about whether Diaz might venture by. And, if he was on duty he could look around. "Say, either of you run into a guy named Diego Diaz? Came into town a couple of days ago. Drives a black SUV with plates from Texas."

The men exchanged a glance before both said, "No."

"Talks with a funny voice," Rafe continued.

"Wait. A strange guy stopped in the Matador the other day," Mayor Foster said, stroking his chin. "Lottie and I were having lunch. He had a funny voice, kinda hoarse? Black sunglasses? He kept 'em on the whole time he was eating. Never talked to anyone except Josie, had lunch and left."

"That's him."

"So?"

"He gave Naldo a ride the other night. When I asked him later, Naldo said he knew him but that he was leaving town. I haven't seen him since, but he's been hanging out near the Palladium. People saw him there yesterday. Maybe I'll take a quick drive out there tonight and then come back and keep watch."

"Yeah, sure."

The men walked away and Rafe gave one last look around. Cere remained beside the fence, along with Jerry, Monte, Bill, and a couple of others from the neighborhood. He didn't know what they were discussing, but he could see the impact of their words. He hadn't known her long, but he could sense her rapt interest.

"Cere, how about if I give you a ride home?" he said, holding out his hand to take her arm. "I'm not going to let you stir up trouble."

A quick smile crossed her lips, and his breath quickened as a dimple showed on one cheek. She lifted her hands, eyes wide and pleading innocence as she stepped out of his reach.

"I'll behave, Sheriff. Honest."

He wasn't certain he believed her, but he didn't have time to argue. He tipped his hat and walked to his vehicle. Maybe this was for the best. If she got caught up in the talk of buried gold, she might forget Marco Gonzales.

****

Cere didn't stay long after Rafe left. She spoke to a few neighbors, asking questions and introducing herself. Most people agreed with the men. Someone was looking for Naldo's hidden treasure. Was it a story that might interest *Scope?* Probably not. This was just another death in a small town. But the evening wasn't a waste of time. Now people knew who she was. Next time she asked about Marco, a few might be more willing to talk.

She said her farewells and walked away. Her feet throbbed in pain from too long in her stiletto sandals, and she had several blocks to walk. Rounding a corner, she gave up and stopped to remove the offending shoes.

A black SUV approached as she straightened. She gripped a sandal tightly as the vehicle slowed and the window came down.

"Hey, what's going on down there?" a whispery voice asked.

She could barely see the man but she knew that voice.

"Hey, I ain't gonna hurt you," he said with a strange laugh.

"Damn right, you won't." Cere felt no fear, not with a crowd down the block. She waved a sandal at him. "These heels are really sharp and I can yell really loud."

Again the unsettling laugh. "You got me really scared. What's happening down there?"

"Some old guy got killed. Mr. Naldo?"

He gasped and leaned forward. To her surprise, despite the darkness, he wore sunglasses. "Naldo Sanchez?"

"They said he was shot. They're waiting for the coroner."

Abruptly the window rolled up and the SUV roared off. To her surprise it didn't go toward the crowd. With tires screeching it rounded the corner onto the main stretch of road that led out of town.

Chapter Twelve

Rafe leaned back against the headrest and fought to keep his eyes open. He checked his watch. 6:15. Less than an hour and his relief should be coming and he could go home and sleep. His plan to catch Diaz had not paid off. The Palladium had been eerily silent and the black SUV had not come by Naldo's house during the night. Most of the crowd was gone by the time Rafe returned, and he recognized the few cars that drove by.

Josie had brought him a container of coffee on her way to open the Matador and he poured another cup before opening the car windows. The crisp morning air washed over him. He loved that clean, natural scent of pine trees, so different from the grimy stench of LA traffic. Rosy streams of sunlight streaked the sky above the rim of the mesa to the east.

The streets were quiet, except for a faint tapping behind him. It grew louder and he glanced in the mirror. A lone runner jogged down the street and he jerked up, nearly spilling his coffee. At first he thought it might be Lottie. Then he realized it was her daughter.

Cere stopped in front of the house. She wore a T-shirt and wrinkled cotton boxer shorts. Her auburn hair was pulled into a messy pony tail. She pulled a small rectangular object from her pocket and pointed it toward the house. A cell phone. He couldn't help himself.

"What the hell do you think you're doing?" he called.

She jumped, fumbled with the object and whirled around. When she saw him, she held up her phone and smiled. "Taking a picture."

"Why?"

"Just to do it. I'm not bothering anyone and I'm within my rights. I mean, I'm on public property." She gestured at the sidewalk.

"That's not going to turn up on TV, is it?"

"A national news program interested in a small town murder? Hardly of interest," she said with a shrug.

"You're up pretty early, aren't you?"

Shoving the phone into her pocket, she walked toward his Jeep. "I'm an early riser. What are you doing here? You look like you've been up all night."

"I have been. I'm keeping an eye on the place until the state crime scene folks get here." With a yawn, he put his coffee into the cup holder and climbed out of the car. He knew he must look like hell but she didn't look like a highly paid reporter either.

As though guessing his thoughts, she tugged at a wayward strand of hair. "I thought it wasn't your jurisdiction."

"I'm helping out BJ, the police chief."

She looked from him to the peaceful yard. "Why were you here all night?"

"You heard that crazy talk about treasure. I wanted to make certain no one tried to get into the house. Naldo might not have gold but there are valuable objects inside. Not to mention there are probably people dying to find out if he still had stuff they lost to his old pawn shop."

"He had money?" Her voice carried a note of surprise. "I heard he worked as a janitor."

"I didn't say he had money. He had valuables. No telling what everything was worth. He probably didn't know."

"Why was he living in that little house and working?"

Maybe the exhaustion was getting to him, but he resented her condescending tone. At second glance, she might appear rumpled, but diamond studs adorned her ears and a designer watch circled her wrist. Her shoes were far from Walmart specials.

"He liked working. Called it his *dinero loco*. But he didn't care about fancy clothes or an expensive house."

She pressed her lips together, obviously catching his note of disapproval. "Gee, Sheriff and to think, Freeda thought you were flirting with me yesterday."

"Were you hoping I was?" The change in her tone was subtle, but he read the flirtatious nature and his senses buzzed with electricity.

A hint of a smile quirked at the edges of her lips. "Were you?"

A sudden giddiness overwhelmed him. Or maybe the exhaustion had finally claimed his good sense. "I don't think I'm going to answer. At least not right now when I look like crap."

Her fingers slid over her T-shirt and back up to her hair. "I don't look so hot either. I didn't expect to see anyone. I don't even have on eye makeup."

"You look good. Especially for this early."

"You *are* flirting."

Despite an outright laugh, he shook his head. "Just

tired."

"You're not going to offer to watch over me like you do everyone else?"

"Who do you need protection from? Besides ghosts, of course?"

Her sudden shiver surprised him. "Maybe that man in dark glasses from the Palladium."

"Diaz? You saw him again?"

"Diaz? That's his name? He drove by last night when I was walking home."

Rafe stepped around the side of the vehicle as his sense of duty took control. "He drove by here? Did he stop or talk to anyone?"

"No, I was walking home, at the end of the street." She pointed down the block.

"Did he know Naldo was dead?"

"He didn't act like it." Another shiver ran through her as though she felt a chill.

"Next time you see him, no matter what time, call me. I'll give you my cell number." He took out a card and handed it to her. Damn, he kept missing the guy! But at least now he knew Diaz had been in town the previous day.

"Do you think he's dangerous?"

"What do you think?" He was curious about her take on Diaz. Rafe didn't trust him, and he could see the man bothered her too.

"I don't know." She tucked the card into her pocket. "But I'll call."

He hated seeing her looking so concerned. His lips twitched and he lightened his tone. "Maybe you should call even if you don't see him."

She bit her lip and smiled up at him. "Even if I

have questions about Marco Gonzales?"

Before he could answer, a vehicle came around the corner and they turned to see a white van with the state seal of New Mexico approaching.

****

Cere sat at her mother's kitchen table, tapping on her laptop when Freeda and Lottie rose. Her mother trudged to the coffee maker on the counter. She touched it before reaching up to the cupboard and taking out a cup.

"Thanks for making coffee, sweetie. You girls are wearing me out. I normally do a morning jog, but the last two days I've been too exhausted."

"Well, I've been up for more than an hour. And I did take a run and Roxie for a walk. Now I'm working on a blog."

"Roxie misses you." Lottie leaned down and petted the terrier that resembled an unkempt rag doll of a dog. She yapped in appreciation. Roxie had become a fixture in the Medina household after Cere went to college. Sometimes she wondered if Roxie didn't consider her a rival for her mother's affection.

"Did I hear you're doing a blog?" Freeda entered the room with a yawn. "About what? You're suspen... I mean, supposed to be on vacation."

Cere's head jerked up and she shot her cousin a cool look. "I'm writing about my vacation. I don't want viewers to forget me. It'll show Alan my dedication and demonstrate I have followers, even when I'm off the air." The idea had come when she first woke and solidified as she ran. It was why she stopped at the murder scene to take a picture.

"What are you saying?" her mother asked, settling

across the table from her.

Cere summoned a bright smile. "It hit me this morning how peaceful it is here, how quiet. No freeway noise. No ambulances."

Freeda yawned again. "My dad used to say that was what he liked about New Mexico."

"It's what I like too." Lottie tugged at Cere's hair, loosening the pony tail. She began combing through it with her fingers. "I like these highlights in your hair, hon."

"Mo-om."

"Yeah, *Tia,*" Freeda joked. "Don't mess her two hundred dollar hairdo."

Her mother pulled her hands away with a laugh and got to her feet. "Wait until I tell Millie. She hasn't raised prices in years. I'm taking my coffee outside and going out to clean the rabbit cages. Coming, Freeda?"

"In a minute. I'm going to fix a cup of tea."

"Cups are in this cabinet," Lottie said as she disappeared through the back door.

Freeda found a mug, filled it with water and put it in the microwave before walking over to stand behind Cere. "Are you really blogging about this little town? Why?"

"To build interest, of course. I do want to show Alan that viewers miss me. I'm not going to let this suspension stick."

"Are you ever going to tell your mom what happened?"

She swatted at her cousin behind her. "Yes, today, before you blurt it out, big mouth."

"I won't be around. Daphne is driving to Rio de los Muertos and has offered to take me."

"Do you think your dad is there?"

"I don't know, but I want to see where we used to live. He always talks about it like it's such a special place."

Cere didn't mind her cousin leaving. It would provide the opportunity to chat with her mother about what had happened at work. "Oh, yeah, New Mexico is special all right."

Freeda leaned forward and looked at the words on the screen, reading over them. "'Even a small quiet town isn't peaceful. It knows murder.' Wow, you gonna send that?"

"Yes! Last night a guy told me it was the first murder since Marco."

"Except Marco's death wasn't murder," Freeda said.

"I don't know. This guy sounded like he knew something."

"I thought you said no one wanted to talk."

Cere fished a white slip of paper out of her pocket. "Take a look at this. I found it on my car windshield this morning. I have a feeling someone changed their mind but didn't want to tell me last night."

She unfolded the note and held it out to Freeda. *I will tell you about Marco,* it read in barely legible pencil. Below the statement was a phone number.

Freeda gasped. "You think they left it last night?"

"I don't know when it was left. The car has been parked on the street since we got here. Someone knew it was mine. I'm going to call in a few minutes. I wanted to let them wake up."

"Wow. Could be the answer you've been looking for."

"Yep." She giggled gleefully. "Between that note and this blog, I might be able to convince Alan I have something going."

The microwave buzzed and Freeda got to her feet and went over to get the mug. She plopped a tea bag into it and headed for the door. "I'm going out to feed the rabbits."

Cere put the finishing touches on her blog and sent it off. At least it would let viewers know she was still working. She opened her email account from work, checked for messages, answered a few and put in a notice referring people to the blog page. Hopefully, by the following morning she could tell Alan there was viewer interest in Rio Rojo and mention the note. After that, she just had to introduce Marco Gonzales.

Chapter Thirteen

The first thing you notice in Rio Rojo, New Mexico is the quiet. No sirens in the distance, no hum of the freeway. It is so silent you can hear crickets in the evening. When was the last time you heard crickets in Los Angeles?

Small towns can provide an interesting contrast to city living. No bumper to bumper traffic, no fear of drive-by shootings.

But small towns have their share of trouble. They don't see violent death often, but it happens.

Like last night. A long time citizen died. Gunned down by an unknown assailant inside his home. Police are investigating and I am not a crime reporter.

I report on people. Like Naldo Sanchez, who lived here all his life. He was once a business owner but for the past few years, what might be considered his retirement years, he has been a janitor. He cleaned City Hall, local schools, and the library. He did odd jobs around town, shoveling driveways and sidewalks and mowing lawns for free for the elderly.

The people in this town don't rely on TV or the Internet for local news. They get it by walking to the scene and stopping to talk about their old neighbor.

"He used to shovel our walk." Greta Lawrence said her mother was his next door neighbor for years. "I was away at college and she could barely get around

because she'd broken her leg. He would do her chores and check in with her to see if she needed anything at the grocery store."

And he did it for free. She and others informed me old Naldo never charged for services to needy individuals, though he made only minimum wage at his janitorial duties. If high school kids were looking to earn money, he'd let them help and somehow managed to pay them.

That's probably the biggest difference between the city and this small town. In the city we move at such a fast pace we never bother to meet neighbors. If someone offers to help, we wonder why and what they want from us.

Here, an old man is remembered for helping neighbors and asking for nothing in return.

Unfortunately the small town can mirror city life, though.

Here, an old man can still die alone.

But he won't be forgotten, or just another body on the coroner's table.

Tonight when the crickets come out and sing their rowdy tune, I'll think about old Naldo and the people he helped.

I'll keep in touch, viewers. I won't forget you while I'm on vacation. Let me know your thoughts.

Rafe stared at the computer screen. The depth of Cere's thoughts and the blog's content surprised him. He had no idea she could be a decent writer. She had included the cell phone picture taken of the house that morning.

"What do you think?" Willie rounded his metal desk in the center of the newspaper's editorial office and poked a finger at the screen.

"I'm surprised," Rafe admitted.

"Lottie told me to check it out, but I figured it was just her being a proud mother."

Leaning back on Willie's worn leather chair, Rafe nodded and rubbed tired eyes. "She's right, though. The quiet was one of the first things that hit me when I came back."

Willie perched on the edge of the desk. "Do you think I'd be out of line to ask her if I could reprint it next week?"

The thought jolted Rafe, and he blinked. "This says she's doing others. Are you planning to reprint those too?"

"Hell, I don't know. You met her. What do you think? Maybe I should talk to Lottie. Invite her to lunch or something."

Despite exhaustion, Rafe smiled. "I see. This is a ploy to get Lottie's attention."

Willie tapped the side of his short hair. "Ploy? Like she would notice me when she's being squired around by Mayor Bradley Foster. Hell, even Tony Gennaro won't take him on."

Rafe found himself chuckling at his uncle's petulant voice. "You bunch of old geezers. Mom's right. You're all still chasing her, like you're still in high school."

Willie shrugged and leaned forward to straighten items on the desk. "Not at all. But Tony is interested in her. She came by the other day to take out an ad about rabbits, and Tony was passing by, saw her and immediately came inside. He walks by every day and never even waves. All of a sudden, he comes inside. I swear the man was drooling. Does he come by the house?"

Rafe shook his head. "I'm not getting mixed up in this. You guys are acting like kids. Before long you'll be using my place to stake out her house or hanging out in my back yard so you can take off your shirt."

Willie patted his growing middle section. "Hell, I'm not taking off my shirt."

"You should have gone after her in high school instead of marrying your gold digging first wife."

"Very funny. Like her family was going to let her date a poor kid from the other side of the tracks. Her dad was bank president and her brothers were going to fancy colleges. I ran the press at the town newspaper. Not much of a future there."

Rafe nodded and looked at the computer screen one last time before clearing it. He got to his feet. "Yeah, I know what you mean."

And unfortunately, he did. Cere, with her expensive tastes and city life style, was not going to look at a small town sheriff. Not much of a future there either.

****

"Yeah, I saw it," Alan said, sounding harried as usual.

Cere hunched over her phone in the car. Two blocks up the hill from her mother's house she actually got decent reception. She'd been trying to reach the person who left the message on her car. So far no one had answered so she called Alan.

"Well?" she asked.

"Well, nothing. You can tell everyone you're on vacation, but you're not getting paid. One more thing, you need to clear out your voice mail and put on an out-of-town message. Your mail box is full."

Cere rolled her eyes. She gave her cell number to people she wanted to call her. The office line was for viewers. "Okay, but keep an eye on my blog. It should get viewers ready for my Marco Gonzales story."

"No more blogs. The Waverly lawyers will see it and claim you're working."

"But, Alan—"

"No buts. I'll let you know when things change. Sorry, gotta go." He hung up.

Cere waved the phone in frustration. No more blogs? She was counting on them to gain support. But she knew better than to battle Alan. She'd wait a week and call back to see if she could write another. In the meantime she'd gather material. She called her voice mail and sat poised with a pencil to take down any important information as she listened to messages.

Most were viewer comments about her last story. She was hoping for responses to her blog. Alan might have second thoughts about her suspension if viewers missed her. The final message began in a low, strange and guttural voice. A shiver ran through her at the gravelly sound.

What the hell? Was it that man Diaz? She replayed it to make certain she heard it right.

"Forget Marco or you'll be sorry."

Chapter Fourteen

"They don't like flowers, but they love the greens." Lottie slid a handful of dandelion greens into the first of three rabbit cages. "Meet Bonnie and Clyde. They're lop rabbits. See the floppy ears? They're pretty rambunctious."

Cere shoved her hands in her pockets, afraid her mother would ask for help. Freeda might enjoy them, but tending the rabbits wasn't on her agenda. Too bad Freeda disappeared shortly after breakfast with her new friend, Daphne.

"I haven't named these two yet," Lottie continued. Two smaller rabbits huddled in a third cage. They ignored the food until Lottie's gentle coaxing convinced them to hop over and sniff at it. Only then did their noses twitch and they greedily gobbled up the greens. "This is one of the high points of my day."

"It sounds as if you like it here."

"Baby, I love it. This is where I belong."

The comment surprised Cere. She would never have imagined her mother away from shopping malls and museums, but Lottie seemed content in her sprawling backyard. The cages occupied one corner, while neat rows of a vegetable garden took up another. Masses of brightly colored hollyhocks, snap dragons, and pansies bordered the neatly trimmed lawn. A patch of dandelions seemed out of place, except her mother retrieved the greens she fed the rabbits from that thatch. A brick patio near the house held a set of wrought iron furniture which once sat beside the pool in Los Angeles.

Cere's skin prickled. They were being watched. Diaz? No, a pair of bright black eyes peered through a crack in the back gate.

"Hello?" Cere called, her alarm vanishing.

Lottie's face jerked up, and she whirled toward the gate. "Oh, Ginny, there you are. I thought you weren't coming today. I started the feeding, but will you please bring more greens?"

A small girl stepped tentatively into the yard. Uncertain eyes examined Cere, before the girl dashed toward the dandelions.

"A neighbor?" Cere asked.

"Rafe's little girl," Lottie explained with a warm smile. "Didn't you meet her at the restaurant?"

Visions came of the half eaten food as disturbing thoughts crossed Cere's mind. He was married? She shook off a small stab of disappointment.

Lottie tapped Cere's arm, blue eyes twinkling with mischief as she spoke in a low voice. "I forgot to ask what you thought of our sheriff."

An unsettling vision of the dark, handsome face danced in Cere's vision. She had been trying not to think of him, and now she had a reason. A child meant a wife.

"Kind of full of himself," Cere grumbled.

Lottie's tanned face frowned in disapproval. "I've always thought of Rafe as very nice. He does a great job with Ginny, given that he's a single parent."

Her insides leaped, though she reminded herself his

marital status shouldn't matter. She studied the girl more closely. Ginny bore a strong resemblance to Rafe, especially her long, thick eyelashes. Twin plastic barrettes held back shiny brown hair and she wore baggy jeans and a light blue T-shirt.

"Cute," Cere said, thinking *single parent* as she noted that one of the pink butterfly barrettes had slipped and the part in her hair was crooked.

"He's a devoted father, despite his job," Lottie continued.

Ginny skipped toward them, clutching two handfuls of greens. "May I put them in?"

"Of course, sweetie." Lottie raised the wire door, and Ginny dropped a pile of limp stems into the cage. The girl looked up at Cere through bangs that nearly hid her eyes and Lottie performed an introduction.

"Hello, Ginny," Cere said, holding out her hand.

The little girl accepted the handshake smiled and whispered a quick "Hello."

"I'll leave you to get acquainted," Lottie said. "I need to get a hose to clean water dishes. You are going to help me, aren't you, Ginny?"

The girl gave an eager nod.

Cere had little experience with children so she wasn't certain what to say. "How old are you?"

"Six." She began hopping on one foot and twirling in a circle.

"Where do you and your dad live?"

"Down the block. But not Mommy... she lives..." Ginny stopped her dance and gestured up with a small thumb.

"In heaven?"

The girl nodded and spun again.

Cere smiled at the child's antics. It must be rough being a single father to a little girl, especially for a macho guy like Rafe. Lottie returned, and she and Ginny took turns washing out water bowls with the hose.

"Staying out of trouble?"

Cere was so involved watching her mother and Ginny, she hadn't noticed Rafe enter the yard. She inhaled softly as she looked him over. In full uniform, he was an impressive sight. The tailored cut of the beige shirt made his shoulders appear wider, his chest thick and muscular. The slim slacks with a thin green stripe gave his legs a long lean look. The brim of a peaked cap shielded his dark eyes as he approached.

"I'm behaving. For now," Cere retorted saucily, aware her heart was beating quicker. "How's the cop business, Tafoya? Did you recover from being up all night?"

Rafe shrugged, wishing he didn't feel so pleased to see Cere. She had been on his mind much of the day. When he realized Ginny was missing from the back yard, he knew where she would be. He'd been excited to search for her at the Medina house. He forced down the wattage of his smile.

"It happens sometimes. I got a couple of hours sleep, then I had to go to court to testify on a case. Gin, are you hungry?"

"We're almost finished," Lottie called, waving her hand. "You two visit."

Cere dropped her head, and Rafe noted a roll of her eyes. "Your daughter seems like a good little girl."

"Like her dad," he replied with a chuckle. What the

hell was he doing flirting? Why couldn't he stop that? She shifted, and Rafe grew uncomfortable, shoving his hands in his back pockets. He tapped the grass with a polished boot trying to think of something clever to say.

"Who takes care of Ginny for you? I would think a sheriff's hours are unpredictable."

"My sister and Mom. Sometimes she stays at the café with Josie or with your mom."

"Her mother is...dead?" Her eyes were wide, inquiring.

"Yep." He hoped she caught his curt, reluctant tone. Discussing Carmen was not something he did with strangers. He changed the subject. "Where's your crazy cousin?"

Something shifted in Cere's eyes. "She's on a mission to find her father. Who knows when she'll be back."

Was that jealousy he heard in Cere's tone? He couldn't stop the sudden light mood that overwhelmed him. "How did you spend today?"

"Visiting Mom's friends. But all anyone talked about was the murder."

"Figures." Naldo's death had been the main subject at the courthouse too.

"How's the investigation going?"

"Are you asking out of curiosity? Or as a reporter?"

How did she manage to look so fresh in the late afternoon? Her hair was neatly pinned behind her head and held in place by a floral silk scarf. Her beige slim fitting sundress looked like she had just put it on. Not even her nose was shiny.

"I'm not working on *that* murder case," she

Rebecca Grace

replied, flashing a withering look that spoke volumes. "My relatives agree it was robbery, like those guys last night were saying. Is that what you think? In your professional opinion?"

A smile twitched at his lips as her eyes grew wide with open curiosity. "Why do your questions always sound as though I'll be quoted on TV?"

"Why do you always sound as though you don't take me seriously?" she retorted.

"I do. Maybe too seriously. By the way, my uncle liked your blog. Did he call you today?"

"Mom and I had lunch with him at the Matador. He seems nice. Why didn't you tell me you had relatives in the media? He and your dad run the newspaper? Why didn't you go into the family business?"

The question surprised him. At times his uncle and dad made him feel guilty for choosing law enforcement. He'd thought about it, but he didn't like writing as much as he liked investigating. "Why didn't you go into teaching, like your mom and dad?"

She laughed and shook her head. "They were better at it than I could ever be. Besides I like this better."

"I bet."

As she edged closer to him he could smell a hint of lilac. His pulse quickened as she turned a brilliant smile on him. "I got a note from someone wanting to talk about Marco. It was unsigned, just a phone number and I've been calling all day, but no one answers. The number appears to be unlisted and it just rings, doesn't even go to voice mail."

He fought the sharp pang of disappointment that ran through him. "May I see the note? Maybe I'll recognize the handwriting or the number."

She hesitated. "I think it might be that Diaz man. I mean, he is probably the only person in town who knows my car."

"Maybe it was a prank. You're not going ahead with this Marco thing, are you? I thought you were doing another blog on Rio Rojo."

"I am. I can use this new murder as a peg for the other story. You know, first murder in years, but the town is no stranger to violent death. Now that I set that up, I—"

"No!" His voice came out louder than he wanted, but was she serious? "You can *use* this murder? Well, I'm glad Naldo's murder wasn't in vain. Damn, are you really that callous?"

He didn't wait for an answer, he whirled away and called to Ginny. "Let's go, hon. I'm sure Cere has a story to write." He put a large hand on Ginny's head in an affectionate gesture, fearing she had heard his upraised voice.

As they walked toward the back gate, Lottie approached, holding a gallon jar of sun tea. "Would you like to come inside for iced tea, Rafe?"

He smiled at Lottie, but found he couldn't keep his cool when he turned and saw Cere watching him, eyes challenging. "I'm sorry, Lottie, we have to go. If I'm around your daughter much longer, I'd be tempted to throttle her."

Chapter Fifteen

"What in the world did you say to him?" Lottie asked, as they sat at the kitchen table with large glasses of iced tea. "He looked angry."

Cere shook her head and sipped her tea, unable to answer. She still smarted over Rafe's comments. Was she being callous? She'd heard the complaint in the past, but it never stung as it did coming from him.

"I should invite him over for dinner," Lottie said. "What do you think?"

"Mother, you heard him. He wants to strangle me!"

Lottie laughed and patted her hand. "I'm sure he's teasing. Rafe's a nice man. You two have more in common than you realize."

"Yeah, right." Cere shook her head in disbelief.

"What were you discussing?" Lottie asked, her voice taking on a conspiratorial tone.

Cere sighed. She had finally admitted her suspension to her mother, but she hadn't indicated her reason for choosing Rio Rojo for vacation. Perhaps her mother could help. She would have been away in college when Marco died, but maybe she knew his family.

"I told you I'm trying to get back into Alan's good graces at *Scope*. You know we do those cold case stories?"

Her mother's brow furrowed. "So?"

"I'm trying to do a story on Marco Gonzales."

Her mother coughed softly, and her head jerked up as her glass dropped to the table with a thump. Her bright blue eyes looked stunned, then...confused. "What? Why in the world would you want to do that?"

"There were questions about his death. Did you see the story Gary Riggins did in the Santa Fe newspaper? You emailed it to me."

Lottie jerked upright. "Oh, my word. I send you links to the paper to read about our bowling team. Why don't you do something on how the town is becoming more like Taos? There's a new artists' colony and I hear they're talking about building a fancy spa on the old Hollister place between here and Casitas. Hon, there are so many things you could do."

"It's just an idea."

"Good." Lottie's voice grew cool, the authoritative teacher in charge. "Then put it on hold. You should relax. I'll invite Rafe and Ginny over some night."

"Ginny told me her mother is dead?"

"She died just before he came back here. I'm not certain how. He's never told me, and I've never asked Ginny. She's a quiet child, doesn't say much."

"Her father probably doesn't let her. He's the macho sheriff, probably bringing her up to be the proper little lady who knows her place—subservient to men."

"Don't shrug him off because he's from here, Cere."

Her serious tone brought a bubble of laughter from Cere. "You're playing matchmaker. Big city reporter and tiny town cop? It's never going to work, Mom."

"Rafe is not small town. It's why we get along. We

enjoyed the city, but we came back to our roots. I know I belong here."

Cere wanted to question her mother further, but she held her tongue. Her gaze slid around the kitchen, trying to make sense of familiar possessions in strange surroundings, like the old cuckoo clock on a bright yellow wall instead of on the mantel in a formal dining room.

"I'm glad you're here," her mother added. "I want you to get to know my family. I've always loved Nena and the Medina family, but you need to know the Winslows too. This is where the other half of your roots are."

She couldn't imagine any part of her being based on the tiny town, but she kept silent as her mother continued in a wistful voice.

"I didn't think I'd get used to California. I was such a small town girl."

Cere studied her mother's reflective pose. She had never before noticed the line of wrinkles forming on the edges of her mother's lips and eyes. Lottie's age was showing. She was nearly Marco's age. How would he look now? Visions of her dreams popped into Cere's head. The Marco she envisioned was the young man of the picture. Maybe she should have an artist do an aging portrait of him.

"What are you thinking? You look a hundred miles away." Lottie leaned toward Cere and took her hand. "I can tell something's wrong. What is it? This suspension?"

Cere sighed. "I am concerned about it. That's why I need to do this Gonzales story."

"Why?" Were her hands shaking? She frowned at

Cere. "Why that particular story?"

"It'll be a great piece. The hand print is a town legend, and it left so many unanswered questions. No one knows how he died or what happened to the money that he supposedly stole."

Lottie's lips set in a firm line and her eyes blazed as she dropped Cere's hand and waved hers in dismissal. "Don't be silly. Everyone knows how it ended. He got depressed because everyone was against him, so he shot himself. No one ever proved he took any money or that he burned those buildings. There were lots of strangers in town because they had just opened that commune in the hills."

Cere stared at her mother in surprise. Maybe she had been talking to the wrong people. "So you know the story? You were around when he died?"

Her mother ran her hands over her thighs as though straightening her neatly pressed slacks. Her blue eyes remained glued to her glass of tea. "That was a long time ago."

"How did those ghost rumors get started?"

Lottie's laugh was soft and sad. "That handprint. If someone had washed it off before it stained the wall, none of that nonsense would have taken hold. Now, honestly, Cere, the sooner you forget this, the better."

"Don't be a spoil sport, Mom. Maybe we should go out there now. I bet you know how to get inside and where the hand is." Pushing away from the table, Cere hopped to her feet. "I can do a blog on it. Think of how much fun it will be, an evening adventure!"

To Cere's surprise, her mother gasped, a look of horror crossing her face. Her curls shook violently as she twisted her head back and forth in a negative gesture. "Certainly not! Cere, I don't think you should do the story. The 60's and 70's were a bad time. Lots of upheaval. The town went through so much turmoil and it didn't end until he died. I think everyone was frightened by the violence and we just wanted peace. The town was rebuilt, and the wounds healed. I don't think anyone wants to recall those days."

The negative reaction disturbed Cere, but it didn't deter her. "I'll bet the change was good. Don't you want to find out if he was murdered? There could be a killer in this town who has gotten away with it for years. Obviously this town harbors some bad guys. Look at whoever killed that old man. You probably know the person."

Lottie drew a deep breath and shivered despite the warmth in the room. "That's ridiculous. And if it isn't, what if you're right and there's someone who won't want you dredging up that old stuff? Have you thought of that? You could be in danger." Her voice had risen with every word, shocking Cere. Her mother seldom betrayed emotion, but her carefully made up face was pinched with distress.

"Danger," Cere repeated breathlessly, her interest even more piqued, thinking of the message on her voice mail. "Do you know something? Suspect someone?"

"Of course not." Lottie stood, shaking her head and holding up her hands. "Now, I am finished with this discussion. I'm going up to change. I promised Bradley we would join him for dinner. Please don't bring up this subject."

"Bradley again?" Cere teased, trying to lessen her mother's unhappiness.

Lottie's cheeks grew pink, and her eyes avoided

Cere's, but a smile played over her lips. "We usually have dinner on Tuesday. I go over to his house and cook for him since he has a late afternoon council meeting. You can go with me now, or you and Freeda can join us when she gets back."

While she was curious about her mother's new relationship, Cere couldn't imagine another evening with the pompous Mayor Foster.

"Do you mind if I skip it? I don't know if I'm up to another long dinner. The last few days have been hectic."

Lottie put her hand to Cere's face, the picture of motherly concern. "You do look tired, sweetie. We can do this tomorrow night. I'm sure he'll understand."

"Why don't you go alone? I don't want to spoil your routine."

"But it's your third night here," her mother protested.

"I'm going to be here a couple of weeks. What I'd like is to take a bath and unwind."

A gentle smile crossed Lottie's face. "All right, but I better get busy. I promised I'd cook *arroz con pollo* and I need to run by the market."

"You better not be using Nena's recipe to feed another man."

The smile turned sad. "Your grandmother knows about him. I can't keep secrets from that old bat. She told me when I moved that I needed to get on with my life. She knows that's what Del would have wanted. I hope you give Bradley a chance. He wants to get to know you better."

"I want to get to know him," Cere said, trying to muster enthusiasm. "Have he and his family lived here a long time?"

"His great-great-grandfather was one of the founding fathers and now his son is the police chief. Bradley was sheriff for years."

Cere didn't respond. She'd watched the big man glad hand people at the murder scene as though it was a political occasion.

His pudgy face had been filled with concern, but it appeared to be a mask. The comments she overheard him make were patronizing, but the crowd seemed respectful, in awe.

"I'd like to have him over for a special dinner some night."

"Sure, Mom. That sounds good."

****

The house echoed with emptiness once her mother was gone, despite its cramped size. The familiar furniture jammed into the tiny rooms created claustrophobia that threatened to overwhelm her. Cere wandered from room to room, restless energy driving her. The thought of soaking in a hot bath no longer appealed to her.

Eventually Cere settled on her favorite chair, leaning back. Her gaze fell on an old magazine rack beside the chair. It had been an early shop project of her father's. She smiled at it fondly, touching it gingerly since it had always been known for its instability. It teetered, and Cere grabbed at it, jerking it forward and sending newspapers and magazines spilling across the wooden floor.

She began picking them up and stopped. Stuffed into the pile was the newspaper article about Marco. Cere pulled it out, careful not to tip over the rack. The newspaper looked like it had been folded and unfolded many times. Why had her mother kept the paper and then acted as though she didn't even remember it?

Across the room, the phone rang and Cere let it ring. Her mother's machine would take a message. Then she heard Freeda's voice.

"*Tia,* I decided to stay here over night. Daphne will pick me up tomorrow when she comes back. Tell Cere to behave. And if she hasn't told you, ask her about her ghost and her dreams."

The line went dead and Cere frowned at the machine. Damn Freeda! It was a good thing she had told her mother about Marco Gonzales.

Cere picked up the newspaper again. Marco's hypnotic eyes reached out to Cere, drawing her in. She nodded at the smudged photo as though answering a call.

Why did no one want to talk about his death? Even Rafe seemed reluctant to discuss the old case. As sheriff, wouldn't it be a feather in his cap to solve the old mystery? Marco's defiant eyes blazed from the paper, piercing space with a silent appeal for truth.

"Only you can help me."

Just who was Marco Gonzales? And why couldn't she let go of this mystical hold he had on her?

"Okay, Marco, show me what I need to know," Cere whispered, as though he was in the room with her. A vision popped into her head as though it had been placed there by Marco.

The Palladium.

Its sagging structure rose in her mind's eye and she turned to the page that showed the building. That was where she needed to go. She glanced through the window. It was early evening. At least two hours of sunlight remained.

Why not go there now as she had suggested earlier to her mother?

Chapter Sixteen

After changing into jeans and tennis shoes, Cere grabbed her purse and video camera case. At the last minute she tucked a can of mace into the pocket of her jeans. If she ran into Diaz again, she was going to be ready. As she backed out of the driveway, she shivered with anticipation. She was going ghost hunting!

The streets of downtown Rio Rojo were nearly deserted, despite the early hour. Only the packed gravel lot at the Matador showed signs of life. Even the lot at Gennaro's held only a few cars. The town ended abruptly, giving way to open, grassy fields dotted with stubby cedars.

Despite knowing where she was going, Cere nearly overshot the turn off for the dance hall. Only at the last minute did she spot the weathered sign and trail of twin ruts. The car lurched in protest as she guided it down the road, drinking in the surroundings, thinking about how it might be photographed.

The road stretched across a mile long patch of prairie before rounding a bend. At that point she caught sight of the long building of pale gold sandstone that she recognized as the Palladium. Her heart skipped. In the golden evening twilight, it looked like it could harbor a ghost. As she neared it, she stopped the car and got out her video camera. Without Freeda to distract her she could take her time and appreciate the overall ambience.

She studied it through the camera lens. The long building hunkered on an open plain, forlorn and empty, surrounded by thin strands of prairie grass. The stubby piñon trees she'd once feared were demons chasing her provided a benign backdrop toward rolling hills of amber sandstone. The roof was a steeply pitched length of rusting tin, though one end appeared to have been added on later. That portion of the roof sagged, its wooden shingles gray with age. Posts marked the porch below the shingles.

Her gaze examined the area near the building. No sign of Diaz or anyone else. Good! After putting away the camera, she slid into the car and inched it forward, stopping where they parked earlier. Nothing stirred but the breeze, a scene so serene she couldn't understand why she had been so terrified as a child.

Grabbing her camera bag from the back seat, she dropped in her keys and video camera. Her mind was on the story and it began to form visually as she approached the building. The dying sunlight cast long shadows, making the setting perfect for shooting at sunset. The dance hall would be dark enough to look like a spooky outline. Maybe if she stayed longer she could shoot enough preliminary video to give Alan a taste of what could be produced. He might relent and let her go back to writing the blog.

She circled the building, phrases and ideas popping into her head. Cere knew the hand print was in a room on the second floor and she would have to go inside to see it. At the back of the building, she hesitated, but tonight no strange man lurked beside the door. Too bad he hadn't left his crowbar. The door was padlocked.

Cere hoisted herself onto the porch using a sagging post, since the stairs looked nearly rotted through. The wooden veranda creaked under her weight. Some of the floorboards had broken completely, and weeds sprouted through the open areas. She stepped carefully, not wanting to fall underneath. Her nose wrinkled at the thought of what might be under there. Snakes? Spiders? Neither was an appetizing thought.

Reaching down, she touched the latch that held the lock and was surprised when it pulled away. So! Diaz must have gotten in. Inside, two sets of prints were visible in the dust. The interior was cool and gloomy and the tracks disappeared. The scent of rotting wood filled her nostrils.

A narrow band of light from the broken plank of a boarded up window cast the only light into the room. Damn! She needed a flashlight. Was there one in the car? There was no light kit for the camera and she couldn't shoot in this darkness.

Slowly her eyes adjusted to the gloom. A rusted sink and a long counter occupied one side—some sort of kitchen. Something scampered in one corner. A rat? A lizard? Cere shivered, but she wasn't afraid. She stepped gingerly toward the dark door. It opened onto a large open room that ran the length of the building.

This was the dance hall itself. The interior was dusky, though rays of dying sun streaked the hall through narrow strips where boards had been ripped off windows. A hardwood floor retained a dull polish in spots. The ceiling was two stories tall, with a narrow balcony and rail ringing the second floor. A raised platform which must have been the bandstand occupied a corner.

Cere closed her eyes, and in her head she could hear music. She could picture a dance band of men in cowboy shirts with jaunty bandannas tied at their throats while a thin blonde with teased hair wailed a tune about her cheating husband. On the polished floor, gaunt-faced men in new jeans and gingham shirts whirled women in floral dresses over stiff petticoats.

And Marco? Her heart thumped, and it was as though she could sense his presence. She could see him leaning against a wall, in a tight white T-shirt and rolled up jeans, his black hair longer than the other young men. Why had she thought of that? Except for the newspaper article she had no idea what he looked like. Continuing her advance, she crossed to a sweeping set of stairs that curved up into darkness.

The stairs were wide, but much of the hand rail was gone. Rotting posts held a few feet of a wide rail in several places. As she began climbing, the steps creaked in protest even though she stepped gingerly. Several cracked ominously. Despite a slow ascent, her heart banged against her chest by the time she reached the top step.

The upper story was almost dark, and she stopped to get her bearings. Chico, no, Rafe, had led them along the upper landing toward a narrow hall at the end. One of the rooms off the hall held the handprint. Keeping the rotting stairs in mind, she stepped daintily along the warped floorboards, noting broken planks. In several places, the bottom floor was visible through cracks. No wonder Rafe kept people out.

The building creaked, as though it was being violated. *What was that?* Cere stopped, listening, but all she heard was wind whistling through the boarded up windows.

The dark hall loomed. Chairs and tables were stacked to one side. To her left was a partially open doorway; to the right, a closed door. Cere couldn't remember in which room she would find the hand print.

She could almost swear something guided her to the right, but she didn't want to believe she was hearing or feeling ghostly happenings. The sensations might be useful in her story but they wouldn't help now. Ignoring the sensation, she turned left toward the open door.

A musty scent teased her nostrils, and gloominess surrounded her as she stepped inside. Again it took a few seconds for her eyes to adjust. Only dim outlines were discernible. The hand would never be visible in such low light, but the spookiness of the room chilled her.

"Talk to me, Marco," she whispered. "Tell me your story."

Nothing. Or was that a creak she heard? She fumbled for her camera and tried to scan the dark walls, but saw only ghostly shadows. A sudden swish behind her startled her.

Bam!

The sound reverberated around the room, and the old building shook as though hit by an earthquake. Cere jumped as the room plunged into blackness. The door behind her had slammed shut. Had the wind done that? Her heart thumped as she moved in the direction of the door. Did she hear creaking outside in the hall?

Something hit her foot, and Cere stumbled, pitching forward and bumping into a solid surface. She cried out, but there was no one to hear. Or was there? Did she hear shuffling? She thrust out her hands in front of her, like a blind woman.

Touching a flat surface was a welcome discovery. The wall. She moved sideways and her shaking fingers sought the door knob. Darkness didn't frighten Cere, but this was different. A cry of relief escaped her as her fingers found the outline of a door jamb and then the knob. She twisted it and yanked. To her horror, just as when she was a child, the knob didn't budge.

Cere rattled the knob, pushing at the door at the same time. No! She couldn't be locked in. The door was jammed. The knob refused to turn, and the wood, for its old smell, and for all the rotting timbers around her, proved surprisingly strong when she thrust her body against it. She pounded against it again and again, stopping only when her fists grew raw.

Her heart was pounding from exertion, but she also felt a slight edginess. What if she was trapped? She stood very still. The only sound was her labored breathing, though she felt her thudding heart was also audible in the room. She reached for her bag to get her cell phone and emitted a cry. The phone was in her purse, which she'd left in the car.

"This isn't going to scare me," she whispered into blackness. Nothing here could harm her, right? Unless there were snakes. Could one be around? Sensing her and inching along the floor toward her?

Something moved beyond the door, and her breath caught. *Was someone out there?*

Cere pounded on the door. "Hey, you! Let me out! The door is stuck!"

Stillness was the only answer.

She pounded again. "Whatever you were trying to do, you made your point. Now let me out. Diaz? Is that you?"

What was that sound? Footsteps? Cere pressed her face to the door, but if there had been footsteps, they had retreated. There was only silence. She was alone.

She turned back toward the room and realized one end of the room appeared lighter, as though a window might be hidden somewhere. She stepped in that direction only to bang her thigh on an unknown object.

"Damn!" Tears stung her eyes and she drew a deep breath, fighting pain. For a minute, she couldn't move. Frustration crept in like a gathering fog. Why hadn't she propped that door open or brought a flashlight? Why hadn't she put her damn cell phone in her pocket? Even if it didn't work, it would provide a tiny light.

The stillness returned, pressing in like a compacting wall. She'd been in dangerous situations for stories. She wasn't going to let this frighten her.

What about ghosts? Like Marco?

"I'm not afraid. I'm here to help you, Marco. You wanted me to come. Now get me out of here!" An eerie calm settled over her, as though she had nothing to fear from spirits. If this place was haunted by Marco, he was on her side.

Ghosts? She shook her head; she didn't believe in them, but another, more frightening thought touched her. *What about the scratchy voice on her voice mail?* It had warned her not to pursue this story. Could that person have followed her and locked her in? That was more likely, and it was probably Diaz.

Something sticky clutched at her face. "Yuck!"

Okay, spiders and other creepy things like that might bother her, but she could defeat them too. She peeled away the clingy net. Her heart had stopped pounding, and her leg no longer throbbed.

The stillness was broken momentarily. *What was that? A car engine? Was it coming closer?* The noise vanished. She didn't think she could hear traffic from the main road. If she'd heard a car, it had to be nearby. If she could find the window she could call for help.

Putting her hands in front of her, Cere inched forward like a blind woman until her fingertips touched the wall again. Pressing her palms to the wall, she moved sideways until her body collided with something solid. A faint ray of light seemed to come from beyond the object. She yanked at it, but it refused to move. It appeared to be some sort of large wooden box.

She attempted to get a grip on the side and front, but the surface was too slippery and her fingers dropped through the air. They landed on something flat and smooth setting off a musical crescendo. She jumped, but fear turned to humor as her laughter rang out. The heavy wooden object was a piano.

"Untuned," she said with a forced laugh. Cere put her back to the side and braced herself flat against it. With a cry worthy of karate class, she shoved as hard as she could. A loud screech of protest came from the rotting wood floor and the base of the heavy instrument, but it shifted. She took off her bag, set it on top and shoved her fingers behind the piano. Bracing herself again, she yanked it toward her.

Another screech and another halting move, but a gray band of light filtered into the room. Pushing her hand into the space between the piano and the wall, she tried to get a better grip. Maybe those workouts using weights could come in handy. Her wrist caught, and she struggled to pull free. She might be bruised by the time she got out, but she sensed progress.

Leaning over, Cere saw the edges of a boarded up window behind the piano. Sensing an escape route, she attacked the instrument with renewed vigor. Dust flew as the piano scraped against the floor, but it moved with each assault. After a few intense minutes, Cere managed to get the piano far enough from the wall to wedge behind it.

Her body felt battered by the time she reached the weathered boards blocking the window. Dim light was visible through slits between the boards. Night was falling outside. She jerked at a board, but it refused to budge. That didn't deter her. Bracing her back against the piano, Cere kicked at the boards. The screeching sound of rusted nails giving way brought a sigh of relief. She was going to get out.

She drew her legs back and propelled them forward again. *C-r-a-c-k*. Those leg exercises were paying off too. Another thrust and wood began to splinter.

"Think of it as your evening workout."

A few minutes of steady kicks freed enough boards so she could poke her head outside. A small glow of twilight remained on the western horizon. In a few minutes, darkness would swallow the valley. The only way out was to climb through the window and drop to the ground. It looked a long distance away, even in the gloom.

"I can do this." Summoning courage, she hauled herself through the window. With a twist she gripped the window sill and stretched as far as she could down the stone side of the building. With a cry, she let herself drop.

One foot caught on a rock and twisted, tossing her

down. She collapsed on her backside, but at least she was free.

Stars popped into the evening sky above her.

"Thank you, Marco," she whispered.

Chapter Seventeen

Her ankle was tender as Cere struggled to her feet. Something grabbed at her ankles—tumbleweeds clawed at her. She jerked free, but their stickers remained, coming through her socks. Removing the prickly thorns didn't work. It would be easier to remove her socks. She leaned against the building and removed her shoes to take off her socks. She sensed a lecture from her mother when she got home. Freeda would probably find it funny as hell.

When Cere bent over to put her shoes on, the first went on easily, but as she fought with the second, her ankle buckled. She hopped away from the wall, lost her balance and fell backwards. Needles pierced her backside from her thighs to her waist.

Was there no end to this? She twisted and discovered she had tumbled into a cactus patch. She struggled to her feet, but despite her troubles a smile came to her face as a familiar sound became audible.

A car engine! This time she was certain. It grew louder, until twin spikes of light sliced through the parking lot.

Cere stumbled forward, waving, hoping for a carload of curious kids. They might laugh at her predicament, but maybe a girl in the group could pull the stickers from her sore backside.

The vehicle stopped, headlights blinding her. A

door opened. "What the hell?"

So much for the carload of kids, she thought, wrinkling her nose as she picked up Rafe Tafoya's deep voice.

"What are you doing here?" he demanded, walking toward her. He had changed from earlier. He wore jeans and a light colored shirt. A black cowboy hat rested on his dark hair.

"What are you doing?" she countered. "Playing sheriff and looking for kids to chase away?"

"Far from playing. I'm on duty, more or less. Your mother called when she found you gone. She figured you'd come out here."

Cere didn't know if she felt betrayed or relieved. "My mother knows me too well. I thought she had dinner plans. How did she know I was missing?"

"She didn't say. She was concerned that you had disappeared and worried you might get lost."

"I'm not lost. I got locked in that damn hall."

"Locked in?" His gaze shot to the sagging building. "How did you manage that?"

"Look, could we hold off on the Q & A for now? I have a problem." She winced from the cactus prickles.

"What?"

"I fell in a patch of cactus," Cere explained. "And don't you dare laugh and say I deserve it, Tafoya!"

He chuckled. "You probably do."

"Fine. I'll pull them out myself. Just keep your headlights pointed this way."

The door closed, and Rafe walked over to her. "All right, Medina. Let the sheriff help you."

"I should warn you," she said with a grimace. "These stickers aren't in the most appealing location."

He stepped behind her, and emitted a soft whistle. "I see. Actually it's kind of appealing."

"Scumbag!"

His laugh was low and intimate as he took hold of one arm to steady her. "I hope you're not squeamish about where I touch because I really can't help it."

Cere chewed on her lower lip as pain shot through her. "Just get them out."

"No problem. What the hell happened to your shoes?"

Rafe listened to Cere's rambling explanation with half an ear. He was amused by her predicament. Several times he fought back laughter. She did deserve it. And he didn't mind at all as he took hold of the long needles which protruded from her nicely rounded rump and pulled them out.

She yelped and hopped slightly, and he tightened his grip on her, pulling her against his body to hold her still. She was light, and he caught a whiff of delightful perfume. Something expensive. Rafe inhaled as she dug her nails into his arm in her quest for support.

"You okay?" he asked.

"Yes." Her breathless reply came quickly through bared teeth.

Rafe smiled as he caught a glimpse of her in the silvery glow of headlights. Her delicate face was set, and she bit on her lip as though to keep from crying. The sight of her vulnerability picked at him like the pluck of a guitar string.

He pulled another needle out, and she twisted again. "Cere, just hold on to me. Or I could sit down and put you across my knee. That might be more natural."

She slapped his arm, but it was a teasing blow. She took hold of his shirt, catching the material in her hand.

"Don't move," he ordered, very aware of the warmth of her body against his. Her scent was growing intoxicating—a mixture of the perfume and the warm female smell of sweat.

"That hurts."

His fingers skimmed over her jeans, seeking more stickers. He tried to be as gentle as possible as he plucked them out.

"Ow!" she cried.

"Sorry." He found another and rubbed his hands along her backside, trying to convince himself he was looking for more needles. The nicely rounded curves felt good beneath his fingers and sent a ripple of awareness through him. He shouldn't be enjoying it this much. Too much time had passed since he had touched a woman so intimately.

"Hey!" She slapped his arm again. "What do you think you're doing?"

"I was feeling for more thorns. Yes, there's one!" He pulled it out, but after that, they were too short to pull out.

"You're not taking anything out," she said, pulling away. "You're just feeling me up. Is that how you examine female prisoners?"

He ignored her sarcasm. He adopted his best official tone. "You're going to have to take off your pants."

She shook her head, all traces of humor dissipated. "Not on your life, buddy."

"I can't get all of them out, and you'll never get

them out yourself. Come on, let me help you take those off."

"I'll bet you're good at that, aren't you? Taking off a woman's pants?"

"Fine. Try to sit. There are still some fine needles and I don't have fingernails to pull them out."

"I do." She lifted her hand, but the glamorous nails she had displayed before were almost invisible. Three were broken and another was hanging. "Damn. I just had those put on."

"Take off the pants. I'll help you find your shoe and follow you back to town so you don't get in anymore trouble."

Irritation flickered in her eyes. "You expect me to drive in a T-shirt and panties?"

He chuckled. The vision that popped into his head was appealing—too appealing. "I'll give you my shirt, just to show I'm a gentleman."

"How kind," she said sarcastically. All the same, she unzipped her pants, and still holding onto him, tugged them off. He had seen the tanned length of legs earlier, and while he knew he shouldn't be doing it, Rafe admired them again. He had to stop that. *Why was this woman so tempting?* It had been years since he'd had this sort of attraction to anyone.

Without the expensive sandals and with her toenails as scuffed as her fingernails, Rafe found her even more tempting. Her tanned legs glowed in the headlights, shapely and muscular. Her panties were pink silk, and she pulled her T-shirt over them. His blood grew warm as his breath came a little quicker. A tightness pulled at his groin.

"Some gentleman. I know you're looking."

He couldn't deny it, and he chuckled again. "I may be a gentleman, but I'm also human."

"Neanderthal is more like it. Now what about the shirt you promised, Mr. Gentleman?"

He slid out of the shirt, eyes on her face. Cere dropped her eyes as though she couldn't take the thought of seeing his bare upper torso. For all her city-girl airs, was she actually modest? At least today he had put on a tank top undershirt. He held out the shirt, and she wrapped it around her. The long tail fell nearly to her knees. The picture drew him like a magnet.

"I like the look," he offered with a smile.

Her lips tightened into a straight line. "I'm sure you do."

Rafe kept hold of her hand as they walked toward the building to find her other shoe. He found it and helped her put it on, noticing her trim ankles as she used his thigh as a foot rest.

She wiped her hands and stood with her hands on her hips staring at the ghostly outline of the building. "Maybe we should go back in," she said, bending over to pick up a black shoulder bag.

Rafe stopped admiring her body. "What? Hell, no!"

She flashed an impish grin that struck him harder than the slap of a fly swatter. "Don't tell me you're afraid? Have you been in there at night since you were a kid?"

"Of course," he said.

She rubbed her hands on her legs, eyes on the building. "Do you have a flashlight?"

"Haven't you had enough of this place for one night? Didn't you say you were locked in a room? Weren't you afraid?"

"Only when I thought someone had done it on purpose. You didn't happen to see Diaz on the road when you were driving here, did you?"

He jerked upright, putting his hand on his gun as though the man might be around. "What makes you think someone was here?"

"I thought I heard footsteps or a car."

He rolled his eyes and shook his head. "It's like that night we were out here. We were all convinced we heard something and ran. The place does that to people."

"You saved me." Her voice was suddenly soft as she turned to him. "I fell down, and I was afraid those ghosts would catch me. Then you picked me up and carried me to the car."

"Huh?" He didn't remember much about that night, except that they ran. It wasn't the only time that happened during his many sojourns, but he'd never helped anyone. He shook his head. "Picked you up? I don't think so. I ran so fast, I was the first one back to the car."

She blinked and he could see confusion. "Then who picked me up?"

He couldn't help but smile. "Maybe the ghost of Marco Gonzales. I remember we found you sitting on a rock by the car.

She slapped at his arm and muttered a swear word. "You can be such a jerk."

"Maybe that's why he's haunting your dreams. He wants payback. Or perhaps he locked you in because he doesn't want you doing the story after all."

"Stop being funny. And don't tell me I'm an excitable female, Tafoya. I've been in tricky situations before. I don't panic."

"Well, maybe you should."

She shot him a glare so sharp it would have wounded him if it had been a material object. They walked back to her car. Cere started to toss in her clothes but stopped. "Oh, no, look at that."

"What?" He followed the direction of her pointing finger.

Her front tire was flat.

"Do you still doubt me?" she asked. "Someone locked me in that room and flattened my tire."

"I doubt that. This car wasn't meant for off road driving. You probably hit a rock or an old nail or something." The situation was beginning to perturb Rafe, but maybe this would teach her a lesson. The open prairie was no place for her rental sedan. "I'll change it for you."

He almost expected her to tell him she could do it herself. Instead she opened the trunk and stepped back.

"Damn rental company," she said with a grimace. "There isn't a spare in there."

He looked into the empty well. "I doubt someone did that to you."

She let fly a curse that surprised him.

Rafe smiled. She was moving up in his estimation. Not that he enjoyed women who cussed. It just made her less prissy.

"Hell!" She pushed hair from her face, twisting it at the nape of her neck. "Is there a towing service I can call?"

"They'll be closed. Why don't I drive you home and we'll get a tow truck to come out in the morning?"

She hesitated, her hand on the door. "I'd rather not

leave the car here, even if it is a rental."

"The car will be safe. I doubt anyone will be out this way tonight."

"Except whoever flattened the tire," she argued. "I have insurance, but I don't want the car damaged or stolen."

Rafe was growing weary of arguing. "You're not in the city. It will be fine. And don't worry about insurance. The rental company is responsible since they didn't provide a spare."

"I don't know…"

Her face was set, and he could read her reluctance, but he was losing patience. He needed to get home to Ginny. "If you won't leave it, you can spend the night inside. I'll send a tow truck in the morning."

Despite her earlier show of bravado, he didn't think Cere would opt to stay alone near the abandoned dance hall.

She tugged at her lower lip and then sighed heavily. "Oh, all right, let's go back to town."

Rafe stepped over to check the tire before leaving. Maybe it wasn't as critical as she thought. He stared at it and leaned closer. His stomach rolled over. A long clean slash was cut along one side of the tire. She could not have driven far if a rock had caused the damage and the cut would be jagged. This had been done by a knife blade or box cutter.

No doubt about it. Someone had cut Cere's tire.

Chapter Eighteen

"You know that was stupid, don't you?" Rafe asked as he drove back toward town. "You didn't find what you were looking for."

"How do you know?"

Rafe met her eyes and grunted. Intense curiosity burned in her beautiful eyes, and he dropped his gaze. It fell to the crossed bare legs visible in the dim glow of the dashboard lights. A hot river of desire flooded his veins, like lava unleashed. This was something he didn't need—physical attraction to a snobbish spitfire.

"I looked around. The hand print is in the room on the other side of where you were. Tell me what you thought you heard."

"Someone was in there," she insisted. "Maybe they followed me."

"Were there any cars on the road behind you? Did you look?"

"There weren't any cars. I checked my mirror before I made the turn off."

"The wind probably blew the door shut."

His gaze flickered to her legs, and she smoothed the shirt over them as though she noticed the direction of his glance.

"I'm sorry you had to come out here. Where is your daughter?"

"Your mother stayed with her."

She sighed and shook her head. "I don't understand why Mom was looking for me. I thought she was on a date."

"With Bradley Foster?" he asked.

"How did you know?"

"Everyone knows everything in this town. You'll find that out quickly enough."

"I won't be here that long. I just want to get my story and get out."

A spark of irritation grated at him. "That damn story is going to get you in more trouble than just getting locked in a dark room."

Instead of frightening her, the comment seemed to spur interest. "What do you mean by that, Tafoya? Is there something you're not telling me? Did you or your family know Marco?"

"He died long before I was born and by now you should know no one wants to talk about him."

"What about his relatives? Are they all gone?"

He drew a deep breath. No sense lying; she'd find out the truth on her own. "He has a few cousins still in town."

She sat forward, a tense nervousness driving her to tap her fingers on the window rest. Her voice took on extra vigor. "So if I call every Gonzales in the phone book, I should run across his relatives?"

"Probably."

"Why don't you save me time and give me names?"

"Uh, uh, I know how media people work. You'll call and say, 'Sheriff Tafoya told me you're related to Marco and might talk to me.' Isn't that how it goes? You can make all the calls you want, but they won't

161

talk. They were unhappy about the newspaper story."

She sat back, but he could feel the intense energy emanating from her. Something was on her mind. "Do you really think I'm callous?"

Rafe had regretted being so perturbed, though her comment had been a harsh wake up call for who she really was. "Perhaps I overreacted, but Naldo was more than a murder statistic to me. I'd known him since I was a boy. He didn't deserve to be murdered. He wouldn't hurt a fly."

"Someone killed him, and someone might have killed Marco."

"Don't try to tie the two together!"

What if she found out there was a connection between Marco and old Naldo? He didn't like thinking about that himself.

She turned wide eyes to him, and he realized he had made another mistake. She'd caught the undertone in his angry proclamation. "Look, Cere, why don't you drop this and enjoy visiting your mother?"

"Talk about culture shock. Seeing her in this town, with that man..." She shook her head, and Rafe perceived an opportunity to turn the conversation in a new direction.

"You don't like our mayor? He's such a sweet old guy."

"It's not that I dislike him. I want her to have a new life, be happy. Somehow it seems disloyal to my dad."

Disloyal? A quick vision of Carmen appeared in his brain. *Was he being disloyal by looking at Cere?*

The lights of the city grew closer and they fell into silence. Cere tried to relax, but her moments in the

Palladium kept coming back to her. She had heard a noise. Not the ghost of Marco. She started to thank Rafe again and stopped. His large presence filled the interior of the Jeep. She smoothed down his shirt. The light scent of shaving lotion rose from it, sending butterflies through her stomach. It had been a while since she'd worn a man's shirt.

She glanced at his implacable face. His finding her had been a godsend, and she could imagine what he thought about her sojourn. Still she wasn't going to give up her enterprise. She would have her mother drive her to get the car in the morning and have a look at the hand print.

Rafe pulled into a garage on the edge of town. The lights were out, but when he honked, a side door flew open. A rotund man in a greasy T-shirt approached them. Cere recognized him as one of the men at the counter the previous day, but she hadn't heard his name. He had turned his back to her, concentrating on his tamales.

"What's up, Tafoya?" he asked, looking from Rafe to Cere.

"Hey, Len. The lady here is gonna need a tow from the Palladium."

"Garage is closed. I can get it for you in the morning."

"That's what we figured. She's gonna need a new tire too."

Rafe opened his door and stepped outside, guiding the man away from his open window. Their voices carried back to her, but she couldn't make out the words. When Rafe opened the door to slide inside, she blinked at the bright light from the overhead bulb.

Her gaze fell on the finely honed muscles of Rafe's arms and shoulders. She had been too distracted to notice before, but now she noted the white undershirt against tanned muscular skin. Its tightness emphasized powerful shoulders and a wide chest with a fine matte of black hair. He must work out. Too quickly he shut the door and the car plunged into darkness.

"Len says he knows you," Rafe said as he settled into his seat.

"I met him at the restaurant," she admitted.

"Did you tell him about doing the Marco Gonzales story?"

"I mentioned it to the guys at the counter, but I told you, no one would talk to me."

He drew a sharp breath. "They may not have talked to you, but that doesn't mean everyone isn't talking about your project."

"What did he say?" Cere thought of the message on her phone and the paper stuck to her car. Her hour at the café seemed to have drawn a lot of attention.

A sharp rap on the window stopped Rafe from answering. He lowered the window, and Len shoved a piece of paper at him.

"Here's a receipt. We'll pick it up in the morning if you give me the keys."

Cere pulled her keys from her purse and handed them to him. "Thank you."

His eyes stayed on her, dark angry circles that bored into her. "If I was you, lady, I'd stay away from that Palladium. Next time you might not be so lucky to have the sheriff rescue you."

He pulled back before Cere could respond. She was aware of his hulking figure watching as Rafe eased out of the driveway.

"That guy was spooky," she said, trying to make her voice light, fighting shakiness in her stomach. "It was like he was warning me. Why should he care if I'm at the Palladium?"

Rafe pointed at a sign as they pulled back onto the road. It read "Gonzales Auto Parts."

"Len is Marco's second cousin. And before you start another open discussion at the Matador, you ought to know that Frank, who owns it, is also a Gonzales."

Damn. She should have known all these people would be related. "Hmm, well, speaking of spooky, how does that man, Diaz, fit in?"

He grimaced and glanced over at her. "You want the truth?"

She thought about the note again—and the phone call. Why had he been at the dance hall that day she and Freeda stopped by? "Did he know Marco?"

He inhaled sharply and turned toward her. "To be honest, I don't know."

"Is he from here? That truck he was driving last night had Texas plates."

"That's where he's from, I guess."

"Is he new in town? You haven't checked up on him?"

Rafe stared straight ahead, but when he spoke, it was through gritted teeth. "I haven't had a reason, other than he is hanging around and being a general pain in the ass."

"Someone new in town and someone gets murdered and you don't check him out?"

Rafe's laugh was harsh. "Well, see this town has strange people go through it all the time. We're not that far from Taos and prime camping areas. Tourists come by, get gas, have lunch and some hang around for a few days. We have a campground at the edge of town and decent motels with pools. We don't make a habit of checking out everyone who wanders into town."

She drew a deep breath. "You said you were curious about him."

"Well, number one, the Sanchez investigation is not my case and number two, he hasn't done anything illegal in the county."

"He broke into that building. Did you notice that when you walked around it? How do you think I got in? The latch was broken."

"If I was going to arrest him for trespassing, I'd be taking you in too. Want to share cell space with him? Our jail only has two cells and they face each other, though both have toilets."

She could tell he was teasing. "I'm just saying! And I just got in once. There were two sets of prints inside that building. I saw them. Which means he'd been in there more than once."

"Actually the other set was mine. I was curious about why he might have wanted to go inside."

Cere jerked upright, though it was painful on her still sore bottom. "Aha! So you know he's not simply an ordinary visitor to town."

He gave her a sharp look. "Give me a little credit, Medina."

Cere smiled back at him. She had a feeling that in the morning—if he hadn't already—Rafe would make a call to the Texas Department of Motor Vehicles to find out exactly who the man was.

Chapter Nineteen

"Help me. Please!"
The glowing eyes burned brighter. Cere jerked herself from sleep, forcing the apparition from her as she struggled to sit up.
"Don't give up."
She hadn't had a dream since arriving in Rio Rojo, but it seemed more real now. She had visited the dance hall where Marco died. Had she felt him there? No, but she hadn't found the hand print either.

Sunlight stroked her face and she shifted, becoming aware of how much her body ached, from using her sore arms to move the piano, to her rump where stickers still tingled, to her thighs from kicking the boards, to her sore ankle. She wanted to roll over and go back to sleep but instead glanced at her wrist to check the time. Her wrist was bare.

Where was her watch? A quick patting of the sheets uncovered nothing. Thinking back, Cere didn't remember wearing it when she showered and got ready for bed. Thinking further back she remembered checking it on the way to the Palladium but she couldn't remember it after that. She either lost it in that fiasco inside the dance hall or in Rafe's Jeep.

The heavenly scent of coffee hung lightly in the air and her stomach rumbled. She hadn't eaten the night before. Cere stretched and got to her feet. A black and blue bruise was forming on one thigh and her ankle hurt when she tried to walk.

"And you still want me to go on?" she said out loud as though she could converse with the phantom from her dream.

She attempted to move with as little awkwardness as possible as she approached the kitchen. Her mother wouldn't offer sympathy this morning.

Lottie sat at the table, blonde hair neatly in place. A mug of coffee rested in front of her and she stared straight ahead, deep in thought. She blinked at the sound of footsteps and hopped to her feet immediately.

"Good morning, sweetie. Let me get you some coffee."

Cere dropped onto a chair at the table. "Thanks, Mom."

"I hope you're over this foolishness." She poured a cup of steaming coffee and brought it to the table. "Would you like something else? Did you eat last night?"

"No, but I can make myself an omelet."

"No, relax. You're on vacation."

Cere lifted the mug to her lips and sipped the fragrant liquid. Luckily some things never changed, like her mother's strong coffee. It provided an instant jolt. She clasped her hands around her mug and frowned at her shredded nails.

Her mother bustled around the kitchen, getting eggs and cheese from the refrigerator. "What would you like to do today?"

"I need to go back to the Palladium and pick up my car."

At the stove, her mother's lips pressed together in

disapproval. "I can take you this afternoon. I have a doctor's appointment this morning. I should be back by one."

Cere didn't want to wait. "I'll call Rafe. I might have lost my watch in his car."

"Good idea. Tell him I'll return his shirt after I wash it. Honestly, I can't imagine what you were thinking last night."

Her shoulders slumped. At times her mother could still make her feel like a recalcitrant teenager. "How did you know I was gone? I thought you were out with Mr. Foster."

"Bradley had to run an errand, so I put dinner in and came back to see if you might change your mind or if Freeda had come back. When you were gone, I knew immediately where you were. When you didn't come home, I called Rafe."

"Mo-o-om, I can take care of myself. I've been doing it for years. I don't need Mr. Macho Sheriff to look after me."

"Hmph! Look at you—all bruised and cut up. Freeda left a message to ask you about a ghost. That's what she was talking about, wasn't it?"

"I had a couple of bad dreams about the Palladium after you sent me that newspaper. Freeda and I went out there with Normie and Pat years ago when we came to get her."

"They weren't old enough to drive."

"Rafe… took us," she admitted. "He was at their house and told us about that ghost."

Lottie burst into laughter and clapped her hands together. "Well, it serves him right then." She dished up the omelet and brought it to the table. "I'm going to get

169

dressed. Take your time with breakfast and then sit outside with the rabbits. You can check on your watch later. Why don't we meet for lunch at the Matador?"

Cere held up her broken finger nails. "I might see if Millie's manicurist has an opening this morning. Have you heard anything from Freeda?"

"That crazy girl. She really thinks she's going to find Fergie this time. I shouldn't have let her go with Daphne. I should have known she'd take off on her own."

"Mom, she's also old enough to take care of herself."

Lottie wrinkled her nose. "You, I kind of trust. The only thing that might get you in trouble is chasing a story. We both know Freeda does a horrible job of taking care of herself."

Cere laughed. "We'll hear from her when the money from her last paycheck runs out, or her credit card gets maxed and cops pick her up for sleeping on a park bench."

Lottie sighed and walked to the door. "That's what I'm afraid of. Nena will never forgive me if I let harm come to her precious little girl on my watch. "

With her mother gone, Cere concentrated on the omelet. She didn't have time to worry about Freeda. If Rafe wasn't around she was going to head for the beauty parlor. Without her mother to hold her back, she might ask Millie and the other stylists if they knew anything about Marco. Diners and beauty shops. She had already tapped one resource. On to the next.

She was finishing breakfast when the phone rang. She felt butterflies in her stomach when she heard the deep voice on the other end of the line.

"How is Lois Lane this morning?" Rafe asked with a chuckle.

"Sore, and thanks again, Tafoya. I'm glad you called."

"Really?"

"I have another problem—I lost my watch. Is it in your Jeep?"

"I'll check. Or you can look for it when I pick you up."

"Pick me up?" Her heart skipped. He wanted to see her?

"I've got some time this morning. I thought I'd take you to get your car. Len towed it in and when I drove by a few minutes ago I saw that he was putting on a new tire."

The offer was nice but had a patronizing ring to it, and she disliked the excitement she felt at the idea of seeing him. "I can walk over to get it."

He drew a deep breath. "We need to talk. I might as well tell you because you're going to find out when you see the bill. That tire didn't go flat. It was slashed. I noticed it last night."

"Slashed?" Her heart skipped. "Like on a rock?"

"No, like with a knife."

"I was right! Someone was there and you knew it all along."

"I didn't want to worry you last night. Since it happened on county land, I'm looking into it. Can you be ready to go in half an hour?"

"You don't suppose it was the ghost of Marco who did that?"

"Don't be smart. This has nothing to do with Marco. Someone was playing games, and it needs to be

171

stopped."

"Diaz?"

"Maybe. I called Texas this morning and gave them his plate number, so we should get some answers about him by the end of the day. If he's still around. No one has seen him since you saw him near Naldo's."

Cere drew a quick breath, thinking of the gruff voice on the phone. Maybe the time had come to tell Rafe about that call.

****

Rafe tried to pretend he wasn't fascinated by the sight of Cere's rounded rump disappearing into the dim light through the Palladium door. He didn't want to admit any sort of fascination with her, even though she was constantly on his mind these days. He dragged his eyes away, guilty for enjoying the view.

The drive to the Palladium should have further discouraged him. She peppered him with questions about who might want to stop her story about Marco to the point of vandalism. He had few answers for her—at least few he would give her.

Rafe let her lead the way, knowing he couldn't stop her. He should have fixed that lock so she couldn't get in the previous night. She turned to him.

"Something on your mind, Sheriff?"

Rafe couldn't resist a smirk. "I was thinking about you sitting on your rump out back with all those stickers in you, then crawling out of that cactus patch."

Her quick smile made his heart beat faster. "Are you flirting with me, Tafoya? Or do you just like the idea of me on my hands and knees? Or my aching butt?"

He didn't know what he was doing. He felt

lighthearted just being with her. In jeans, a T-shirt, and walking boots, and with her thick hair tied back, minus the red nails and theatrical make up, she didn't resemble the city woman who had looked disdainfully around the restaurant two days ago.

She was waiting for his answer to her playful question, an inquisitive look in her eyes, a twist to her full pink lips that made his blood run warm. He turned away.

"You wish I was flirting, Medina."

Cere laughed and dropped her gaze to the dusty floor. Thin outlines in the dust showed evidence of her earlier entrance. Her breath caught suddenly, and she pointed at the floor.

A knot twisted inside him as Rafe followed her finger. Beside her footprints were other prints in the dust. Larger. Several of them covered hers. Their eyes met. Her eyes were wide brown orbs, curious, but not frightened. Rafe felt an insane desire to touch her, but he kneeled down beside the footprints instead.

"Looks like boot prints made after you were here," he pointed out.

"So they prove someone was here," she said with a shudder, voice barely above a whisper.

"We don't know it was Diaz." He picked out the prints he had made several days ago and then found the prints he judged to belong to Diaz. "These boots look bigger. But I can't tell. This heel is rundown at the back. See? Those over there were probably made by Diaz and those boots are new. I saw them when I was in here the other day." He rose to his feet, slapping his hands together to get rid of the dust.

Cere turned to him, and her fingers brushed his

wrist, setting off electric impulses. The touch was gone as quickly as it came.

"Please don't tell Mom about what happened out here. I don't want to worry her."

"She was right. Coming out here was a bad idea."

A look of determination came into her clear brown eyes as she stared at the prints. "Whoever it was wanted to frighten me. They could have hurt me if they wanted. I was alone, vulnerable, but they only tried to scare me. Well, I don't scare easy."

"That's too bad," he replied wryly.

She whirled around and walked into the main room. Rafe followed her, keeping an eye on the foot prints which disappeared on the dustless dance hall floor. At the top of the stairs gloominess enveloped them as she pointed out the room where she had been locked.

"Damn, I forgot my flashlight. Will you be okay while I run down to get it?"

"Fine, Sheriff," she said with a bright smile.

He turned and hopped down the steps until the crack of wood slowed him. Perhaps he should barricade the stairs before someone fell through and sued the county. For certain he needed to put up fresh barricades on the doors.

She waited until she heard Rafe exit the building, leaving her in total stillness. The dusky smell was overwhelming, but the old building was not as frightening in the morning light.

Sun filtered in through cracks, settling on the rounded wooden railing that was dusty but looked like it could still gleam with a good coating of varnish or furniture oil. The walls were faded and yellowing, the door moldings a dirty, faded green. What had this place looked like forty years ago? Again, she could almost hear the twang of a Hank Williams song or maybe Glen Campbell or Willie Nelson.

She looked at the door where she had been. It remained closed and she tried the door. It was locked, but she saw no sign of a latch. The door's only locking mechanism was an old skeleton keyhole. Someone would have needed a key to lock it from this side. She had felt no key on the inside so she had not locked herself in. Had she heard someone turn the key?

Her breath caught and she turned away. She'd wait until Rafe came back. Maybe he could pick the lock or knew where they could find a skeleton key.

Across the hall, another open door beckoned. Now she remembered being twelve years old, accompanied by her cousins, Freeda and Chico-Rafe leading the way. She moved toward the door, as though she was being drawn to it.

By Marco's ghost?

No, if there was a ghost, he'd have led her in the right direction the previous night.

"Stupid," she whispered. The ghost with the built in GPS.

She moved forward, hearing the creak of the wind on the roof, the rustling of leaves through the broken boarded up windows, the squeak of her boots on the floor boards. The building seemed to shudder, or maybe that was Rafe opening the door downstairs.

She forced herself to walk faster, palms growing damp and she wiped them against her jeans. The dark room yawned black in front of her and she pushed her way inside.

The only sound was labored breathing—hers. Dust hung thick in the air, and the room smelled musty. Light filtered in through cracks in boarded up windows. Pieces of furniture were piled around three walls, but the fourth, at the opposite end of the room was bare. A dark smudge took up one corner.

"Cere?"

The voice was Rafe's and came from the hall.

"In here."

"Did you find it?" he asked, standing in the doorway.

"I think so," she said, throat parched, voice threatening to break. "Do you have your flashlight?"

The light shined on the wall.

Cere could hardly breathe as she looked at it—the hand on the wall.

Chapter Twenty

She stared at it for a minute, fighting the uneasy feeling that coiled in her stomach. The print was a dark, brownish smudge on the faded, dirty wall, though the outline was unmistakable—a palm print surrounded by four outstretched fingers and a thumb. Small dark specks and a smear below it spoke of bloody violence, though real color was long gone.

She moved closer to it, but didn't touch it. Her initial moments of elation were followed by a blanket of disappointment.

"Damn," she whispered, aware her voice shook slightly. She wasn't certain if she was overcome by what she was seeing or so disappointed she wanted to fall down and cry.

"You okay?" Rafe asked, standing beside her.

"How do you suppose Riggins shot his picture?"

"What's wrong? Afraid it won't look good on television?" Sarcasm filled his voice.

"It's not as obvious as I thought it would be. I had visions of this ghostly print, but this would need..." She made a face, sizing it up. "I guess I could bring in very bright lighting."

"Or enhance it digitally," he finished dryly.

She had been thinking just that, but she wasn't going to let him know. She stiffened and fixed him with a cold, tight lipped frown. "Hey, Tafoya, I don't embellish!"

Turning her attention back to the hand print, she followed the bloody trail down to the words written below. She took the flashlight from his hand and moved forward, playing the light over the smudged words.

"Todo por amour. All for love," she read, translating into English. "This is something. The last three words on his mind before he died."

"Yeah, right. They say he died for love."

She looked up at him. His gaze was fixed on the words. "Is that why they say he might have committed suicide? Because some woman spurned him?"

"Something like that."

Another thought struck her. "If it was suicide, don't you wonder who the woman was?"

Rafe drew back as though she had slapped him. "What?"

"Even if he wasn't murdered, we should find out why he died."

He stood back, placing his hands on his hips. "You mean like maybe that's why the ghost is haunting you? He wants you to find out who killed him or who he killed himself for?" His bitter laugh rang out in the empty room.

She stifled the word she wanted to call him.

Rafe watched her agitation grow. He shouldn't have left her alone. Of course she would not stay still. The damn woman had to keep investigating. Naturally he would find her in the room where the bloody mark stained the wall.

He stared down at Cere. She tugged at her lower lip, small face set. Somehow he knew she was looking for an angle since she must now realize the hand was going to be tough to photograph. And without the dramatic picture of it, she might not have a story.

He'd been ten when he first saw the print, and it had been a big disappointment, his introduction to false advertising. Perhaps that was why he had become the ghost guide, ready to trick others as he had been tricked.

Rafe turned away in disgust. He could almost see her story now. Despite her protests, he knew how TV worked. She would embellish or enhance the print and the story. Damn, he didn't have time for this and he'd lost interest in her appeal. "Can we look for your watch? You said you weren't in here."

With one final glance at the hand print, she straightened. Without warning, she tripped, pitching forward. He caught her as she collapsed against him.

The feel of her firm breasts against his chest sent a surge of awareness through him. Rafe caught her wrist and wrapped his other arm around her, as though they were dancing.

For an instant he held her, aware of warm breath on his chest, and her thudding heart. The sweet smell of her perfume drifted up to him. He doubted he'd ever forget that scent.

She lifted her face to him, and Rafe had the wild urge to kiss her. To lean down and taste those very pink, plump lips. To see if he couldn't erase from her brain all thoughts of that damn hand print.

Her eyes rested on his lips. Was she thinking the same thing? No. She jerked away, pulling free. "You tripped me!"

He grunted. "Nope. I'm beginning to think you're a natural born klutz."

"Am not," she cried in a childish tone.

He doubted that Cere Medina was off balance very often, but he liked seeing it when it happened. Then again he wasn't usually so off balance himself. Maybe he had been without a woman too long. Carmen had been gone for three years.

"Your watch," he repeated, walking toward the other room.

"That door is locked."

He wrenched the knob. It stuck but after a few jerks, it turned and the door swung open. He turned to her and flashed what he hoped was a triumphant smile. "Locked? Really?"

Her face fell, and even in the dim light he could see color shoot up into it. He played his flashlight over the dusty floor, hoping to prove to her that only her footprints marked the floor, but his smile froze. Boot prints mingled with hers, boot prints with a worn heel. Someone had been here.

"What the hell?" Her hushed, shaky voice came from behind him, and she touched his side as she moved around him. It was a soft touch, but it set his nerves to tingling. "The piano's back in place."

"What?"

"The room is dark, but it should have been light because I moved the piano and knocked out the boards. Someone put the piano back."

He stepped toward the hulking instrument, the narrow beam of light playing on the dusty floor. Near the piano, a triangle of dust prints streaked the floor.

"Oh, look at those dust marks. It looks like it had been moved in front of the window recently." Her voice was insistent.

Rafe leaned against the piano and attempted to push it away from the wall. It was difficult to move, even for him. Whoever had moved it was strong. He shoved again. The room flooded with light as he inched it away from the wall.

"This is weird," she said. "Why would someone move it and then move it back?"

"Who the hell knows?" He started to turn away, and stopped. The back was dusty except a portion in the middle where she must have rubbed against it, but what caught his eye was the corner panel, which looked loose.

He tugged at the panel, and it fell away, clattering to the floor. Cere jumped and squealed. Rafe might have teased her, except his breath caught at what he saw. He reached in and removed a black box. He could barely breathe as he examined the familiar outline of a white bucking stallion. He had never touched the box before, but he knew it well. Naldo's box!

"What is that?" Cere's voice was a breathless whisper.

Rafe untied the worn clasp and opened it. He wasn't surprised to see packets of bills held together with rubber bands. Below the cash were thin stacks of yellow envelopes, tied with string. She reached for it, but he caught her hand.

"Is that... the stolen money? Marco's treasure?" she asked, eyes flying to him, wide and hopeful.

He shook his head, mouth dry, throat tight. "Naldo's."

Cere paused for a second. "Naldo? The man who was killed? Why would that be here?"

"That's what I'd like to know."

Rebecca Grace

She again reached for the box, but he held out an elbow. He could understand her curiosity, but he couldn't allow her zeal to get in the way of a murder investigation.

"Don't touch it. This could be evidence. I doubt Naldo hid it here, so it could have fingerprints from the killer. It needs to go to the crime lab."

"You touched it," she pointed out in an accusing tone.

"A mistake," he admitted, cringing at making such an amateurish blunder in front of her. He knew better—his only defense was shock and curiosity. Gingerly, he placed the box on top of the piano so it didn't become more contaminated.

"I wanted to see if it had the money. Will you do me a favor?" He pulled his keys out of his pocket and held them out. "Go to my Jeep and get some evidence bags and plastic gloves out of the back. They're in a blue case. I'll check to see if there might be any other evidence around."

"Evidence?" Her voice grew breathless, and he could see the sparkle in her eyes even in the gloomy room. "Do you think there's a connection between the hand and this current murder?"

Rafe could sense her growing excitement. He held out a calming hand. "Don't run to the bank with that. This could be nothing more than coincidence."

"This makes everything better!" she said in a high, excited voice. "The hand print, and now we've found money stolen in the new murder." The words tumbled out as though ideas were taking form.

"Let it go," he ordered.

"I needed more substance. That hand print is not as

obvious as I thought it would be. This could be just perfect."

Rafe's stomach tightened. The sad sight of Naldo's box and her enthusiasm at what its discovery meant ate at him like acid. "Will you stop with your damn story and go get those bags? This is serious."

Her dark eyes flashed at him. "And my job isn't?"

"I'm chasing a killer right now. You chase frightened boys."

She drew back as though he hit her. "What the hell gives you the right to be so self-righteous? Have you ever faced ethical questions in this podunk town?"

Her angry queries were like tossing down a gauntlet and he faced her, speaking through gritted teeth. "I faced plenty of ethical questions when I worked in Los Angeles for seventeen years. But you know what? The five thousand people in this podunk county are every bit as important. They deserve my protection and dedication and I intend to see they get it. All those people in your exciting city didn't give a damn when some teen punk gunned down my wife. They drove by her, while she was bleeding in the street because they didn't want to get involved. People here care about each other. They wouldn't do that."

Cere drew up, face pale. Compassion bloomed in her eyes. For an instant he feared she would touch him, and he moved behind the piano. He didn't want sympathy from her.

"Rafe, I had no idea," she said in a soft tone.

"I know you didn't." He needed to get space between them and she seemed to sense that. It only upset him more. "You have no idea about this place. These people care about Naldo's death for more than gossip. They cared about Marco too. That's why they won't give you the titillating story you want."

She stiffened as the words seemed to sink in. "I'll get the bags."

Rafe grimaced as he watched her walk stiffly out the door. He shouldn't have allowed anger to get the better of him, but his feelings were sincere. His wife had been caught in the crossfire in a gang shootout as she waited in a fast food drive through.

A thick pain nearly choked Rafe. Thoughts of her death still hurt. To think he'd been ogling Cere's legs. That self-centered woman would never understand sacrifice. Carmen had chosen to work as a teacher in that blighted neighborhood because she wanted to help underprivileged teens. And she'd been killed because of it.

Rafe drew a deep breath and shook away thoughts of Carmen. He focused back on Naldo's box. Had it been placed here after Cere left? Had someone been placing it when she showed up and interrupted him? That didn't make sense.

If he killed once for the box, he would have killed again. And why flatten her tire and keep her there? Or perhaps he had been leaving and wanted to make certain she couldn't follow.

At least finding the box on county land provided an excuse to get involved in Naldo's murder investigation. It was no longer only a city case.

A sharp retort, like the popping of a firecracker, startled him. It came from outside, and he heard a cry of alarm.

His hand dropped to his Colt 45 Cobra. For an instant he was back on the streets of Los Angeles. He bolted down the steps, ignoring their creaking.

He paused just inside the door when he heard Cere's labored breathing. She huddled by the porch rail.

"Are you okay?"

"Someone's shooting at me," she cried as he inched onto the porch in a crouch.

"Where's it coming from?" He squatted beside her. A pinpoint of blood dotted her cheek and he brushed it. "You're hit."

"No, I'm fine. Wood chip." Her gaze stayed on the mesa across the valley. "It's coming from over there."

For a minute, stillness filled the valley, then a thin cloud of smoke rose from behind a piñon tree on the hill. Rafe yanked Cere flat as wood splintered above them and another pop rang out.

"Shoot back. He's going to kill us!"

Rafe took aim at the tree. His shot made the dirt dance in front of it. He fired again, then a third time. He waited for a minute and when no shot was returned, he told Cere to stay down.

Using boulders and trees as shields he raced from one to the other, moving steadily toward the hillside. No more shots came at them, and by the time he reached the tree, the gunman was gone.

Behind the bushy piñon, a flat outcropping of rocks led to the top of the hill like a golden sandstone staircase. He climbed the rocks to the crest, but found no sign of anyone along the ridge or on the other side. The gunman had disappeared.

He turned and hopped back toward the bottom of the hill. Cere was searching the ground near the tree where the gunman had been hiding.

"Find anything?" Rafe asked

Silently she pointed down and a glint from the sun caught his eye. Using his pen, he lifted an empty shell casing. "Thirty-thirty," he said quietly.

"Was it Naldo's killer?"

"I have no idea. Naldo was killed with a handgun, which was found. This is from a rifle. Did you see anything when you came out of the building?"

"No. I heard the shot hit. He's not much of a marksman."

Rafe said nothing. The shot had been well above his head on the porch. He had not aimed to kill the gunman because he had a hunch that the person didn't mean to hurt them. This rang of scare tactic.

He reached in his pocket and pulled out a small paper bag. Carrying them had become a habit when he worked homicide. Now they served mainly as receptacles for Ginny's uneaten candy bars. He dropped the shell casing in the bag, aware of Cere watching him.

Her auburn hair glinted in the sunlight, and despite his earlier anger, a river of warmth ran through his blood. He had to give her credit for tenacity. She was actively looking around instead of cowering. He walked toward her.

"Stop!" She held up her hand. "There are footprints in the dirt."

Rafe started to tell her she had to be wrong. He had checked the area. Maybe she was mistaking his boot prints. "Now you're playing detective?"

He moved forward, ready to tease her and point out they were his, but he stopped as he looked down at where she pointed. He could see faint imprints, bigger than his size tens.

"What do you think?" she asked. "They look like

the ones we saw before."

Rafe kneeled for a closer view. These were more defined than the prints at the Palladium, but unless he was wrong, they were close to the same size. The same person?

"Stop playing Nancy Drew, and stop hopping around. You're going to screw up the crime scene for the lab guys." He tried to be gruff, but was not able to pull it off. "Intrepid reporter solves her own crime. Is that your angle now?"

Her face was tight, her coffee-colored eyes serious as she looked up at him. "For your information, I've been to crime scenes. Did you notice there's a mark on that boot heel? And do you see the way the left heel is worn down on the side?"

Rafe examined the prints again. She was right about the mark. And while she appeared unfazed by his criticism, she took his warning to heart. As they walked down the hill, she followed his steps, careful to stick to the rocks so they didn't leave extra footprints.

"What are you going to do now?" she asked.

"I have to call BJ, and the state investigators. Maybe you should take the Jeep and head back to town. I'm going to be out here for a while."

"I can wait with you."

Rafe wasn't certain that was a good idea, though he welcomed her company. As they arrived at the Jeep, he pulled the phone from his belt holder. "Don't wander too far."

"You think he could still be up there watching us?"

"Maybe." He found himself smiling suddenly, though he didn't feel particularly humorous. "Maybe you ought to go back inside the building. Perhaps your ghost will protect you."

The look she gave him sent his stomach roiling.

"Don't laugh," she said. "I thought I heard someone warn me to duck just before that first shot."

Chapter Twenty-One

Rafe tried not to think about Cere's strange comment as he punched in the numbers to call BJ. He doubted she had heard anything. The breeze in the trees could do strange things. Fearing the gunman could still be around they both sat inside the Jeep while he made his call.

"I'm at the Palladium and have a new development in the Sanchez case."

"This is a city case, Rafe." BJ didn't sound pleased to hear from him.

"Not anymore. I found Naldo's money box in a room out here."

BJ sounded like he was sputtering. "You found it? Just like the gun? You think you're gonna solve this thing first or something?"

Rafe stifled his annoyance. When would BJ realize their jobs should complement each other, not provide competition? "Could be."

"Listen to me, Tafoya—"

"No, you listen. This is my jurisdiction, and I'm calling the state boys back and I want to be copied on everything they find from the in-town investigation. Not only that, but I'm going to have them look into why someone took a potshot at me and Cere Medina today. Now, if you want to get a look at this box before they take it, come on out. I'm calling them as soon as I'm off the phone. Until they get here, I'm posting a deputy to keep everyone out."

He followed through, calling a friend at the state criminology lab in Santa Fe. It would take a few hours for technicians to show up, but he would feel more comfortable with them conducting the investigation. He knew he could handle it himself, but this would give him an excuse to ask for reports on Naldo's killing. He knew better than to expect BJ to share them.

"Who do you suppose killed that Naldo guy?" Cere asked as he slid his phone back into its holster.

"I wish I knew."

She pulled at her lower lip, deep in thought. "Why hide the money out here?"

"No one normally comes out this way. I believe Naldo was killed for the money and he couldn't afford to be caught with that box. Maybe he's been watching the place and saw you come inside."

Her pretty face was set, but again it was not troubled or frightened. "Why lock me in the room where the money was?"

"Maybe he didn't know what you were doing and wanted to scare you off. Or perhaps he had accomplices and went back for them because he feared you might take the money. He wanted to keep you locked up until he could get help. Hell, who knows?"

"How much do you think is in that box?" she asked, looking toward the sagging structure, again pulling at her lip.

Rafe followed the direction of her gaze. He leaned a boot back against the Jeep, folding his arms. "Hard to tell. Naldo never had a bank account. He'd cash any checks he got for his odd jobs. He did everything in cash and lived off the money in that box. He had no pension so he expected that money to take care of him for the rest of his life."

"No bank account?" she said incredulously.

Rafe shrugged. "Lots of people who grew up out here didn't trust banks after the Depression. Hell, he was his own banker when he ran the pawn shop. Always kept cash on hand."

"People in town knew this?"

"Of course."

"So it was someone from around here," she concluded. "I mean, the townspeople are pretty guarded. They don't talk to strangers, right?"

Since he'd come back to Rio Rojo, he'd met everyone in town. He couldn't imagine anyone shooting the old man—even for the money.

"That doesn't necessarily mean the killer's local. If I have one complaint about this town, it's that people talk too much, too loudly. You should hear that group at the Matador. They used to tease Naldo all the time. Maybe he told someone himself. He loved to gossip. Maybe he told Diaz. He said he knew the guy."

She nodded. "That was the impression I got when I told him the old man was dead. But for some reason I thought he was upset—like he didn't know."

"If he knew him, if he even cared, why not go to the scene and get the details? Unless he already knew the details." He turned to her, his hand on the seat. "Listen, do you want to take the Jeep and go back to town? I hate to strand you out here until a deputy can come out."

She glanced toward the Palladium and then turned to him and gave him a radiant smile that made his heart

191

skip. "Why don't you tell me Marco's story while we wait? The one Gary Riggins didn't get right?"

Damn, this woman never quit. And that smile was merely a ploy. She knew its potent effect. Cere Medina, reporter-charmer in action. Rafe turned away, and stroked the scar under his beard thoughtfully. Still, maybe he'd give her a few details—just enough to make her bored.

Cere could tell she might finally be getting through to him. She increased the stakes. "I'm beginning to wonder if there's something you're trying to hide. It isn't fair either. Someone shot at me. Was it because I want to do that story or because of the money?"

Rafe seemed to consider her comment and finally nodded. He gestured toward a piñon tree. "Let's go sit in the shade. Maybe … a few questions."

With the Jeep on one side, the tree on the other side and the Palladium sheltering them from the hill, no one could shoot at them except from the wide open space of the road. Cere found a flat rock near where he perched to serve as a seat. He picked at the grass at his feet, eyes averted from her.

"To tell the truth, I don't know much about the case, but what do you want to know?"

"Riggins made it sound like murder in his story. Do you think he was right?"

"He wrote what he thought would sell. Suicide is too benign to sell."

Cere recalled the blazing eyes that called out to her in the night, the voice that wouldn't leave her alone. "I think Marco's story deserves to be told one way or another. Riggins' assistant says you started helping him and stopped. Is that true?"

His booted toe kicked at a rock on the ground. "I sensed the story wasn't going to serve any purpose except stir up trouble. From what I know, it appears there were two Marcos. He was a hell raiser when he was young. Riggins barely touched on that, but Marco was sent to state prison for breaking into a bunch of stores."

"Riggins said he was arrested for crimes he didn't commit."

He grunted and tossed down the piece of grass. "Yeah, well, he claimed Bradley Foster framed him."

"Mr. Foster? Why would he do that?"

Rafe's large shoulders lifted in a shrug. "Exactly. What would be the point? He was deputy sheriff. He'd have more to lose if he got caught framing some silly kid."

Rafe was right. She might not like Bradley, but he didn't seem the type to take such a chance.

"The thing is," Rafe continued, "and this is only hearsay I got when I was young and told those ghost stories, when Marco was convicted, he apparently put on a big show in court. Jumped up on a table, waved a fist and promised revenge, that he'd come back and get even with the town."

Cere gulped. Why had Riggins left that out of his story? It was a wonderful anecdote. "Who might be able to tell me about that?"

"I don't know. It was one of those urban legend type things. We all said it, but no one knew who started it. Or anyone who heard it."

Which was probably why Riggins left it out. "And then? He went to jail?"

"Back then some hard-case kids ended up in

prison, not juvie hall. He served time with felons and supposedly changed. Educated himself and turned activist. When he came back, he claimed he wanted peace, equality for minorities, but no one trusted him or believed his motives. He tried to shake things up, organizing marches, giving protest concerts. He was a songwriter and wasn't afraid to openly challenge the status quo with his music and speeches."

He paused, and she thought of the defiant figure in the newspaper picture, fist upraised. The man looked unafraid.

"It must have been a jolt to this sleepy little place," she said.

"Exactly. And right after he got back, another round of burglaries started up, similar to those earlier ones. Stores reported break-ins at night with cash registers robbed. Foster was sheriff by then and found no concrete evidence of the culprit, but everyone remembered Marco's vow of revenge. He got blamed."

She took a deep breath. "I heard... he might have burned down the old newspaper office. That's why there aren't news stories about him."

His lips pressed together in a straight line and she wondered if he knew where she'd heard that. "Over a period of a couple of months, the violence escalated. Someone threw Molotov cocktails into businesses. Half of Main Street got hit. A hardware store, a couple of restaurants. The theory was that Marco did that in secret while preaching peace during the day."

"Quite an enigma."

"He did some good. My dad and uncle were college educated, but they worked as janitors, doing odd jobs, like running the presses at the town paper.

Marco urged them to start up their own paper since that one was failing. After it burned, they did just that."

A sudden realization hit her and she shivered despite the warm morning breeze. "Marco was a hero to your family. I don't understand why you didn't want to tell me about that."

Rafe looked lost in thought, tugging at his beard. He seemed to weigh his words before responding. "People still disagree about his motives."

"I see why Gary posed his story as one big question."

"One more thing. Some people say he got hooked on drugs in prison and got depressed because things weren't changing. They think his comment about love wasn't about a woman, but was aimed at how he felt about the town. They say he tried to destroy it and then killed himself because it wouldn't change."

Cere touched his arm. "Will you do an interview for me? Tell the story about how he helped your family?"

Rafe drew back, startled. His black lashes flew up and down. He lurched to his feet, and wariness invaded his dark eyes. "You never quit, do you, Medina? Hell no!"

The request had come too soon. Another couple of minutes and she might have had him. "I understand, but who might talk? Len and Frank seem pretty adamant. Is there anyone else?"

"Marco didn't have a mom or dad. He was brought up by an uncle, Frank's dad. I don't think he had anyone who would claim him by the end." He shook his head, as though casting off the taste of something bitter. "Let it go, Cere. Let the ghosts rest in peace and maybe they'll leave you alone."

Cere hesitated, not certain how to proceed. Rafe had opened up a new side of himself when he admitted the truth about his wife. She could see now why he had come back to Rio Rojo. The pain as he spoke of her death was palpable. The idea of the uncaring city was not new; she had grown used to its indifference over the years. But to have it brought home in such a graphic manner must have made a big impact on him. She thought of Ginny with her crooked part and well washed T-shirt, and a wave of sympathy surged through her. She wanted to reach out and attempt to share in his anguish.

"Cere?" he prompted, bending down toward her.

She pushed away thoughts of his pain. She needed to forget the personal issues. Her own safety was at issue. "I need to tell you something and this isn't about a ghost. It's real. Someone left a message on my voice mail, telling me not to look into Marco's death. That I could put my mother's life and mine in danger." She described the creepy voice.

"You should have told me this immediately."

She chewed on her lower lip. "I knew you'd use it as an excuse to get me to stop."

"And now?"

The truth was she was tired of being his adversary. But she didn't know what else she wanted.

Before he could respond, a plume of dust rose in the distance and the faint sound of an engine came from the road.

Sunlight glinted off the windows. For an instant she feared it was Diego Diaz in his big black SUV.

Chapter Twenty-Two

BJ Foster stepped from his car and hitched up gray pants. He lumbered toward them trying to look official, but with his blue shirt pulling out of his wrinkled pants, the image didn't fit. He reminded Cere of the stereotypical small town sheriff.

"So tell me about this evidence you found," he demanded, giving Rafe a skeptical look. His light blue eyes slid over to Cere, and Rafe introduced them.

His gaze lingered on her a bit too long, and Cere shifted uncomfortably as she said hello.

"You want to see the box?" Rafe asked.

BJ's attention swiveled back to Rafe. "Yeah, the strange thing is, you're the only one who's told me about that money box. Most everyone else seemed to think he had it spread out in bundles underground. We've been chasing people away from his yard."

Rafe's jaw tensed as he shook his head. "Look, I wasn't the only kid who ever worked for him. I watched him get money out of that box. I'm certain other people saw him do that too. They just haven't told you."

"His coins in there too?"

"I didn't see that little pouch he used to carry around, if that's what you mean."

"Uh-huh and you're the one who knew where the murder weapon was too." His hard eyes narrowed.

"Seems to me you're my top suspect."

Rafe shook his head, disbelief visible on his hard face. Cere could imagine the two men battled quite a bit. Or maybe the police chief was just trying to put on a show for her. Rafe's phone beeped. He checked the number, held up a hand, excused himself and stomped away, a scowl on his dark face.

BJ turned to Cere with a wide smile. Tall and sturdy, tending toward pudginess, he stood over her like a towering oak. "I hear you was locked in a room out here last night?"

Cere wasn't used to being on the asking end of questions. She countered with a question of her own. "Do you have any suspects who might have killed that old man?"

He drew back as though shocked she would ask. Sunburned, with a scattering of freckles across the bridge of his nose, BJ Foster looked like Huck Finn grown up, a well fed Huck Finn.

"Well, missy, not right now."

"Rafe certainly didn't do it."

His wide, ruddy face lit up. "I know, but little Chico there gets too full of himself sometimes. Acts like I don't know what I'm doing just 'cause he spent a few years in the city."

"I see." Cere donned a grin that she hoped showed her understanding. It wouldn't pay to get on the police chief's wrong side. He might be useful in answering some questions.

"My dad told me about meetin' you."

"I enjoyed meeting him." Another bright smile—her reporter smile.

"Whatcha doin' out here today with him?" He

gestured toward Rafe who was walking in a large circle, talking on the phone.

"I wanted to look at the hand print. I should talk to your dad about that. He was sheriff when Marco Gonzales died?"

BJ's pleasant smile dissipated. "My dad won't talk about it. That boy made lots of trouble for the town."

"What if I said he was murdered, and I could prove it?" she asked, hoping to get a reaction from him.

His response was a clenched jaw and a redder complexion. Animosity filled his clear eyes. "That opinion ain't gonna make you popular. Everyone knows he killed himself."

"The story in the paper seemed to suggest otherwise."

"That writer was a damn fool. Tell me about the other night." Exasperated, he pulled a notebook and pen from his pocket.

Cere didn't press for more answers. She could hold her questions until later. For now, she recounted the story of getting locked into the room.

"Can you take me upstairs and show me?" BJ asked.

"You don't want Rafe to do it? He found the box."

His blue eyes flickered to Rafe who had finished his business and was putting away the phone and coming toward them. "Yeah, I guess."

Cere regretted her suggestion as soon as the two men entered the Palladium. She should have gone too. If state investigators took over the case, there was no telling when she would get another look at the hand print. She waited patiently until they came out. Rafe dangled a black leather band as he approached.

"Is this yours?"

"My watch. Where was it?"

"Under the piano."

His grim look stopped her, and she realized he held up only half of the band. There was no watch attached.

"It's all we found. And you can't go back in," he said as though guessing her thoughts. "It's now a crime scene. It may hold the key to finding Naldo's killer. And that killer may worry you saw him. You need to be more careful."

"Rafe, are you worried about me?" The question was accompanied by an impish grin and a flash of her bright eyes.

He fought back the warmth that surged through his blood as his gaze fell to her upturned lips. He leaned back on the hood of his patrol vehicle, kicking at pebbles in the road. He dipped his head, hoping she couldn't see his face under the brim of his hat. "I protect all my constituents."

The burst of laughter that erupted from her small frame only drew more heat into his blood, and he shifted uneasily, aware of an urgency spreading through his lower regions.

"I'm glad you find this so amusing," he replied, through gritted teeth. At times he wanted to shake some sense into her. Why didn't she realize she might be in danger? "We may be dealing with a killer here and he may have kept your watch for a reason."

The flirtatious smile froze, and her face sobered somewhat as she lifted the broken watch strap. She slid it into a pocket without saying anything.

"Look, Cere, all I'm saying is I doubt they intend

to sell it."

"If they want to use it to threaten me again, I won't give in."

While she refused to be cowed by threats, and he admired that quality, she needed to stop being foolish. If only he could convince her to go back to Los Angeles before she got hurt. In the distance a car turned off the road.

"One of my deputies is coming. I'll have him drive you to get your car. I better stay out here."

"I can…" she began, but he crossed his arms across his chest, gave her a hard look and shook his head.

"There will be a lot going on. As a civilian, you'll be in the way. Not to mention your mother is going to be worried when she hears about the shooting."

She looked ready to protest further but at his comment about her mother, her eyes widened and she shrugged. With a deep sigh she turned toward the arriving car. "You're right. She will be worried."

He walked her to the patrol car and made the arrangements to get her back to town. As she settled onto the seat he leaned over to speak through the open window. "You need to stay out of trouble, okay?"

"I will go home, take a shower to get rid of the dust, then get a manicure and have lunch with my mother. How much trouble can I get into?"

Rafe's rumbling chuckle sent a tremor of awareness through Cere. "Trouble finds you. See you later, Cere. I'll call you."

The low, intimate sound of his voice sent another shiver snaking along her spine as the car bumped over the prairie to turn around. The thought of seeing him later shimmered like a piece of promised jewelry. His concern for her was obvious, but she wasn't certain how to feel about it. She'd always taken care of herself. Having someone else worry set off sensations she didn't particularly like.

As they reached the main highway, her cell phone buzzed. The display showed the call came from Freeda. She tapped the talk button.

"Hi, sweetie, are you back?"

"Well, I don't know what to do." Freeda's voice cracked. "I was having breakfast at a diner and I heard that he was here a couple of days ago. They don't know where he was going or if he'll be back. But he was here!" She sounded near tears.

"Hey, you better give it up and come back, okay?"

She sighed heavily. "I suppose. I'm out of money. My payment from that last job didn't go into the bank today like I expected, and Daphne is heading back. Nena is going to send money, but it won't arrive until tomorrow."

Cere shook her head. She should have known. "Things aren't going so well here either. I lost my watch, someone…" She stopped, unable to tell her story in front of the deputy. "I'll tell you about it when you get back."

She tapped the phone off and started to put it away, but it still showed coverage bars. She scrolled to the number from the note left on her car. Despite Rafe's warning, she still wanted answers about Marco. She needed to find the person who wanted to talk to her. Rafe had given her some of the story, enough to further whet her appetite. She wanted the rest. The number rang on and on. No answer and no voice mail.

She turned to the young deputy. Rafe had introduced him as Zeb. Short and wiry with thick glasses and a pale complexion, he looked more like a banker than a law enforcement officer. Even his cowboy hat looked too big for his narrow head.

"Are you from Rio Rojo, Zeb?"

"Yep."

"Your family's from here?"

"We moved here twenty-five years ago when I was three. They came to live in a commune near Casitas. They didn't like the living arrangement but they loved the area. Lots of ex-hippies live here."

She thought of the older men in their rock T-shirts and long hair. "Is your mother an artist?"

He laughed, displaying small white teeth. "How did you guess? She runs a studio on Main Street in a brick building that was a five-and-dime until the insides burned up."

She shivered. Was it a makeover of one of the buildings Marco might have destroyed? She'd have to check. Maybe some good things had come from Marco's alleged reign of terror. She had Zeb point it out as they passed through town on the way to the Gonzales garage.

Len wasn't around and a young counter man handed her a receipt and the keys to her car. "It's around back. I guess the rental company is paying the charges," he said.

Her mother wasn't home yet and in a way she was pleased. Her ride with Zeb had given her a new idea. Instead of taking a shower, she grabbed her camera bag. Given the problem with the hand print her story needed other visual options—like rebuilt stores downtown and

Naldo's house. She didn't know which stores had been rebuilt, but she could get shots of the house.

Leaving her car at home so she didn't attract attention she walked the few blocks to the murder scene. In daylight, the property she'd originally considered shabby gave a different impression. There was no sign of violent death except for the ring of yellow crime tape strung around the driveway and through bushy shrubs to the edge of the unattached garage. Fresh green and white paint on aging wood and trim on the garage doors and the scattering of ceramic figures on the lawn demonstrated loving care. That made the yard painful to view. Rose bushes were trampled, and piles of dirt sat beside shallow holes.

Wow, were people digging up this place in search of treasure? What would they think when they found out that the money box had been found? Was it a coincidence that the box was found in the building where Marco had died?

Discovery of the box enhanced her story. The cash would provide great pictures—if she could convince Rafe to let her photograph it. The focus would remain on Marco, but the new murder provided a fresh angle to the old mystery.

She surveyed the street. Seeing no sign of anyone she slipped under the tape and into the yard. An outline for the story leaped into her head—she would open with a walking shot in the yard with its holes, talking about the search for treasure.

"But this isn't the first time murder has visited Rio Rojo," she murmured. The scene would shift from the colorful yard to a gloomy interior. "Thirty five years ago, a man met his doom in this room. And this is all that is left." The camera would then zoom into a spotlight framing the hand print.

She would recite some of Marco's story and the camera could follow the trail of blood down the wall, as she read the words he left in Spanish. "Words of love, but meant for whom?"

Cere stopped her soliloquy. Anything else here? Maybe she should check the back yard. Holes back there might be bigger since a fence blocked the view from the street. She hurried along a broken sidewalk on the side of the garage until she was sheltered by the fence in the backyard.

"You ain't supposed to be in there."

Cere whirled around. An elderly woman with bright alert eyes peered over the fence, a frown twisting her leathery face.

"I'll report you to the cops." She stood less than five feet tall with startling white hair and wrinkled skin over a bony figure. A thin hand waved a wooden cane with surprising vigor.

"I wasn't going inside. Just looking."

"So's everyone else." She pointed her cane at more holes in the yard.

Recalcitrant neighbors were Cere's forte. She transformed into the understanding reporter, calling forth her brightest smile. "I bet it's tough for you as a neighbor. Hi, I'm Cere Medina, Lottie's daughter."

"Lottie?" A frown of confusion crossed the wrinkled face.

"Her brothers are the Winslows. My Aunt Millie runs the Mane Attraction beauty shop."

The old woman nodded, connection made. She moved closer to the fence. "You lookin' for someone?

Your mom don't come this way. Her brothers neither."

"I'm a reporter. Did you see anything?"

The silver head shook. "I was in bed. My grandson, Robby, found the body, you know. I guess it was pretty bloody."

Bingo! Her heart quickened, reporter's senses coming alert. "Is Robby home?"

"He's at work. He'll be home tonight. Do you want to talk to him?" The alert eyes grew even sharper.

"I might. I'm doing a story on the murders..."

"Murders?" The bent elderly woman straightened, a look of fear shading her eyes. "There are others? Like a serial killer or something? I see that on TV all the time."

Guilt shot through Cere at the startled reaction. "Nothing current. I meant Marco Gonzales."

"He used to live back there, you know."

"Back where?"

The neighbor's cane came up and pointed at the brick side building. "The garage. Used to be a little room. Naldo fixed it up for him."

"Marco lived here at one time?" She cast a glance toward the Sanchez garage, trying to disguise her eager interest.

"After he got out of jail, his folks wouldn't have nothin' to do with him. No one wanted him around. His sister used to come by sometimes."

"His sister?" This was getting better. She'd heard of cousins, but this was a closer connection. She tried not to sound too eager. "What was his sister's name? Is she still around?"

The woman waved a leathery hand. "She died a coupla years ago. Her kids are still around, Gus,

Sophie. But Linda stopped comin' by after they had a fight. I heard 'em. She was tellin' him to stop being a bum. He said no one would hire him. That's why he worked the ranches and did odd jobs. Sometimes he gave speeches at the VFW Hall or at the church. Always talkin' he was. Sometimes I could hear him in the garage, singing. He had a pretty voice. He shoulda been a singer. Even Naldo told him that."

Her heart pounded so loud she feared the neighbor might hear. A connection between Naldo and Marco? Why didn't anyone ask about it? *Why hadn't Rafe asked?* The answer was simple. He had known all along.

Chapter Twenty-Three

Cere donned her warmest smile as she approached the fence. *Damn Rafe*. He hadn't wanted her to know about this connection, but now perhaps she had found a good source for her story. "Did you know Marco?"

"Nope. He never talked much to me, but he spent lots of time with my boy, Nick. Wanted him to go to college. Like an education was gonna do Nick any good."

Cere held her breath, triumph rising inside her. "May I speak with Nick?"

She shook her head, dismay turning her features more gray. "Nick's dead. He was wounded in Vietnam and never recovered. Now there's just me and his boy, Robby."

"But you've heard what they say about Marco, right? Do you think he killed himself?"

The woman leaned forward on her cane, wizened face growing set, voice low and filled with disdain. "He didn't kill himself. Naldo knew it. I think Naldo knew who did it."

"Do you think that's why Naldo's dead?" Cere asked, nearly choking.

The elderly neighbor snorted. "His killin' had nothing to do with Marco. They wanted that money. I told Naldo over and over not to keep cash around. And them gold coins he used to brag about..." The white head shook from side to side.

"Everyone knew about the money, right?"

A grizzled finger shot up. "Wait, I gotta go. I hear my story coming on." With surprising speed, she turned and hobbled to the house.

Cere's glance zeroed in on the brick garage. Finally! A way to tie the old death to the new murder. Looking around to make certain no one else saw her, she dug out her camera and shot video of the garage, the hole-covered lawn and the little house.

****

A relationship between Marco and Naldo! Cere couldn't get the thought out of her head as she showered and changed into silk shorts and a matching top. She also couldn't forget that Rafe withheld the information. With time remaining before she had to meet her mother for lunch, Cere drove back to the Gonzales garage, a faded red brick building that hugged a street corner at the edge of town. Its signs had been painted over the logo of a gasoline company now out of business. Several older model cars huddled on the cement pad in front. Open hoods yawned on two of them. The upper half of a portly body disappeared into the engine area of one while the young mechanic who had given her the keys to her car earlier twisted a wrench under the other open hood. Inside, Cere found Len working on a car engine that rested on a counter. He didn't look particularly surprised to see her.

"May I ask you a few questions?" she asked.

Len shoved back a faded baseball cap on his head. "The rental company paid for the tire."

"I know, but I have a couple of questions for you."

He leaned against the counter and wiped the grease

209

from his hands with a grimy rag, giving her his full attention. "Yeah?"

"Rafe told me someone sliced my tire."

"Yeah."

"I'm trying to figure out who did it. Do you suppose it might have something to do with my questions about Marco?"

Surprise widened his dark eyes and he stopped wiping his hands. "Why would you say that?"

"Because I was asking questions at the Matador the other day. I think someone followed me when I went to the Palladium last night. Even you indicated I could be asking for trouble."

One side of his face scrunched up in a scowl. "I'm sorry for that. I was trying to scare you."

She summoned her most forgiving tone. "Scaring the city girl, huh? But I'm serious about whether someone might not want me asking about Marco."

He relaxed visibly, leaning back against the counter. "I can't see anyone following you because of it. Marco got a bum deal for sure, but no one cares about it anymore. I don't talk about it, 'cause it ain't worth discussing. Can't change things."

"Did you know him well?" He seemed young to know much about Marco personally, but it didn't hurt to ask.

"I was four when he died, but his songs are good. One of my cousins was talking about trying to get them published."

"Really? I might be able to help with that. What's your cousin's name? I'll call him." She wasn't certain what she could do, but her offer might open some doors.

"Gus. He's working up at the Hollister Ranch so you can't reach him. You got a card or something? I'll have him call you."

She pulled a card out of her purse and added her mother's phone number. He took it and shoved it into greasy jeans. She could feel his curious eyes on her as she slid into her car and drove away. Finally, she felt like things were moving along!

****

Even the menu at the Matador with its wilted salads was no obstacle to Cere this time around. Now that she knew Frank, the owner/cook, was related to Marco, she was determined to talk to him again.

Against its background of Western music, the restaurant buzzed with voices when she entered. The same handful of men she'd met before sat at the counter, and several nodded at her. One even smiled. The waitress, Josie, handed her a menu and told her to grab any booth.

She glanced around. Her mother wasn't there yet, and she debated whether to sit at the counter, but she saw Ginny alone at a table in the corner, a coloring book and crayons around her. She spotted Cere and smiled, waving small fingers.

Cere walked past the counter. "Hi, Ginny, why don't you join me? Mom's going to be here in a few minutes."

The girl nodded, straight black hair falling across her face. Someone had made an effort to comb her hair and put in barrettes again, but again the part was crooked and one barrette clung to a thin strand of hair. The orange jeans were new, but her matching striped T-shirt bore a ketchup stain on the front. A pang of sympathy tugged at Cere as she thought of the small girl losing her mother in a shootout. Ginny's little hand found hers and together they walked to an open booth.

She settled the girl next to her. "How are you today, Ginny?"

"Okay," she murmured, head down. Orange polish dotted her nails. Had Rafe done that? Cere smiled at the thought. She tried to think of what to say to the girl.

"Did you see the rabbits this morning?"

Ginny's head jerked up, long lashes fluttering. "I helped feed them."

"Which is your favorite?"

"All of them. Mrs. Lottie said I could name them." She waved and Cere turned to see her mother coming through the door.

Lottie swung into the booth as the waitress approached with plastic glasses of water. She put them on the table and glared at the girl. "Ginny, you're supposed to be coloring, not bothering the customers."

"I asked her to join us." Cere said. "We're becoming good friends."

Ginny nodded enthusiastically.

"I always wished Mom had bunnies back when I was growing up," Cere said, smoothing Ginny's hair.

Josie still stood over them, shifting her weight back and forth impatiently. "Do you know what you want?"

"Is the *chili relleno* on special today?" Lottie asked.

"Of course."

"We'll split an order along with a big salad."

"A salad?" Cere asked when Josie left with their order.

"I've invited Millie and your Uncle Norm and

Bradley over for dinner."

Ginny shifted to her knees and Cere couldn't help herself. She reached over and smoothed the girl's hair back from her face, removing the drooping barrette.

Her mother pulled a brush from her purse and held it out. "Why don't you fix her hair? I'm sure Ginny would like that."

Taking the brush, Cere glanced around. The table was no place for this, but lunch had not arrived, and she had a feeling ceremony was not observed in Rio Rojo. Fixing someone else's hair was not Cere's forte, but she brushed through the silky strands, straightening the part. Ginny sat obediently as though she was used to it. At the end, Cere finished by re-fastening both barrettes.

Lottie winked at Cere with a knowing look as she took the brush back. "I knew you had a few maternal instincts."

"You did that on purpose."

"How's the coloring today?" Lottie asked, turning attention back to Ginny.

The little girl smiled. "I have a new picture for you."

"I'd like to see it," Lottie said.

With childish agility Ginny slid off her perch and skipped across the restaurant. She returned with a sketch pad and crayons. She climbed into the booth on Lottie's side.

"It's not done. I couldn't decide on colors for the flowers."

With the two occupied, Cere excused herself and crossed to a glass case near the front counter. It held trinkets and souvenirs, but they weren't of interest to her. She pretended to be looking at them before turning to Jerry Orozco who was digging into a plate of green chili.

"Hi, have you heard anything new on old Naldo's killing?"

"Nah," he said, jerking a thumb to his left. "But me and Sam keep chasing kids away from his yard."

"I was by there this morning and saw all the damage. Have either of you come up with any new theories on who might have done the killing?" She looked from Jerry to the round-faced Sam who sat next to him.

"You investigatin'?" Sam asked. "We saw your article. Pretty good."

"Thank you. I want to do another one. I met his next door neighbor today. She said her grandson found the body."

"Mz Padilla," Jerry said with a nod, sopping up green chili with a tortilla. "Robby found him on the floor. What did she tell you?"

"Not much. I'm going to talk to him later."

Frank came out of the kitchen, wearing a tight gray T-shirt that strained against his huge middle and was covered by a dingy apron. A white sliver of a cap sliced across the top of his thinning salt and pepper hair.

"Hello, Mr. Gonzales," she said with a nod, hoping he'd read the blog too. "I hear your *chili rellenos* are great. That's what my mom and I just ordered."

His hazel eyes were wary as they examined her. There was no hint of the welcome the others had given her. He nodded and turned away to put a steaming plate of enchiladas in front of another man at the counter.

"I'd like to talk to you," she said, leaning toward him as he neared her.

"Uh huh." Despite the cool tone, he slowed.

"I hear you're Marco Gonzales' cousin?"

"So?"

"I know you don't like answering questions, but I hear he was a talented songwriter, that he tried to do good things for the town. I hear he wouldn't commit suicide."

His lips tightened, but for once he didn't walk away. "He was railroaded," he said in a low voice. "Town leaders didn't like his music, his ideas and blamed a bunch of robberies on him. Just like the first time. They convicted him anyway. The town would've deserved it if he burned down buildings, but he didn't."

A bell sounded and he waved his hand. "Look, I don't have time to talk." He stomped back to the kitchen.

Sam put a couple of bills on the counter and headed for the door, while Jerry looked more interested in his lunch. Across the restaurant, Lottie was viewing Ginny's latest creations.

Frank's comments had stirred her interest. Cere stepped behind the counter and followed him into the kitchen. "I understand you're busy right now. May I set up a time to talk to you?"

The kitchen was hot and smelled of fried onions and chili. Her stomach growled, but she didn't look to see if their order was up. Josie stood in a corner chopping vegetables for salads.

Frank didn't look angry that she'd followed him. He gestured toward the back of the kitchen with his chin. "Listen, you want to know Marco, go look at his writing. There are a couple of clippings in the office on the bulletin board. Check the top drawer of the desk.

There's a book with some of his stuff."

"You keep it handy?" Cere asked. After the reluctance to talk about Marco, the offer to view his work was refreshing.

"A reporter had it. His assistant just sent it back."

"May I borrow it?" Cere held her breath, but she had to ask, knowing she might never get another chance.

He studied her for a minute and then flicked his hand. "Sure. Go ahead."

Following his directions, she walked into a musty office. A beaten up metal desk sat along one wall, heaped with piles of folders and packets of receipts. Above it, several newspaper clippings lined a bulletin board pitted with age.

One held a picture of Marco. Despite the rumpled, yellowing paper, his face stood out. He wore a beret, his handsome features proud and regal, His dark eyes seemed to leap from the picture, fiery and alive. Another clipping showed him standing at a podium, one arm held high in a dramatic pose. She recognized it. This was the picture Riggins had used. Perhaps she could get a copy.

"Marco Gonzales urges calm at an outdoor rally," read the headline. She skimmed the story.

Marco Gonzales preached a message of law and order as he addressed a crowd of more than 500 Chicanos on Saturday. He told the throng that instead of shows of civil disobedience they should strive to work with law enforcement to help find perpetrators of the latest round of fires and burglaries in downtown Rio Rojo.

"Why give in to violence?" he asked. *"I've seen*

what it can do to people and it doesn't help. It won't make you feel better. You're law abiding citizens. You believe in truth and justice. Don't let the lawless or The Man drive you in that direction."

Most of the message followed that tone. But hadn't he just come out of jail after making a pledge for revenge? Was his peaceful message aimed at everyone else while he waged a secret battle against the city?

She took down the clippings and opened the top drawer of the desk. A worn brown leather book rested on top. She opened it, recognizing one of the clippings pasted onto a yellowed page. Had this scrapbook belonged to Marco? Who had made it? Subsequent pages held pasted up pieces of typewritten copy. A shiver of excitement surged through her. She placed the clippings inside the book and before returning to the table, she carried it out to the car and stashed it in her trunk. She would just as soon not tell anyone what she had. Maybe she could convince Alan to let her do another blog in a couple of days.

Back inside, the lunch was tasty, but she kept thinking of her trunk. A ghost seemed to fill her ears, whispering to her to look through that scrapbook.

As they rose to leave, Cere turned to Ginny. "Why don't you spend the afternoon with us?" The girl would keep Lottie busy and give Cere time to go through the scrapbook.

While her mother took Ginny and Roxie for a walk, Cere opened the scrapbook. Would she find any answers here? She was almost halfway through when her mother's phone rang. Cere didn't answer. Better to let it go to voice mail. She could hear if someone left a message that was an emergency—like Freeda.

Her mother's pleasant request to leave a message came from the other room, then a rough voice set her skin crawling.

"Quit snooping, bitch, or you'll end up like Naldo. Next time I'll aim for your head."

Chapter Twenty-Four

"What are you doing?"

Cere almost squealed, but instead, she forced a benign grin to her lips to hide her shaking hands. She had not heard her mother and Ginny come into the house. Only moments earlier she had erased the horrible message.

"I'm looking over some old information." She wanted to shield it from her mother, but Lottie's sharp gaze had already zoomed in on the scrapbook.

Her eyes widened as her face grew pale under her tan. "Marco? Where did you get that?"

"Frank let me borrow it. Want to go through it with me?"

Her mother whirled away. "No, and I wish you'd get over this craziness. It's..."

"Not dangerous, is it?" She tried to sound calm, despite the threatening messages and gunshots.

"If I say yes, will it stop you?"

Cere's gaze rested on Marco. What was it that drove her on? Her quest for a major story? No, she could pursue other ideas. The ghost in her dreams begging justice? Maybe. At times she felt a palpable presence beside her, pushing her forward.

"Only you can help me."

"Maybe this scrapbook will answer my questions, and I'll give it up."

Lottie's lips pressed together until they formed a white line of disapproval. "I wish you'd give it up now. You're playing with fire, and if you don't stop this ..."

"Miz Lottie, can I wash the cages now?" Ginny's high voice interrupted the tension.

Lottie's pained look dissolved, and she forced a smile to her lips as she turned to the girl. "In a minute..." She licked her lips as though she didn't know what to say. Fine frown lines etched her mother's jaw and cheeks.

A wave of guilt swept through Cere. "Mom, why don't Ginny and I clean the cages? I know you need to start dinner preparations."

"Thank you." Lottie's blonde curls shook as she pointed at the book and clippings. "And put that away."

"I'll be right out." Cere smiled at Ginny, folded up the clippings and shoved them into the book. She took it to her room and stashed it in her empty laptop case, which she then shoved under the bed.

As she headed outside, she stopped to kiss her mother's cheek and murmur an apology. In the back yard Ginny kneeled in front of the cages, dark eyes intent on the animals.

"Whatcha you doing?" Cere called

The grave look on Ginny's face was heart wrenching. Six year old girls should be having fun. Her small hands opened to reveal palms of crushed greens. "I'm feeding dandelions to the bunnies. Do you want to help?"

Cere drew back, fearing stains on her beige shorts. Perhaps she should change before she helped her clean the cages. "I may need your help. I've never done this before."

"I'll get the hose," Ginny said. She dashed to the side of the house, turned on the water and tugged a lime green hose toward the pens. Its weight sometimes brought her to a standstill as water shot into the air.

Cere was torn between smiling at Ginny's efforts and feeling sympathetic. She took the hose, frowning at its muddiness. She should have changed clothes. She settled for removing her sandals. "Do you have friends, Ginny?"

"Your mom." She sank onto the grass to take off her tennis shoes and socks so she was also barefoot.

"It must be rough with your dad working all the time. Do you always stay at the restaurant?"

"And my grandma and Aunt Lou, but her kids are older."

"I bet you miss your mom, huh?"

Ginny's face grew more somber, and for an instant, Cere feared she was going to cry. "All the time."

"I've missed my mom too since she moved here."

"My mommy didn't move. They shot her and she died."

A jolt ran through Cere, as though the gunshot pierced her heart. How much did she know about her mother's death? She gave the girl's thin shoulder a gentle squeeze of support. "Show me what to do next."

Ginny's grim face relaxed into a childish grin. "You move that bunny into the other cage while you wash his cage, and then you move them both into the clean cage. I'll hold the hose."

The playful smile was reminiscent of Rafe's, and Cere's heart lurched. Momentarily distracted, she missed grasping the rabbit and it hopped past her. Ginny squealed and dropped the hose, dashing after the rabbit. The untended hose took on a life of its own, becoming a stalking snake as it squirted first Cere and then Ginny, sending them into squealing gales of shouted laughter.

"What the hell..." Rafe stepped through the back gate, surprised to see Cere and Ginny at the mercy of a jerking hose. Cere grabbed the hose and whirled in his direction, but she didn't spray him. Every male hormone jumped to life, and his uniform trousers grew tighter. He barely recognized her. Her hair was an auburn helmet plastered to her head, and her silk shorts stuck to her tanned legs like a second skin. Water drops glistened on her heaving chest and for an insane instant he imagined what it would feel like to lick them off. Every line of her delightful body was visible through the thin material stuck to her, including her erect nipples. This was a sight he didn't need to see, one he doubted he could soon forget.

Ginny was soaked too, but what struck him about her were her giggles—wild and uncontrolled. He couldn't recall the last time he'd heard her laugh like that.

"What are you doing here?" Cere asked, still wielding the hose. Ginny dashed for it and Cere showered her with a weakened spray. Ginny screeched with laughter and threw herself to the wet grass and rolled away.

"I was looking for my daughter. That is my daughter, isn't it?"

Ginny spied a new defense and darted to Rafe. She took shelter behind his legs, clinging to his knees, shaking from the cold water. "Save me, Daddy!"

Cere pointed the hose in their direction, but still

didn't squirt. She adopted a fake tone of warning. "Okay, Sheriff, get off my land. You can't evict me or use that innocent child as a hostage. "

He held up his hands in mock surrender. "Okay, ma'am. I'll let you stay, but put down the weapon, okay?"

Ginny still clung to one leg, her high toned laughter filling the air. "Yeah, put it down."

"What started this?" he asked Ginny.

She watched Cere who feigned one way and then the next. "She was cleaning cages, and the hose got away and I squirted her. Now she's after me."

Cere advanced, stepping around him to get a clear shot at Ginny who released him and ran laughing to the cages.

"You girls cut that out!" From the back door, Lottie appeared, waving towels. "Cere, don't you dare squirt him."

Her smile was open and daring, and he again felt heat shoot through his loins. Her expressive eyes looked him over as though considering how much she could douse without retaliation. Her gaze lowered and she seemed to realize what her drenched clothing was doing to his male anatomy.

She whirled, sprinting toward Ginny wielding her hose. "I'll get you!"

Before she could reach her, Lottie shut off the water. She approached and handed him a towel. "I hope she didn't get you wet. One minute they were working and the next they were behaving like kids."

He was pleased to see Ginny's playful antics. "Come here, Gin."

Ginny ran to him and let him wrap her in a towel.

Her teeth chattered from the cold but she was still giggling. "We're just playing."

"Give her to me. She's going to get you wet," Lottie said.

He tipped his hat toward her. "I'll go home and get Ginny some dry things. I wanted to see if you could keep her a little longer. I have to help out at the paper."

"We'd love to have her. Millie, Norm, and Bradley are coming to dinner. Why don't you come by when you're finished?"

"Maybe." He wanted to get out of the yard before Lottie saw his sorry state and he embarrassed himself. Starting toward the gate he found Cere next to him, a beach towel draped around her wet body.

"I need to talk to you." Her voice was low, all jovial traces gone as she fell into step with him. Water drops shimmered on her shoulders, giving him a crazy urge to touch her.

"Sure, later." He stepped through the gate. He needed to get away from her. He felt like he'd escaped a danger worse than the gunman who fired at them hours ago.

****

"I don't want this Marco business to come up tonight, do you understand?" Lottie's voice was high and spots of pink dotted her cheeks as she carried a covered beef roast to the oven. "I want that book out of sight. I don't want it suddenly turning up."

"But Mom, they were all here when Marco died..."

"Cere, please stop."

The oven door slammed, and Cere jumped. They were alone. Ginny, exhausted after their water fight, was asleep on the sofa in fresh, dry clothes.

Lottie fanned her face with her hand and drew in a slow, deep breath as she removed her pot holder glove. "I'm sorry. I didn't mean to get angry, but sometimes you're so stubborn."

Sitting at the table, Cere flicked potato peelings from a peeler. She had been debating whether to ask her mother if she might invite Mr. Foster or her uncle Norm to go through the book, but Lottie brought it up first.

"This story is taking up too much of your energy. I know it's your job, and I respect your work, but I'm asking you to forget it for now."

"Sure, Mom. Mr. Foster was sheriff then, wasn't he?"

"See? Will you stop? This is supposed to be a fun dinner. I don't want my guests questioned like interview subjects. Bradley would be unhappy enough, but Norm would go right through the roof." Lottie's face flushed and again, Cere noted a few wrinkles across her mother's forehead she'd never noticed before.

"Uncle Norm? Why would he—"

"Enough! I want your promise. No questions about that story tonight."

She had no wish to anger anyone, but her mother had raised another question with no answer. What connection could Norman Winslow have to Marco? She didn't ask. Instead she decided to change the subject.

"Say, Mom, do you know a man by the name of Diego Diaz? He looks about your age. Drives a big black SUV?"

The tension in her mother's thick body lessened as her brow furrowed in thought. "Diaz? No. I don't remember any Diaz family in town. Is he from here?"

"I don't know where he's from. His SUV has Texas plates, but Rafe says that old man Naldo knew him. Is it okay if I ask Uncle Norm or Mr. Foster about him?"

"Why?"

"He was at the Palladium the other day. Apparently he broke into the place."

Lottie's hand came down hard on the table. "There you go! No, no Palladium questions."

"Okay, okay, but have you seen him around? He has an eye patch."

Lottie sank down at the table and began cutting up the peeled potatoes. "Eyepatch? Wait, yes, I might have seen him in the Matador a few times. He tipped his hat to me once. Hmmm. I guess I should tell Bradley. I saw him talk to Naldo."

Cere almost dropped the potato peeler. "Really? Like they knew each other?"

"I don't know. But now that you mention it, Naldo looked uncomfortable, like… I don't know, he didn't want to talk to him. I figured he was someone who had moved to town after I left. I didn't realize he was new or from Texas. Have they questioned him?"

"Last I heard they can't find him."

Her mother stopped cutting the potatoes and leaned toward Cere. "What's your interest in him?"

She could sense her mother's interest, but didn't want to admit he had scared her or that he had seemed to know who Lottie was. "I just wondered if you knew him. He's got a strange voice. Anyway, did Rafe say if he was coming by for dinner?"

The change of subject was welcomed by her mother. Lottie visibly relaxed and she reached out and tapped Cere's hand. "I hope so. He likes you and he's the only person who can make you behave."

"Right." Her cheeks grew hot at the thought of him. Yes, he liked her, as witnessed by the fire in his dark eyes when he saw her sopping wet. The worst part was that her bones had grown weak at the sight of his open desire. She'd wondered what it would feel like to toss her wet body at him and have that hard body touch hers.

She shivered slightly and noted that her mother was watching her and ready to laugh. "Oh, Mom, stop trying to pair me up with him. He's just a part of this story."

"Sure, and Ginny is simply another little girl, even though you brushed her hair and played with her. I've never seen you behave that way. Normally you run from children."

"Don't get any ideas." She waved the potato peeler at her mother. "That was a one-time thing."

"Just like you're helping me cook?" Lottie chided. "I've never seen you hold a potato peeler before, much less use one. Are you sure you're not trying to impress Rafe with your skills? Making garlic mashed potatoes was your idea."

"What skills? I'm skilled at picking up food or ordering it delivered. But I am a gourmet chef compared to Freeda. She'd burn the place down if I let her cook."

"Speaking of your wayward cousin, when is she getting back?"

"Anytime, unless she figures out a way for Nena to send money directly to wherever she is. She needs to get over this search for her father. If Fergie wants to see her, let him make the effort."

Lottie's smile was slow and sad. "Oh, hon, she's driven by a desire to spend time with him. Kind of like you are always driven by a desire to get the next story."

****

"You can't even get up there now," Millie said, her plump face scrunching into a frown. "The road past the Palladium is no longer maintained and with old Mr. Hollister dead, I've heard his heirs are talking about turning that whole area into a health spa and bringing the road in from the north."

Cere jerked to attention at the mention of the dance hall. Across the table, her mother's eyes narrowed into a warning look. Until now she'd been half listening to the memories her mother and aunt shared about how they once loved to spend summers at nearby cabins near the base of the mountains.

Naldo's murder was mentioned, but only briefly. Lottie adopted her best school teacher voice and told her guests she wanted more pleasant dinner conversation than murder, especially with Ginny present. She and Millie guided the conversation to talk of the past and their teenage summers at a nearby lake.

Lottie put her hand on Bradley's arm. "Hon, do you suppose the developers might change their mind and build a road from this side too? That would mean more tourists for Rio Rojo."

Cere cringed at the touch and the word, "hon." Why did her mother have to use the pet phrase she had once called her father?

Bradley cleared his throat and smiled at Lottie, issuing a wink that disturbed Cere further. "Well, I've been talking to them Tres Padres people. Big corporate bunch. Don't you gals worry. I'm lookin' out for this town. If there's a way to get them to build from this side too, we will."

"I hear there's lots of new construction near Casitas," Norm added, his thick fingers waving a fork at the table. "We could use some of that new business at the bank. Dick's always complaining we need new customers."

Dick was the oldest of the Winslows, president of the First Bank of Rio Rojo, but her mother had never been close to him. Lottie and Norm were the two youngest siblings and had been close from childhood, a relationship cemented even more when he married her best friend. Norm's rotund figure and thick jowls made him appear the oldest. Black glasses gave him an owlish appearance. Together he and Millie resembled twin bowling balls on thick, stubby legs.

She nodded in agreement to his comments. "Then maybe we can convince whoever owns that old dance hall property to tear that damn building down."

Lottie shoved back from the table with a loud screech of her chair. "Cere, let's leave them to their discussion of town business and get dessert. I'll call Ginny in." Rafe had not made dinner and the little girl had been excused earlier to play with Roxie in the backyard.

Cere threw her mother a pained look, but Millie was already pushing her fleshy arms against the table and getting to her feet.

"I'll help. I need to move."

Lottie squeezed Cere's shoulder enough to bring pain as she walked by and Cere rolled her eyes, but nodded in silent agreement.

Bradley turned to her as the two women disappeared into the kitchen. "I hear someone took a shot at you out at the Palladium."

"I guess everyone knows about that." She glanced at the door, wondering how much she could get away with before her mother returned. And he brought it up.

"News went around City Hall like wildfire," he said with a growling laugh. "I hope you don't think we're inhospitable, but I don't understand what you were doin' out there."

This was dangerous territory. Both men watched her with expectant looks and she couldn't help herself. "I'm doing a story for *Scope* on Marco Gonzales."

The room grew silent, like the emptiness after a bomb explosion.

She expected the reaction to come from Bradley, but though his jowly face grew florid, her Uncle Norm, the perfect banker who never displayed emotion, turned a dull shade of gray, eyes wide, lips thin and slack.

"My god, what would ever make you think of such a ridiculous thing? Don't you realize how much damage you could cause? You're going to drop this idea immediately! Don't even think about it!" He looked toward the kitchen door and then leaned toward her, his voice low and shaking. "Don't ever mention it again! Especially to Lottie!"

Chapter Twenty-Five

"Cere, you're making something out of nothing." Rafe shook his head as he sank onto a worn, brown leather chair. He took a sip from a mug of beer and leaned back with a sigh. Damn he was tired, probably too tired to be dealing with Cere, but she had brought Ginny home along with a welcome roast beef sandwich. She'd put the little girl to bed while he ate. Now they sat in the family room drinking beer when all he wanted to do was sleep. She'd insisted on talking so he poured them both beers.

"Is that why you never told me?" she asked

"It was a long time ago and it's not related to the current case, but I knew you'd blow the whole thing out of proportion. Someone here right now killed Naldo."

"Isn't it possible there's a correlation? Someone killed them both and took Naldo's box to make it look like a robbery?"

"Why wait thirty-five years if Naldo knew something? It doesn't make sense."

"You think I'm trying to tie them together to embellish my story?"

He didn't answer because that was what he thought and why he hadn't told her. There was so much information she could spin in the wrong direction if he told her everything and he wasn't going to help her. He was too damn tired. A swivel fan spun toward him, flicking warm air across his face and then back to her.

"Why do you suppose my Uncle Norm is opposed to my doing the story?"

Rafe squeezed his eyes shut and fought to keep them open. "I have no idea. Did you ask him about it?"

"I didn't bring it up. Mr. Foster wanted to know about the shooting today so I mentioned my research. He didn't seem surprised, but my uncle went ballistic. Even before they came over, Mom warned me not to mention it."

"Who knows? Maybe 'cause Marco burned down his brother's hardware store?"

Her gulp was audible. "What?"

"No one told you that, huh?"

"Well, no… Damn!"

He wanted to tell her she needed to do more research, but that would only make things worse. He twisted slightly in his chair and shifted. She was looking around the room and he could almost imagine what she was thinking. The sprawling ranch style house was fine for him and Ginny but it was probably different from home back in California. His mother kept the place neat, but the furniture was dated and thrown together for convenience. He'd never bothered to unpack personal effects, except Ginny's toys that littered half the room.

"What did BJ think about the box? His father thinks an outsider killed Naldo, but if it was robbery, then why leave the money?"

"Bradley doesn't like the thought of anyone in town doing it. I don't either. The idea that someone I know might shoot at us... That's not the Rio Rojo I remember."

"This town isn't as placid as you think," she said softly.

"What do you mean?"

"Nothing really, though I'm curious about my uncle. I'm having my nails done at Aunt Millie's shop tomorrow. I may ask her what she knows."

"The intrepid reporter strikes again."

"Did you have casts made of the footprints up on that hillside?"

He released a deep sigh. In a minute he was going to be rude and ask her to leave. "Are you trying to tell me how to do my job? Of course I did. But they may not be important. Lots of people hike in those hills. There's a picnic and camping area up on the mesa."

"I'll know that print if I see it again. It was worn on the back left heel and had an oval in the center of the heel."

Her words surprised him and he sat forward. "You noticed that much?"

She pointed at her head. "Very observant intrepid reporter here. What about the money box?"

"What about it?"

"What was in it besides the money?"

Rafe shifted, draining his beer. Enough! He lifted his arms and stretched. "I don't mean to be inhospitable, but I need to call it a day. It's almost eleven."

"You should have called me to help you at the newspaper office. I'd have come down."

Despite his exhaustion a smile creased his full lips. "The national TV star would lower herself to write for a local weekly?"

"Hey, Tafoya, I worked at my college paper. I

know about newspapers. We probably put out more stories in a week than your uncle does..." She stopped as he shook his head and pushed to his feet.

"You have to keep putting down the town, don't you?"

She drained her beer and stood, picking up his mug and walking toward the kitchen as she replied. "Actually I'm getting to like the town. When I walk down the street, people say hello even if I don't know them."

He followed her. "That's why I came back. People reached out to me after Carmen...letters, condolences. Most of those people I hadn't seen in years. When I heard they were looking for a sheriff, it seemed natural. This is the best place for Ginny too. I'd like to think that when she grows up, she can stop for a burger at one in the morning and not worry about random gunfire."

At the sink she rinsed their mugs and put them in the drainer. He examined her for a minute in her slim fitting sleeveless dress. Despite being so tired, he found his earlier arousal returning. How the hell could she look so damn good this late at night? Or maybe because it was so late.

She approached him and stopped in front of him. Her eyes swept over his face and she reached up to touch where his beard met his cheek. "I'm sorry for keeping you up. You look exhausted."

The touch was like a hot poker and he stroked the side of her face with his forefinger, making her tremble. "And you look fresh as a damned daisy."

Her eyes focused on his lips, and she moved forward, her breath quickening. Her fingers rested on the hair at the top of his shirt and he shuddered.

He wanted her. And the realization shot through him along with a wave of guilt. He couldn't continue. His finger dropped, and he stepped back. The moment, whatever it had been, was gone. He turned sideways, jamming his hands in his back pockets.

"Why don't we talk in the morning?"

She stepped back, understanding. "Was your wife's death the only reason you left L.A.?"

"Get me drunk some night, and I might tell you."

****

"Still playing the role of city bitch, huh?" Freeda threw herself into the empty manicurist chair across from Cere.

"Well, nice to see you too. What are you talking about?" She hadn't seen her cousin in days, but naturally Freeda would show up unannounced at The Mane Attraction and start lecturing her.

"Here you are getting your nails done instead of being with your mom. I'll bet you're here to pump Millie and her gals about your story."

That was true—she'd been stewing all night about her uncle's anger over Marco, and she had looked forward to questioning her aunt, but another manicurist stepped forward to help while Millie busied herself with another customer. The young woman spent most of her time talking on her hands free device while working the file.

Cere held up her drying nails. "I had a royal emergency. My nails looked like yours, all chipped and torn. You should see if they can take you while mine dry."

Freeda curled her fingers into fists to hide her blue-black chipped and chewed nails.

"Later, maybe."

"When did you get back? We were expecting you last night."

"We didn't get in until two or three so I stayed over at Daphne's. I called *Tia* last night. She said you were over at the sexy sheriff's house. I think she figured you might stay the night." She leered, lifting and lowering her brows.

"As if."

"How come you didn't go out to the lake with her? Or are you afraid you can't wear your spikey sandals?"

"Lake?" A sudden spark of annoyance pricked at Cere's scalp and she jerked upright. "Did she say she was going to the lake?"

"Yep. She was putting a cooler in the car as we pulled up. Gave me a key and told me where you were."

"Damn!" Cere shot to her feet. Having already paid her manicurist, she waved at Millie who was across the room putting a gray-haired woman under the drier. "See you, later."

Freeda followed her to her car that was parked right outside. "What's up?"

"She didn't tell me she was going to the lake. She waited until I left. That means she didn't want me to go with her."

"Why?"

"I have no idea, but let's find out. I was so focused on talking to Aunt Millie I didn't pay attention this morning, but Mom did seem kind of spacey."

"Sounds like you outsmarted yourself. What are we going to do? Follow her? Do we know where this lake is?"

"They said it was beyond the Palladium. That you follow that road, though I don't remember a road beyond the parking lot."

"Sure, I saw it the day I had to pee. It's not much of a road, mainly ruts, but you can see there was something there. Tell me what's been going on since I left. You and the sheriff, huh?"

"Forget the sheriff. Wait until I tell you what I found out about Marco." As they drove to the Palladium, Cere filled Freeda in on her scary night at the dance hall, plus the shots that had been fired at her and Rafe.

"See that dust cloud?" Freeda shouted as they turned the corner that led to the dance hall.

The cloud was several miles ahead, rising against the backdrop of the foothills. It disappeared into a wedge in the line of hills.

"Do you suppose that's her?" Cere picked out twin trails through the grass beyond the parking lot. What was once a road was now mainly patches of gravel overrun by grass. The going was slow as she dodged rocks and ruts that scarred the former road.

"Someone's been driving along here." She pointed to tire tracks in the dirt. "Besides Mom."

As they neared the edge of the mesa, she could see the slice into the mountain and the beginning of a small creek bed wedged along one corner. Only a narrow ribbon of water meandered through it. She came around a corner and slammed on the breaks. Her mother's stopped car was just ahead.

Lottie stood at the rear of her car. She walked toward them as Cere opened her door. "You damn girls! I don't know whether to kick or kiss you for following me."

Her car was parked at the edge of the road with the back tire entrenched in sand.

"Are you okay? What happened?" Feeling shaky from the close call of almost hitting the car, Cere climbed out and approached her mother.

"I was trying to get around a big rock in the road and got stuck."

She waved a finger at Lottie. "This is what happens when you take off without telling anyone. I'll bet your cell doesn't work out here, does it?"

Lottie didn't answer but her look of chagrin provided the answer. "See why I always tell you to let me know where you're going?"

"*Tia,* what are we going to do with you? Oh, hell. Look at this." Freeda frowned down at the side of their car. "For the past couple of miles I've felt like we were pulling to my side. I figured that was just the road, but the tire on your rear wheel is flat."

Chapter Twenty-Six

"No," Cere wailed. "I just got it fixed." But sure enough as she rounded the car, she saw the tire was flat as a pancake, but it wasn't the new one. That was on the front wheel.

"Hope you got a new spare when you got the tire replaced," Freeda said.

"It's a rental car and doesn't have a spare. I'm going to raise hell with that company."

"Do it later," Lottie interjected. "In the meantime, we better figure out how to get out of here. Check your phones to see if they work. We may have to walk out."

Cere could imagine what Rafe would say about this. She pulled her cell phone from her purse, but as usual it showed no service.

Freeda shook her head as she stared down at her phone and slumped against the back of the car. "I'm beginning to think I'm a jinx."

Hands on her hips, Lottie scanned the horizon and squealed. "Hey, look. Who's that?" She jumped like a cheerleader, waving and shouting. "Hey! We need help!"

A lone rider on a black horse galloped toward them.

Freeda's muttered curse before Lottie's sudden gasp warned of the identity of their oncoming rescuer. Or was he coming to rescue them?

Diego Diaz pulled up his horse a few yards away. As usual, he was dressed all in black, from his battered cowboy hat to scuffed boots. Sun glasses covered his eyes and a toothpick dangled from a pouting lip. He didn't resemble a faux city cowboy traveling around in a Caddy SUV. The black horse was magnificent, but the leather saddle was well used. Diaz's black shirt and jeans were faded and frayed around the cuffs. He trotted his horse around both cars before stopping next to Lottie. He cleared his throat before speaking, but his voice still came out in that raspy croak. "Having trouble, ladies?"

"Thank goodness you happened by," Lottie said. "I'm stuck."

"And my tire is flat," Cere added.

"What are you doing up here? This is private property." Using his toothpick, he pointed at a fence that bordered either side of the road a few yards behind their cars. The wire gate was pulled back to one side and sagged on the ground. "That gate is kept closed and surely you must have noticed the 'Private Property' sign on it."

Lottie folded her arms across her chest, like a little girl caught doing something naughty. Her head lowered and her voice filled with chagrin. "I saw it...before I opened it."

"I see. Probably not a good idea. And definitely not a good idea to leave it open behind you. Never know who might follow you in." The sharp sarcasm was made doubly strong by his raspy voice as his face swung toward Freeda and Cere.

She refused to accept his superior attitude. "What the hell are you doing here, if it's private property?"

"Don't owe you an explanation, but I happen to work for the owner." He dismounted his horse and approached the cars.

Lottie threw Cere a perturbed look and leaned toward her, gripping her arm until it hurt. "Don't anger him. We need help." She walked over to Diaz who examined the flat tire.

"We really appreciate any help you can give us, Mr…"

His head jerked up. "Diaz."

"Good to meet you, Mr. Diaz. I'm Lottie Medina." She held out her hand and he straightened and stood facing her for a moment. His hand rubbed his faded black jeans and for a split second Cere wondered if he was going to be rude and ignore the outstretched hand.

Then he reached over and shook her hand before jerking around toward Cere. "I can change your tire if you want and, Mz. Medina, if you have a blanket I can get your car out of the sand."

"Unfortunately this car doesn't have a spare tire. It's a rental."

"And they know you keep driving it up to the Palladium and over all these rocks n' things?"

"How do you know I've come up here more than once?" she demanded.

His black sunglasses turned to her and their shiny blackness reminded her of a bug's hard emotionless eyes. "I ride all over these hills. Patrolling. It's my job. I see lots of things."

She gulped as her gaze swung around to his horse and she noticed a rifle sticking out of a leather holder. "What else do you do? Maybe a little target practice?"

"I'm a good shot, if that's what you're saying."

Lottie came up beside her and pinched her arm. "Cere, don't accuse the man. He's going to help us."

"Is he?" Sudden fear raced through her. Hadn't he once bragged bodies were buried in these hills? Bodies that had never been found? How hard would it be for him to kill them right now and bury their bodies? They might never be found. She swallowed hard and decided to lie. "Just so you know, Mr. Diaz, the sheriff knows where we are. And he's checking on you too."

He'd been leaning over the tire and now he jerked up. "Really?" Offering no other response, he ambled over to the other car to check the stuck wheel. "You got a spare, Mz. Medina?"

"Yes."

"The wheel rims are the same size. Maybe if we put it on your daughter's car, she can drive back to town. You still haven't told me why you went through that gate."

Lottie tugged at her hair, looking nervous. She pointed to the torn up road. "I wanted to go up to the lake. We used to stay at the cabins up there. It's only twenty miles out of town, but thirty years ago, it seemed much farther. The air is so cool, lots of grass and sometimes we'd see deer. I wanted to see it again."

"Well, this road ends at the base of the next hill. The creek changed course and took it out. You would have had to turn back anyway. The only way to get there from this side is on horseback."

"Oh, drat."

His sudden bark of a laugh made Cere and Freeda jump.

"Yep," he said. "Oh, drat. Got a blanket?"

"Certainly." Lottie unlocked the trunk and

produced a green and blue striped stadium blanket. While he worked with it, placing it around the wheel, Cere and Freeda took out the spare. The tire wouldn't go far, but Diaz was right—it would get them back to town.

With the blanket under the tire, he had Lottie drive forward and back up slowly until she freed her wheel from the sand. Then he walked back to where Cere and Freeda were struggling with the nuts on her wheel.

He made quick work of the changing process, though he barely used his left hand. A long jagged series of scars ran across it. But his right hand showed amazing strength. If he wanted to choke someone to death, he could probably do it.

She also noted his old boots. Both heels were worn. Was there an oval in the center of the heel? Trying not to be obvious, she studied the ground looking for familiar prints in the soft sand. Nothing.

Finally, he straightened, and shook the dust from his hands. "That should get you back to town. I'll lead you to an open area where you can both turn around."

Lottie hesitated, gazing down the canyon with longing. "I guess I'll never see the lake again."

"It means that much to you, Mz Medina?"

Her sad smile was answer enough. "Yes, it does. And please, call me Lottie. My students call me missus. It always made me feel old."

"Well, Lottie, tell you what. I could arrange to get you up there. You ride?"

Her laugh was quick and almost girlish. "Are you kidding? I did when I was a kid. I could even ride bareback, but I haven't been on a horse in years." Sighing, she turned away. "Oh, well, it isn't that

243

important. Thank you, Mr. Diaz. I'm sorry my daughter's been so rude and hasn't thanked you."

"It's okay. I never mind helping ladies. Especially good looking ones. And you can call me D-V. Mr. Diaz makes me feel old too." He smiled, a sincere grin that for once wasn't mocking.

Freeda elbowed Cere's side and whispered. "Wow, your mom just made another fan. I'm telling you, she's doing a whole lot better than either one of us."

Bradley Foster was bad enough. No way would Cere let this jerk charm her mother. She pushed forward.

"Mr. Diaz, were you up here yesterday? Did you hear the rifle shots?"

His smile vanished as his face jerked toward her. "Rifle shots? What the hell are you talking about?"

"Someone shot at me. Came close to shooting my head off. You mean you didn't see that while you were *patrolling*?"

He drew back as though she slapped him. "You think I did it?"

"I'm not accusing anyone. But who else is up here regularly?"

He didn't reply as his lips tightened into a straight line. He looked from one to the other, but only Lottie spoke.

"Cere didn't mean to accuse you…"

"Right." The sarcastic tone was back in his voice and he walked over to his horse. After heaving himself up onto it, he tipped his hat to them. "I'll lead you over to a place to turn around. Then I suggest you get the hell out of here and stay the hell out. Next time you might not be so lucky."

****

"Well, you were right. The prints on the shells match a set of prints on that old box."

Rafe's stomach twisted at the pronouncement from Jack Landis, his connection at the state crime lab. So the person firing at Cere had handled the box—and probably killed Naldo. When had the box been put there? The night before? Or just before they arrived? Had the shots been an attempt to get them to leave? Maybe they had interrupted him on his way back to retrieve the box.

"Any hits on the prints in the database?" he asked.

"Nope, sorry."

He reached for the antacids in his desk. Part of him had hoped the prints would hit on a man by the name of Diego Diaz. Maybe he'd been caught drunk driving or been locked up on some petty charge in the past. But it appeared that wasn't the case. He popped a couple of tablets in his mouth.

"You want me to keep trying?" Jack asked.

He liked working with Landis because the man was thorough, but he had no idea what else he could do if the prints weren't in the criminal database. "You have other places you can check?"

"I have some things up my sleeve."

"Go for it. Did you get anything on that name I sent you? Diaz?"

"Diego Velasquez Diaz. Texas DMV lists his address as north of Dallas. One of the gals says it's a pretty upscale area. Ranch living and horse farms. Two vehicles registered to him. White Mercedes convertible. Black Cadillac Escalade. Sounds like a man with money."

"But no criminal history?"

"Nothing I can find. Want me to check for employment history? See where all that money came from?"

"Yeah, do that. And give me his exact address."

After he hung up Rafe turned to the computer on his worn desk. He called up Google maps and typed in the address for Diaz. It zeroed in on a location and he tapped up the street view.

He popped another couple of antacid tablets as he studied the gates and fenced walls that hid most of the homes.

Chapter Twenty-Seven

Smoke rose from a grill in the middle of Lottie's back yard. The tangy scent of barbecued ribs, seared hot dogs and hamburgers swirled through the warm evening breeze. Tinny country music wailed from oversize speakers in one corner of the yard and provided a low background for voices and the steady swell of laughter.

Surveying the festive scene, Cere cursed her bad luck. This would have been the perfect place to ask questions. Because the crowd was made up of her mother's friends and relatives, many were Marco's age. But she'd promised no Marco tonight.

The guests circulated around tables heaped with ribs, burgers and buns, bowls of potato salad, and platters of appetizers. Others gathered near a keg of beer that squatted near tubs of ice covered soft drinks. Guests with filled plates congregated at long wooden tables with benches running along both sides. The day's prickly heat was dissipating and in the distance, thunderheads loomed over the line of mesas, shielding the yard from the setting sun but holding no threat of rain.

Cere and Freeda strolled among the serving tables, making certain the platters didn't get too low, and bowls stayed filled with chips and dips.

"Try the guacamole." She pointed out a bowl to her

cousin, Pat. "I made it."

He dropped a couple of spoonful's onto his paper plate. "Where have you been? I thought you were coming by the bank."

Cere pointed at the table as she unwrapped a tray of deviled eggs and miniature quiches. "For the past two days Freeda and I have been up to our elbows helping Mom." After the drama at the Palladium and the close call in the canyon all three agreed they needed something frivolous to occupy their time. The party presented a great distraction as well as an opportunity for Lottie to see old friends and get to know neighbors better.

Her Marco story had received minimal attention. Cere emailed Alan pictures of the Palladium and hinted at writing a blog on what she had uncovered so far. Locked in her room alone, she went through Frank's book but it didn't contain much help. The type in the articles was faded and smudged due to the liberal use of paste. One comment scribbled in blue ink under an article about the trial stood out.

Farce. That trial was a FARCE!

Riggins had still not surfaced. His stay in Mexico had been extended and the phone number from her car remained unknown. She received no more threatening calls, but she had the uneasy sensation of being constantly watched. Could it be Diaz? His appearance as a ranch hand had surprised her and shocked Rafe even more. According to him the man had no criminal record, not even a parking ticket.

Lottie appeared beside her and whispered, "Bradley's here. Be nice, okay?"

The portly man smiled as he waddled toward them.

"Evening, ladies. Looks like a good party."

"It will be better now that you're here, Bradley. May I get you something?"

"It's good to see you, Mr. Foster," Cere added as her mother hurried off to get him a drink.

"Bradley, please. Are you enjoying your visit? I hope you haven't been back to the Palladium. There's no telling what kind of mischief's in that place. They say there's ghosts." One side of his jowly face creased with a wink.

"I think I made friends with any ghosts."

A hearty laugh rang out. "I bet you did."

"I've been thinking of coming by City Hall to see you."

"Certainly. I'll be happy to show you around."

Actually she wanted to view the courtroom where Marco had been convicted. She might shoot an on-camera stand up there, holding up the typed, yellowing sheet so the camera could zoom in on the word, *FARCE!* Maybe if she asked Bradley in that setting, she could get him to talk about arresting Marco or his trial, particularly the shouted threat. He might know if Marco had an attorney and provide his name.

Her mother returned with his drink and Cere excused herself to fill her own plate and find a place to sit. Freeda perched on the edge of a lounge chair, entertaining her cousins Pat and Normie with tales of nightlife in Hollywood. She didn't feel like joining them. Spotting her Aunt Millie, she approached and held out her plate.

"Mind if I sit with you?"

"Please do." Millie shifted her wide hips and waved a rib at the bench. She was Cere's favorite aunt.

Honest and fun loving, the plump woman thrived on gossip and food.

"What do you think of Bradley?" Millie leaned toward her, sharp eyes focused on the pair.

"I'm pleased to see her dating, and he seems to like her."

Millie seemed to sense her wariness and waved a chubby hand. "Bradley's okay, but he likes to run everything. I tried to set her up with Tony Gennaro. He's been so lonely since his wife died and he had a crush on Lottie in high school. Course lots of boys did. Lottie was very popular."

"So I've heard." Cere struggled with a rib, wiping greasy fingers on a napkin.

Millie cleared her throat as she leaned closer, speaking in a low voice. "Speaking of the old days, I hope something I heard was wrong."

A warning bell went off in Cere's head. She had a good idea what was coming. "What?"

"You're not really doing a story on Marco Gonzales."

Drawing a quick breath, she cast a glance in her mother's direction. Lottie was laughing at something Bradley was saying and could not overhear them. And it wasn't like she raised the subject. Instead of answering, she posed a question. "Did you know Marco?"

Her aunt's round face grew pink. "What does your mother say about this?"

"She thinks it's a terrible idea."

Millie's nod was curt, silver curls dancing on top of her head. "Course she would. It's bad enough we have a new murder."

"Could they be related?"

"Heavens no! Course if Marco was still alive, he'd be the first person I'd suspect. Now you forget all this talk about death and murder."

"Mom, murder is all anyone is talking about these days." Pat playfully tapped his mother's shoulder and slid in across from them. "Great guacamole, Cere."

"Thanks. It's an old family recipe from my dad. Did Freeda give you an earful?"

"She's quite a pistol. I don't know how the two of you survive. Makes our little town sound so boring. What do you hear about the murder? We don't get much gossip at the bank."

"Pat, don't!"

"Mom, this town needs a good mystery," he said, rolling his eyes. "Hasn't had one in years."

"Since Marco Gonzales?" Cere asked.

He tapped his mouth as though yawning. "B-o-ring. That was no mystery."

"Remember when we were kids, and went to the Palladium?"

"I remember we got scared as hell. Scattered like jack rabbits. I haven't been out there in years. I hear kids vandalized the place."

"They vandalized her car out there the other night." Millie waved a rib at the table.

"What were you doing?" Pat asked. "Looking for ghosts again?"

"I'm thinking of doing a story on Marco for *Scope.*"

Pat drew back, his forehead wrinkled in confusion. "Wow, going national? Some newspaper just did a story and I didn't see anything new. You think a national audience cares about some suicide in a tiny town?"

Millie nodded an "I told you so" at Cere.

"Did you go to his trial?" she replied, focusing on her aunt.

Millie's rapid blinks indicated her surprise at the question, but her next response was a forced laugh. "Oh, heavens, no! We were more interested in flirting with boys at the lake than sitting in a hot courtroom in the middle of summer."

"Did you think Marco committed suicide?"

"Of course not." Then as though realizing the alternative, she shook her head. "But you never know. He was always crazy. Probably wanted to make a statement. Didn't know it would kill him." Her voice had grown mocking and a thick hand patted Cere on the arm. "I'm sorry. He was so... so full of himself in those last days."

At that moment the back gate swung open, and Rafe stepped into the yard, preceded by Ginny. While she'd been hoping he would come, Cere's stomach still jumped. All her senses went on alert as a smile spread across her lips. Even though she had not seen him for two days, he had been constantly on her mind along with those final moments at his house. Had he meant to kiss her? Should she have pushed it?

He didn't see her, moving into the crowd, nodding at guests, a wide grin on his dark face. His white polo shirt emphasized wide shoulders, and tight faded jeans outlined long, hard thighs. His thick black hair ruffled in the evening breeze.

Ginny bounced beside him, shiny black hair tied in pigtails held in place by thin yellow ribbons that matched her shorts set. She made a beeline for Roxie, who was tied to a tree in the corner.

Cere self-consciously stroked her hair, tucking it behind her ear. Suddenly she wondered if her sundress was too revealing. Perhaps she should put on a jacket, even if the evening was warm. Rafe stopped to talk to her Uncle Dick and several other men. He didn't seem to notice Cere, and disappointment flooded her.

Ginny had seen her and ran over. "May I untie Roxie and play with her?"

"I think Mom wants to keep her tied up so she doesn't jump on everyone."

"I could hold onto her leash."

"Why don't I get you something to eat, and then you can play with Roxie inside later."

"Can I go eat by her?" Ginny countered. "She looks lonely."

"Yes, you may." Cere excused herself and led Ginny to the food tables. As she filled a plate to Ginny's order, she caught the spicy clean scent of Rafe's shaving lotion.

"For some reason, I didn't think of you as the maternal type," he murmured close behind her ear.

Giddy sensations filled her at his nearness. "I know a hungry girl when I see one."

"Cere says I can eat with Roxie and then play in the house."

Rafe made no protest, and as soon as Cere handed Ginny the filled plate, the little girl carried it toward Roxie.

"I have a feeling she's hungry but she still may feed some to the dog," Rafe said, heaping ribs onto a plate.

Lottie appeared, ever the efficient hostess. She threw an arm around her daughter. "Is Cere taking care of you? Be sure to try the guacamole. She made it herself."

Rafe gave her another appreciative look that set her insides twitching. "Domestic too? Maybe I underestimated you."

Knowing her warm cheeks were growing pink, she retorted, "I'm a damn good reporter too. Wait until you see that Marco story."

Before he could reply, her mother gripped her arm in a tight hold. "Don't you start."

"I'm behaving." Cere held up her hands.

"See that you do, missy. No one wants to talk about that."

"No one wants to talk about what?" Her Uncle Dick had joined them. A wavy crop of snowy hair made him appear older than his sixty years. Ever impeccable in a polo shirt and Dockers, Dick Winslow looked every inch the bank president.

Despite her mother's hovering presence, Cere spied an opening. "We were talking about Marco Gonzales. I'm thinking of doing a story on him."

Dick glanced at his sister, who had visibly stiffened. "So I hear. That newspaper article was bad enough. Stirring it all up again is stupid."

Cere felt a rush of irritation, but she wasn't going to argue. She was more surprised that so many people knew what she was doing.

"Maybe you can talk some sense into her," Lottie said. "Excuse me, I better circulate."

Given her mother's backhanded blessing, Cere turned toward her uncle. "You knew Marco, didn't you?"

Dick's pale blue eyes grew surprisingly cold. He seemed to consider the question for a minute, but unlike Norm, who had gotten so upset, he answered. "We all grew up together. Went to school together, well, sometimes he went. He was a bad apple. I was glad he went to jail even if he didn't commit those crimes. It got him out of our lives."

"You don't think he committed the original burglaries?" Marco's cousins claimed he was falsely imprisoned. Did others believe it too?

Her uncle's face turned stiff, disintegrating the weathered lines along his lean cheeks. His hard voice was chilling, despite the warm breeze. "Whatever happened to that guy, he had coming."

"Did you go to the trial?" she asked.

"Why would I be interested? We weren't even in town. We went up to the lake right after he was arrested as I recall." He leaned toward her and spoke in the quiet voice of a bank president explaining why he must turn down a loan. "Do us all a favor, Cere. Let it go. There is nothing to be gained by stirring up trouble."

Cere twisted around toward him, not at all ready to let go now that someone was finally talking to her. "I understand that Uncle John's hardware store was one of the buildings that burned."

His eyes turned to blue-gray granite and his voice was just as hard. "Lots of buildings burned and lots of money was stolen."

"And everyone is convinced he did it?"

"Who else? Everything bad happened while he was around, and it stopped when he died. Your mom says you're a smart girl. Put it together."

Chapter Twenty-Eight

Cere's cheeks burned but she clamped her mouth shut to keep from swearing at her uncle as he turned and marched away. She couldn't cause a scene at her mother's party—especially not over Marco.

Whispering a curse, she glanced around to see if anyone had heard their exchange. Rafe had disappeared at some point. Now he was engaged in a laughing conversation with a portly, balding man and a taller man with a salt and pepper beard and flowing silver hair.

Feeling deserted, Cere searched for company. Freeda stood in a corner playing darts with Pat. Lottie and Bradley sat among a group at the edge of the house while Millie was now holding court over several women. Her Uncle Norm stood alone nibbling on a rib and watching the scene.

His smile as she approached was somewhat of a surprise. "Good party. How ya doin' tonight? I've been meaning to apologize to you for my behavior the other night."

"I'm fine." Still smarting over his brother's angry words she couldn't help but jump right back into the topic. "Why did you get so upset?"

His smile lessened. "It's just a ridiculous idea is all."

"My mom knows."

His pale face clouded over. "And?"

"She doesn't like it."

"Of course not. Did Naldo put you up to this?"

The comment shocked her. "Naldo? I never talked to him. Would he have talked to me?"

"He didn't take kindly to strangers but loved to gossip when he drank. See, Naldo always said Marco was innocent. Wouldn't surprise me if he got that reporter to do the newspaper story."

Cere drew a quick breath. Could that be a reason for Naldo's murder? Because he talked after years of silence? How much had he known about Marco's death?

"I hear he had songs and letters from Marco in that box they found," Norm continued.

A shaft of anger pierced through Cere. "Who told you that?"

Rafe had not let her see what was in the box and sidestepped her questions about it. Why didn't he want her to know the contents related to Marco?

"BJ. But you should drop the Marco talk. You'll only rile people up."

Cere caught Rafe's eye. He smiled at her and waved a chip laden with guacamole, but she didn't smile back. She excused herself and stomped over to him.

"Why didn't you tell me what was in that box?" she demanded. "I understand it held papers and letters from Marco!"

His eyes grew hard as pieces of coal as he looked down at her. "Says who?"

"BJ told my uncle. Why didn't you tell me? Doesn't that show a connection?"

Rafe faced her, grim and unapologetic. "I knew how you would take that information, and here you are. The letters just happened to be in the box. There were other mementos in it too, clippings about his son, letters from his son."

"Put it together, Rafe. Naldo was the only one who believed in Marco. He took him in, kept his letters. What if he knew something..."

Rafe held up his hand. "Leave the investigation to the professionals. Excuse me, I need to check on Ginny."

For the second time in minutes she muttered a curse, but what she wanted was to take off her stiletto and fling it at him as he walked toward the house. She was growing more convinced that the only violent deaths in Rio Rojo in thirty-four years were related. She could feel it and her instincts were seldom wrong.

"I'm giving you one final chance to make a play for the sexy sheriff and then I'm going after him myself." Freeda's arm came around her rigid shoulders and beer sloshed on her arm. From the way Freeda wobbled she'd imbibed too much.

Cere scrutinized the immediate area, fearing someone might overhear them. "Lower your voice."

"Did you meet his uncle and folks? The uncle's kinda cute, hippie looking. I thought he mighta met my dad, but he says he never did."

"Cere, I want you to meet someone."

She pivoted at the sound of her mother's voice. Lottie stood with the man Rafe had been talking to and a short, stout woman. She would have been pretty except for an overabundance of black eyeliner that made her resemble a pudgy raccoon. Cere recognized her—the woman at the Matador who said Marco burned down the newspaper office.

"I'd like to introduce you to Rafe's mom and dad."

Rafe was nowhere to be seen. Why hadn't *he* brought over his parents to introduce them earlier, before their tiff?

She held out her hand. "Mr. and Mrs. Tafoya, it's so nice to meet you. I really enjoy your granddaughter. She's a sweet girl."

The woman nodded eagerly as she took Cere's hand. "She's my angel. Rafe's doing a good job with her."

Cere turned to Mr. Tafoya, as her mother excused herself and yanked Freeda away. "Rafe told me you and your brother own the newspaper?"

Pride surged into his warm brown eyes as they shook hands. "Willie handles the editorial side. I do sales and composing. I used to do the printing, but we send it out now. We always wanted Rafe and Willie's little girl to take it over eventually, but she's gone to Albuquerque and Rafe, well, at least he's doing what he enjoys." His eyes found Rafe who stood in deep conversation with a tall, slim woman with long black hair.

An unwelcome spark of jealousy raced through Cere. She forced her eyes away. "You wanted him to be a journalist?"

"He majored in journalism, worked the police beat. Then the law enforcement bug bit him and he went to a police academy in California. Being a law enforcement officer is hard work, but he's good at it. He could have done well in the city. Always been smart, dedicated."

Cere let her eyes drift to Rafe. He laughed at

something the woman was saying. Even from a distance, she could make out the thick black lashes as he winked at her. Her muscles tightened, and Cere fought off the unwelcome sensations piercing through her. "I'll bet you're glad to have him back home, Mrs. Tafoya."

"Please," she said with a light touch of Cere's shoulder, "we're Art and Stella. I was afraid he'd never come back, but it's good to have him so close."

"He told me about why he came back, how his wife was killed."

The couple traded glances, and Stella looked her over again. "He really came back for Ginny. She shouldn't grow up in a violent area and she needed to be around family. That little girl means more to him than anything."

"Taking care of Ginny, people. That's Rafe. That's his life," Art added. "What do you think of our town? Besides that it's too quiet. I read the blog we reprinted."

"You write pretty good," Stella said, her warm smile widening.

"*Well*, Stella. Well—not good." The tall man who had been part of the Tafoya group earlier had come up behind Stella. He nodded at Cere and held out his hand. "Hello, Cere, I'm Willie Tafoya. Thanks for letting us reprint your article. Stella is correct. You do write well. Next time you do a blog, let me know. We're always looking for material. I'll give you a byline. But, pardon me, you were telling Art about the town?"

The praise surprised her and she shook Willie's hand with a beaming smile. "I've never spent much time in little towns, so it's different. When I go to the store, they call me by name. I cashed an out of state check and no one questioned it. Of course, my uncle runs the bank."

Art nodded. "That's the way things are in a small town."

"Everyone knows everyone," Stella agreed.

She made a quick decision, one she hoped she didn't regret. "Like Marco Gonzales? I heard that he helped you and your brother found the paper, Mr. Tafoya."

All three smiles vanished and Willie grew rigid while Art shifted uncomfortably. They exchanged glances, but Willie was the one who spoke. "Like hell, he helped. Maybe he talked about it, but we worked for old Mr. Clarkson long before he came back to town."

"So you knew him?"

Stella fidgeted, her gaze lowering. Cere noted that her black lashes were as long and curly as Rafe's.

Art looked across the yard, eyes purposely avoiding Cere. Again, the response came from Willie, whose pointed jaw had grown noticeably tight. "It was hard to miss him. He made certain everyone in town got to know his name."

"But no one wants to talk about him. Why?"

Stella brushed her fingers through her neatly curled hair. When she looked up, her brown eyes were hard as marbles. "That's another thing about small towns. It's like a family, you know. You keep your secrets from strangers. Marco talked a lot, but not all of his ideas were wrong."

Cere sensed undercurrents in the conversation. Willie fixed Stella with a pointed glare and looked ready to correct her again. Art folded his thick arms across his chest in a position of defense. All three were visibly uncomfortable.

Cere turned to Stella. "The other day you said he burned down the newspaper office. Did someone see him do it? Or ask him about it?"

"Kinda hard to ask," Willie answered, "since he died that night. Someone did see him running away from the building with his shirt singed. Old Mr. Clarkson was working late and he barely got out. I remember when Marco was a kid he used to say someone should burn down the whole damn town. Urban renewal, he called it."

"Yeah, right," Art added with a harsh laugh.

A chill ran through Cere. No one had told her that someone saw Marco start the fires. Why had that information not appeared in the Riggins story?

"Cere, are you trying to impress my parents?" Rafe's voice was light, and his arm touched her shoulder in a gentle, playful touch. "Is she regaling you with stories of being a fearless reporter?"

"We were talking about Rio Rojo and its storied past," she said.

His mother frowned, while Willie snorted in disgust.

Art swiveled away and placed his hand on Rafe's shoulder. "Ginny keeps telling us about the rabbit pens. Lottie's busy so do you mind showing them to us? Come on, Mom, Willie. Please excuse us?"

****

Needing a rest, Cere sank onto a chair near the edge of the patio. The party was winding down. Her gaze roved around the remaining guests. Rafe and his parents stood in a group at one corner of the yard. The clustering included the tall, dark-haired woman he'd been laughing with earlier. Stella seemed to know her well since they kept laughing together and playfully jostling.

She studied Rafe, tall, handsome and commanding. Why had he hidden the information about Marco living with Naldo and that Marco's things were in Naldo's box? What else did he know? He was hiding more. She could see it in his dark eyes. What was it about Marco that made everyone close up or become hostile?

"Cere?"

She jerked up and searched for the name of the tall, lanky man with the silver-blond hair and quick blue eyes behind wire-rimmed glasses.

"Mr. Gennaro, won't you join me?"

He sank onto the chair beside her. "It's Tony. I wanted to welcome you and offer you and your mother dinner any night."

"Thanks."

Freeda claimed the man had a crush on her mother, and her aunt confirmed that he'd had one in the past. From his nervous look, Freeda was right.

"Your mother is pleased you're here. I hope you stay for a while." At Lottie's laugh across the yard, he jerked around. Cere followed his glance. Lottie leaned close to Bradley, and Tony's face reddened. Who would have thought her mother would have two men pursuing her?

"I saw your article you did in the paper," he continued. "I hear it was put on the internet. Are you going to put us on the map?"

"Maybe. I'm working on the old mystery of Marco Gonzales. Did you know him?"

Like the others, he drew back, and a curtain seemed to come down over his blue eyes. "Why dig up that particular thing?"

"Do you think he committed suicide?"

"I never really thought about it."

"But you were here when he died?"

"I was away, in Europe, studying at a culinary academy, but I wish I had been here." His placid face hardened into a grim mask, and a muscle twitched along his jaw line. "Maybe I could have made a difference. He burned my dad's restaurant the night he died. Maybe…"

He blinked, shook his head and rose, wiping his hands together as though clearing away the subject. "No use talking about it. I just wanted to extend an invitation to you and your mother. Good night."

Another closed door in her face. She studied the guests remaining, morose that she hadn't learned anything new about Marco. Or had she? She had been right about one thing. Most of these people had known him and all had strong reactions to his name. Their blunt refusals spoke volumes even if no one would talk.

On impulse she took her cell phone out of her pocket and punched in the number she had been calling. Perhaps it belonged to someone in the backyard. No phone rang, she got no answer, and no one checked their phone. Heaving a sigh, she hung up. Another dead end.

Seeing no sign of Freeda, she began to clean up, throwing trash into the big plastic containers at the edge of the yard. As she worked, thoughts of Marco appeared in relation to the party guests. These people were his age. Where would he have fit in with this crowd in the present world? Would that quest for civil rights have transformed into civic responsibility? Maybe he could have ended up mayor instead of Bradley Foster. Or would his reputation as bad boy have proven stronger? Would he have become a hardened felon when he went back to jail?

The photo of the fierce young man with the raised hand returned. What happened to Marco? Had the town beaten him down to the point of despair? To suicide? His cousins thought he was railroaded but they hadn't known him. Her uncles knew him and called him a hell raiser; her aunt labeled him crazy. Willie and Art made him sound like an outcast.

Cere put the last of the trash in the bins and rolled them one by one to the back gate. She opened the gate and pushed them through. As she slid the second barrel into place, a breeze stirred and a plastic cup flew out and fell to the ground. She reached down to pick it up and her breath caught. In the soft dirt between the gate and the alley was a footprint. An oval marked the center. The side of the left heel was worn. A shiver ran through her. She knew that boot print.

Was one of the guests the person who shot at her and Rafe? A more sinister thought hit her. Could one of their guests be Naldo's killer? She started to look over the fence but an engine came to life at the end of the block. The lights of a vehicle came on, spotlighting her before backing away. As it turned, she saw it was a dark SUV. Diaz? Had he been parked in the alley? Maybe spying into the yard? She shivered and hurried back through the gate.

Chapter Twenty-Nine

Rafe watched Cere from inside his office with more interest than he cared to admit. She stood in the main corridor of the courthouse, chatting with old Mrs. Peabody from Public Records. The thin, elderly woman was smiling patiently and nodding at Cere. Every so often she took a pencil from behind her ear and made a note on a yellow pad. He knew the topic of their discussion.

Damn Marco Gonzales.

He drew his gaze away, thinking about the party the previous night. He hadn't spent much time with her, though he had been constantly aware of the pleasant tinkling of her laugh. She had looked very good in a pale yellow sundress that turned her skin the rich color of a caramel sundae. This morning she wore a gold blouse and matching slim skirt that not only showed off the tan, but her curves as well. A bright lime green bag with a designer pattern stamped across it was slung over her shoulder, pulled tight against one breast. He fought off the rush of desire that went through him every time he looked at her.

Mrs. Peabody turned from the counter and stepped away in brisk precision, her low heels clicking on the marble floor. Cere stood alone, staring down at the polished top as though the blank surface was interesting. Her delicate fingers tugged at her lower lip, face set, eyes unfocused.

He pushed away from his desk and approached her. "What are you thinking? You look a million miles away."

Her head jerked up like a frightened deer and she glanced around the hall. "Rafe! Where did you come from?"

Disappointment surged through him as he pointed at the office door and then the entrance to his personal office. "You didn't notice my office is right across the hall? I thought maybe you were hoping to run into me."

Her face colored slightly and her lashes swept down. Shyness? From her? His earlier excitement returned. Then a playful gaze swept up to him.

"You wish, Tafoya. You know damn well why I'm here. I'm getting information about Marco and the fires he *allegedly* set."

For an instant, he was jealous of a dead man. Did she ever think of anything else?

"Did you learn anything last night?" He was afraid of the answer.

Her eyes became troubled, stormy as sea water churning up sand. "People are hiding things. Even you."

He couldn't dispute that, but he wouldn't enlighten her. "If you're expecting me to spill all about a developing murder case, you should know I'm within my rights to silence."

"It's not all the murder case and you know it."

He stood up straighter, hitching his thumbs in his belt. He couldn't tell her all he knew. Too many lives were involved; too many people might get hurt. If he trusted her, he might say more, but he didn't think she would keep a confidence where a story was concerned.

"I'm not sure I follow you."

"You claim Marco's death and Naldo's are not related. How do you know? Did you read the letters in the box?"

"What good would it do? Like I said, there were a number of things in there, like letters from Naldo's son. I didn't read those either."

"May I see the letters from Marco?"

"Hell no! What are you really doing at the courthouse?"

She gestured toward the heavy wooden staircase that split through the center of the century old building and her eyes roamed around the wide gloomy halls. "Actually I wanted to get a look at this place where Marco's trial was held. Is this where the jail is? Would he have been kept in a cell somewhere?"

"If you're looking for a stone wall with his name chiseled on it, you're out of luck. The jail was in the basement, but it's no longer in use. We share space down the block with the city. The area below was covered with drywall and turned into a museum that is only open on weekends. I'll take you down there if you want."

She shrugged and pointed upstairs. "What about the courtroom? That's where he was tried, isn't it? When he was seventeen? Didn't that old man Naldo work here?"

"Not back then. He was operating a pawn shop. I think the court room is open if you'd like to see it."

Before she could answer, Mrs. Peabody came out of the records office and approached the counter. She carried several sheets of paper that she handed to Cere.

"I found the list you wanted, Ms. Medina. I'm not sure if it will be helpful. That whole block was demolished. When it was rebuilt, none of the original owners moved back. They either rebuilt elsewhere or went out of business."

Cere sighed. "I see. But the list will have the original owners, right?"

"Of course. Most still live in town."

"Can you put me—"

"I'm sure Mrs. Peabody can't reveal personal information," Rafe interrupted, knowing where she was heading. "You'll have to play intrepid reporter and get info from a phone book."

Mrs. Peabody's face grew pinched. He didn't know if she was pleased he'd kept her from having to refuse the request or if she might have provided the personal information. The woman was normally protective of privacy, given her position in the records office, but the spotlight of a national television show might have tempted her to let down her guard.

"You know, dear, nobody really suffered as a result of those fires," she said. "The businesses that rebuilt were in bigger, nicer places. That block was very old. In fact, the fire might even have helped make our town what it is today. Some people, like your Uncle John, left town and got much better jobs. I hear he has a big hardware facility down in Albuquerque."

Cere's lips twitched in irritation, but she smiled and thanked Mrs. Peabody as she stuffed the pages into her bag. She turned to Rafe, her smile widening. "May I see the courtroom?"

He nodded and led her up the stairs to the second floor. The door was open so she could have gone in on her own.

"May I take pictures?" She produced a small metallic pink digital camera from her bag.

"It's public property. Be my guest."

She stepped inside, looked around and frowned at the small interior. Only the heavy wooden judge's bench remained from the previous century. It had been updated a few years earlier with new cushioned chairs for jury members and all the old wood paneling had been pulled out and replaced with white painted walls and modern art.

She snapped several shots before swinging toward him. "I have a feeling this is different than back then."

Rafe had seen her face fill with disappointment at Mrs. Peabody's statements about the fire's aftermath, and he nodded, hoping to totally dash her hopes. "Newly renovated. Just like Mrs. P. said. We're a better city because of all that happened."

She sighed and dumped the camera into her bag in a motion of disgust. "I was afraid of that. I need to figure out some good visuals for this story. Nothing seems to hold up."

Rafe leaned back against the railing of the jury box, folding his arms across his chest. "Give it up, Cere."

A small furrow appeared on her forehead and the corner of her lips twitched. She plucked at her lower lip again. "I may have to. I can't get an answer out of my boss about doing another blog and everything I try hits a dead end. I'd hoped someone would talk. Frank gave me an old scrapbook and newspaper clippings, but there wasn't anything useful there that Riggins didn't have. I went to the library this morning to look for old stories about Marco's trial, but no archives exist from the old newspaper. I don't know where Riggins got that quote about Marco swearing vengeance on the town. Maybe Mr. Foster? I'm not sure how much he'll tell me and court records for juvies are sealed so I can't even find out who his attorney was."

Rafe knew better than to crow in triumph. That would make her more determined. He opted for a change in subject. "You made quite an impression on my folks last night. All good."

The furrow smoothed out as the corner of her lips turned up. The sight sent a buzz of awareness through him. Suddenly he was conscious of the way the skirt clung to her tiny waist, and the rounded lines of tanned cleavage visible at the neck. Bright eyes met his.

"They're nice. You have your mother's eyelashes," she teased, winking at him.

Warmth spread in his lower regions. She was so lovely when she smiled like that. Tempting. He lowered his gaze. "My sisters curled them once."

She laughed, a soft pleasant sound that tickled his stomach. "Ginny will thank you for them in a few years."

"Probably."

"What happened to your friend?" she asked.

"My friend?"

"The woman you spent most of the evening with?"

Her voice sounded snappish, and it set his heart thudding. "Are you jealous, Medina?"

"You wish."

Despite feeling pleased at her reaction, he didn't want to give her the wrong impression. "Susan's a nice lady. I've known her since high school. That's the thing about this town. Everyone knows everyone."

"That's what your mother said. Most people knew Marco."

Back to Marco. "But that doesn't mean they want to talk about him."

A corner of one lip crooked up in annoyance. "If only I could find the person who left a message on my car the first day I was here."

Surprise pricked him like a barb, and he jerked toward her. "What? You never told me about that."

Her expressive eyes challenged his. "Just like you never tell me things. One day we should be totally honest."

Before he could respond, she glanced down at her wrist where she wore a slim gold watch. Naturally it carried a designer logo. The watch she'd lost was probably expensive too. If Naldo's thief-killer had found it, he might have taken it to sell.

"Oops, I have to go. I promised Mom and Freeda I'd meet them at the sandwich shop for a quick bite and then we're going over to the auto shop."

He couldn't keep the disgust out of his voice. "You're not going to question Len about Marco again."

She laughed, and the tension began to dissolve like a drifting cloud. "We have to get another tire fixed, plus Mom wants him to look at her old Honda so Freeda has her own set of wheels. You think I'm driven. Freeda's much worse. She is now convinced her father is somewhere nearby so she wants to go hunting for him."

"Must be a trait that runs in your father's family. Your mom is so…well, calm."

"You think so? She was the one who got us trapped in the canyon the other day. Hey, did you know Diaz is working up there?"

"Huh?" Rafe's senses went on instant alert. He hadn't seen Diaz in days and even if the background check had come back clean, in his mind the man remained a suspect.

"We saw him up the canyon on the other side of the Palladium on horseback. He said he was working. For whom would he be working?"

"I'm not sure. I think that's the old Hollister place, but it's all Tres Padres land now. I'll check and call you later if I find out anything." He gave her a wave and turned toward his office. Diaz working nearby? He wanted to find out if the lanky Texan was still around.

****

"What are you doing this afternoon, Mom?" Cere asked as they watched Freeda drive away in a fifteen-year-old Honda. Freeda claimed she wanted to go for a short drive to see how the car handled but they knew better than to believe her.

Lottie tapped her lip, forehead creased in concern. "Maybe you should have gone with her. I'm not sure about that car. You know she won't turn around until she gets to wherever she and Daphne were."

"She'll call if it breaks down. Maybe we should go shopping in Taos. It would serve her right if it does break down and we're not here. You look like you're dressed for some leisure time." Perhaps during a drive with nothing to do but talk, her mother might loosen up about the mystery of Marco.

Lottie jammed her hands into the pockets of her turquoise jogging suit. Despite the casual attire, her blonde hair was neatly coiffed, make-up in place. "I'm supposed to bowl this afternoon, but I may skip it.

Team Gennaro can do without me for a week. I don't know if I'm up to a trip to Taos though. Why don't we go home and you can sit in the sun while I do some gardening. You need to relax. You girls did a lot of hard work last night."

Thinking of Tony and his wistful glances, Cere grinned. Was her mother clueless about his interest? He had offered to help cater the party and bring over a crew to clean up afterward. Lottie settled for letting him provide dessert.

"You should go bowling, Mom. You owe it to Mr. Gennaro. That tiramisu and those cannolis were wonderful. Don't worry about me. I'll go home and relax in the sun."

She dropped a hand to Cere's arm and squeezed it. "Good idea. It's time you took it easy."

Cere was only partially sincere about relaxing. Mainly she wanted time alone. With her mother and Freeda occupied she had time to study the list of burned businesses that was stuffed in her bag. Was Mrs. Peabody right? Had no one suffered as a result of the fires? That would eliminate payback for the fires as a motive for killing Marco. Why would anyone want Marco dead? To stop the fires? That was rather extreme. What could Naldo have possibly known that might have resulted in his death? If he had known the truth about Marco's death, why keep quiet all those years? And why speak out now?

Her phone beeped. Freeda must be stranded already. Her pulse quickened when she saw Alan's name on the display instead.

"Hey, boss, did you get the pictures? I was thinking of doing a blog—"

"Not on that Paladin place." He mispronounced the name—probably on purpose. "That idea is crap. You're not a crime reporter, Cere. I pay you to work the Hollywood beat."

"You're not paying me at all, remember?"

"Yeah, and I won't be, if you don't do what I tell you. Stop sending me stuff. You're on vacation. Act like it. Go to Taos and do a blog on galleries. I might pay for that."

A sudden spark ran through Cere. "Really? I could get off suspension?"

His laugh came through the phone as a bark. "Maybe. Listen, hon, I had dinner with a couple of network guys last night. I get the feeling they're unhappy with Gail. Her work has suffered since you left."

"I kept telling you she was stealing my stuff."

"I think they're discovering it wasn't just Audrey's pictures making the stories work."

"What are you saying… I could…" Her breathing had grown quick and shallow and she wasn't even moving. She'd stopped, fearing a loss of the phone signal.

"Don't get your hopes up, babe, but Audrey's been talking you up."

Her heart rate accelerated as a jolt of pleasure surged through her. Thanks, Audrey! She'd owe her camerawoman a bottle of champagne if this came through. "Do you want me back tomorrow?"

"Stay there. Look around. You're good at coming up with story ideas. Find something to blog about, you know, some Hollywood aspect."

Cere felt like she was exploding with glee and her

insides felt like a bubbly cauldron of joy. A sudden thought hit her. "How about Tres Padres?"

"Trays what?"

"Tres. As in Three Padres. Don't ask me what it means, but the other day I heard about this new luxury spa they're building nearby. It's supposed to be aimed at attracting a Hollywood clientele. How about that? No one's done anything yet. We could get the first look."

"Yeah, sure, great! Get some pictures and work up a blog. Make me proud, babe."

Chapter Thirty

Cere felt like dancing on air all the way home. She tried calling Freeda but got no answer and left a message asking her to call. She knew better than to say they might be heading home. Her goofy cousin definitely would take off for parts unknown.

Wow, she could get back to work! Or move up to the network! She set up her laptop on the dining room table and plugged into her mother's internet connection. The words "Tres Padres and New Mexico" went into the search engine, but turned up "no results." She tried "Rio Rojo, New Mexico" and got only the map listing and the newspaper website.

Perhaps she should call Stella or Willie Tafoya. A check of Tres Padres on the newspaper's search box again came up empty. Hadn't the men at the Matador joked about the place? Hadn't Bradley Foster mentioned it? A quick call to his office failed. He was out.

She tapped the side of the computer in disgust. Now what? She twisted in her chair and spied the leather book inside the laptop case. She would have to return it to Frank before she left. She picked it up and opened it, peering at the picture of Marco. His smudged eyes stared accusingly as though he knew she might abandon her search for the truth about his death. Poor Marco. Would he haunt her again when she returned to

Los Angeles?

She shoved the book away from her. "Leave me alone!"

The book slid sideways falling from the table to the ground. As it did, several sheets flew out. Damn, she'd unglued the pages. She reached for it and found the sheets hadn't been pasted in. They were separate musical sheets that were tucked into the book. The yellowed pages were filled in with penciled musical notes above smudged words that were almost unreadable.

"Damn ghost," she muttered, standing. She wasn't going to strain her eyes. She was going to forget Marco and spend the afternoon getting a tan and reading through the brochures Freeda had picked up. Perhaps one of them was about Tres Padres.

If she couldn't find any information, she'd head for Taos in the morning to look for stories. After donning a bikini, she grabbed a towel and a tube of sun screen. Stopping in the dining room to pick up the brochures she glanced again at the scrapbook. A blast of air from the air conditioner vent ruffled the pages as though Marco called out not to be forgotten.

With a sigh, she touched the clippings and the sheets of songs. Maybe a quick read? Her mother kept glasses all over the house. They could keep her from suffering eye strain from the smudged words. Oh, hell, why not?

The afternoon sun warmed her skin as Cere stretched out on a chaise. Butterflies flew lazily, teasing her hair. From overhead came the cry of a turtle dove. In the distance the steady buzz of a lawn mower churned out the pleasant scent of newly cut grass. She applied sun screen, sat back and began reading the yellowed pages. Had Marco written these lines?

All we want is justice, freedom, the right to love
Built of skin and bone by our Lord above.
We strive for lives of harmony and peace.
Believing in dignity, rights and our equality.
We battle for honor through words and deeds
Enduring pain, as we fulfill our daily needs.
Beliefs should not be lost, ideals cannot be bought
We want to grow and live, like our fathers taught.
In freedom, with justice, for what our fathers fought.

She studied the notes above the smudged words, but she wasn't good with music so she couldn't imagine how his song would sound. The sentiments were touching and she could almost see him singing them accompanied by a worn guitar. Perhaps Freeda could borrow a guitar and sing them. Her phone buzzed and she grabbed it. Speak of the devil.

"Hey, babe, I was just thinking about you. Where are you? I need your musical talents."

"I'm on my way to Taos."

She shot up on her lounger. "What? Why?"

"You know my dad loved to paint. I've been thinking maybe someone there has seen him."

"When are you coming back? Do you have money? Where will you stay?"

"Nena is making reservations and picking up the bill. She'll wire money if I need it. *Prima*, I know what you're thinking, but I gotta do this. Besides, you have Marco."

"Actually, Freeda, Alan may want me back."

"What?" A screech came across the line. "Not yet!

We're on vacation."

"*You're* on vacation. I'm on suspension. If I come up with a story idea I might get back on the payroll. He's letting me blog again. And there's more. Audrey's been talking to her network boss. I might get Gail's job."

Freeda's shriek almost made her drop the phone. "But we can't go back yet. I just need a few more days. Come on…"

Cere could read the sound of desperation and it touched her. "Okay, how about doing me a favor in Taos?"

"Sure, babe, anything."

"This is serious, Freeda. Don't blow it off or we will have to go home."

"You can count on me."

"I need a story, something with a star angle. If you come up with an idea, we could stay a few more days. I might even get Alan to send a video crew."

While Freeda wasn't particularly trustworthy, she could be remarkably versatile when she wanted. This might also provide time to complete Marco's story. If Alan didn't want it, maybe the network chief might. Cold cases were a big thing on the network magazine programs and it would demonstrate she was more than a Hollywood reporter.

"I don't know, Cere, I'm gonna be busy…"

"While you're wandering around, ask about Hollywood stars, if anyone has a good story, you know what I'm looking for."

"Hey, that's a good idea for cover. I'll flash my press pass and tell them I'm working for *Scope.* Can I use your name and number?"

"Of course."

"Okay, cuz. I'll get back to you with the goods."

As she sank back onto her chaise lounge, Cere felt uneasy, like she was being watched. The back gate jiggled and she shot up as a pair of bright black eyes focused on her. At first she barely recognized him. Rafe had trimmed his hair to a short, fashionable length and shaved his beard. Without them, he looked younger— and even more handsome. Why hadn't she noticed the lean, chiseled lines of his face before? The strong jaw? A jagged scar zigzagged down the edge of one cheek, keeping his face from perfection, but giving it a rugged appearance. An unsettling buzzing set her senses spinning, and warmth flooded her.

"What are you up to, Tafoya?"

He drew back, clearly defensive. His eyes darted away. "I'm looking for my daughter. She likes to play with Roxie." His fingers tugged at his chin, the trademark of a man used to facial hair.

"Roxie's inside. I haven't seen Ginny."

"I left her with a neighbor while I got a haircut, and she disappeared."

Cere felt warm under his gaze and she reached for a gauzy cover up. He turned away, face slightly red. Was he affected by the sight of her in a bikini? The idea sent another spark of awareness through her.

He scanned the yard, eyes anywhere but on her. "Tell her to come home if you see her."

"I'll keep an eye out for her. She's a sweet little girl. Must take after her mother."

Rafe shoved his hands in his back pockets. "Actually she does. I hope she grows up to be just like her. Her mother was a wonderful woman. Smart too."

Rebecca Grace

His wistful voice touched Cere. Here was a man who still loved his dead wife.

"I'm sorry. That was a cheap shot. Do you miss her?"

"Naturally. So does Ginny. She needs a mother. Mom thinks I should remarry for that reason."

The thought startled her. "That's crazy!"

"Maybe. Hell, forget it. I have to find Ginny." He flicked a hand as though swatting a fly, the macho man caught in a personal discussion that required a show of emotion.

"I'll watch for her."

The buzzing of the mower stopped, and stillness enveloped them. Cere waited for Rafe to leave, but he hesitated. Was he waiting for her to comment on his appearance? Why had he changed his looks? Could it have something to do with her? She thought about the electric sparks she felt when she was close to him.

Rafe fought to slow his quickened breath. The sight of a partially-clad Cere stretched out on a chaise was not what he had expected when he let himself into Lottie's backyard. Seeing her in a bikini started a racing in his blood. He fought the sensation plus the tightness in his jeans. The sheer force of his physical reaction stirred up disturbing fears of disloyalty to Carmen. It didn't seem right to find another woman so desirable.

He told himself she wasn't the reason he chopped off the beard and hair. His mother had been hounding him for months to do it, but after seeing Cere that morning, something had just hit him to do it. During his lunch hour he'd gone for the works. Now he felt exposed. The beard and hair had been with him since Carmen died.

282

Looking down, he noticed a leather book at her feet. "What are you reading?"

Cere picked up a sheaf of pages. "Frank gave me some of Marco's songs. Considering his background and that he didn't graduate from high school, they're actually impressive."

"Some of us homeboys are pretty smart. Even if we didn't go to fancy schools or graduate from expensive universities."

"I'm not being patronizing. I think it proves my point that he was special." She rose from the chair and moved toward him.

Below the cover up, a thin layer of sweat welled in the golden valley between her breasts. Heat seized him. Then cold. He felt quivery all over. He dragged his gaze from the tempting sight.

"Let me know if you see Ginny."

The sudden touch of her fingers on his bare arm was like a searing burn, but he savored it even as it scorched his senses.

"Rafe, I am sorry for my stupid comment. Actually, I think you're a pretty special guy."

His heart skipped as his breathing accelerated. Rafe wanted to lift the hand and hold it. Touch it to his lips. He wanted his fingers or lips to explore her velvety skin, but that wasn't going to happen.

He flashed a quick smile, purposely adopting a teasing demeanor. "You're not so bad yourself, Medina. At least now I know there's a woman in there."

Her breathing grew shallow and her parted lips tugged at him. Then she slapped his arm. "More woman than you can handle, Tafoya. I treat romance like I do reporting. If I go after a story or a man, I get the job done."

Her lips drew him. The temptation was too great. He leaned forward, and his lips brushed hers, a fleeting touch aimed at teasing her. Like a magnet her lips caught his, held them. A sudden surge of desire raced through him, stronger than he had felt in years. Then images of Carmen floated across his eyes and guilty pangs pulled him back.

"Yep, I bet you do treat a man like a story. Use him until you're finished and then move on to the next." He touched her soft lips with a finger before jerking away and turning to the gate.

Cere sank to the chaise, shaky fingers on her lips, knees weak. What a strange encounter. Her lower body tingled with desire. She wanted Rafe to kiss her, *really* kiss her.

She'd seen fire in his dark eyes, and they warmed her skin more than the summer sun. She'd wanted to feel his hands on her bare skin, to feel his hard body against hers.

Why had he pulled back after that brief touch? Thank goodness he had left—before he noticed her hard breathing or saw the hardness of her nipples. A few more minutes and she'd have thrown him to the ground and they would have been wrapped around each other's naked bodies.

No! She couldn't get romantically entangled. Long distance relationships didn't work, and she would not give up her dream of working at the network for anyone.

A sudden movement in the corner of the yard drew her attention. Ginny bolted from behind the house, a mischievous grin splattered across her face. "Hi."

Cere summoned a stern voice. "Your Dad is looking for you."

"I know," she said, wrinkling her nose.

How long had Ginny been lurking? Had she seen them? She studied Ginny, recalling his comment that she needed a mother.

In a pastel play set of shorts and T-shirt, with hair held in pigtails by pink and blue ribbons, she looked like a little girl who was loved and cared for down to the red, white and blue bandage on one knee.

His parents said he gave up his career to get Ginny out of the city. Would he put his own happiness on the line and marry simply to give her a mother?

"You shouldn't hide from your dad."

"He was going to leave me with Aunt Lela. I'd rather be with Roxie and the bunnies." She shrugged her thin shoulders, a wistful expression on her young face.

A feeling of sympathy overwhelmed Cere. The girl appeared so small. It must be tough growing up without a mother. "Ginny, why don't you make new friends?"

Her innocent smile was disarming. "You're my new friend."

"I meant kids."

Ginny's shiny hair danced around her head as she shook one pigtail loose. "I don't like the kids. My cousins are big and mean. They pushed me in the dirt last time I was there."

Cere recalled instances with older cousins who pushed her and Freeda around when they were little. Those experiences had bonded them. "Come here. Let me fix your hair."

She approached and Cere brushed through the

strands with her fingers and pulled out one bow that was about to fall off. She started to re-braid her hair, but Ginny pulled away. "That hurts."

"I'm sorry. You had a tangle."

"My dad never hurts when he fixes my hair."

She chuckled. "Your dad is better at this. I'm not used to taking care of little girls."

Wide, searching eyes turned up to Cere. "Do you like my dad?"

"He's nice."

"My grandma asked him if he liked you."

Her heart did a wild flip flop. Was his mother playing matchmaker? "What did he say?"

A thin shoulder lifted in a shrug. "He said you're okay. Too obsessed with work."

Obsessed? Was that how he saw her? Her efforts to retie the ribbon failed and Ginny fidgeted until she gave up. How did Rafe manage?

The gate jiggled, and Rafe came through. He ignored Cere, stern eyes on Ginny.

"I knew I'd find you here. Didn't you hear me calling? Come on, Munchkin, the lady has more important things to do than deal with missing children." He patted Ginny's shiny head gently.

The small face jerked to Cere, her black eyes pleading. "Can't I stay here? I'll be good."

She felt her insides melt at the appeal. "Why don't you let her stay? I'm not doing anything except sitting in the sun. She can play with Roxie and Mom will be back soon."

His dark eyes met hers, and a smile tugged at his lips. One eyelash fluttered like a raven's wing. "I'm going to take you up on that just to keep you out of trouble. Why don't you bring her to the Matador later and I'll buy dinner. Call if she proves too much to handle."

Cere fought a sudden bout of giddiness as her bones turned liquid, threatening to deposit her on the grass in a puddle of sunscreen. Was he asking her out? Her nod was quick.

Rafe leaned over and kissed Ginny's head. "Behave, baby. Don't get in trouble and do what she says." His eyes flicked up at Cere. "I think this might be better for you than her."

For the rest of the afternoon, Ginny played with Roxie while Cere read the smudged words of the songs. Damn ghost. She could feel his cold fingers reaching out to reclaim her interest. The man who wrote these words of peace was not the sort to despair and kill himself. He had no material goods, but did he care? He worked on ranches—what kind of a threat could he pose? Or maybe it was a charade. He preached peace while breaking into stores, taking his revenge, stealing money with the idea of moving on.

She shivered as shadows began to cover the back yard. Ginny sat on a chair, skinny arm stretched out, and eyes blinking. Some babysitter. She hadn't noticed the little girl was falling asleep. Cere carried her inside and put her on the sofa, covering her with a blanket.

A sudden noise startled her and mail slid through the slot on the bottom of the front door. She walked over to pick it up. A medium sized manila envelope caught her eye. It was addressed to her. Who would send her mail? The postmark was Rio Rojo the previous day. The envelope rattled as she shook it. Cere slit it open and peered inside. A shiny gold circle was visible.

She poured out the contents. The smashed face of her lost watch slid into her hand. A single piece of paper fluttered to the floor. She unfolded the note and gasped.

Don't let this happen to you.

Chapter Thirty-One

Cere fought to calm her nerves as she slid into the booth across from Rafe. She couldn't keep from looking at his lips. Why hadn't she noticed them before—nicely formed, pouty, kissable? She folded her arms to hide goose bumps. She had more important things to think about than kissing.

She had pretended she wasn't dressing special for him as she put on a denim skirt and a pair of her mother's huaraches. The skirt was short enough to show off the newly acquired tan on her legs. A fitted sleeveless white cotton blouse also showed off her tan, as it nicely outlined her breasts. She chose the simple combination because she knew he wouldn't look favorably on silk and spiky sandals. After taking time on her make-up and pinning up her hair, Cere decided she looked good.

Would Rafe notice? Why did she care what he thought anyway? Was this a real date? Or just a payback for babysitting? Besides, she didn't have time for frivolity. She had more serious things on her mind.

Ginny settled onto the bench beside him. His big fingers began fixing her bows, which were falling again.

"Did you behave?" he asked.

Ginny's young face was solemn as she nodded. "I fed the bunnies and Roxie, and Cere fixed me a peanut butter sandwich and an apple."

Cere shrugged at his questioning look. "After you called to say not to bring her until seven, I decided she needed to eat."

"Can I go play?" Ginny asked.

"Sure. Grandma's coming to get you in a few minutes."

Ginny slid off the bench and hopped over to the play area in the back of the restaurant. Cere glanced around, surprised at the thinning crowd.

"Is it always this quiet? I'd have thought this place really got going once the sun went down."

"People eat early. It's busiest at five. I'm sorry I'm late. That happens…"

"You're talking to a journalist, Tafoya." She leaned across the table, speaking in a low voice so no one could hear. "Anything I need to know? Like about Diaz?"

He grunted and leaned forward too, clasping his hands together. "There's something there, but I can't pin it down. He's not working at Tres Padres. They're contracting out their project to a Santa Fe company. I called them, but he's not on their work rolls. It looks like that parcel of land may be privately owned through some deal that I haven't been able to track down. All I know is the owner is from Dallas, and that's where he's from so maybe he works for them."

Before Cere could reply, Frank brought out an order for a customer and waved toward their booth.

"Hey, Rafe, Cere, be with you in a minute."

"Take your time," Rafe called back. "Just get Ginny a little cheeseburger to go."

"Actually I'm not very hungry," Cere admitted.

The thought of food, even one of Frank's delicious bowls of chili, didn't appeal to her.

He seemed to sense her unease. "Something wrong?"

Cere tugged at her lip, not certain how to tell him what had happened.

"Did you find something in the songs?"

In reply she removed an envelope from her bag and poured the contents on the table. The broken crystal of her watch and its insides made a tinny sound as they rolled across the surface.

"You found it?" Surprise turned to anger. "You didn't take Ginny to the Palladium and then instruct her to tell me that story about the rabbits."

Cere licked her lips and swallowed hard, trying to get some saliva into her dry mouth. "It came in the mail." She turned over the envelope and pointed at her name and address.

"You're thinking whoever locked you in the room sent it?"

"It had to be. How else would they know it was mine?" Cere pulled out the note that accompanied the watch and handed it to him.

Rafe read it over, handsome face tense and concerned. "Damn, this is getting crazy."

"It's worse," she admitted.

"Huh?" A frown furrowed his brow, and Rafe glanced quickly around the room, as though afraid their words would be overheard.

The time had come to be totally honest. "I told you about the message warning me not to look into the Marco case? The other day someone called the house and left another—that if I keep asking about Marco, I could end up like Naldo."

Trouble brewed in his dark eyes as he slid the contents back into the envelope. "Why the hell didn't you tell me about that call as soon as it happened? Or this? Maybe you should give up on the story."

"I knew that's what you'd say. That's why I kept quiet. Don't you think this is further proof the deaths are related? Maybe that's why they're trying to stop me."

"Whoever sent this watch wants you to stop investigating. It could be the person who hid the box, but we don't know that. Nor do we know it's the same person who warned you off Marco or who shot Naldo. I can't deal in supposition, Cere. I need facts."

"Why would two people do the same thing? Leave messages like that? I've been thinking. Maybe the money in that box was the stolen cash, Marco's treasure."

"You're not thinking of putting that theory into your story, are you?" His disgusted tone left no question of what he thought.

"I'm just trying to come up with different ideas." Cere pressed her hands together, trying to shake off the feeling of unease she'd had ever since receiving the envelope.

Frank came out of the back and approached the table, carrying plastic glasses of water and two menus. "Got the cheeseburger going. Do you need menus?"

"I'm just going to have green chili," Cere said, despite her lack of hunger.

"I'll have the *carne asada*," Rafe said, "and can you bring us a big manila envelope if you have one?"

Frank looked from one to the other. "Envelope?

Yeah, sure, I got some in the back."

When he was gone, Cere leaned forward again. "So you recognize that it's evidence."

"I'm being thorough but I'm not going to get involved in a wild goose chase trying to link Marco to Naldo's death. I don't think they're related." His dark eyes shot arrows at her across the table, face becoming set, a nerve pulsing along his jawline.

Frank returned with a large manila envelope and handed it to Rafe. Once Frank turned back toward the counter, Rafe used a napkin to lift the other enveloped by a corner. He slid it into the larger mailer and sealed it.

"It may be a long shot, but I'll send it to the crime lab in Santa Fe. We found the watch band in the same room as the box so it stands to reason the watch was there too. Has anyone else touched this envelope? Your mom? Freeda?"

"No. Think about it, Rafe, if they aren't related, you could have two killers in Rio Rojo. No one wants to think that violence happens here. It's why everyone is so eager to say Marco committed suicide. But Naldo's death shows bad things do happen."

Rafe looked away, hands clenched on the table. "You don't know what it's like to fear you can't keep the people around you safe. I'm supposed to keep order. That's my job. To look out for people."

Her fingers slid over his fists. "You're doing your job, but you can't make the world perfect. Even here."

His dark eyes flashed on her angrily as he jerked away. "You do your stories and never worry about people getting hurt. You don't realize there are real people behind those stories."

His anger stunned her. "Don't turn this around on me."

"Do you ever think about it? When you chased that actor kid, did you consider you might be hurting him? That you were invading his privacy when you interrupted what should have been a happy, private moment of homecoming?"

"You're changing the subject. What about Naldo? Are you ignoring the truth so you can pretend this is a safe town?"

He flinched as though she had delivered a major blow.

"You can't save the world, Rafe, any more than you could save your wife. You do your job and keep order as best as possible."

He grunted, shaking his head. "You'll never understand."

"You're right. I don't understand why you won't help me. Even just a little."

Behind him, the door opened with a jingle of the bell and he turned as his mother entered and walked toward them. Rafe's face softened in a look of relief and he rose to kiss her cheek when she got to the table.

"Thanks for coming to get Ginny, Mom. Frank's fixing her a burger."

Stella placed long burgundy nails on the edge of the table and smiled as her dark eyes swept from one to the other. "You two have a nice dinner. What do you think of his new look, Cere? *Muy guapo*, no?"

Cere grinned back and put her thumb and forefinger together in a gesture of approval while Rafe's face grew red.

"I'll go get Ginny for you."

Once Stella and Ginny were gone, Frank brought out their meals. The spicy fragrance of chili and the smoky scent of grilled meat drifted up in a pleasing aroma, but Cere wasn't hungry. Rafe dug into his meat, chewing slowly, but she only pushed the pork and chili around. Finally she tapped her spoon on the bowl.

"There's something else I need to tell you."

He put down his fork, a look of resignation on his face. "I was hoping that break finished that discussion."

"Last night after the party, while I was cleaning up I swear I saw a boot print outside the yard. The same one from the hill by the Palladium." She grew cold just saying the words.

"Is it still there? Why didn't you tell me earlier?"

"It was gone this morning. That was why I haven't said anything, but think about it, the person who was shooting at us could have been at our party. Or peeking in from outside the gate. I thought I saw Diaz's car parked down the block."

"Cere…"

"Okay, okay," she said holding up her hands. "I know, I'm accusing him again, but to be honest, I don't know or remember half the people at the party, but one of them may be the person sending these notes. Think about that person in your safe little town."

He stiffened and his jaw tightened but he didn't answer. Fire rose in his dark eyes and for an instant she feared an angry reaction. Instead when he finally spoke, his words came out in a low monotone.

"Okay. Marco's sister was probably the person closest to him, besides Naldo. Her son has the letters he sent her. He let me read a couple, but they were so private, I couldn't keep reading, and I sure as hell wasn't giving them to Riggins. Gus might show them to you if I call him." His black eyes swiveled around to catch hers, pulling her in until she felt like she was drowning.

She dropped her gaze, her body warm. "I've called him, but Len told me he's working up at a ranch. I've left several messages, but he's never returned my calls."

"I'll call him and ask him to answer your questions."

"Thanks." She reached over and touched his hand, and he turned his hand up and caught her fingers, giving them a slight squeeze. Her heart began to thud as he smiled and winked.

"Maybe you deserve a little help. You did take care of Ginny for me. Who knows when I'll need another favor."

Sparks of fire ignited on her skin from her hairline to her toes. The fingers he still held were on fire. "Remember that, Sheriff."

"But can we change the subject? Isn't there anything else we can talk about?"

Her heart was thudding and she held onto his hand, squeezing it. She felt a smile splash across her face, like the sun bursting through a cloud. Another idea hit her, a safer one. "I keep hearing about Tres Padres. Is there anything you know about it? You said they're-building."

"No ghosts out there," he said.

She slapped his hand away playfully. "I might want to do a blog."

"There's not much to know. You should talk to Uncle Willie. He's written stories for the newspaper. Why are you smiling like the cat that just ate the canary?"

Cere couldn't admit it was because of a lead on Tres Padres. Or maybe it was because he had finally agreed to help her. Hell, actually she just suddenly felt giddy.

He wagged a finger at her, but in a playful way. "Don't take my help on those letters the wrong way. I still don't want that story blown up into a tabloid expose. If I think you're heading that way, I'll come after you worse than whoever sent that watch."

The words sounded like a threat and she started to fire back at him, but a slow smile drew his lips up, and she felt herself melting inside as his eyes grew warm.

"You don't want me to come after you, Medina," he said, in a low voice that made her tingle all over. "Because I always get what I want too."

Chapter Thirty-Two

A tense, skinny man of about twenty stood outside when Cere answered a sharp rap on the door. With a thin, almost pretty face and long sweeping lashes, he reminded her of waiters in Los Angeles who wanted to become actors.

"Hi, I'm Gus." He extended an elegant, fine-boned hand. "Rafe said you wanted to see these?" He offered a worn thick manila envelope held together with a rubber band.

"Thanks, I'm Cere. I could have come by your house. Would you like to come in?"

"I'm on my way to work." He wore the orange-red uniform of a discount house.

A twinge of disappointment touched her. Cere had been pleased to see the packet, but she wanted to talk to Gus about his uncle. "I thought you worked up at a ranch?"

"Part time. Mr. Diaz lets me work there when I'm available."

The name grabbed her, and she stiffened. "Diego Diaz? He's in charge?"

He lifted a thin shoulder. "I guess."

"How long has he been working there? He doesn't seem to know many people in town."

"Most of the Hollister Ranch people don't come into Rio Rojo. The main road from the ranch goes west into Casitas."

"May I call you later? If I have questions?"

"Yeah, but I don't know much about the songs. I just found them." His head dropped, a long lock of hair falling over his eyes. "See, my mom died a coupla months ago. I found these songs and letters when I was cleanin' out her house."

Anticipation buzzed in Cere's head. What if these new letters held the key to Marco's death? "Thank you so much for bringing them over. I can't tell you how much I appreciate it."

The instant the door closed she carried the envelope to the dining room table. Luckily she had the house all to herself. Her mother was getting her hair done and Freeda remained in Taos.

She tore open the package and dumped out two packets of envelopes. All were old, the ink faded with age. The envelopes were standard, and the stationery was the cheap lined variety that came in a tablet. The letters to his sister were poignant, and tears filled Cere's eyes as she read through them. They were written when he first went away to jail. The uneven scribbling portrayed a teenager unskilled in proper grammar or spelling.

I miss you all more then I knew I could—I wish I could bring it all back and do the things they want me to do. Don't ever go to jail. It's a sad empty place.

One of these days the truth will came out and I can came home. I don't know why I am send here for something I didn't not do. Someday everyone will know they was wrong about me.

The letter sounded as though he had been telling the truth when he said he did not commit the original crimes, but slowly the tone changed, from one of hope to one of resentment.

I hate this prison and being here. Being locked up is the worst that can happen to a man. I can't do nothing without permission, cannot go outside when I feel like it. I don't know why no one could tell the truth. I'll never forgive the people who put me here. You'll see. I'll get them all. Expecially her.

The words chilled Cere. *Her?* Who was he talking about?

Cere did not find much new information in the letters, except Marco became an angry, bitter man. He also grew intellectually, taking classes and working on his writing. In the end he focused his anger not so much on a personal level, but at the system.

I can see why I was an easy target. Rebellious and too immature to see and recognize that I was nothing special, just another cheap hood.

History has always dealt harshly with rebels. My reasons were not even valid. My actions were a show, the vain performance of a confused adolescent.

Cere picked up the second packet and began going through it. These letters were different. They contained songs, but not folk or protest songs. One letter explained them.

I know you think I'm crazy, but I think she regrets what she did. Why would she write me that letter? I wrote this song. I had to do it in Spanish so the guards can't read it. I can't give it to her, but maybe you can. Type it on the old typewriter and translate. Make it nice for her and then give it to her, okay? Tell her to think of me singing it to her, just like the old days down by the pond.

These were love songs, some very touching. A few were written in Spanish. Cere fought tears as she read them. Marco had been a sensitive young man, in love with the wrong woman.

Only one letter referred to the mystery girl as writing to him, but he kept sending love songs to his sister. Had Rafe seen these? What was his take on Marco's ill-fated romance?

Thoughts of Rafe brought a bout of physical awareness. Cere tugged absently at her lip. He always seemed to be on her mind these days. He was like Marco in a lot of ways—putting on the gruff show but she could see the sensitive side. She envied his wife whom he described so reverently. It was obvious he kept a warm place in his heart for her. Could anyone ever replace her? Cere chased away those thoughts. Someone might, but it wouldn't—couldn't—be her.

****

Carrying her video camera, Cere walked from one end of the downtown Rio Rojo main street to the next. She stopped on one corner to photograph the street that had once burned, noting the newer buildings. Only at one end where she could see exposed brick that was painted over with white could she tell where the old town ended and the fire stopped.

On one side block she saw a sign for the *Rio Rojo News.* She walked down the street until she was in front. The name was printed across the plate glass window in gold script and she could see Stella behind a high counter inside.

While her mind was on the Gonzales story, Cere hesitated. Since she was here, perhaps she should stop in and see if Willie had time to talk to her about Tres

Padres. Rafe hadn't provided many answers the night before. Mainly they'd flirted and verbally sparred.

Stella looked up, saw Cere and waved. "How nice of you to come by," she said, walking around the counter as Cere entered. "Ginny told me about her afternoon with you. Quite a little handful, isn't she?"

Cere grasped her fingers and squeezed them. "She's fun. I'll do it any time."

"You looking for Rafe? Or Ginny?" She tilted her head to the side. Beyond the counter, Cere saw an open entrance that yawned into the back area, which hummed with activity. The scene was chaotic, reminiscent of *Scope* at deadline, except on a more modest scale. Several people sat at battered desks in front of computer screens frantically typing on keyboards. Their faces carried identical looks of determination and concentration.

To Cere's surprise Rafe sat at one of the desks, tapping at a keyboard with two fingers. They moved like pistons. He was concentrating so hard on his work he didn't notice her arrival.

"The sheriff is writing for the paper?" she asked, pausing by his desk. Hadn't his father mentioned that Rafe had a degree in journalism?

"I help out every so often," he acknowledged, stopping. He surprised her with a warm smile. "This becomes a family operation when help is short and there's a deadline."

"I won't interfere."

He hit a key and looked across the desk to his uncle, who was also at a keyboard, horn-rimmed glasses perched on his nose. "There's the story on the high school requirements, Uncle Willie. Got anything else?"

"Thanks. Hi, Cere." Willie waved and tapped his keyboard, his face carrying the demeanor of a man with too many things on his mind. He turned to a thin-faced blonde who was toiling away at another keyboard.

"Caroline, where's the story on the drugstore closing? All I have here is the press release from their Santa Fe office. Did you ever call the place?"

"I didn't have time. We can use the release and follow up later."

"I hate using straight releases," he said with a heavy sigh. "Maybe I'll hold it until next week."

"Want me to do it?" Rafe asked.

Willie whirled toward them. "I need you to do the water rights story and road closures."

Rafe snapped his fingers and sat back at his keyboard. Cere drew a deep inner breath and stepped forward.

"I can do the drug store story," she volunteered.

Rafe drew back, dark eyes wide with surprise. "You?"

"I can write. Besides, you helped me. Gus brought by the letters so I owe you; I might as well repay your uncle."

"You helped me too." He gestured toward Ginny who sat in a back corner at a small, plastic desk, dark head bent over a coloring book.

"I know, but maybe we can talk later about the letters."

He rolled his eyes and chuckled. "I should've known. You wouldn't volunteer without an ulterior motive. Take the help, Willie. I want to see if she is a reporter, like her card says."

The rebuke was issued in a teasing way, and Cere took it in that spirit. "Maybe I want to show you I can write."

"Okay." Willie held up a sheet of paper. "Here's the release. Give me two inches."

"Two inches?" She wrote in minutes. How long was a story that ran two inches?

"Newspaper talk," Rafe said. "Just write it. We'll let you know if it's long enough. And try not to make it too tabloid."

Cere tossed down her purse. "I can write, Tafoya! Prepare to be dazzled."

Willie punched the keyboard of a nearby computer and the screen flashed to life. "I've got you logged on. Just click on the post button and it will come to me for the final edit and I'll send it on to composing. Do you mind explaining to her how to use the word processing system?" he asked his nephew.

Rafe's glance swept over her, and her heart thudded. His dark eyes smoldered as he agreed. He leaned down and she caught the tangy scent of his aftershave as he brushed across her to capture the computer mouse. Luckily she had a vague idea how to use the program. She certainly wasn't learning from him. Her senses were too aware of the big hands maneuvering the mouse, the dark hair sprouting from the neck of his white shirt, which was open at the collar and the muscles of his biceps as he moved.

"You all set?" he asked finally, looking down at her.

Cere blinked, fearing he might notice how distracted she was, so she simply nodded. As he moved away, she settled herself at the computer and read the release. It explained the local chain drug store was one of dozens being closed in the state. Cere looked for Rafe, but he was on the phone. She turned to Willie.

"What about current prescriptions? This doesn't say when the drug store is closing."

Willie gave her a blank stare. "That's why the release should be rewritten."

Cere nodded. What a stupid question. That was why he had been looking for the re-write. She needed to get the information, and given his busy demeanor, she had to do it on her own. "Is there a phone book around here?"

"Phone book?" Willie asked, brow furrowed.

"I want to get a quote from the local manager." She would have looked it up online, but she wasn't certain the computer linked to the internet.

He tapped a pencil eraser on the copy. "Yes, but you don't need to take that much time."

"Is she causing trouble?" Rafe had the phone to his ear, but his attention focused on them.

"She's looking for a phone book to get quotes," Willie said.

"Don't make up quotes if you don't get the guy," Rafe warned.

She started to protest, but a full smile crossed his lips, followed by a wink that set her pulse racing. Cere crumpled a piece of paper and threw it at him. "I don't make up quotes."

He tossed back a thin book that contained white and yellow pages. She located the number and made the phone call.

Twenty minutes later she looked over at Willie. "I've emailed that story to you. Anything else I can help write?"

He stopped typing, a surprised look on his face. "You got quotes and wrote the story?"

"I'm used to daily deadlines. I could run over and take a picture of the store if you want. I have a digital camera with me."

Willie turned to his computer. "Let me look it over." He punched a couple of keys and busied himself reading. When he looked up after reading it, she saw approval in his eyes.

"Nicely done." He flashed a sign of approval to Rafe. "Thanks. You brought me a winner."

Rafe's nod warmed Cere, generating an unwelcome heat in her lower body. She glanced around, pretending to be indifferent. "Do you have a soda machine?"

"In back," Willie said. "I'll buy if you'll help me with a couple of other stories."

"Deal."

As she walked by, Rafe brushed her arm. "Nice going. He isn't easy to please."

Chapter Thirty-Three

Sitting back on the hard wooden chair, Cere rubbed her eyes. She was too tired to move. A glance at the clock above her told her why. The red digital numbers read one-thirty.

Rafe placed a cup of hot chocolate in front of her and leaned against the desk. Willie had left moments ago after sending the weekly edition to the printer.

"Thanks for the help," he said. "It's usually not this hectic, but one of the reporters quit last week and Uncle Willie is taking his time replacing him. He's hoping my cousin, Estrella, returns from Albuquerque. She got laid off last month and hasn't found anything. He doesn't pay much, but she'd have a place to live."

Cere started to comment that Estrella probably wanted to make it on her own, but stopped. Instead she gratefully sipped the warm, sweet liquid. "Maybe she knows how tough this job is. I didn't realize a weekly newspaper could be so difficult."

"Some weeks it is." He turned a chair around, straddling it, arms resting on the back.

She tried not to focus on the thick forearms with their mat of dark hair. She feared he could hear her heart thudding. The large cluttered room was unnaturally silent.

"What a tough life—long hours as sheriff, taking care of Ginny, working for your uncle."

"I don't mind. Reporting was my first job. When I went to Los Angeles I worked the crime beat. It helped me decide to change careers. I could see how hard Carmen was working as a teacher. I wanted to be one of those directly doing something so I went into law enforcement."

"Now you want to help this little town?"

A heavy sigh escaped him as his gaze traveled around the darkened room. "This place means a lot to me."

She licked her lips, curious about how much he might open up. "Was your wife from here?"

"No. We met in college. We talked about coming back, but I wanted to stay in the city."

"She must have supported that."

He lowered his head, hesitating before giving his answer in a soft, almost cracking voice. "She'd go wherever I wanted."

She could hear the pain and regret in his tone. Would she ever meet anyone who made her feel that way? "Your dad is pleased you're back. I bet your uncle is too."

"Uncle Willie was the one who urged me to leave. Mom and Dad lived in Albuquerque when I was born but Willie stayed here. He always lived for the paper." Rafe stood and stretched, rubbing his face. "Need a lift? Didn't you say you walked over?"

"This isn't L.A. No need to worry about..." She stopped. She'd almost said "violence."

Reaching for her bag she noticed the envelope with Marco's songs. "Oh, Marco's cousin brought me these. I don't think you've seen them. Do you have time to take a quick look?"

Exhaustion sat on Rafe like a heavy cloak, but he couldn't refuse her request. She had helped out and he owed her. She'd looked so focused as she worked. The stories might be inconsequential to her, but she gave each her full attention. Now she looked at him with a hopeful smile. He took one of the worn pages and read it. He had never seen it before. The words surprised him.

"You're certain this is his?"

"Yes, why?"

"Frank showed me some of his stuff—all folk songs. My Spanish isn't good, but this is a love song."

"I know. Remember the spurned girlfriend? Apparently Marco wrote these when he was in jail and mailed them to his sister so she could type them and give them to the girl."

The hair rose on the back of his neck. "Who was she?"

"I don't know. I read every letter, but he never gives her name."

Rafe was too tired to think about the meaning of the love songs. He wished Cere would simply drop this. What difference did any of it make?

She rose to stand beside him and he caught a whiff of perfume. A slow steady pounding began in his temples. She leaned close, brushing his arm as she read the page in his hand. He forced himself to ignore her creamy caramel skin.

"I wish my Spanish was better," he admitted.

Taking hold of his hand she pulled the page closer to her. "The loose translation goes something like: 'My life doesn't exist except for you, moments stolen in the night, wanting something that isn't right.' And this one says, 'life isn't worth living without you, but loving you is like reaching for the sun, brightness I can't hold for long.' Very sweet, don't you think?"

Cere dropped his hand, and picked up another page. Rafe attempted to ignore the light that came into her eyes as she read the page in silence. Marco's words seemed to thrill her.

"This is beautiful." She began reading in hushed voice. "'Life has no meaning without love. My love has no meaning without you, my sole reason for living.' He was a poet in a lot of ways."

Her eyes met his, and the night stood still. Marco's tender, soulful words hung between them—lacy, fragile lines. Cere jerked her eyes away. She too seemed to feel the spark.

"There are musical notes here," she added in a high voice that sounded unnatural. "Like he tried to put them to music."

Rafe couldn't stop himself. He leaned down, catching her chin with his hand. Her pink tongue shot out, licking her lips, as his body grew heated and hard. Her eyes closed, and a quickened breath exhaled through parted lips. He leaned toward her. He had to kiss her or explode. Her lips were warm under his. They tasted sweet, like hot chocolate. Images returned of her glistening body in a narrow bikini, and he pulled her into his arms, enjoying the softness of her skin.

His lips gently coaxed hers open until he fully claimed her mouth as her arms wrapped around his neck. His tongue explored her lips then slid inside to touch the hot, moist inner areas. His heart pounded, and hot desire raced through him. He had not wanted anyone this badly in years. No, he wasn't certain he had ever wanted someone so badly.

Her breast filled his hand, and she moaned. Rafe wanted to possess her but he stopped. He'd never been the type to take sex lightly. This wasn't going anywhere, and it was wrong to act as though it might.

With a groan he pulled his hand from her breast and took hold of her shoulders, breaking the kiss. "Cere, wait."

Her eyes were liquid with desire as she opened them. He drew back, dropping his hands from her shoulders. "I'm sorry. I didn't mean to do that."

Her eyes examined his as though searching for something. She seemed to find the answer and turned away, picking up the pages. "Marco's love songs were too much for you to handle." Her tone was light, but the pages rustled. Her hands were shaking.

What would she do if he kissed her again? Took her to bed like his body wanted? Willie had a sofa in the backroom for late nights. No, he couldn't. Instead he drew back and adopted a sarcastic attitude.

"Yeah, he was quite a guy. Hell, look at the time. I need to pick up Ginny. Want a ride?"

"I can walk home." She squeezed his arm and reached for her bag.

Rafe hesitated. "That may not be a good idea. Remember those…"

A finger touched his lips, cutting off his protest as an impish smile crossed her face. "No one's going to hurt me. I have a can of mace in my purse. I dare Diaz to show his face again."

He jerked his head back as though her touch scorched him. He needed to let her go before his

Rebecca Grace

throbbing body took control of his brain.

Cere was stricken by how alone she felt as she walked down the gloomy main street. All the stores windows were dark and even the few neon signs in town had been turned off. Her footsteps clicked hollowly on the sidewalk. Despite her bravado with Rafe, she had to remind herself that the town was safe, even at two in the morning. Behind her, a car started. As it glided around the corner she recognized it as Rafe's.

She pressed her lips together, thinking about their kiss. What would it be like to spend the night with him? His body had been hard against her, and she could feel the desire surging through him. But she had been excited too, aroused by his hand on her breasts and by the sensual touch of his fingers on her skin. She had nearly lost control and begun whimpering with want.

Too bad he had stopped—she certainly wouldn't have. She'd been half teasing when she said she got what she wanted. The only problem was her relationships never worked out. Like Marco?

The words of his love songs filtered through her brain. They were sweet songs of teenage angst. Who was the girl behind them? Surely she could solve that riddle. Stella had said everyone knew each other and their business. Had it always been that way?

The sidewalk gave way to gravel. Damn, she'd been so lost in thought she hadn't paid attention to where she was going. She'd missed the turn home. A quick turn and then another pointed her back in the right direction. The street lamps were spaced farther apart in this outer part of town and there were no sidewalks, but the darkness didn't bother her.

The sound of a car came from behind her, and she smiled, prepared to tease Rafe for his concern. The car picked up speed as it approached and she looked back over her shoulder. The headlights were blinding. That wasn't Rafe.

Her heart pounded as she quickstepped around a corner. The car followed. Damn, what was the driver doing? If it was someone who knew her, wouldn't the person call out the window? But if someone meant to scare her, she wasn't going to let them intimidate her. She fumbled in her purse for the mace, drew out the can and stopped walking. She held the can out toward the lights. At least the car wasn't a black SUV. She could make out a light colored van. Hadn't she seen it, or one like it, parked outside the Matador? Who did it belong to?

She walked toward it, wielding her can, and it shifted into reverse, wheels screeching. Its headlights pointed at her, and the van moved again—this time straight at her. It picked up speed, forcing her to frantically seek refuge. She managed to duck behind a thick tree trunk as the van barreled by.

It roared down the street as her heart thumped loudly. What was the driver trying to do? Frighten her? Hurt her? She turned down a nearby alley and jogged the remaining two blocks to her mother's house, a fearful eye constantly glancing over her shoulder.

To her surprise, lights blazed in the house as it came into view. Fear choked her and she sprinted the final few yards, arriving at the door breathless. First the van, now this. Her mother normally went to bed by ten.

"Mom?" she called, bursting through the door. No

answer. Prickles of dread filled her as she dashed from empty room to empty room.

"Hello?"

Still no answer.

As she stepped into the kitchen she saw several boxes beside the open door to the basement. It yawned with light shining from below. She hopped down the narrow stairs, fearing what might be at the bottom. She drew a breath of relief when she saw her mother sitting between an open footlocker and a wastebasket, sifting through papers.

"Mom, what are you doing?"

Her mother looked up, surprised. "Cleaning."

"It's two in the morning."

"I need to throw this away. My brothers brought it over when I came back, but it's all junk." Her mother appeared agitated.

"Would you like help?" Her brush with danger was forgotten as she faced her distraught mother.

"I can do this alone. You go to bed."

"You can finish tomorrow. Let's both go to bed."

"I want it gone." Lottie waved at the papers. To Cere's surprise, her face looked tear streaked and red. "This is all your fault."

"What do you mean? Did someone threaten you? Say something?"

"No." Her mother sank onto an unopened box, wiping her hand across her face. "It's this...this...hand thing. Why can't you let it go?" Her voice rose until she was nearly shrieking. "He's dead. Stop this before someone else gets killed!"

Cere's heart thumped with dread. "Someone else? What do you mean? Besides Naldo? Or did you mean

Marco?"

Lottie's flushed face stiffened. She looked ready to cry and seemed to battle for composure. With a sniffle, she rose, blinking as though waking up. "I'm sorry. You're right. Let's go to bed."

She started to repeat her question, but her mother brushed by her and pulled the light cord, plunging the basement into shadows.

Chapter Thirty-Four

"Cere? Lottie? Are you down there?" Rafe's voice sounded from the basement door.

"I'm down here," Cere called and his feet clattered on the stairs.

She averted her eyes as his legs came into view, pretending his sudden appearance didn't affect her. Her pulse had started racing the minute she heard him call her name. Memories of his kiss still haunted her.

"What are you doing?" His foot shoved a broken wooden tennis racquet and sideswiped a battered brown trunk. Piles of books, old clothes and trinkets littered the floor next to empty packing boxes.

"Spring cleaning in June. I'm helping Mom. She wanted this stuff thrown out so I'm trying to sort it for her." She brushed a hand over her damp forehead to push her hair out of her eyes. After the uproar of the previous night, she'd been determined to get the area into some semblance of order. She still didn't know why her mother had been so upset.

At least the physical effort kept her mind occupied—away from fears about the van that chased her and the person threatening her. The work also kept her from thinking too much about the man across the room and the tender moments they had shared.

While his presence was welcome, she was suddenly and painfully aware of her mother's cotton boxer shorts and threadbare T-shirt she wore. And she was barefoot. Her hair was partially covered by a scarf, but some of it still managed to escape and fall in her face.

"What is that?" Rafe asked, settling onto a piano bench across from where she sat on a hassock in front of a footlocker.

"It's my mother's old yearbook." Her hands brushed over the embossed silver cover. "This place is a treasure trove. It's a whole side to my mother I'd never seen from her younger years before she went to California."

Rafe reached into the trunk and pulled out a dried corsage. "This really says something." It disintegrated in his hands.

"Rafe, that meant something to her," she scolded.

"How meaningful can it be if she left it behind?" He pulled out a vibrant pink blouse dotted with purple flowers. "People wore this?"

"Look." She held up the book and pointed at a picture on the yellowing page. A pretty blonde teenager with a bow pinned to her long hair smiled at the camera. "That's Mom. Wow, she looked young. And check out that hairdo."

She started to laugh but realized Rafe was frowning at the page. Her eyes focused on the book, and she saw what had caught his attention. A boy with thick black hair smirked at the camera as though he knew a secret no one else shared.

"Marco!" She jerked the yearbook toward her to see the picture better. Even without the hair, Marco would have stood out. He wore tight bell bottom jeans and his shirt was open almost to his waist. A dark choker of some sort, perhaps leather, wrapped around his neck. Like the newspaper picture, intensity burned in his dark eyes. His curled lip indicated a defiance of authority.

Excitement pulsed through her as she flipped pages, seeking more pictures of him. "I can use these pictures. I *knew* they had to be in school together. Maybe Mom knows who Marco's girl was."

Rafe nodded, dark eyes unreadable. He stroked his chin as though the beard remained. His fingers moved on to touch his lower lip.

She dropped her head as memories of their fevered kiss sent a shiver of awareness racing through her.

"May I look at that?" he asked.

Handing the book to him, she scrambled to her feet. The open basement area seemed to shrink as his large presence filled the restricted area where she'd been working. His tangy aftershave overshadowed the dusky sent of dampness. As he flipped through pages, she turned away searching for more material in the trunk.

"Look at this." His call jerked her around. A long finger jabbed at a picture in the yearbook. "Is that or isn't that your mother? And look at who she's dancing with."

Leaning over his arm she read the caption, "Winter Prom." The picture showed dancers below strips of crepe paper. The photo was blurry, the figures tiny, but she could see her mother's unmistakable blonde hair and Marco's thick black hair.

"They're all over the floor. It's hard to tell who she's dancing with," she said, though she wondered why her mother had never told her she knew Marco well enough to dance with him.

"I'm amazed at you, or has your reporter brain stopped working? Has it occurred to you that the mystery girl might be your mother?"

She swallowed hard, shaking her head in denial. "No. According to Marco's letters, that girl betrayed him. My mother wouldn't do that."

He tilted his head toward her, doubt written in his eyes, but at the same moment both seemed to notice how close they were. His gaze moved to her lips and she turned away, fighting the tremble that slithered down her spine. Was he about to kiss her again?

Attempting to put space between them, she stepped behind the footlocker. "What are you doing here anyway? I thought you were going to Santa Fe to deliver my watch and that envelope to the crime lab."

"I took it but I'm afraid lots of people touched the envelope before it got delivered and we don't know if the watch has anything to do with Marco or Naldo."

She held up her hands. "You told me that already." Perhaps she should tell him about the van that followed her. No, he would only criticize her for insisting on walking home alone.

"Okay, I'll get going. I just wanted to let you know it may be a while before we get results back from Santa Fe."

"Thanks for letting me know."

She returned to her task, but despite his comment, Rafe lingered. He wandered around the rows of unpacked boxes and covered furniture that had been too big to fit upstairs. From time to time he picked up items, examining them and putting them down. She fought to ignore him as she flipped through a scrapbook of yellowing pictures of David Cassidy and John Travolta cut from magazines. A shoe box held a neatly arranged row of envelopes, and Cere lifted out a letter. The girl's name was unfamiliar and the postmark was Germany. A pen pal. Cere replaced the letters.

Another shoe box. More letters. Most of these were unopened. She was about to close the box when an envelope caught her attention. Her hands began to shake as she reached for it. She knew the unmistakable scrawl. It belonged to Marco Gonzales.

Her breath caught as she read her mother's name on the front of the envelope. It carried no address or postmark. Drawing out the folded pages with quaking fingers, she felt like a thief. The familiar cheap paper was yellowed with time, almost brittle. She wanted to stop, but she had to know. A shiver ran down her spine as she read the first line.

Lottie, my love, I'm sending you another song...

She dropped the paper with a cry as though it was hot, springing to her feet.

"What?" Rafe asked, approaching her.

Tears clouded her eyes as she turned to him and handed him the page. "Rafe..."

He read the letter while she pulled out a piece of typing paper that was also inside the envelope. It was a typed version in English of one of the love songs she had read the day before.

"You knew," she accused in a shaky voice.

His stunned face told a different story. "No, I didn't. I was just being a jerk."

A spasm of dizziness shook her, and he slid his arm around her. She clutched at him, needing a connection of some sort and he helped her to a seat on the piano bench.

"Is that why she's been so against my doing the story?" Bewilderment grasped her in a tight vise.

"I would think so." He sank onto the bench beside her, taking her hand.

"Why didn't she tell me? I would have understood."

"Would you have stopped asking questions?"

"Well, no but she could have helped me, given me information..."

He grunted. "See? That's exactly why she didn't tell you. You wouldn't give up. You'd be asking more questions, and it's obvious she doesn't want to talk about him."

Across from them, the yearbook stood open, as though presenting its secrets. She reached over and touched it gingerly. "Is this why my uncles hated him?"

"Probably."

"But how did she betray him? What did she do?"

He drew a deep breath. "Think about it. They were teenagers when he went to jail. I bet she didn't stand by him. That she didn't stand up to her family and answer his letters. Look. Only a few of them were opened."

Cere got to her feet as though she might be sleepwalking.

"Where is she right now?"

"At the Matador. She was meeting Mr. Foster for lunch. I wanted to surprise her and clean the basement while she was gone."

He sighed unhappily. "What a surprise. It looks like you managed to open up a whole new can of worms."

Cere picked up the yearbook and the envelope with

the typewritten songs. "I want to talk to her, but maybe I should ask my uncles about these letters first. Maybe I can get someone to tell the truth." A sudden thought hit her. "You don't suppose one of them hurt Marco?"

"What do you think?"

She recalled the anger both her uncles demonstrated when Marco's name came up. "But why?"

"Are you kidding? Look at that picture. The town hood? The sweet younger sister?"

"They wouldn't kill him to keep him away from her. Besides, this was high school. She was in college when he died. I don't know if she was around that final summer."

"Well, if you insist on questioning them, I'm going with you."

For once she didn't feel like tackling things on her own. She put her hand on his hard forearm. "Thanks, Rafe. That's very sweet of you."

Her smile nearly melted him and he covered her hand with his. He wanted to do more than that, he wanted to take her in his arms and hold her. The discovery had hit her hard. "Have you ever been involved in a story that affected you directly?"

"What do you mean?"

"Maybe you should pull back. Now that you know your family might be personally involved, isn't it a conflict of interest?"

Her reply was to pull her hand away from his touch. "I can still gather the information and figure it out."

He could see he would not deter her. She wasn't

thinking about the emotional toll of the story, even yet. "Why would you put your mother through this? Name her as the girl who betrayed Marco? This story doesn't need to be told."

"As a journalist I have a responsibility to uncover the truth and tell it."

"No matter who gets hurt?"

Tears emerged at the corners of her brown eyes and he sensed her wavering. He pressed his advantage.

"You don't have to do this, hon. Let it go. No one is going to criticize you."

She gazed up at him, dark eyes haunted. "I can't play favorites. Besides, now I know why I have to do it..."

Damn, he wanted to shake her. Why didn't she walk away while she could, the way he wished he had when he looked into Marco's story for Riggins? Maybe he could still limit the damage. He'd been unable to discover the unknown woman and he'd suspected that might be the key that unraveled the entire mystery. But now that he knew, did it really help?

Chapter Thirty-Five

Norm and Dick Winslow worked in Rio Rojo's main bank, a golden sandstone structure of five stories that dominated the downtown area. It sat on the central corner of Main and First streets. Cere didn't see Rafe or his Jeep so she parked in front to wait. They had agreed to meet at the bank in an hour, giving her an opportunity to shower and dress and him time to check in with his office. She remained in her car, watching traffic pass, checking for white vans. Unfortunately she counted five before Rafe pulled into the parking spot beside her.

"Ready for this?" he asked as they walked inside.

"I'm always ready," she declared, though her stomach fluttered like it buzzed with butterflies. She had no idea what she was going to ask or if her uncles would see them. They had not called in advance.

Rafe led her to the executive offices at the back of a cavernous lobby. The plush, elegant surroundings were a surprise. Her feet sank into thick emerald carpet and the burgundy wing chairs beside the receptionist's cherry wood executive desk looked like they belonged in a gentleman's club. Muted green walls gave the room a somber appearance, and she wondered if the wall and carpet colors were selected to make visitors think of money.

A tall thin woman who resembled a sleek cat in a

well cut suit looked over the top of rimless glasses as they approached. Her graying hair was pulled into a severe bun. She had been at the party, but Cere had not met her. In cool precise tones she assured them Dick was in a meeting and couldn't be disturbed but Norm was available.

"I'll let him know you're here," she said in a crisp tone, gesturing them toward a side door as she picked up her phone and pushed buttons.

Stepping through a dark walnut door they entered a world of chaos. Norm's cluttered desk had no empty space and two visitor's chairs beside it also held files. His pudgy face creased with a wide smile as they stepped through the door but he didn't rise.

"Cere, Rafe, nice of you to drop in. What can I do ya for? Have a seat." He waved toward a dark green and burgundy sofa that lined a wall to the right of his desk. The window above it framed downtown in the foreground and a blue ridge of mountains in the distance.

Drawing a deep breath she plunged forward. "This isn't a social call, Uncle Norm. I'm curious about my mother and Marco."

The smile disintegrated, and Norm sat back. His black leather chair screeched in protest. "Whoa. That's a strange thing to say."

"You're not going to deny she dated Marco, are you?"

His plump hands raised in protest. "She never dated that thug. Where did you get that idea? Sure, he wanted to go out with her, but we never let her. He was a loser. We all knew that."

"You didn't like that she wanted to see him?" she

pressed.

"I discouraged it from the get go. And she never went out with him."

"He sent her letters and songs while he was in jail."

His head gyrated back and forth. "Did you ask Lottie about this? I can't imagine she wants you prying into private matters."

"She doesn't know I found his letters and songs. They were in a trunk Uncle Dick returned to her when she moved back."

"You mean that stuff from Mom's basement? Damn! If we'd known that we'd have thrown them away."

"Did you ever see the two of them together?" she asked.

"Well, maybe once or twice, but it was innocent. Just him walking her home from school once. Daddy made it clear she wasn't to see him again. When that boy left our house, he knew better than to come back."

She drew a deep breath. What had the Winslows done to discourage Marco? Thoughts of his poignant words came back to her. It was hard to reconcile them with the photo of the rebellious youth in the yearbook. "Who did she go out with?"

"Lots of boys. Hell, she could have dated any boy in the county. Lottie was a looker."

"Even Mr. Foster?"

"Well, no. Bradley was married then. He was a deputy and he'd come by the house all the time to see Daddy."

This wasn't getting them anywhere. She doubted a romantic rivalry had anything to do with the current situation.

"Did she see him after he got out of prison?"

"Nope. She was in college and sure wasn't going to date a con. I think she was seeing a pre-med student. Seems like I remember she wanted Daddy to get him a job at John's hardware store. No, any foolishness with that crazy kid ended when he got arrested."

****

"I don't think he was telling us everything," Rafe said as they stepped through the bank doors into a blast of hot summer air. He was good at judging people who were being questioned and being less than truthful. Norm met all the criteria. He kept fidgeting and his eyes rambled from his disheveled desk to the window, refusing to look at them.

"What do you mean?"

"Let's go over to the Matador and talk. We can leave your car and I'll bring you back."

She glanced at the clock on the bank façade. "It's nearly three, a little late for lunch."

"I want to talk to Frank. Actually I should do this alone."

"Don't tell me you're suddenly interested."

"Maybe." He didn't want to admit it to her, but the letters and that interview had piqued his interest. He didn't like unanswered questions, and right now he had plenty of them.

Could she be right about Naldo's murder being tied to Marco somehow? When they'd entered the bank, he'd noticed a few smears on the marble floors of the lobby. Old Naldo had kept those floors spotless when he was alive. One of his many odd jobs. In the middle of Cere's questions, Rafe had a sudden recollection— the gleam in old Naldo's eyes when Rafe mentioned

Cere wanted to do a story about Marco. The old man was always looking for ways to earn money. What if he had known something about Marco's death? What if he had tried blackmailing the wrong person?

Her hand touched his arm. "You know something."

"No. I'll call you later." He started for his Jeep, but she was right behind him.

"I have time. I'll go with you to the restaurant."

He shot her a cool look. "On one condition. Frank may not want to talk in front of you. If he balks, let me do it alone."

"Will you tell me what he says?"

"Not if he wants it kept confidential. And not if it jeopardizes the investigation."

Her eyes lit up in triumph. "So you do see a connection!"

"No comment, Ms Reporter," he said, unlocking the door for her. "And if you misbehave I'll make you walk back."

****

Only two booths were occupied when they entered the restaurant. One held a couple with two lively children in bright vacation garb—probably tourists, Cere decided. Josie sat in another booth, two stacks of bills in front of her. The spicy aroma of chili wafted from the kitchen.

"Frank around?" Rafe asked as they took stools at the counter. "We'd like to talk to him."

Josie picked up the bills, got to her feet and tucked her order pad into the back pocket of her tight jeans. "He's in the back. I'll get him. Can I bring you anything?"

"A couple of sodas."

Cere leaned forward and called, "Make mine diet," but Josie had vanished.

Frank came through the swinging doors to the kitchen wearing an apron spotted with red chili. He nodded at Cere before turning to Rafe.

"Hey, *compadre,* what brings you around at this time of the day?"

"We've been looking through Marco's stuff. Gus brought her his songs."

"Yeah? So?" He looked from one to the other, openly curious.

"I'm trying to find out who Marco didn't get along with."

Frank leaned on the counter, dark face scrunched in concentration. He might not say anything to her but she could see he wasn't going to refuse Rafe's questions. "Well... let's see..."

"What about *her* uncles?"

Frank's eyes flickered to Cere as his head bobbed up and down. "They didn't like him and he didn't like them. I was a little kid when he came back but I remember hearing that before he went to jail they beat him up pretty bad. I guess Dick and John grabbed him outside the Palladium, but I hear that place always had fights."

"Was it over a girl?" Cere asked.

"I never heard why they did it."

"Did you ever hear if he had a girlfriend?" she continued.

Frank's glance slid to Rafe. "Didn't you once tell me he dated your mama?"

Cere gasped and swung to Rafe who refused to meet her eyes. "You never told me that."

329

"It wasn't important." He slid off the stool and got to his feet as Josie emerged with their drinks. He dug into his pants pocket and tossed money on the counter. "I gotta go."

Cere wasn't about to let him out of her sight. Dropping her own money on the counter, she quick-stepped after him to his vehicle. She yanked open the door and threw herself into the front seat as he started the ignition.

"Why didn't you tell me about your mother?"

Refusing to look at her, he pressed his lips into a tight straight line as he backed out the Jeep. "She wasn't the girl who betrayed him, the mystery woman. She told me he was involved with someone before he went to jail, someone he kept secret. I think we both know who that is."

No wonder he had been so secretive from the beginning. Her thoughts raced. "What about when he got out of jail? Was that when he saw your mother?"

Rafe's dark face could have been chiseled out of one of the nearby rock faces of the mesas. He wasn't going to reply. But he didn't need to. His silence provided confirmation.

"This is why you didn't want me looking into the story, isn't it? You knew your mother's name might come up."

His head jerked toward her and his dark eyes were like drills boring into her. "What about you? Your mother *is* involved, and you're still trying to uncover secrets. When I found out about Mom, I stopped feeding Riggins information. If I had known from the beginning, I wouldn't have talked to him, period. I regret hurting her."

"So she dated him. What's the big deal?"

"That's the way you see it, isn't it? This is a game to you, with rules made by a dead man. Your damn ghost. What if it was your mother's rejection that led him to suicide? What if someone killed him out of jealousy over her? Are you going to report that? How far are you willing to go, how many people are you willing to hurt just to get this story?"

Chapter Thirty-Six

Turmoil dogged Cere as she drove home. Rafe's words echoed in her head. What should she do? Tell all of Marco's story, including the part about her mother? For years she had chased people suffering from horrible grief to get their stories. How much pain had she caused over the years? The thought brought a shudder.

But Rafe didn't understand that more than the story drove her. Thoughts of her ghostly companion filtered through her mind. She understood now why the vision had come specifically to her. Had her mother betrayed Marco? Had he been murdered because of his connection to her?

A blur of white to her right jerked her back to reality. She'd been driving too slowly and a white van zipped by her. Her heart skipped a beat as she caught sight of the driver—Len Gonzales from the garage. Was that the van from the previous night? Why would Len want to run her over? Why would Marco's family want the truth hidden?

She had never understood that relationship. The family disowned Marco when he came back. But he had tried to help the town, hadn't he? Wouldn't the Gonzales family want that story told? Unless they feared he was behind the last string of burglaries and the buildings that burned. Did they fear she would uncover the truth?

****

Cere found her mother sipping iced tea on the shady portion of the patio when she arrived home. A soft breeze rustled leaves overhead and the yard smelled of marigolds and geraniums. She poured a glass from a pitcher on the table and sat down. "How's your day going?"

A smile tugged at Lottie's lips. Fine laugh lines crinkled around her eyes and mouth. "Quiet. Where have you been all afternoon? Freeda called from Taos. She's staying over a couple more days. She said she's working on ideas for you. What's that about?"

"I might do a blog on Taos. Mom, what if I give up on the Marco story?"

Lottie's tongue flicked over her lips as her smile widened. "I'd be pleased. I don't know why you're interested in the first place."

Sitting back, Cere held up her hand. "I didn't say I'm giving up. But if I do, will you tell me about him?"

A look of confusion crossed Lottie's face. New rivers of wrinkles appeared on her tanned cheeks. "Why would you want to know if you're giving up?"

"It's become…well…a personal issue."

Her mother stiffened and when she placed her glass on the table Cere noted her hand shook slightly. "I see."

Perhaps honesty was the best argument. "I went through your yearbooks today. I saw pictures of you and Marco dancing together. I saw his letters."

Lottie's face blanched despite her tan. "Those letters were private."

"I didn't read them. But I know he wrote to you, that he was involved with you."

"He was involved with a lot of girls," Lottie

interjected with a wave of her hand. "He was cute and he got around."

"But he wrote songs to you."

Her mother grew very still, refusing to meet her glance, eyes fastened to her half-finished glass of tea. "It was a teenage crush. My dad, my brothers worried he was obsessed with me. He wouldn't leave me alone."

A question pricked her curiosity, but Cere didn't ask it. She went in another direction. "Someone said your brothers beat him."

"Several times. He was stubborn and wouldn't stop calling. Dad was ready to have the phone taken out." Her voice cracked and she took a quick sip of tea.

Cere couldn't wait any longer; she had to know the truth. "Mom, tell me. Did you care about him?"

Her eyes misted with tears and she swallowed hard before replying. "I was young. Silly."

Sensing more to the explanation, Cere waited patiently.

Slowly Lottie smiled, voice vibrating with energy when she finally spoke. "He was so exciting, full of life. Fun. Very special."

"You did care."

"Not enough." Her eyes glazed over and she clasped her hands as though they were cold.

"Why won't you let this go? What difference does it make? Your father was the right man for me. He was everything Marco should have been, everything he couldn't be with me."

"What does that mean? He wrote those songs to you. It sounds to me like he could have been a talented songwriter."

Lottie wiped her dry cheek as though expecting tears. Turning away, she pulled on sunglasses that had been sitting on the table. "Marco could have been anything he wanted. Songwriter, poet, politician, he could have done so much. But the young fool put all his energy into chasing me. Look how well he did once he got over that foolishness. He came out of jail ready to make a difference."

"Yes, maybe, but I get the feeling his heart was broken."

Her voice turned icy. "Don't try to make me feel guilty, Cere. I've always felt guilty about him. I will until the day I die." Her hands began to shake, and Cere realized she was on the verge of crying.

"Mom, what is it? Do you think you're responsible for his death?"

"No, he was over me when he came back. I hadn't answered his letters. I had never seen the songs."

"Why didn't you read the letters?" She recalled the forlorn boxes of unopened letters in the basement.

Lottie's thin shoulders sagged. "I never knew about them. Rosalie… kept them."

"Who's Rosalie? His sister?"

"Stella's sister, my best friend." She pressed her lips together as a tear rolled out from under her sunglasses. "I never realized she…she was in love with him. She wanted him that whole time he chased me. It was silly. I sent him one letter and told him to send any replies to his sister or Rosalie because I couldn't receive them at home. I never heard from him so I thought he hated me. Apparently he wrote those letters and songs but I didn't find out until the day he died. Rosalie admitted that she and his sister conspired to keep them from me. Linda never approved of me any more than my family liked him. Anyway, Rosalie gave me the letters she received. I never saw the ones that went to Linda. Poor Marco. He didn't understand why I never answered... But I didn't know... I never opened them after he died." Her breath caught and she gulped back tears.

"But you kept them all these years?"

"I put them into my keepsake trunk and forgot them. I guess Mom put my belongings into that same trunk. Dick gave it to me when I moved back."

"Was that what you were looking for last night?"

Nodding, she coughed slightly before reaching over to pick up her glass and take a gulp of tea. "I wanted to throw them out. I don't know why I kept them. I guess I thought one day I might be brave enough to read them. Marco was such a romantic fool. A sweet, silly idiot. Everyone said he was mean and angry." She paused to take another drink, draining her glass.

"That wasn't Marco. Just the opposite. He put on that tough exterior so people wouldn't know the truth. Sometimes he even believed the show he put on. But I always knew he was sweet. We used to sit up there at the lake...and he'd play his guitar and sing to me."

Cere bolted upright. "Was that why you were trying to drive up there?"

"I wanted to see how much it had changed. See if it was as magical as I remember. But it's probably gone and so is he. All we have are those letters..." Her voice trailed off.

"He was very special to you." She caught hold of her mother's hand. Its coldness surprised her and she squeezed it.

"Yes. But not enough."

"I don't understand."

"This all happened so long ago, Cere. It doesn't matter now."

She wanted to agree, but there was still Naldo. What if Marco's death and his were related? She pressed on, squeezing her mother's hand again. "I read some of Marco's letters to his sister. He sounded as though he came out of prison ready to make a difference. Do you think he committed suicide?"

"Honestly, I don't like to think of the alternative— that someone killed him and has gone unpunished for years."

"Do you have any ideas who might have done it?"

A sudden stillness seemed to take possession of Lottie. Above them, rustling leaves made the only sound. She looked as drained as her empty glass. She blinked and stared at Cere, as though surprised to see her. Pulling her hand free, Lottie wiped her damp cheek.

"Let's forget this," she said, getting to her feet. "Why don't we go out for dinner? I'll see if Bradley will join us. We can go to Gennaro's. Why don't we invite Rafe too?"

Her heart skipped at the thought of inviting Rafe to dinner. Given what her mother had told her, perhaps she should give up the story. And she would enjoy telling him that in person.

"I'm sorry for all this trouble," she said, putting her hand on her mother's arm as they walked down the hall.

Lottie attempted a smile. "It's okay. You had no way of knowing. I should have told you."

A thump on the porch startled them both, but Lottie smiled. "It's the paper." She opened the door and brought in the *Rio Rojo News*. Cere tried not to act eager, but she looked over her mother's shoulder as she unfolded it.

"My gosh." Cere pointed to a small headline on the front page about the drug store closing. "He gave me a byline." A thrill rushed through her at the sight of her name in print.

Lottie gasped. "You wrote a story for the paper?"

"I helped out. Where do you think I was last night? I didn't know he was going to give me a byline." A giggle escaped her. She had appeared on TV screens all across the country, but seeing her name in type was special, even if it was only seen by three thousand people.

"Maybe you've found a new career. Now that you're giving up on the Marco story, you can find other things to write."

"Maybe."

But even as she spoke, a pair of dark eyes burned into her brain. *Would he let her go?*

Chapter Thirty-Seven

Dinner with Cere should be no big deal. Still, as Rafe fumbled with his silk tie, he studied his reflection in the mirror. As sheriff, he seldom dressed up, so why was he putting on his best blue suit for a date with her? Was it even a date? They would be dining with her mother and Mayor Foster. Rafe didn't normally socialize with him, but he wasn't about to refuse. After the angry way they parted, he'd been surprised by her call and pleased she forgave him for being so blunt.

He gave his tie one final tug as his mother stepped into the room. Her nut brown face wore a bright smile.

"You look good, son. That girl is going to be impressed."

He grimaced at the mirror. "I'm not trying to impress. It's just a friendly dinner."

"I've never seen you so dressed up. Even when I set you up with nice girls." She brushed his arm and his back with a lint roller. "It's good you're going out. You've seemed a lot livelier since she came to town."

His fingers caught her pudgy cheek in an affectionate squeeze. "Don't get the wrong idea, Mama. In a week, she'll go back to LA. Then life can get back to normal."

"Sure, *Mijo.* She told me she likes taking care of Ginny. I thought you said she wasn't the motherly type."

"She isn't. Too involved in her career. Not at all like Carmen."

"No one is going to be like Carmen." She leaned toward him with her most fierce look of disapproval. "You need to remember that. Going out with a woman is not going to ruin memories of Carmen. That part of your life is finished. You need to move on. The past is gone and the future is waiting."

Over the years he had grown used to her simple lectures. Ever since his return, she and her family had been lining him up with women. He had never been interested, even if Ginny needed a new mother. His daughter liked Cere, but he doubted he could marry someone so career obsessed.

Leaning down, Rafe kissed his mother's graying hair. "You're an angel to look after Ginny on such short notice."

"Since when does taking care of my grandchild make me special? I should be taking her more often. Stay out as late as you want. Ginny will be fine with me all night."

"I'm not staying out all night."

Her short fingers gave his tie a quick tug and tapped his chest. "Have fun. I saw the way you looked at her the other night. I'm not so old I can't remember what it was like to be young and in love."

"That isn't what's happening. She's using me to get her damn story."

"That's what you think."

"That's what I know." Even if Cere made his body come alive, he couldn't forget she only wanted a story—a story that could hurt people he loved.

****

Cere was aware of everything about Rafe as he helped her with her chair. The sight of him in a dark blue suit was a surprise. Suddenly she wondered if her own cream colored sleeveless sheath was too simple. She had bought it because its slim lines hugged her figure in just the right places. The scooped neck had an open strip crisscrossed with X's showing just a hint of cleavage. The light color nicely accentuated her newly acquired tan.

Tony helped her mother with her chair and Cere bit back a smile. Why didn't her mother notice his attentiveness? Why didn't he find a way to demonstrate his interest? He seemed as stiff and formal as the restaurant with its crisp linen table cloths and candles at every table. But he looked as fresh in his black suit as the carnations in small bud vases. The burgundy carpets and dark wooden paneling made the room gloomy but in an elegant manner that whispered romance. Why couldn't he personally express that?

"I saw your name in the paper," Bradley said to Cere after their order was taken. "Are you writing for Willie?"

"I was helping." She beamed at Rafe, a sudden surge of heat flowing though her body. "You can tell your uncle I'd be happy to volunteer while I'm here. I liked seeing my name in the paper."

"He'll be pleased to hear that."

"How's everything in your department?" Foster asked Rafe after approving the wine Tony had brought. "Things seem pretty quiet."

"That's the way I like it," he said.

Tony glanced at the mayor as he poured wine. "Pardon my intrusion, but what about the murder,

Mayor, Sheriff? Is there anything new on that?"

Foster flicked him a condescending glance. "Don't worry, BJ'll catch the boy who did it."

"How do you know it was a boy?" Cere asked.

"Boys keep digging up his yard. BJ has to keep sending deputies over to chase them off. Naldo was killed by someone who believed the story he had money. They almost got it."

Cere chewed on her lip, wondering if she should ask what was on her mind. She couldn't help herself. "Mayor, do you think that money in Naldo's box was Marco's money? I hear there were letters in there from Marco."

Lottie gasped, and under the table Rafe nudged her knee. The touch was electric, and her eyes flew to him. He shook his head slightly.

"Money?" Tony asked. "What money? What box?"

The mayor froze Tony with a cold look. The tall man drew back as though he realized he'd intruded. He excused himself and moved to another table.

"Talking about that boy having money is foolish," Bradley said in a low, demeaning voice. "He never had a cent to his name."

His dismissal of Tony and his tone irritated Cere. "But if he looted those stores before he died, shouldn't he have had some?"

"Probably spent it. Blew it on drugs. He never had any sense. I don't know why you're still asking questions about him." His eyes flashed at Rafe as though this was his fault.

She refused to back down. "I think someone is hiding information. Someone's trying to scare me into stopping my questions."

All three focused on Cere. She could sense their doubt. Rafe shook his head, but only Bradley protested. "That's the craziest thing I've ever heard."

Feeling trapped Cere poured out details of the phone messages, the smashed watch and then told them about the van that nearly hit her.

Lottie gave out a little cry. "Cere, you need to stop. You could get hurt. If whoever killed Naldo—"

"Naldo's killing had nothing to do with that boy's suicide," Bradley interrupted. "Sounds like someone wants you to stop being nosy. But Lottie's right. You better stop this right now."

"Why didn't you tell me about this earlier?" Rafe asked.

"It's not your jurisdiction. Do you think Len would have done it? I saw him driving a white van today."

"Did the van have a dent on the left side?" Rafe asked.

"Yes."

"Then it belongs to Frank," he said. "He leaves the keys on a hook just inside the back door. Anyone could have taken it at any time."

"Half the people at City Hall borrow that van when we need to deliver supplies," Bradley said. "I even use it at times."

Cere laughed, attempting to be good natured. "Mr. Mayor, were you trying to run me over late last night?"

His blue eyes twinkled as they fixed on her. "If it made you stop upsetting your mama, I might throw a scare your way."

Cere drew back, despite the twinkling eyes. There was something sinister in his words. Could Mayor Foster be involved? But that was silly. He was the mayor. Why would he kill Naldo? Or try to scare her?

She turned to Rafe. "Would one of the Gonzales men do it?"

"Why? You're trying to prove he didn't commit suicide. Your story would only vindicate him. Besides, they're helping you. They gave you his songs."

"Maybe they know he committed the burglaries. They want to sell his songs, and while the works of a tortured soul might sell, who wants love songs from a petty thief?"

"Love songs?" Bradley's voice was louder than normal.

Lottie twisted in her chair, and Cere immediately realized her mistake. No one had known about the love songs.

"There was talk there might be love songs," she said quickly. She did not want to embarrass her mother.

"Let's forget this," Lottie said, patting her lips with her napkin. "Didn't you say you're giving up on that story?"

"Thinking about it," she said, wishing her mother had not brought up the subject like that. She could feel Rafe's eyes on her, and she refused to look in his direction.

"Sounds like a good idea to me," Bradley said.

Perhaps if he had not sounded so smug, Cere might have agreed. "Even if I don't pursue the story for air, it doesn't mean I won't continue to investigate. I'm not convinced he committed suicide."

Bradley stiffened and he gripped the edge of the table so hard his pudgy hands turned white. His blue eyes grew frosty as icicles. "That was my conclusion as sheriff and that of the coroner. Are you saying we were wrong?"

"Maybe you didn't have the proper information to uncover the truth," she offered, trying to appease him.

"The truth was right in front of us. Same as with the burglaries the first time he went to jail. I knew that boy did it, no matter how much he protested his innocence."

Rafe cleared his throat. "What was the evidence? Were there fingerprints?"

"He was seen near the jewelry store and he had cash and a diamond ring. Where else would he have gotten it? There were no fingerprints. I bet he wore gloves."

"Can we change the subject please? It was so long ago. This isn't why we came to dinner," Lottie protested in a high voice. Her face was pale except for two pink splotches on her cheeks.

Guilt swept through Cere. In her haste to battle the mayor, she had ignored her mother's wishes. A quick glance at Rafe told her he felt the same way.

"Mayor, tell us about Tres Padres," he said, changing the subject. "I keep telling Cere it would make a much better story."

Bradley drew back, the tension lessening. "Yes, it would. I talked to those folks this morning, in fact. That project could bring good things to the valley."

Cere forced herself to show interest, making a few notes and the conversation got them through dinner. When Lottie excused herself to go to the ladies room Cere went with her.

"I'm sorry for bringing up Marco," she said, taking her arm as they entered. "Did Mr. Foster know he chased you?"

Lottie's arm was tense, her voice dry. "Of course. Everyone knew. When we were juniors, that nut spray painted 'Marco loves Lottie' across the side of the Palladium. Dad had a fit and Bradley made him clean it." Despite her tense answer her face broke into a sad smile.

"Do you ever dream him?"

Her mother blinked rapidly. "What a strange thing to say. Why would I dream about him?"

She pressed her lips together, unable to reply and simply shook her head. "No reason."

As they stopped to wash their hands, seeing her mother's sad eyes in the mirror she decided to cheer her up. "What do you think of Mr. Gennaro?"

Lottie's brow wrinkled. "No more Marco. I told you he was too afraid of him to stop him from chasing me. All the boys were."

"I mean now." Cere grinned at her mother. "Haven't you noticed how he keeps hovering around the table?"

Her cheeks turned vibrant pink but she laughed. "You and Freeda. Stop playing matchmakers. But...well, don't take this the wrong way... I may not be home tonight."

"You're going to spend the night with Mr. Foster?"

Lottie glanced around as though someone might be listening. "It's not like that."

Her mother's face flushed brilliantly, and Cere felt a lump in her throat. She refused to contemplate her mother and Bradley as lovers. It seemed disloyal to her father. But after her earlier behavior, all she could do was squeeze her mother's hand.

"Do whatever you would do if I wasn't here. Rafe

will take me home. I promise not to tell Freeda. She'd never let you hear the end of it."

Lottie's smile was one of gratitude. "You behave yourself."

"I have to, and you don't?"

"That isn't what I meant. Rafe doesn't want you investigating any more than I do. You should have seen his face when you were talking about threats. He cares about you."

Chapter Thirty-Eight

"You should have told me about the van," Rafe said as they strolled along Main Street and turned onto the block where the van had shone its lights on her.

"I didn't want to worry you." She kept her tone light, as though she considered the matter inconsequential. "This is where he backed up and that's the tree I ducked behind."

"You knew it would worry me." He leaned down for a look at the street surface, but the pavement gave up no information they could use.

"Maybe I hoped it would," she said, attempting to banter.

"Cere." He straightened and took her hand. The moonlight was all the light they had, but in its silvery glow she could see the flame of desire in his dark eyes as he spoke in a soft, intimate voice. "I do worry about you. Believe me, I'd rather not. You're quite a handful."

"I don't need anyone to take care of me," she protested.

"Caring about someone makes you want to take care of them." He tugged her hand, pulling her toward him. "Damn, I'm not sure what I want to say."

Her senses buzzed as her heart skipped. He was saying he cared about her. Cere reached up and stroked his face with her free hand. She was beginning to care too. Did things happen that fast? Could it be possible she was falling in love?

He leaned down and kissed her quickly, just a soft touch but it quickened her breathing and set her pulse on high-speed.

"Come on, I'll walk you home, unless you want to go back for the car."

"Let's walk. Mom's not coming home tonight."

"Is that an invitation?" he asked with a chuckle. Playfully he caught her in his arms and held her loosely against him.

Cere leaned against his chest, inhaling his clean scent. Her insides grew jittery, and all her senses leaped to life. Hot sparks heated her skin. "What do you think?"

"You claimed to be too much for me to handle."

She leaned back to look up at him. Shadows hid his eyes, but she could feel he wanted her as much as she wanted him. She touched his feathery lashes with her fingertips. "That's true."

"I'm not into games, Cere. I've always played for keeps."

Her stomach did a wild flip flop, and her knees felt weak. But as she reached up to kiss him, he drew a deep breath, released his hold and stepped back.

"Unfortunately I don't think we're ready for that."

Cere tried not to let her disappointment show. "Oh."

"Let's do something fun. Want to take a drive?"

"To the Palladium?"

"No!" He took her arm and tucked it under his as they resumed walking toward the house. "You enjoy going out, don't you? I bet you miss the noisy atmosphere, the swanky clubs."

"I like going out, but I seldom have time. I used to meet friends for dinner, but it's become a chore. Traffic is horrible, everyone lives miles apart. Did you and your wife go out a lot?"

"Carmen wasn't much for the social scene. She was a teacher and dedicated herself to her students. She'd have tutoring sessions at all hours of the day and night. That's..." Rafe stopped and shook his head.

Cere regretted mentioning his former wife. She kept doing that, and it put him into a thoughtful mood. Had his wife been on a late night tutoring session when she'd been killed? Maybe a change of subject was in order.

"What do you think of Bradley Foster?" she asked.

"Full of himself. Like his son."

"He's very smitten with my mother."

His lips twitched into a smile. "Does that bother you?"

"I never thought my mother might get involved after Dad died. Mr. Foster doesn't seem her type, but she says she had a crush on him when she was young. Mr. Gennaro is closer to her age and seems to like her, but she thinks of him as a brother."

"Isn't that how it always is?" he said with a gentle laugh.

"I guess. Poor Marco had a crush on her and she probably didn't notice him either. Did you hear Mr. Foster? He's so certain Marco committed the burglaries, but I read the letters to his sister. Why would he lie after he'd been convicted?"

"I wondered how long it would take to get around to Marco." Rafe cast a glance at his watch. "Two hours.

I'm impressed."

"Stop it. You looked interested too."

"Maybe a little."

They turned onto Lottie's block and she leaned her head against his arm. "Want to come in for coffee? It might keep me out of trouble. You know if you leave me alone I'll go to the basement and start reading through letters again."

"Let's sit in the back yard and talk."

Rafe wasn't certain if he was doing the right thing agreeing to stay. As he stood in the back yard, lighting a torch at one end of the patio he could see her inside the kitchen, pouring glasses of port. She turned on her mother's stereo, which was still set up to feed music outdoors, and came through the door with glasses in hand. She put them down on a table at the edge of the patio and playfully grabbed his hand.

"Dance with me, Tafoya. I need to keep moving."

"I don't dance well."

Cere was not to be denied. She pulled his hand until he was against her. The touch of his chest and thighs against her body shot a bolt of electricity through him. She leaned her head against his chest, and he thought about what he'd told her—he didn't believe in casual sex. Did she? His body was coming alive in a way it hadn't in years and he could feel the thud of her heart beneath his hand which enfolded hers against her upper chest.

His palm gripped her back, and he could feel warmth penetrating through her thin dress. What would it be like to feel his hand against her bare skin or maybe his lips? A hot wave of desire splashed across his lower regions.

Closing her eyes, Cere gave in to the music, her body swaying against his. All too soon the song ended. Rafe's lips nuzzled the top of her head, and Cere lifted her head for a kiss.

The touch was warm, gentle and carried promise of things to come. Too soon he had to break it or beg her to take him to the bedroom.

"Cere," he whispered into her hair. "You know how much I want you."

"I can feel it," she said with a giggle.

He jostled her and pulled back, only slightly embarrassed. She wrapped her arms around his neck and kissed him hard on the mouth.

"I like it," she whispered.

Her radiant smile made Rafe's heart skip. Hell, everything about her tonight turned his insides to butter. Why the hell didn't she just go back to California? He hadn't been joking about one night stands. The problem was he wanted her and not for only one night. He wanted to hold her, but he feared he might never be able to let her go. He would make a fool of himself and try to get her to stay. He had persuaded Carmen to move to Los Angeles. She had gone and paid the ultimate price. He'd never ask anyone to sacrifice for him again.

He jerked away and held her at arm's length. "Behave."

"Want to talk about Marco?" she asked with a coquettish grin.

He laughed. "Maybe."

"I just wish I could hear his songs. I've been waiting for Freeda to come back and sing them for me. I don't know much about music."

"I can play the guitar and sing. Not well, but I can do it." Suddenly he was willing to do anything, even sing Marco's songs if it meant putting distance between them. At least singing might keep them from personal talk.

"Drink your wine and I'll get the songs and Mom's guitar."

He sipped the wine while she retrieved the song sheets. The tunes were simple, and once he familiarized himself with the guitar, he began to put the words to music. A chill ran through him as he sang. He smiled at Cere, perched below him on the top step of the porch.

"Wow," she said with a laugh when he finished the first song. "You're not a bad singer. I didn't realize you had hidden talents."

He touched the folded paper, thinking about the songs and what they meant. "These aren't bad."

"I told you he was special. He accomplished a lot for having the deck stacked against him. There's no telling how far he could have gone if he had lived. Why hasn't it occurred to anyone that a man like that doesn't give up?"

Rafe sighed. She was right, even if she was going about her investigation the wrong way. What could he do? What good would opening up old wounds do for anyone? Marco was dead. He moved to the next song, strumming Marco's written chords.

"You're not going to believe this, but I feel a connection to him," she said. "It's like it's always been there. Remember the first night at the Palladium? I thought you saved me. Now that I think about it, I wasn't carried out. Something, someone led me, let me know I was safe."

His lip twitched in annoyance. "We were all safe. There was nothing there. Are you saying the ghost helped you? Formed a connection? That's why you're dreaming him?"

"Not anymore. I think that was triggered by seeing his picture in the paper. It must have set off my subconscious."

"Better not tell Freeda."

"Don't laugh, Tafoya. Last week when I got locked inside, I knew that I'd get out safely. Sometimes I feel he's watching me or talking to me. It's like I can hear him." She stopped as though she realized how crazy that sounded.

Rafe peered at her over the top of the guitar. "Do you think your ghost will protect you from the person who almost ran you down or threatened you?"

She inhaled sharply, small face growing serious. "You don't need to remind me of that."

"The threats are not from a ghost. They're real."

"I know. I want to stop, but I feel bad for him. Look at those love songs. He poured his heart out and Mom never saw them."

"My mother says her family was against her seeing him."

"Have you asked your mother about Marco?"

He didn't answer, pretending to work on the next song. He wasn't certain how to explain, but he could see her determination. Maybe it was time to be more honest. He set the guitar aside. "When I discovered my mother's involvement, it bothered me. I thought maybe he killed himself over her."

"How did you find out?"

"Bradley Foster told me. It stopped me from

publicly asking questions about the mystery woman."

"Some mystery," Cere said. "Everyone knew Marco wanted my mother. He painted their names on the wall of the Palladium."

"She might not be that final mystery woman. There's something else I haven't told you." He slid down from the chair to sit on the step beside her. "The woman could have been my Aunt Rosalie. She wrote to him in jail and he came to see her when he got out. That was how Mom got to know him."

"And they started going out?"

He shrugged. "Apparently."

Cere put her hand on his arm, gripping it. "Rafe, she was the one who gave Mom his letters. She might be the key. Can you get her to talk to me?"

"I've never met Aunt Rosalie. She moved away years ago."

"Mom said...she was in love with him."

A jolt of surprise reverberated inside him. "What? How does she know? Mom said..." He stopped. Again, there was too much at stake, too much he couldn't reveal. He sighed and shook his head. "All that happened a long time ago. I'm not sure it's worth digging up."

Cere stared at him, but for once there was softness in her gaze. When she touched his arm this time, it was a gentle squeeze. "That's why you tried to stop me from doing the story, isn't it? You didn't want me dragging your mom and her sister into this."

His nod was quick. "Now you can see the problem."

"Rafe, I don't think he killed himself."

His stomach knotted, but he made the declaration

he had been ignoring since the first morning he took up Marco with his mother. "Neither do I."

"As sheriff, Rafe, you have the power to re-open that case."

Rafe sighed heavily, a finger stroking the scar on his face. For years he hid it behind his beard. Now it was a reminder of how things could go wrong while trying to do the right thing. A young gang member had sliced his face in a knife fight while Rafe was trying to save his life.

"I've thought about it. If I hadn't discovered my mother's involvement, I might have done it."

"So now what?"

"I don't know. I don't want more people to be hurt." He leaned toward her and touched her lips gently with his, ignoring the urge to wrap his arms around her and hold onto her. "That includes you."

She stroked his face, touching the scar with exploring fingers. "I'm not as fragile as you think."

He pulled her hand away, kissed it and got to his feet. "That's what scares me. I better get going."

"Before I drag you up to my room?"

He tilted his head toward her, attempting to look as stern as possible, but he feared she could see right through him. "Goodnight, sweet Cere."

"One more thing. How about if I do a story on Naldo?"

"What?" That came out of left field, but he had a feeling she had other things on her mind.

"A feature story." Her eyes came alive as she hopped up and began pacing back and forth on the porch. "I could talk to people. Find out about his life. Heck, get the truth about that buried treasure. Maybe it would stop those people digging up the yard."

"You just want to ask about Marco," he said with a shake of his head.

"I'm good at people features. Naldo was a fixture in town, right? So far all I've seen in the paper is mention that he once ran a pawn shop and now he's a murder victim. There has to be more to him than that."

Rafe groaned, but she was right. Willie had talked about doing a feature, but none of them had the time to work on it so it had fallen by the wayside.

"I'll ask Uncle Willie. We tried contacting his son but no one knows where he is. His grandson is an attorney in Albuquerque but he's back east on a civil case. If Willie agrees, I'll pass on the information."

"Great! Thanks." She kissed his cheek and turned away.

He walked to the gate, almost fearing she might come after him. As he opened it, he glanced back. She was pacing the porch, chewing on a nail. His earlier desire faded. Her mind was elsewhere—on a new story idea.

He wanted to tell her to stop her crazy drive for the truth. Wanted to promise to keep her safe, but maybe she was better off with the damn ghost. That was where her mind was.

Chapter Thirty-Nine

The sun felt good on her bare arms as Cere sank onto a rickety wooden chair on the porch outside Robby's house. The sound of a blaring television came through the open door.

"Tell me about Naldo," she said after tapping the audio record button on her cell phone.

Robby was a gangly youth, all arms and legs with a lean torso covered by a too large T-shirt and baggy Bermuda shorts. A gold earring pierced one eyebrow.

"He was a nice old guy," he said, scratching a bony arm. "Why do you wanna know?"

"I'm doing a story for the paper."

Willie had called her personally to approve the idea, but it meant more than a feature story. She knew what Rafe's acquiescence meant. He was allowing her to ask questions about Naldo—and perhaps Marco—without arousing suspicion. "What was he like?"

"He liked to gossip, but never bothered anyone. He just liked to talk. He was a hard worker. Always fixing things."

This she had already heard from Jerry and the guys down at the Matador where she joined them at the counter to launch her initial round of interviews. Thinking of their claims she posed her next question.

"What about rumors he had buried treasure?"

His thin lips drew into a sneer. "He kept his lawn

so nice there was no way he would dig it up. He kept his money in a box in the house. As for talk about coins, ppffft, he talked about 'em plenty, but I never saw them. I think they're gone."

"Do you think whoever killed him was after his money?"

"Sure. Everyone knew he had cash around. He didn't believe in banks."

"No one ever came to visit him? No family?"

"I heard he had a wife and son. She died before I was born. His son went to prison. He's probably still there."

Rafe said they couldn't find the son. Perhaps he was still in prison. She would have to check.

Across the yard a green-and-white police cruiser slowed and stopped in front of the old man's house. She got to her feet. "Can we talk again? Or would you like to come over to the house with me? Mayor Foster arranged to get me inside."

BJ Foster hitched up his gray pants and lumbered up the sidewalk. He was shaking his head, cowboy hat bobbing. "I told Daddy this isn't a good idea, but he says if you write something in the paper it might get people thinking and shake loose some ideas."

Cere gave an understanding smile. "No new leads?"

He held up his hand, eyes frosty. "Whoa! I'm not giving interviews. You can go through the house, but I'm not saying anything for the record."

"Is it okay if Robby comes?"

Behind her, Robby shifted. BJ fixed him with a cold stare. "I guess. As long as neither of you touches anything."

"What about the house and its contents?" she asked as they approached the front steps. "What will happen to it?"

"We reached the grandson but he can't come right now. Personally I can't imagine Shark with a family. He'd come out of prison every few years and go right back. He'd been in trouble with the law since Daddy was sheriff."

With a jerk of a meaty hand, BJ removed the crime scene tape that sealed the front door. He pulled out a key. "I can't stay long, so don't expect to take your time."

The inside of the house had the musty smell of an area that had been closed up. A thin layer of dust covered all the surfaces of a cluttered, claustrophobic living area. Cere could picture Naldo sitting on the sagging chair in front of a large television. A quilt was folded neatly across the arm. Religious curios and trinkets crammed nearby shelves.

"That cabinet is where he kept his box with the money," Robby volunteered, pointing at a mahogany cabinet with a glass front.

The objects inside were shoved together, remnants of the investigation. A picture frame caught her eye, and she opened the cabinet door.

"What are you doing?" BJ protested.

"I want to see these pictures." The rose-colored plastic frame held three pictures. In one, a young man and a plump woman posed. The woman held a baby. The hairstyles and clothes were out of the 50's. Another was a school picture of a frowning youth of about thirteen. The final picture was a snapshot of the same boy standing beside three other boys. One was Marco.

She looked toward BJ. "Shark hung with Marco?"

He walked over to look at the picture. "That was before my time. Look at those guys. Thugs."

Marco and Shark had long hair that curled over their shoulders and wore tight black T-shirts. The other two boys wore slacks and cotton shirts. Their hair was thick but much shorter.

"Who are those guys?"

He shook his head. "Don't know."

"May I take this picture?"

"Why?" He frowned at her, blue eyes troubled.

"I want to show it to Mom. Maybe she'll know who they are."

He started to shake his head, then shrugged. "Hell, go ahead."

She slipped the snapshot out of the frame. On the back was a date written in pencil—1976. Were these guys still around? Could they tell her about anything?

The murder scene in the kitchen had been cleaned, and the bedroom held no clues. It had a twin bed with a neat quilted spread. The walnut dresser held several pictures of Naldo and his wife and a recent graduation portrait. Probably the grandson.

As they left the house, Cere turned toward the garage where Marco lived the last few months of his life. "May I check the garage?"

"Nothing to see."

"I'd like to see inside."

He opened the door, and she peered into the interior. If Marco had once lived there, any signs of his presence were long gone. The walls held only racks of garden and automotive tools. Tour concluded, Cere headed home, feeling disillusioned.

Her mother was making lunch when Cere returned. "How did it go?" she asked, as she slathered mustard on slices of bread and placed thin pieces of roast beef on it.

Cere sank onto a chair at the table and took out Naldo's snapshot. "Who are these guys? One is Naldo's son, one is Marco, but who are the others?"

Lottie frowned and lifted the glasses she kept on a chain around her neck. She peered through them at the picture. "Why that's Art and Willie."

A shiver ran through Cere. "Rafe's dad and uncle?"

"Yes." She took one final look and handed it back to Cere. "I'm positive."

Cere re-examined the picture but saw little resemblance to the men she knew. "They were friends with Marco?"

"In junior high. Then Berto went to reform school, and the Tafoya boys stopped running around with Marco. I think their parents worried he might lead them in the wrong direction."

"Was that how Marco got his reputation for being wild? Hanging out with Berto? BJ called him 'Shark.'"

"Berto *was* wild. It wouldn't surprise me if he committed those burglaries. He was here when that second round occurred."

She put the picture into her purse. Did Rafe know his father and uncle were once Marco's friends? Or was that yet something else he hadn't told her?

"How was your date?" Lottie placed plates with sandwiches on the table and sat across from her.

"I'm not asking you about how your night was."

"Disastrous. I was home by midnight. You were fast asleep."

She paused with her sandwich halfway to her

mouth. "Disastrous?"

"It was silly. But... I read those songs and letters you left in the dining room."

This time she nearly dropped her sandwich. "You did? Did you learn anything?"

Her mother carefully avoided her eyes, focusing on her own sandwich. "The Marco who came out of jail was different than the boy who went in. But I knew that. He was over me at the end. He even forgave me..."

"Forgave you for what? Not returning his interest?"

Lottie sighed and pushed away her sandwich. "I must tell you something, but it can't leave this room. It can't go into a story."

"Of course not." Cere held her breath as her mother hesitated.

"Everyone thought Marco was obsessed with me, that it was one sided. They still think that." She took a deep breath, eyes glued to the table. "The truth is... I was just as crazy about him. He was so intelligent. His grades were horrible, but he taught himself. He knew all the romantic poets and could quote poetry. No one saw that. He could have done so much. If it hadn't been for me, he would have."

She paused, but Cere didn't prod her. She knew when to not interrupt a reluctant subject.

"I never told anyone about my feelings. Not even Millie." She looked up as tears filled her eyes. "My family hated him so I couldn't admit the truth. He accepted it and let everyone think it was one-sided. He took those beatings...for me."

Cere took her mother's hand as tears flooded her eyes. "Oh, Mom..."

"It's more than that." Lottie swallowed hard, as

though choking on something. "I knew Marco never committed the burglaries."

The hand she held trembled in her grip. "How?"

"I was with him...all those nights. The money was ours...his and my babysitting money...what we'd saved. That ring was mine. He got it at the pawn shop doing odd jobs for Naldo. Bradley caught him with our money. We were going to run away..."

Tears cut a pale swath down the makeup on her cheeks. "I...I never came forward during his trial. I think my parents realized something... They packed us up and took us to the lake. It was only thirty miles away, but I couldn't get to town. We stayed until the trial ended. He went to jail...because I was too cowardly to admit I loved him."

Cere felt tears fall on her hands as her own eyes overflowed. "Oh, Mom..."

"I want to know how he died. I owe it to him. I was afraid to come through for him once. I want to do it now. You do it. Bradley's so sure...but he's not right. I can't prove anything...and...damn, sometimes I'm such a coward."

She stared at Lottie. She had never looked so defeated. Squeezing her hand, Cere nodded. "I'll find out the truth, Mom. For you and Marco."

Chapter Forty

"Did I tell you about the first time I saw that hand print?" Rafe asked as he and Cere arrived at the Palladium parking lot. "It was early twilight just like now. Dad and I were looking for old bottles. He said we might find some in the lot."

"You've never discussed that." She shifted beside him and he fought to keep his eyes from straying to the sight of her shapely legs as she uncrossed them. In form fitting capris, her tanned calves curved in an inviting line.

He turned away and they climbed out of the car. "I was a kid and I'd heard the stories so I asked him if we could go inside. He had a flashlight and shined it on the wall. It was spooky."

She pursed her lips and tugged the lower one, deep in thought. She'd been quiet most of the evening. His pulse quickened as she licked her lips.

"I remember that night we came with your cousins. You were so brave. The rest of us were jittery going home, but you were quiet. Composed."

She stopped and stared at the building, still reflective. *What was she thinking?*

"Did you really have a crush on me?" he asked, adopting a playful attitude.

Her head jerked to him. "What?"

"That's what Freeda said."

She rolled her eyes, and a smile slid across her face. She elbowed him playfully. "Dream on, Tafoya. I was only twelve."

"Yeah, trouble."

They picked their way through the overgrowth and entered the building. Rafe helped her across the broken planks of the wooden floor. Floorboards creaked as they walked into the main room. A small animal scurried off to one side, and she drew closer to him until he could smell her perfume.

"Something scares you now that you're no longer twelve?"

"Creepy, crawly things."

He gave her a mock stern look. "They don't scare Ginny."

"She's been around male cousins too long."

"She didn't want to go to Santa Fe with my sister. She would rather get her nails done by Cere. You're her new best friend."

"After the dog and rabbits. I had fun doing her nails. I never thought of being a mother, but taking care of her, I could do it..."

Rafe whirled toward her, keeping his voice playful although her admission struck a sharp chord inside him. "You?"

"I'll think about it once this is solved."

"Of course." He'd been pleased when she called. He had been trying to think of a reason to get in touch with her. Then she revealed her motive—she wanted to get into the building. Now she stood in the middle of big room, surveying it.

"I'm not sure what I'm looking for. I thought if I saw the hand again, I might get a new clue. Mom liked the idea."

He moved to stand beside her. "I'm pleased you asked me to come. It shows you have some sense."

"I needed your permission to get inside."

"Like you wouldn't climb through the broken door and come in anyway," he said.

Rafe was right, and they both knew it. Cere wasn't certain why she asked him to come. She wanted to ask about his father and maybe while they were here she could broach the subject.

Stepping around cracked steps they made their way to the second floor. The door where she had been locked was blocked with police tape, but she had no desire to visit that room. She stepped inside the room with the hand print and played her flashlight over the image.

The outline and the words under it were dark smudges on the wall. What did they mean? She closed her eyes, thinking about all she knew that she hadn't known the first time. Marco had loved Lottie. He faced her angry family, only to have her betray him. He'd forgiven her while he was in jail, and she said he was over her. Who had the romantic words been written for? Who was the final mystery woman? Rafe said it wasn't his mother. How could he be sure? Lottie said Rosalie loved him. Had he loved her at the end?

"It's strange to think of them all growing up together," Cere said softly, her fingers touching the print gingerly.

"Do you really feel a connection to him?"

She stood still. Wherever Marco's ghost lurked, it wasn't there now. "I've been to places with psychics. It's not like that. I feel like he draws me back here, to see something. But I have no idea what it is. Mom doesn't think he committed suicide. His final letters were filled with hope. He didn't come back for revenge or kill himself out of grief. There was something else. I need to talk to your Aunt Rosalie."

"Good luck. She just took off. I've never asked Mom about her. I guess I can. I'm just not sure what good it will do." His voice was quiet, but she sensed an edge.

"I thought you wanted to learn the truth."

"Marco is gone. We can't bring him back."

"We could help his memory."

He sighed and ran his hand through his hair. "Tell you what. I have a songwriter friend in L.A. I can send some of the songs to him and see if he can sell them."

The gesture touched her. "Mom claims Marco didn't commit any burglaries. She and Mr. Foster had a fight over his comments the other night. She's furious that he's so smug."

"How would she know Marco didn't commit them?"

Cere bit her lip. She couldn't betray her mother's confidence. "She just does. We agreed he didn't commit suicide. Do you think he was guilty of the fires? The thefts? What if Shark committed the first round of burglaries? Naldo's son?"

"I've thought of that. Maybe that's why Naldo gave Marco a place to stay when he came back. Berto went to jail not long after Marco for something else. It's possible."

Cere studied the hand print and the words below it. "All for love." Maybe she could never get to the bottom of Marco's death, but selling the songs could help

Marco's image. *No.* His burning eyes seemed to appear inside the hand print. They blazed from the dingy wall, as though saying that was not enough.

****

After a quiet trip back to town, they drove to Rafe's house and called Gus to ask permission to send off the songs. There was no answer so she called her mother to let her know where she was.

"I was just on my way out the door," Lottie said. "Tony is taking me to dinner."

The news surprised but delighted Cere. "You still haven't made up with Mr. Foster?"

"Not exactly. Maybe we both need to take a step back."

"Mom's going to dinner with Tony," she said as she hung up. "I hope I haven't caused problems with Mr. Foster."

Across the room that served as a home office, Rafe dug through papers that cluttered his desk. "If it's meant to be, they'll make up."

"This place needs organization," she teased, approaching him.

"You want to clean it up?" He tossed papers into a drawer waving at the remaining piles. "Be my guest."

She shook her head. "My office at home is the same."

"I knew it was beyond you to be domestic. Since Ginny is gone and Lottie is busy, how about if I grill steaks for dinner?"

Her insides tightened and she tried to keep the grin to a minimum as she nodded in agreement. "I might even dazzle you with my salad making abilities."

****

"Have you ever thought of going back to L.A.?" she asked as they sat in the living room after dinner, sipping coffee. Dinner had been enjoyable. His steaks had been succulent and he enjoyed her salad. For once they kept the conversation on their parallel lives in the city.

She was aware of how close they were on the loveseat, but it didn't bother her. She liked the feel of his hard thigh pressing against her leg.

"I'll never go back," he said. "That's no place to bring up Ginny. Carmen never liked it actually. I was the one who wanted the city. All she wanted was a home, kids, and to help others."

Cere touched his arm lightly. "She loved you."

"She did everything for others. For me. It was all about me. That was wrong."

"So you'll marry to give your daughter a mother? Now you're doing everything for your family and giving up doing for yourself? That's not right either."

A corner of his lips lifted in a smile. "You speak with such certainty. Like you really know."

"I know giving up your life is wrong. A relationship needs balance. You should both make sacrifices."

"Maybe, but I was selfish, and it killed her. I'll do anything for my family. I'll make whatever sacrifices are necessary. One day you may understand sacrifice."

"It doesn't mean anything if all it brings is pain."

Rafe's hand on her hair surprised her. She turned to him, saw the fire in his eyes and moved toward him. Talk of sacrifice and pain died in her throat. He leaned forward and claimed her mouth with his, his arms wrapping around her and pulling her to him.

"Damn you," he whispered against her ear when he broke the kiss. "You make me crazy. I didn't want to do this, and here I am. I want you."

She moaned and found his lips again. His hands skimmed over her until they fell on her breasts. His palms caressed them.

"I want you too. Can we stop worrying about what's going to happen and just..."

His responding groan was his only response. He began kissing her neck, his lips trailing down from her ear to the neckline of her blouse. His tongue snaked out, outlining the V-neck. Nimble fingers unfastened her buttons, and she cried out as his lips found the bare skin at the top of her bra. Smooth hands pushed her blouse down her arms.

Cere unbuttoned his shirt, her hands enjoying the hard feel of his muscles below her fingers. She rubbed her face against the thin mat of black hair on his chest as it sent an electrifying rush through the rest of her. Her insides were growing warm, liquid, building to a fiery sea of desire.

His fingers found the catch of her bra. Her full breasts swung free into his hands, as his lips found her sensitive nipples. Again Cere cried out. Everything was forgotten but the hot touch of his lips and his hard, throbbing body against hers.

She tugged at his pants, and Rafe pulled back slightly.

"Wait."

"No," she moaned. "Don't say you don't want me."

"I do."

Her hand fell below his zipper. Yes, he did want her, every bit as much as she wanted him. She massaged him gently, fanning the flames inside herself as much as the fire in him.

"Let's go to my room," he said in a husky voice.

Cere shoved down her pants and panties in case he might change his mind. A fevered look of desire consumed his dark eyes. He wouldn't stop this time. Half dressed, clinging to each other, they stumbled down the hall to his bedroom.

He lifted her onto the bed and moved back and removed a small foil packet from the bedside table.

"You keep a supply of those handy?"

His dark eyes glowed. "Don't even joke about it. I may be losing my head, but I won't toss away responsibility."

She might have teased further, but he dropped his pants and shorts. The magnificent sight of his aroused body sent convulsions through her. No more joking. He leaned toward her and their lips met again. They fell back onto the bed, hands learning each other's bodies as he claimed her. She welcomed him inside her whimpering with need. She had never felt so complete.

Their bodies moved together, setting a rhythm as smooth as ballroom dancers for a time and then growing fevered as sweet passion burst into the full blossom of satisfaction. Cere cried out his name, and he responded, until he shuddered inside her. She clasped him to her, nails digging into his skin.

"You're very sweet," he whispered into her ear.

She leaned her head on his shoulder. "You're amazing." Then impishly she added. "Tell me more about Marco."

Their mixed laughter rang around the room.

Chapter Forty-One

Rafe was sleeping when she rose early the next morning. He didn't move as she ran her hand along the rough stubble of his face. Her fingertips teased his long lashes. Tenderness filled her. She wanted to climb back into bed and stay with him. Nothing else mattered.

Much as the thought intrigued her, she couldn't do it. Her mother would get up soon and see she had not come home. After a quick shower, while coffee brewed, Cere walked to his office. The sight of the piles on his desk made her smile. She might not be domestic, but she wanted to show him she could be if she cared.

Sitting on his leather chair she organized piles. In a few minutes she had a system worked out—business on one side, personal on another. Cere searched the desk for folders. The top drawer held pens and envelopes. A second drawer, labels and miscellaneous supplies. In the third drawer she found empty file folders.

She began putting the various papers into folders, until she opened a folder which wasn't empty. Inside she spotted a smudged envelope with Marco's handwriting. Why would Rafe have a letter? Had he taken it from Gus?

She pulled it out. The contents set her heart to pounding.

Stella, I am sorry. I should have been honest. I should have learned long ago that revenge is a petty motive that doesn't help anything. Rosalie was right.

I knew you belonged to Art. I should never have pretended feelings I didn't have. I do care but I can't marry you.

My heart remains elsewhere and I can't—won't ever give up.

Please forgive me.

She re-folded the letter with shaking hands. What the hell was this about? Revenge? Hadn't Marco given up that idea? Why did Rafe have this letter? Frantically she dug through the file looking for answers.

But things were different this morning. She was in love with Rafe. She needed to clear the air between them completely and that wouldn't happen until all the questions about Marco were solved. She'd always wonder and he would fear for her safety.

During the night, she had felt they were holding back. She feared loving him, but she knew he'd held something back too. They didn't totally trust each other.

A sudden noise at the back door startled her. Guiltily Cere slipped the envelope back in the folder and put it in the desk. Stella opened the back door. At least she thought it was Stella. Cere barely recognized her without make up.

"I brought Rafe breakfast." She held out a brown bag.

"I just stopped by...I better go," Cere said, but she feared his mother could see the truth. Her clothes were rumpled from being tossed on the floor, and she wore no make-up either. Not to mention that Rafe's scent clung to her skin. Without looking back she hurried through the house, grabbed her purse and rushed out the front door.

****

Lottie sat in the kitchen, a cup of coffee in hand, watching a small television set on the counter when Cere entered.

"I was about to call Rafe's to see if that's where you were, but I figured you might be having too much fun."

Her cheeks grew warm, but Cere knew her mother could probably see the glow in her eyes. She had never felt so vibrantly alive. Good thing Freeda wasn't around. She'd never hear the end of it.

She poured a cup of coffee and sat across from her mother. "Sorry. I should have called."

"I'm glad I didn't know until I got up. I would have worried. But you're a grown woman and Rafe's a good man. I'm not going to lecture. I just hope you're not playing with him."

She had no idea what she was doing. Rafe had said he cared about her, wanted to take care of her, but he had not said he loved her. One thing was certain—he didn't trust her. And she didn't trust him.

What else was he keeping from her? Now she knew Marco had dumped Stella. A sudden thought hit her. Marco said revenge was worthless. But had Stella taken revenge on him? Could she have killed him? The thought sent a shiver through her.

"You care about him, don't you?" Lottie asked, bringing her back to the present.

"Yes. I don't think it's going to do any good. Where would we live? He won't go back to Los Angeles."

"You sound like me and Marco. We were seventeen, but we didn't think our worlds would work together."

"You were running away. Would that have worked?"

"No, but I didn't realize it until he was arrested. I learned I was too weak to make it work." A faraway look came into her eyes. "And Marco? He was ready to reach for the stars. He was heading for the moon."

"See? I want the moon. Rafe is grounded on earth."

"Nothing wrong with that. You make him happy, and he does the same for you. I've seen how you look after Ginny. I never thought of you as motherly, but you can do it."

"In a haphazard way."

"Mothers don't just sprout. We all have to learn."

A change of subject was in order. She couldn't discuss Rafe. "How was your date?"

Lottie's face scrunched into a mass of wrinkles. "Tony is nice, but I keeping thinking about Bradley. I told you I used to have a crush on him. I guess he had a crush on me too, but he couldn't do anything since he was married."

"Such a dilemma. Two guys." A gray strip of cardboard on the table caught her attention. "What's that?"

Her mother pushed it to her. "I found it in the old stuff. Marco and I once sneaked off to a carnival in Taos."

Cere picked up the strip of four black and white photos. They were the sort taken in a photo booth, but they provided a detailed close up of Marco's face. "Oh, my gosh. His eyelashes."

Lottie nodded, eyes growing misty. "You see it too."

"Mom!" Her voice came out in a high squeal. "Is he...?" A weight descended, like a heavy blanket engulfing her. She jerked her face up to her mother as coldness invaded her. Suddenly the letter on Rafe's desk made perfect sense. "Mom…Rafe…looks like…Marco!"

Her mother didn't seem surprised. "Stella will never admit it, but it makes sense. I saw Marco once when he came back. He was dating her and made it clear he was over me. I could see he was as committed to his causes as he had been to chasing me. He wanted to know why I never responded to his letters. That was when I found out Rosalie had the letters. Neither of us realized how she felt about him. When I went to see Rosalie she threw them in my face. She'd hoped he would turn to her when he got out. Instead he started dating Stella."

"Out of revenge? Against you...or Art?"

"Both, I guess. We were supposed to be his friends. Art was going to help us get away, but neither of us showed and then Bradley caught him with the money. We both let him go to jail."

Everything was starting to come together, to make sense. "How was Stella revenge?"

"She broke up with Art to go out with him."

Her throat was dry and she drank a sip of coffee, hoping to wet it. "Does Rafe know?"

"I don't know. I immediately sensed a special connection to him and his little girl. *I knew.* I don't know if others realize the resemblance. Marco was so long ago…"

She thought of Gus, Marco's nephew with his long fluttering lashes. That was why she had not recognized

Stella earlier. She had not been wearing her long, false lashes.

"Art must know."

"Probably. They got married and moved to Albuquerque right after Marco died."

Everything might be falling into place, but she didn't like the direction things were going. A queasiness filled Cere's stomach. She thought of Marco's letter. *Revenge.* "All for love." Suddenly the words made sense. Could one of those three people have killed him? Stella because he dumped her and wouldn't marry her? Art, because Marco took his girl and got her pregnant? Rosalie, because he'd been unwilling to love her? Was that why she left and disappeared?

Three suspects. All from Rafe's family.

A sudden ringing of the phone was so jarring she jumped. Lottie picked it up and held it out.

"Cere Medina?" said an unfamiliar voice.

"Yes?"

"This is Gary Riggins. I hear you've been trying to reach me."

Her heart skipped and she gripped the receiver like a lifeline. "I am so glad to hear from you. I have so many questions I don't know where to start."

"Start tomorrow. I just got back and I'm up to my eyeballs. Give me a call then."

She didn't like to be put off, but she agreed to drive over to Santa Fe the next day. As he said goodbye, she thought of something else. "Wait! Do you know this number?" She'd called it so often she knew it by heart and read it off to him.

Paper rustled in the background. "Let me check my

notes. Yeah, sure. Naldo Sanchez. Didn't I read he died? That old man knew something, but I could never get it out of him."

A cold chill ran through Cere. Naldo had been trying to reach her? He'd wanted to talk about Marco and hours later he'd been murdered. Someone stopped him from talking. Permanently.

How much of this did Rafe know? She'd sensed there was something else he was hiding. Was this it? Did he fear—or know—his father or mother had killed Naldo?

"He was murdered," Cere said.

The phone clicked and then Riggins' voice yelled across the line. "What the hell? You're kidding? The hell with this mess here. I'll be there tomorrow. I *knew* that old man was hiding something."

"Police say robbery was the motive. He had a money box with cash."

Riggins shouted a curse. "No! He kept going around in circles, telling me to stop studying the hand and study the writing. I never saw a damn thing, and he never let me quote him. You say he had money? That old man didn't have a dime. I had to pay him to talk to him."

"Do you think he was blackmailing someone?"

"What kind of reporter are you? Of course he was. They got tired of paying and offed the poor sucker. Maybe I'll try and get there tonight. I'll call you. We need to get to the Palladium."

Cere hung up, the earth reeling under her feet.

Chapter Forty-Two

"Who was that?" Lottie asked. "You're white as a sheet. Was it another threat?"

Cere faced her mother grimly. She'd been unable to move after hanging up. "Gary Riggins. He's coming to Rio Rojo. He thinks Naldo knew the truth about Marco's death. That's why he was killed."

Her mother's gulp was audible. "Why would he keep quiet all these years?"

"Blackmail? That's what Riggins thinks. It bothered me that there was so much cash in that box. Where did he get it? He was old, retired with no pension, no job."

A shadow of concern crossed Lottie's face. "Maybe you should call Rafe."

Rafe! The one person she couldn't call. Did he know who killed Naldo? Was that why he opposed her investigating? No, that honorable man would never ignore his duty.

Or was this a sacrifice of his honor to protect his father or mother? Had Stella killed Naldo because she feared the truth coming out, not only about Marco, but her son as well? Or had Art wanted to keep the old man quiet? Perhaps he attacked Marco in a fit of rage after learning about his fathering a child with Stella out of revenge. Since Marco had lived in Naldo's garage just before his death, it made sense that the old man knew what was going on.

The phone rang again and she jumped. She moved away, her eyes sliding to her mother in a silent plea. Lottie answered and held it out to Cere.

"Talk to him," she whispered.

So much had happened since she rose from Rafe's bed hours ago. She took the receiver with shaking hands and said a quick hello.

"Good morning, sweet Cere." The warmth in his voice might otherwise have made her melt. Not now. "I missed you this morning. Why didn't you wake me?"

She tried to adopt a light tone as her mother exited the room. "I was trying to keep from scandalizing Mom, but she was already up. She's more worried about you than she is about me."

"I wonder why." His low chuckle vibrated across the line.

"Rafe..."

"I like the sound of my name coming from you, sweet Cere."

His words and tone made her tingle, but she made a face. "Now what?"

"Is that why you ran off? Is that why you sound so strange?"

"We gave all these reasons why we weren't going to get involved and then..."

"Don't say to let it go."

Her throat felt dry, and a huge lump grew in it. "We live in different worlds."

He exhaled sharply. "So?"

"I'll come by later. I'm working on the Naldo story, and I might have new information..."

"Can't you let work go for a while?"

Was he trying to stop her from getting information? If his family was to blame, would he let her tell the story?

"I'll be by later, really."

"Sure," he snapped.

Tears clouded her eyes as she hung up. Maybe she should go to Taos and link up with Freeda. A couple of crazy days might be just the cure for the doldrums. Or heartbreak. Maybe she should simply leave. She didn't think she could prove anything about Marco without hurting Rafe's family or her mother. She'd already come between her and her new boyfriend.

Marco's burning eyes popped into her head, as though reminding her of her promise. What about Naldo? His killer should be found. BJ Foster was in no rush to solve the crime. Even Rafe's attempts seemed half-hearted, though now she knew why.

Lottie came back into the room. "Why don't we get away? We could drive to Taos and look for Freeda."

Shopping held little appeal but Cere needed time to think. "Sure, but I need to get back early in case Riggins arrives this evening."

****

Rafe sat at his desk, reading the report on the broken watch and the bullet shells. As expected, there were too many fingerprints on the envelope, and the shells were easily obtainable in any hardware store. They were still running prints from the watch.

The words swam before his eyes. He glanced at the clock. Nearly three. Where was Cere? If only he'd been awake when she got up. He had not been surprised to find her gone. As wonderful as the night had been, the situation remained awkward. He wanted to tell her so much, yet he had no idea if he should.

Was he in love with Cere? During the moments that led to their passion, he had been convinced of it. Making love to her had been everything he'd hoped it would be. Guilt about being unfaithful to Carmen disintegrated in the face of her beauty and the sheer explosiveness of her desire. Something special had burst forth between them. Carmen would have wanted his life to continue with someone special. Cere filled the bill. Full of life, stubborn and unpredictable, she might not be what he needed, but she was what he wanted.

His father peered inside his door and then entered with a wave. "Hi, guy. Wanna grab a beer?"

He set the report aside. "I'm finishing up some work."

"You work too damn hard. Take the rest of the day off. You can catch up later."

"I was going to see BJ in case there's anything new on the Sanchez case."

Art frowned and dropped into the chair across from him. "You think there's gonna be a break? Willie told me that Cere is writing a story about Naldo. Do you think that's a good idea? There's no telling what she'll do."

"It's a feature." While she could still make dangerous discoveries, he was no longer certain what she would do if she discovered everything. He was beginning to trust her.

"Is that the cop talking or the man who's been looking at her legs?" His voice carried a doubtful edge.

"It makes a difference when you have a personal stake in it. I think of murders I investigated so clinically. Then I think about how hard it was to face Carmen's death. Cere's learning the same lesson." At least he hoped she was. He couldn't imagine the soft, loving woman returning to the tabloid shrew he'd first met. She had changed, or was he wrong thinking he could trust her?

"If she comes up with a sensational story, I'll tell Willie not to publish it. As long as our name is on the masthead, we won't print anything that embarrasses the town."

"It will be fine."

Art ran a hand over his bald head as though he had hair. "You in love with this girl?"

Rafe rubbed his hand across the back of his neck. Who was he kidding? Cere wasn't coming by. "It's never going to work."

His father's voice softened, the earlier cool traces gone. "It can if you want it to. Sure, she's from the city, but so what? You lived there, you could go back."

"I won't live there. I want Ginny in a safe environment."

"You can't always protect those you love. Life isn't that easy. Carmen could have been hurt here. It was her time to go."

A sad smile crossed Rafe's face. He was used to small lectures from both his parents. "I'll think about it, Dad."

Art stood and jerked a thumb at the door. "I'm going over to Lucky's. Come by if you get the urge."

Rafe watched through the window as Art sauntered down the sidewalk, stopping to talk to people. A fierce feeling of protective instinct came over him. He wasn't certain about Cere, but one thing he knew—Art loved his family and would do anything to protect them. Could he do any less?

****

Cere sat on the back porch, fuming. The trip to Taos had been a debacle. First, Freeda wasn't even there. She'd moved on to another small town. Second, Cere couldn't focus on clothing selections. Shopping normally proved therapeutic, but her mind kept going back to her wonderful night with Rafe followed by her terrible discoveries.

Then there was what she'd learned about Naldo. He'd wanted to talk to her. He might have used blackmail to earn money. Where did Rafe fit in? He'd been at Naldo's the night of the murder. Perhaps he'd used the money box to throw off suspicion and then hid it and pretended to find it later. Could he be part of a conspiracy? Or was she putting him in that position as a way of putting a gulf between them?

Her mother was inside talking to Bradley. He'd called as they arrived home as though he'd been watching the house. Sensing her mother wanted privacy, Cere retreated to the porch.

Seeing the guitar leaning against the railing, she touched it, thinking about Rafe singing his father's songs. The burning eyes appeared in front of her. She recalled the first day she saw Rafe, when she thought his eyes belonged to her ghost. Now she knew why.

Lottie came out the door holding Roxie's leash. "I'm taking Roxie for a walk. I may stop at Bradley's."

Cere nodded, watching as her mother disappeared through the gate. The evening stretched in front of her, but she knew she couldn't call Rafe. Not yet. Her phone buzzed and she grabbed it. The number was unfamiliar.

"Cere, it's Gary Riggins. Listen, I'm sorry but I can't make it tonight. I'll get there tomorrow early, okay?"

She sighed. She'd actually hoped he would show up. "Sure, I understand."

"We'll go out to the Palladium, okay? I really want to study those words. Maybe you'll see something."

The dance hall.

Suddenly Cere knew what she had to do. She hopped to her feet as she said goodbye. She wasn't going to wait for him. Naldo had said he should study the words. That was exactly what she was going to do.

****

Tired of working, Rafe shoved his paperwork aside. He checked his watch and popped an antacid wondering for the tenth time in three hours if he should call Cere. He had gone by the newspaper office looking for her in the late afternoon only to be told that she'd called, told Willie her story was on hold and she was going to Taos to shop. What did that mean?

The phone rang, and he grabbed it, hoping Cere was calling back.

"Rafe? Jack Landis at the State Crime Lab."

"Hi, Jack. What's up?"

"I got back the info you wanted on Diego Diaz. I know you said he came up clean in Texas, but I got an interesting result when I ran the name through our state records. By the way, I also got prints off that shell you brought in."

Diaz got his immediate interest, but so did the shell. "If the prints aren't on the shells, he can wait. I thought the shell prints came up blank. I have the report right here."

"I didn't find anyone with a criminal record. But I started going through everyone we have on file. I don't know if it means anything, but..."

Rafe listened with a pounding pulse. He called Cere as soon as he was off the phone. No answer. He tried Lottie's number.

"Is Cere there?"

"Hi, Rafe," Lottie said with a laugh. "Isn't she with you? I came to get her for dinner but she's gone."

A terrible thought hit him. "She didn't go to the Palladium, did she?"

"I hope not. She's been preoccupied all afternoon, but I thought it was because that Santa Fe reporter called her. She said something about Naldo blackmailing someone. Maybe she went over to talk to his neighbor again."

Rafe hung up and rushed to the door. All he could think of was finding Cere.

****

What was that? Cere paused on the steps leading to the second floor of the Palladium, letting the echo of her footsteps die. A board creaked, but it was the step on which she stood.

Creee-aaak.

There it was again. It came from the back of the dance hall. She wanted to call out, but if someone was in the building, they would know where she was. No, she was being foolish. She had nothing to fear. If Marco was her guardian angel he would not let her get hurt.

She proceeded up the steps, stepping carefully around the broken stairs. Another squeak, but it sounded like the settling of the old wooden and stone structure. On the second floor she used light from the fading sun that filtered in through broken windows to walk to the back of the building.

Her flashlight and lantern were reserved for the hand print. She wanted get a look at the room in bright light. The doorway yawned black and forbidding. Stepping through, she flicked on the flashlight. It felt like an eternity since her first visit. She knew more about Marco, but little about why he had come to his bloody demise. Was the answer in this room? Drawing a deep breath, she scratched a match on the floorboard and lit the lantern. A harsh light flooded the room, casting eerie shadows.

She studied the hand print and the words below it. "All for love." What had Marco been thinking when he wrote that? Who was the woman he meant it for? Rafe's mother? Rosalie? Lottie? Why did Naldo say to study the words?

As she stared at them, the truth hit her like a bolt of lightning. Marco had not written them. She'd seen his letters. This was not his handwriting.

Her breath caught. This resembled the block printing on the envelope containing her watch. Was that who killed Marco? Who wrote like that? Art? Stella? She played the light around the room one more time, looking for anything that might hold clues.

Another creak startled her, and Cere whirled toward the door, the flashlight falling from her hand. A dark shadow loomed in the door way, and she gulped. Fiery black eyes came from the glow of the fallen flashlight.

"Cere?"

"Rafe! You scared me." As she fought to bring her pounding heart under control Cere gazed at his black eyes. Marco's eyes. The eyes from her dreams. "What are you doing here?"

"Just a hunch."

"I found something." The words exploded from her lips and she pointed at the wall. "That isn't Marco's writing. He was more interested in peace than love when he got out of prison. There was no mystery woman; that's why we can't find her. He didn't commit suicide, but someone wanted this to seem like a suicide note. He was murdered, Rafe."

Chapter Forty-Three

Rafe crossed to the wall and studied the words. He turned to her, wiping a hand across his face. Again she was stricken by his resemblance to Marco. Maybe she would have realized it from the beginning if not for the beard.

"Did you find out anything else?" he asked.

Her heart rose to her throat, and her voice came out as a squeak. "I know the truth about your mom."

He became very still, eyes still on the wall, his gaze avoiding hers. "And me?" he finished, jerking his head up, rising to face her. "Did you uncover the truth about me?"

She nodded slowly.

Rafe's eyes blazed with something unreadable. "Now what? Are you going to report it? Drag those dirty secrets out into the open to appease your damn ghost? Or because you think it's your job?"

A knot formed in her throat and she stepped toward him and touched his arm. "What if I ask you to trust me to do the right thing? Could you do that?"

"Yes." The flame that burned in his dark eyes was no surprise. She had seen it the previous night in his bed. The flame of love. "Do you trust me?"

All day she had doubted him, but now she saw the truth. It had been there all along, just like the message on the wall. She nodded. "I understand why you've hidden so much."

Turmoil wreathed his face, hardening into chiseled lines. "You don't know what it's like to discover you don't know who you are. All those years I thought I knew my dad. He was good, always there for me. He still is. He will always be my dad."

"How did you find out?"

"After I learned the truth about Mom seeing Marco, I went to her. She didn't realize what I was asking and it all came out. I guess she never got a chance to tell him the truth. He never knew."

Tears filled Cere's eyes. One more tragedy in Marco's young life. "But she told your dad."

He sighed heavily and nodded. "He took her back and claimed me as his own. I'm not even sure why, but he's been as good a father to me as he was to my sisters."

His words were the final piece of her jigsaw puzzle. But it only confirmed her earlier suspicions. She feared she knew the truth about Marco's death. And she doubted she could tell Rafe. He obviously didn't know his father once betrayed Marco.

Before she could say anything, the door slammed shut, shaking the building. They moved toward the door in unison, but an ominous click stopped them. A shiver of fear rippled down her back. Beyond the door, floorboards creaked.

Rafe yanked on the doorknob, but it didn't budge. Cere pounded on the door as the odor of gasoline filtered into the room. Her eyes met Rafe's.

"You don't suppose he'll burn the place down?" she asked. Would Art harm the man he'd raised as his son? Did Rafe even guess?

Rafe banged a fist on the sturdy door. "Foster! You'll never get away with it."

"Foster?" Shock ran through her. "Bradley Foster? What makes you think it's him?"

"They found your fingerprints on the shell casings and her watch, Foster." He pounded harder on the door.

She choked back her terror and joined the pounding. The Mayor? Could Rafe be right? Heavy footsteps sounded in the hall. Whoever was out there was running away. She fell to her knees and peered through the old fashioned keyhole. Tiny as it was, it afforded a frightening glimpse of flames starting to leap up the walls. The building itself might be constructed of stone, but the wooden moldings and floors were tinder dry and would burn in minutes.

Through growing flames she caught a glimpse of Mayor Foster, sweat pouring down his grim face as he hobbled toward the steps. Smoke floated under the door. If they didn't move quickly, they were doomed. She swiveled the flashlight around the room, searching for the window and its rotting boards.

"Oh, no," she whispered, pointing at it.

Rafe shook his head in frustration. "I had the windows boarded up with new wood to keep people out."

A shiver of helplessness ran through Cere, but she shook it off. She couldn't die, not now that she had found Rafe.

"I love you," she said, as smoke billowed into the room. She wanted him to know that in case she was to die. Her mother had hidden her feelings, but Cere wanted hers out in the open.

His smile was grim, and he winked at her as he

turned back to the door. "It's about time you figured that out. Let's get out of here."

Rafe hurled his shoulder at the door. It groaned in protest, but held steady. Cere did the same, summoning all her strength. Pain stabbed her arm. They tried again, and a panel splintered. Focusing on that area, Rafe plunged against the door again. Its crack was a heavenly sound, but smoke floated through a small hole. Even if they got out, they would face the fire.

The door finally broke under their dual effort. Smoke invaded the room as the flames grew more intense. Smoke seared her throat and tears ran down her cheeks. Rafe handed her his handkerchief to put over her nose, and they kept on working.

He gripped the panel and pulled it to form a hole. He lifted Cere and shoved her through. She fell to her knees as she faced a wall of flames. Despite the handkerchief, smoke scorched her throat. Rafe appeared beside her and they crawled to the stairs.

A gaping hole in the middle of the stairs stopped their progress. Flames licked up one wall, and snaked down the railing on the other side.

"Let me go first," Rafe shouted. He sat on the edge of the step and leaped to the floor below. His leg twisted, and he collapsed in a heap, but he sat up and held out his arms for her.

She dropped toward him and he caught her, clutching her to him. Pain contorted his sooty face. They were out of the immediate fire, but she could see he was hurting.

"Are you all right?"

"I twisted my knee." He tried to stand, but stumbled against the wall. She put her hand under his arm and attempted to help him up, but they both collapsed.

"Get out of here," he gasped as smoke swirled around them. "Go!"

"I can't leave you."

He tried to stand, but his leg buckled and he fell forward. The outline of a figure appeared through the smoke. Her ghost? Foster? Fear paralyzed her for an instant. No, the man was too lanky to be the Mayor.

"Help," she cried.

The black clad figure of Diego Diaz came through the haze. He put his arm around Rafe and pulled him up.

"Diaz!" Rafe looked as surprised to see the man as she was, but he didn't refuse the help.

"Get his other side," Diaz ordered, and she put her arm around Rafe's back. Together the trio staggered out of the building. By the time they reached Rafe's Jeep he was about to collapse. He drew deep gasping breaths and she fumbled for a water bottle.

Diaz grabbed the radio microphone and called for an ambulance while Cere sank beside Rafe and gulped in welcome breaths of fresh air.

"Where did you come from, Diaz?" Rafe asked, coughing.

"Patrolling," he replied in a rasp.

Cere was in no mood for the man's sarcasm, but she was happy to see him. She pointed at a horse tied to a nearby tree. "You were riding around in the dark?"

Diaz jerked around and cursed. He turned toward the burning building. Cere looked down at Rafe.

"That's Foster's horse," he gasped. "Don't let him get away."

Diaz quickly hobbled toward the horse. She headed around the other side, hoping to cut off Foster if he ran that way. As she came around the back side of the building she heard a familiar voice, gasping for air.

"Cere?" Bradley Foster slumped below a broken window, shirt and pants torn, face bloody. "I fell through the stairs."

"Serves you right," she said and then realized he couldn't move. In a few minutes, the flames would reach the lower level. They needed to get away from the building.

"Help me," he pleaded, holding out an arm.

"You tried to kill us." But even as she spoke, Cere knew she couldn't leave him. She tried to help him to his feet, but he was dead weight.

His eyelids fluttered. "I…only meant to scare you. Those messages...the watch... I just wanted you to stop..."

"You tried to run me over."

"You were upsetting Lottie..."

She didn't know if she believed him, but his shuddering breath propelled her to try again. Her mother would never understand if she left him to die. As she tugged, another arm came into view. Diaz grabbed him around the middle and jerked him away from the side of the building.

The mayor collapsed onto the ground. "Thanks..." he mumbled.

Diaz stood over him, a grim look on his face. "I didn't do it to be a hero. It's time for honesty." He prodded the supine man with the toe of his scuffed boot. "Tell us the truth, you bastard."

Bradley lifted a shaking hand. "You going to kill

me?"

"If I was going to do that, I'd have left you to broil. I want to hear the truth before God comes for you." Diaz produced a water bottle from his back pocket and dropped it on Bradley's stomach.

The mayor drew a deep shuddering breath and took a gulping drink.

"You framed that kid, didn't you?" Diaz asked.

The question surprised Cere. She thought he would ask about Naldo's death.

"Tell her the truth about Marco. You're the only one who knows it now that the old man is dead."

Bradley shook his head. "He committed those burglaries."

"Like hell!" Diaz sounded as though he knew. Who was this man? "The first break ins?"

Foster's face pinched as though he was in pain. "Not the second bunch...but I caught him...red-handed that first time. He had money. He...couldn't explain it."

"Sure. You never gave him a chance to explain. And then you framed him the second time. Naldo knew. That's why you murdered him."

"He had a gun. Crazy coot was gonna shoot me...if I didn't tell...we struggled...the gun went off."

"You killed Marco too?" Cere asked Foster, her breath catching.

His tired gaze slid from her to Diaz. "I...didn't kill...Marco... Shark..."

"Berto?" She looked at Diaz, expecting him to protest again, but he didn't.

He leaned toward Foster, his husky voice accusing. "The two of you framed Marco for the fires, the burglaries and then you paid Shark to kill him."

"Why?" Cere asked.

"He was...no good...but he could talk...and people listened..."

Diaz grunted and poked a finger at Foster. "You were afraid of his ideas. Afraid he would overthrow the old boy network."

"We wanted him gone..." Foster's voice grew weak as tears streamed down his ruddy cheeks.

Cere turned to Diaz. "Mr. Clarkson saw Marco. He told Willie and Art his shirt was burned...."

Diaz shook his head, his face rigid with anger. "Marco caught Shark robbing the pawn shop, taking the coins and setting fire to the place. He tried to put it out and heard Clarkson next door. He saved him and followed Shark out here to meet his benefactor. Isn't that what happened?"

"Marco had...burns... Shark hit him in the face with a rifle barrel. I...told him to keep the money, get rid of Marco...and left..." Foster stopped and gasped for breath.

"And called it suicide," Cere accused.

"Everyone wanted it...over. Shark took the money, coins and left. He...knew better than to ever come back."

"Sure." Diaz sounded skeptical. "You sent someone to take care of him too, didn't you? What happened to those coins, old man? They never turned up."

"Crazy story...old man didn't have coins any more. Shark took 'em."

"You took his money box to try to make his death look like robbery," Diaz charged.

"Naldo left me a note that he wanted to talk. Is that

397

why you killed him?" Cere asked.

"You'll never...prove anything." Bradley groaned, lifting his hand to his throat. "Maybe...maybe...Shark came back..."

"We both heard your confession." Cere straightened as she heard sirens blare in the distance.

"Tell Lottie..." Foster choked out.

"Leave my mother out of this."

"She was...too good for him... I cared about her when she was young... That kid was no good. She shoulda been mine. Mine!" He wheezed and clutched at his shirt.

"Are you okay?" she asked, leaning over the portly man. "The ambulance is coming."

She could see it turning off the main road.

"Heart," he mumbled, and before either could move, he pitched forward.

Diaz leaned over him, touched his chest then his neck. "He's dead."

She leaped to her feet as the ambulance bumped over the uneven ground toward them. She ran to meet it, directing paramedics toward Foster and Rafe. A fire truck arrived right behind the ambulance.

As Cere paced the parking lot, firemen set up lines, while paramedics worked on Rafe and Foster.

Diaz walked over to join her. He showed no emotion as he spoke. "The bastard is gone. You okay?"

She studied the impassive figure, puzzled by his knowledge about Marco's case. "What made you say Marco was innocent? How would you know? Exactly what is your interest in this?"

He rubbed the side of his face, his visible eye focused on the scene at the ambulance. "Maybe I was an impetuous kid too, serving time in an adult prison with hardened guys like Shark. Scared boys like that crazy kid."

A wave of surprise swamped her. "You knew them in prison?"

"Could be."

"We never found that in your record."

He grunted and rubbed his fingers together. "You should know money talks. Back then it could even get juvenile records expunged."

"Do you know what happened to Berto? You said something about not getting away with the money."

"He never made it out of this valley alive." He gestured toward where paramedics were loading Foster's covered body into the back of the ambulance. "That old man sent someone after him and I'm convinced they took those coins."

"What makes you say that?"

"Just a hunch." Diaz refused to look at her. What else did he know? Did it matter?

She drew a deep breath. "It's over. Finally."

"Not yet. Thousands of dollars are still missing."

"And I repeat, how do you know?"

He lifted a shoulder in a stiff shrug. "Don't worry. You have your Marco story. Now you know his death was not suicide. "

"Shark killed him," she said sadly.

"The town," he said, husky voice filled with sarcasm. "That mixed up kid left prison ready to change the world, and that bastard and this town killed him. There's your damn story."

Tears flooded her eyes. "I don't know if I can tell it. My mother loved him."

His head swiveled to her. For once he actually appeared to be surprised. "Who the hell said that?"

"That money Mr. Foster said Marco had..." She sniffled and choked out the truth. "It was hers. Theirs. She was running away with him."

"Running away or paying him off?"

"She was going to meet him..." She stopped, realizing the confidence she was revealing. "I'm sorry. I can't discuss this. I promised Mom..."

"I won't tell anyone. The kid said something about a girl. She was going to write, but she never did, and the idiot kept writing to her."

"Apparently her friend who got Marco's letters kept them and never gave them to her until the day he died. But the letters, the songs he wrote, they're beautiful... They made her cry." Her own tears stopped her from continuing.

"She read them?" Diaz straightened, the gaze of his green eye blazing into her, as intense as the heat from the fire. For an instant she could hear the pain in his voice, similar to her own feelings over the tragedy of Marco's lost love.

"I guess you're right. It isn't over. See, she loved my dad, I know it...but you never forget the first love of your life." A lump filled her throat and she jerked around and sought Rafe. He sat hunched at the back door of the ambulance, watching her. She started toward him.

"Where you going?" Diaz asked.

Her heart swelled and the words could barely come out, but she wanted to say them. "To tell someone I love them."

"You mean your job?" The emotion was gone,

replaced by his normal sarcasm.

She whirled on him. "You're a fool, Diaz."

His laugh was harsh. "So I've been told. See you around."

As she approached the ambulance, Cere's confidence dissipated. Telling what she and Diaz learned before Foster died was an easy alternative and she launched into the details for Rafe.

"Mr. Foster said Naldo's death was a mistake," she concluded, "but I doubt we'll ever know the truth. I was more surprised that Diaz knew so much about Marco."

Rafe contemplated Diaz as the mysterious man limped toward his SUV. "I suppose I should apologize and thank the S.O.B."

"He claims Berto never got away with the money but he wouldn't tell me how he knows."

"You're moving on to another story?"

"I got my story, but I'm not certain if I'll tell it." She drew a deep breath and licked her dry lips. Without further thought, she moved to Rafe, wrapping her arms around his back, leaning her head on his chest. "Thank you for coming to save me."

He put his arm around her and held her against him. "You're far from helpless, sweet Cere. And you saved me."

"Maybe that's the answer," she whispered. "You can't keep everyone around you safe, but together we make a good team. I love you. I want to be with you, wherever you are."

"Enough to sacrifice for me?"

She thought of her mother and the sacrifices Lottie had not made. Of Marco's sad life. Of Rafe who had shown how much he would give. "Yes!"

"I wouldn't ask it of you." His sober eyes gazed down at her. "Do your story. I trust you to do the right thing. And you're right. Together we can try to keep those around us safe. I love you too, sweet Cere."

She looked toward the Palladium. Despite the efforts of firemen, flames licked its foundation and leaped into the night sky. The building was burning to the ground and taking all its secrets. Fire danced in the window where Marco left his bloody hand print.

"All that's left of Marco is gone," Rafe said, wiping a hand across his face, and she realized he was crying.

Lifting her hand, she stroked the tears away. "No, he lives in you and Ginny. And his writing. If you want to know him, read his songs, his letters. It's all there." She looked one last time at the room where Marco died. In the flames she could almost see his eyes, but they no longer glowed with bitterness. Rafe gazed down at her and in his eyes—Marco's—she saw love. She had helped Marco, but in the end he helped her much more.

Epilogue

Raucous noise filled the Matador, but when bright TV lights went on and Cere stepped forward to speak into the microphone, the room grew silent.

"The political speeches and essays written by Marco Gonzales will be published. To the people who visited the site of his death, he was a ghostly myth built around a bloody hand print. To the people here in his cousin's restaurant, he was a hero ahead of his time who died too young. Now everyone will know the man who celebrated life with his words. This is Cere Medina reporting for *Scope,* in Rio Rojo, New Mexico."

She handed the mike to Audrey, who stepped from behind the camera. "Great story, babe. It might even be the lead tonight."

Wiping her cheek in case a tear edged out of her eye, Cere shook her head. "I doubt it. I had to beg Alan to let me do it as a cold case feature."

She had left out any mention of Marco's doomed romances. As for his love songs, they belonged to Lottie and she wanted to keep them to herself for now.

Audrey winced as her phone beeped. "Alan wants you to call him."

"When are you coming home?" he demanded when she reached him. "Did you hear about Len Perkins, the comedian? His wife drowned in their swimming pool. He claims he was out of town, but someone saw him

403

climbing the back fence the night she died. I need you to climb the wall. Get into the pool area. Talk to the neighbors."

Cere tuned out of the conversation. Rafe was beckoning her to a table where he and Ginny sat beside her mother and Tony Gennaro.

"Alan, I am home. That was my last report."

"You're getting out of the business?"

"I'll send you the town paper with my next story."

A word about the author...

Rebecca Grace is a former award winning broadcast journalist who is now writing fiction. She specializes in romance, romantic suspense and mystery novels, novellas and short stories. She is also the co-author of a how-to book on creating characters and teaches writing classes.

Thank you for purchasing
this publication of The Wild Rose Press, Inc.
For other wonderful stories of romance,
please visit our on-line bookstore at
www.thewildrosepress.com.

For questions or more information
contact us at
info@thewildrosepress.com.

The Wild Rose Press, Inc.
www.thewildrosepress.com

To visit with authors of
The Wild Rose Press, Inc.
join our yahoo loop at
http://groups.yahoo.com/group/thewildrosepress/